T0277567

THE TIME DOOR

THE ETERNITIES DUOLOGY
BOOK ONE

THE TIME DOOR

SHANNON McDERMOTT

Published by Enclave Publishing, an imprint of Oasis Family Media, LLC

Carol Stream, Illinois, USA.
www.enclavepublishing.com

ISBN: 979-8-88605-154-4 (printed hardcover)
ISBN: 979-8-88605-155-1 (printed softcover)
ISBN: 979-8-88605-157-5 (ebook)

Cover design by Lyndsey Lewellen, www.llewellendesigns.com
Typesetting by Jamie Foley, www.JamieFoley.com

Printed in the United States of America.

To my sister Heather,
who has been the reader that I needed

There was an end to Ilium, and an end came to Rome;

And a man plays on a painted stage in the land that he calls home;

Arch after arch of triumph, but floor beyond falling floor,

That lead to a low door at last; and beyond there is no door.

They are reeling, they are running,

as the shameful years have run . . .

—G.K. CHESTERTON,

"THE BALLAD OF ST. BARBARA"

PROLOGUE

Night covered Mars. Stars pricked the black sky, cold points of light, and the moon opened wide a bright eye.

The volcano—incredibly high, incredibly wide—raised a new horizon. Nothing touched the starkness of its cold slopes. Time and ice choked the great volcano, burying its fires under unimaginable years.

Margaret Killiam stared at the night, entranced in spite of herself. She had always hoped they would arrive during the day—at first because she wanted the sight of Mars in all its red glory to meet their landing. Later, she only wanted to be in the sunlight again. She had never wanted to go straight from the night of space into another night.

Still, this night, this darkness shrouding the barren plains and this starlight on the wasted volcano. This had its own glory.

She looked up at the moon—Phobos, she knew, the greater satellite of Mars. It looked as if it were watching them, watching their lonely intrusion onto a planet that had cleansed itself of life untold aeons ago.

Margaret breathed in deep and turned back to the rover. She scrambled up into it, struggling against the clumsiness of her suit and the low gravity. As she settled into her seat, she knocked her legs against the hard-shelled case that contained her personal belongings.

"We're all ready," the commander said, his voice distant and familiar over the transceiver. "Take us in, Colonel."

Margaret looked at David. Her brother sat ahead of her and to the left, in the driver's seat. As the only career pilot among them, that was naturally his place. Donegan Moynihan exercised his right as the mission commander to ride shotgun.

That left her in the back with Gulliver Eamon.

Eamon's expression was invisible behind his helmet's tinted faceplate, but his foot jerked impatiently. He didn't speak, and given some of the exchanges he and David had had in the ship, perhaps that was for the best.

David's hand moved over the dashboard, and Margaret kept her eyes fixed determinedly on him. But she saw, in the corner of her eye, the hatch lowering. Air hissed as it sealed, locking them in, and she did all she could not to be bothered by it.

Not like the ship. We'll be out soon. She articulated the thought very clearly in her mind, but the tension in her muscles didn't ease.

Then David's voice sounded in her ear, reverberated in the confines of her helmet: "Systems go."

A *thrum* shadowed his words—the engine revving. Then the rover glided forward.

"We're close." Eamon sounded breathless, his voice low but charged with intensity. "So, nearly there."

In moments the rover lost its smoothness, bucking as it crawled up the slopes of the volcano. The headlights glared on broken rocks, on the fruitless desert of a water-starved world. Red sand changed beneath the light, its hue growing darker, edged with hostility.

Margaret strained her eyes ahead. There were too many shadows, darkness layered with darkness, but finally she caught a different shadow—deeper, steadier. The rover pressed toward it, and she knew.

"Annie," Eamon said, a strange affection in his voice. He might have been addressing a woman.

The black hole grew higher and broader than the rover. David guided them in, sure and smooth. As the blackness swallowed them, David's voice murmured through the transceiver: "Lead us home, Annie."

Annie wound silently before them, tightly around them, its close, hard walls turning the light of the moon and stars into a memory. The cave led on and on, deeper and deeper into the cold volcano.

"Not long," Margaret whispered, and remembered the transceiver in her helmet too late.

"What, Doctor?" Moynihan asked.

She closed her eyes and phrased her thought for public consumption. "It's not long until we get there."

Silence followed her words, and she regretted their dull obviousness.

"No," David agreed, his tone subtly changed, carrying the warmth he saved for her. "Not long."

"Especially after so long," Moynihan added.

And the journey wore on. The headlights seemed even harsher in the cave than they had aboveground. They starkly lit dust and rock and sent long shadows marching down the cave walls.

David slowed, taking them around a curve, and all at once, the cave expanded into a cavern, mostly filled by a two-story building. The headlights bounced off the drably white sides of the building and exposed its exact, businesslike lines. It looked homely to Margaret, Earth materials crafted into a dwelling by human hands.

David circled around the habitat and docked the rover. They climbed out, toting their travel-cases, and clustered at the door.

Donegan Moynihan fed his code into the security system, and the door opened. They pressed inside to a small room cut off by hatched doorways on either side. One computer screen glowed dully in the wall, facing the hooks that studded the wall opposite.

The mudroom.

David sealed the door behind them, and Moynihan woke the computer. The next minute, environmental controls hissed oxygen into the space.

Margaret set down her case and crossed her arms, tired beyond words of waiting.

Donegan Moynihan turned from the computer and pulled off his helmet. Margaret immediately did the same and breathed in the air around them. It smelled stale and traced with ancient and unguessable chemicals, but she didn't care.

She stripped off her suit, relieved to be rid of it, and hung all its pieces on the hooks. Then she looked at the others.

Moynihan was done loosing himself from his suit, and David was just finishing, but Eamon had gotten tangled up. He finally extricated himself from it, flung it down, and stomped on it. As he bent to grab it up, light ran down his blue jumpsuit to strike the insignia stitched on his upper arm—five stripes and one star.

It equaled the golden leaf on her green jumpsuit. David surpassed them both by a full rank, the silver eagle shining on his gray sleeve.

Moynihan bore no insignia at all.

Their commander twisted open the left-hand hatch. "Let's have a look at our new home."

Eamon finished hanging his suit and brushed his hands off on his shirt. "Home? The exploratory mission forgot to tack up the Home Sweet Home sign."

David walked past him. "I fully expect you to pull one out of your pack and tack it up yourself."

Margaret cast a look at her own pack and decided to worry about it later. She followed the men into the next room.

She knew it was the medical bay; she had memorized the diagrams. Yet the sight of it surprised her—all the solid realness. Black lines on white paper jumped to reality.

"Your domain, Dr. Killiam," said Moynihan. Then—likely because the bay was too small to comfortably contain all of them—he moved on.

Margaret lingered, filling her eyes with the medical bay. She wanted to explore all the equipment, but she put aside the impulse and passed into the lab.

The lab was easily twice the size of the bay, crisscrossed by narrow lab tables, stocky glove boxes, and testing stations. Moynihan stood in the center, running pleased eyes over it all. "And this," he said, "is my domain."

He was as happy as Margaret had ever seen him, but he paused only a moment before stabbing his finger toward the next hatched door. "And there is the engineering bay—Eamon's domain." Then he walked to the stairwell, tucked into a nook of the room, and began the climb to the second level. David went up right after him.

As their footsteps rang on the metal stairs, Margaret took a sideways look at Eamon. Irritation flashed in his eyes, but he motioned Margaret to go before him and then followed, last of all.

The stairwell let out into a common area—two short couches in front of a large screen, a table and chairs mere feet away. A recess on the far side of the room deepened into the galley; the privy ducked out of sight in the corner. Three more rooms, each a private cabin, waited behind their closed doors.

And that was it. Home sweet home.

Eamon slowly circled the room, the light glinting on the plain gold ring on his left hand. He was not married—no married man or woman was even considered for the Mars mission—and Margaret didn't know why he wore a wedding band. In more than two years, she had never gained a right to ask.

Moynihan walked to his cabin and slid open the door, but then he turned back. "It's night in the sky above us, so it's night for us, too. Try to sleep. The morning will come before you're ready."

"You could argue morning never comes in an underground cave," Eamon said. "We'd need to take a trip in the rover to see sunlight. Still . . ." His eyes combed the room.

David smiled. "We're on Mars."

Eamon nodded. "I think this will be a tolerable place to live."

Something—bitterness or pain—ghosted across Moynihan's eyes and vanished. "How does it strike you as a place to die?" And he melted into his cabin.

"Hail to our fearless leader," Eamon muttered, barging into the cabin he shared with David.

David caught Margaret's eye, dismissed the commander's gloom with a shake of his head, and hurried after Eamon.

As second-in-command, David ought to have gotten a cabin to himself. But since Margaret was the only woman, she got it instead, and David had to bunk with Eamon. With guilty gratitude, Margaret slipped into her cabin.

She perched on her bunk. It was larger and softer than the bunk on the spaceship, and she felt a wash of satisfaction. Margaret untied the black laces of her boots, tugged at the heavy shoes, and let them *thump* to the floor. Then she peeled off her thick socks.

Beneath it all, her feet were small and white and cold. She pulled them up onto the bunk and tried to absorb her new reality.

Two years of intense preparation. Six months of getting here. And now they were ensconced in a habitat on Mars, with four years of study and experiments and exploration ahead of them.

Pleasure at their triumph warmed her, and excitement for the work and glory ahead tingled her skin. She stretched out on the blanket and closed her eyes, letting herself dream. But then she thought of lifeless Mars, unforgiving to the point of desolation, and the millions of black, cold miles that separated them from Earth, and a faint trace of panic polluted her joy.

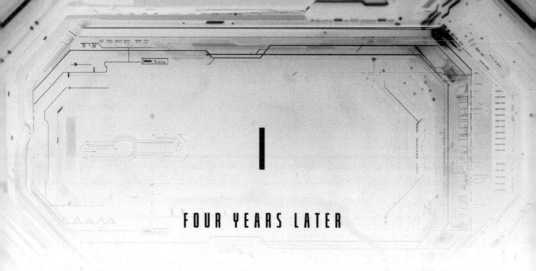

I

FOUR YEARS LATER

Dollar bills filled the truck—bound into neat bundles, stacked floor to ceiling.

Manasseh Cruz stood on the concrete lot and gazed into the open back of the truck. The artificial lights of the building in front of him shone balefully on the concrete, exposed the deep-inked green of the bills that seemed to be within the paper more than on it. The mints of the U.S. Treasury always did good work.

Night air whispered cold around him, seeking to slip beneath his clothes. Cruz kept his hands deep in his pockets, but his face was growing numb.

A man came around the truck, slinging an assault rifle in his hands. "We've got the gates opened," he announced, his breath puffing white clouds in the air between them.

Cruz stretched out his hand. "Give me your knife."

His face unflinching, the man pulled a knife from his belt and gave it over.

Cruz grasped the hilt and, stepping forward, slipped the blade beneath the plastic bindings of a cash bundle and yanked.

The bindings split; the knife was well-honed. Cruz flipped its hilt toward the other man and offered it back.

The man took it, but his eyes stayed on the cash bulging from the cut bindings.

Cruz buried his hand in the tear and pulled it back, clenching bills. He rifled through them—a few new and crisp, the rest ragged. A thousand-dollar bill, a few hundreds, a few tens, one or two ones.

He stuffed them back into the truck. "I keep hoping for higher denominations."

The armed man grunted. "People part harder with those."

Cruz knew that, but he still hoped higher bills would be procured—still thought they could be. He stared at the towers of dollar bills, remembering those he had gathered in the past, imagining those he would gather in the future. Then he motioned sharply toward the other man, not bothering to look at him. "Proceed."

Cruz walked to the gray door of the building in the lot's center and watched as the truck backed up, sliding its cargo of money through the gates. Then he ducked inside.

Ancient light bulbs lit the drab walls and hard floor, shining bare and harsh from the ceiling. The effect was more depressing than if the place had been left altogether dark.

A long window opened up one of the walls, grime caking its edges where glass met wall. A woman stood by it, an electronic notebook in her hands. Cruz joined her, looking out at the truck trundling to a black, metal shed of a building.

It ground to a stop, and two men hopped down from the cab. They walked to the rear of the truck, black shapes in the fitfully lit back lot. But Cruz saw the rifles dangling at their sides.

The men opened the chute cover, unlocking it on either side and letting it fall to bang against the shed. Then one man climbed into the truck, yanked down a bundle of cash, and lowered it to his partner. The second man shoved it into the chute.

As they emptied the truck, Cruz turned to the woman. "How much this time, Rochelle?"

"Three hundred seventy-three million."

"You always stop at such neat, round numbers. Is it a sign of OCD?"

"No. Laziness."

Cruz looked at her, her alert eyes and adamantine features, and knew that whatever reasons she had, laziness was never among them.

The men finished and closed the chute. They returned to the cab of their truck, and it fired to life and rolled away.

With a jingle of metal, Rochelle tossed the key in her open palm and held it out. "Do the honors?"

Cruz took the key and stepped to one end of the window. He opened a steel panel, slid the key into the slot, and twisted. For a long minute, nothing happened.

Then the explosion boomed beneath their feet, muffled by yards and yards of earth. The floor trembled, and the window shivered.

They stared at the shed until reddish light began to glow through the seams of the building, leak from the roof vents. Hot air streamed out of the vents, occasionally carrying bills up out of the shed. Fire limned some of them, flames tracing the paper against the night.

One bill drifted toward the main building, riding the warm current, and then it fluttered down before their eyes.

Cruz got a long enough look to know that it had escaped the fire untouched, and he knew Rochelle noticed, too. "Well, that messes up your account."

She raised her notebook, full of precise numbers. "I'll go out and tear that bill into tiny pieces."

Cruz didn't doubt that she would. He turned away from the window, his pleasure at the immolation of the bills dampened by that part of his brain that never stopped running numbers. Three hundred seventy-three million—out of tens of trillions.

He sighed, digging his fingers randomly in his pockets for the cigarettes he'd long since given up. "It's like emptying the ocean with a spoon."

"Not quite that bad; maybe a pitcher." But Rochelle's brown eyes softened a little, flicking to him. "When will you come again?"

"When I can. This is far from the only train I have to keep on the rails. And far from the hardest." He held out his hand, and she placed an info chip in his palm. Cruz closed his hand around it, nodding to her. "They're holding a plane for me at Cheyenne. It's time for me to go."

Rochelle turned to the window again. "Have a safe trip, Congressman."

"Until next time, Rochelle." Manasseh Cruz walked out the door, into the night-filled parking lot. He hurried over the concrete, thrusting his hands back into his coat. A sleek car waited for him at the edge of the lot to take him to the military plane, to carry him back.

To Washington.

Reuben Jackson stared out the window. Four stories down, snow clogged the streets of Washington. Dirty grooves formed narrow paths for tires on the road, for feet on the sidewalk. The brown stains were almost pleasant beside the black patches soiled by garbage.

White snow was too much to ask.

"Can't be much of a view, Jackson."

Reuben kept his back turned. "Oh, I don't know, Congressman. I think I can see the Capitol from here."

"Veterans shouldn't talk like tourists."

Reuben stared at the dirty snow. "Tourists? Who has money these days to be that?"

Leather creaked behind him, no doubt as the congressman stood up from one of the conference chairs. "Now you're talking like me."

Reuben forewent a response.

Footsteps echoed the congressman's way toward the door. "I'll give you credit, NASA Man. You do a lot of talking with your back."

Reuben finally turned around, mostly to see if the congressman really would leave before the meeting began.

The congressman stopped at the service cart and picked up a pitcher, beads of condensation rolling down its glass sides. He poured out a cup of ice water and looked up at Reuben. "The stronger stuff is at the bottom."

Reuben regarded him. Manasseh Cruz, the chairman of the Mars Appropriations Committee, one of the most powerful men in Washington and—in Reuben's book—always up to something. The heritage his surname proclaimed left its mark in his skin, in his dark eyes and black hair, but Reuben always thought he saw traces of other legacies in the congressman's face. What chaos of nationalities and ethnicities ran in his blood Reuben could only guess, but they combined to give the congressman the happy advantage of looking good in his campaign ads.

Reuben let his eyes drift to the service cart, drift down to where Cruz alleged they smuggled the strong stuff. And he shrugged. "I'll take a shot if you will."

Cruz saluted him with his glass, making the ice cubes tinkle. "I could make a politician of you, NASA Man."

Reuben disliked the nickname, probably because he disliked the congressman, but he smothered his irritation and tried to be semi-friendly. "I wonder when the Four First Names are going to get here."

Cruz walked back to the table and sat down. "Within five minutes, or I'm out of here. I've got more to do than they have."

On the trail of his words, the door opened, and all four scientists came in together. Dr. Karl—his eyes like iron, in color and hardness—sat at the head of the table. Opposite him, Dr. Francis, his red hair fading into gray, took over the other end of the table. Dr. Noel, with his distant eyes and perennially crooked collar, grabbed a chair beside Dr. Rudolph, who still wore glasses although he really could afford proper eye treatment.

These were the Four First Names, the Mars Discovery Steering Committee.

Reuben took the seat alongside Cruz, the only chair still open, and they filled up one side of the table, as if allies.

Dr. Karl laid both hands on the table. "Let's get this show on the road. Jackson, begin."

Reuben took a moment to answer, carefully schooling his feelings out of his voice. "Nothing has changed since our last meeting. Except that instead of being two weeks late, the relief convoy is now three weeks late." Which they knew—and had caused.

No one responded to Reuben's words, and it took Karl less than half a minute to close the opportunity. "Chairman Cruz?"

"Congress," Cruz answered, "is still unwilling to appropriate funds for a spaceflight to Mars and back. America simply cannot make such an expenditure. You must bring down the funding request. It's dead in the Appropriations Committee."

Reuben drummed his fingers against the table and looked at Karl, waiting for him to drop the second shoe.

Dr. Karl obliged. "The steering committee has canceled the relief convoy."

"We'll send a supply capsule." Dr. Francis hurried the words out of his mouth, looking toward Reuben but not quite at him. "It will bring the colonists five years' worth of foodstuffs. They'll be taken care of."

'Colonists?' Reuben repeated. He looked at the scientists, who had been part of the project far longer than he. "When did they become *colonists*? They signed up for four years of exploration, nothing more. It's not right to simply leave them on Mars."

"No, it's not right," Cruz said. "It also isn't right that our grandparents and great-grandparents shoved us into a hole trillions of dollars deep."

Reuben sighed. Somehow, Cruz could never hold a conversation without clambering onto his hobby horse. "The debt's gone."

"But we're still in the hole. We'll be years more climbing out."

Reuben shook his head, not wanting to hear more of Cruz's endlessly gloomy diagnoses and prognoses. "Let's stay on topic. The Mars team has lived four years trapped in a handful of rooms, one mistake away from death every day. It's time to bring them home. We said we would. And don't you remember? It was you who made the promise."

Cruz swiveled, pointing to the window that opened onto the wintry gray and white of the city. "Jackson, if you cared to follow that road out there a mile or two, you would find whole neighborhoods of people burning dollar bills to keep warm. We aren't helping them. Why should we help the Mars team?"

"The troubles of being trapped on a death planet like Mars—"

"Are among the many troubles we can't afford to fix." Cruz pushed up from the table to look down on Reuben. "Congress will not approve the convoy to Mars. My committee will kill it for them."

Reuben also stood. He looked from the congressman to the First Names, all of whom were traitorously mute.

Because, no doubt, everything worth saying they had already said to Cruz before they called the meeting. They were only here to tell him what they'd already decided. "If," Reuben said, "there's nothing to talk about, you could just have sent me a memo." He walked away from them and right out the door, his anger rising with every step.

"Neither Cruz nor Karl has any give in him. Now that they've united against the convoy, there will be no convoy."

Jephthah Baines, standing behind his desk, went on sorting papers without looking up. "And that's bad?"

Reuben studied Baines, trying to read the nuances of his words. "Of course. We're breaking the promise we made to our people on Mars. They've gone from explorers to colonists, and they don't even know it. But what can we do? Too many people are suffering here."

"I heard you kicked up a fuss."

Reuben folded his arms. "Who talked?"

"That same little bird who always tells things to the president's chief of staff." Baines looked at him for the first time since he began his report, and the light of the desk lamp glinted in the chief of staff's eyes. "So, why did you turn the meeting into a fight?"

Because Baines wouldn't sit, Reuben stood and leaned against the top of the chair. "They got me with the word *colonists*. Do you see how they make decisions? They don't ask for our agreement. They don't want our advice. Sometimes they don't even announce their decisions. They just do what they want, and eventually we figure it out."

Baines pointed a finger at him. "That's an old problem. My new problem is that stories are flying all over Washington about how the president's NASA liaison insulted the First Names, yelled at the great Manasseh Cruz, then stormed out of the room."

"I didn't—"

"It doesn't matter what you did or didn't do. What matters is the stories. Don't make problems for the president, Jackson. He has enough already."

Stung by the rebuke, Reuben leaned forward. "When did the president lose control of the space missions? NASA is part of the executive branch, and the president is the chief executive. So, how did he lose control?"

"Lay it at his predecessor's feet, Jackson. He was the one who set up the First Names and agreed to a special appropriations committee that funds the mission item by item. That is all the trouble, except—" He stopped.

Reuben eased off the back of the chair, and it creaked as his weight came off it. "Manasseh Cruz. Manasseh Cruz came to town and finished you off."

"How long until you launch the capsule, Jackson?"

Reuben rubbed his neck and acquiesced to the change of topic. "A few more days. Down at Cape Canaveral, they were dusting off *Artemis* for a return flight to Mars. Now we need to find the key for whatever warehouse NASA locked the capsules in after Project Adam. It will take time to prep."

"But the Mars team will be all right."

Reuben nodded grudgingly, but had to add, "Rationing will carry them through with minimal pain."

"Then see that the capsule is launched quickly."

Reuben heard the dismissal in the chief of staff's tone, and he stepped back from the desk, grabbing up his coat. "I'll shoot you a memo when we have a launch date." He let himself out of the office and, shrugging into his coat, wove through the halls of the West Wing. Finally he came out onto the snow-covered lawns. The gray winter sky dully faded to black, a sunset with no colors.

Reuben trudged his way to the gate, crunching snow. Secret Service agents standing guard there let him out, and he began the walk home.

As he left Pennsylvania Avenue behind and entered the real city, the landscape changed. Suddenly people were all over the streets—crammed into the alleys, where makeshift shacks leaned against buildings, standing on the sidewalk. Vendors, faces red with the cold, offered their wares.

Reuben stopped at a woman holding a basket, his nose telling him she sold dinner. He gestured to the basket, and she pulled back the cloth for a brief moment. Before she covered up the food again, he noticed two things—a pile of evenly browned pastries, and the steam rising into the February dusk.

He buried his hand into his pocket and brought out five or six coins. He showed them to the woman, hoping she would want them. Many people still accepted coins, especially the older and heavier ones.

She shook her head.

Reuben slipped the coins back, caught the cigarette lighter between his fingers, and drew it out. He held out the lighter and pressed down, making the flame jump skittishly in the winter air.

She shook her head.

Reuben tucked away the lighter and yanked a scarf from his pocket. He shook it out, demonstrating how wide it was, how thick.

The woman nodded.

Reuben passed the scarf to her. She stuffed it into her coat and uncovered her basket, taking out a pastry and giving it to him.

It felt beautifully warm, and Reuben loosened a button to slide the pastry beneath his coat. He nodded to the woman and walked away, hurrying home.

II

Margaret Killiam peered into the microscope. Stroking the adjustor with her finger, she increased the magnification until, finally, she saw.

Or, more accurately, didn't see.

Margaret stepped back and said, "This one is negative, too."

She didn't get an answer, and she didn't expect to. Since Donegan Moynihan had taught her to perform the tests, they had worked together like this—in focused quiet, planets orbiting a sun in fluid, untouching harmony. If Margaret turned, she would see Moynihan bending over his work with absolute concentration.

She did not turn; she stayed in her orbit. Margaret slid out the small petri dish, giving a last glance to the five or six drops of discolored water pooled at its bottom. Six months ago, they had chiseled it as ice from Gusev Crater, in an expedition that mined hundreds of ice samples from the Tharsis region. The work of obtaining the ice had given way to the longer, slower work of analyzing it. Now they were approaching the end.

With nothing to show for it.

Margaret returned the petri dish to the freezer and walked over to the computer. Moynihan's log of the ice-experiments was open, and she selected the specimen she had just tested and entered her findings. It took barely a moment.

Driven by a glum impulse, she tapped the screen, bringing herself back to the log, and sorted it by negative results.

Hundreds scrolled out of sight below the screen.

She sorted the log again by positive results.

None remained.

With another tap, Margaret returned the log to its normal organization. She walked to the freezer but stopped before touching it, turning to where Moynihan worked not three yards from her. He looked intently into the microscope, and she waited for him to straighten before speaking. "Do you think we'll find it, Dr. Moynihan?"

He reached for something lying flat on the shiny steel table. "Find what?"

"Microbes. Bacteria. *Life*." There was no greater discovery to be made on the Red Planet.

The scientist slowly pulled his hand back, slowly turned his gray eyes to her. "It doesn't seem likely, does it?"

Margaret looked him in the eye, wanting him to give her more. "Four years, Commander. Four years of expeditions and experiments, and not a trace of even the lowest forms of life."

"This planet is hostile to life. It may be that nothing—not even the most simple organism—ever lived here. But there is also some evidence that Mars once was habitable, and the planet could have hosted life then. Maybe all these years of radiation and a subzero climate scoured all life from Mars. And maybe life is still here somewhere."

"Perhaps in Jeanne?"

He shrugged. "Perhaps."

"So, why did you abort our expeditions to Jeanne?"

"You know why, Doctor. The cave is so deep our radar couldn't sound it, even ten kilometers in. To explore Jeanne, we would have go to so far into the volcano—and so far under it—that any mistakes would be fatal."

"And yet that's exactly where we would find life on Mars, if it's here to be found."

"True," Moynihan agreed. "Maybe Jeanne would lead us to bacteria living underground, or microbes frozen in the ice. But if we die making the discovery, will it be worth it?" He turned back to his microscope, making his question rhetorical, and that rhetorical question the last word.

Margaret felt him withdrawing again, tucking his spirit away into whatever place he kept it safe.

Safe from, among other things, her. She turned to the freezer—and back again to Moynihan with a question. "Did you ever want to be famous, Dr. Moynihan?"

He stopped and looked at her. A slow half smile quirked his lips, but she didn't know what he smiled at. "I admit I've wanted to see my name bandied with respect in scientific circles. What about you, Dr. Killiam? Did you ever want to see your name written in a history book?"

She turned away. "No. I've seen other names written in history books, and it wasn't good." Margaret opened the freezer, suddenly wanting to be busy, but her words boomeranged back at her. Two names stood before her eyes—written on her heart even more surely than on that awful page of history.

"Y'know, I always wanted to be famous. I'd settle for infamous."

Margaret turned around and saw Eamon, lounging in the hatchway to the engineering bay. His posture was as lazy as his drawl, but his blue eyes were wide awake.

As Margaret wondered if he'd heard all their conversation, Moynihan adjusted his microscope. "Don't worry, Lieutenant Commander. You've got your place in history."

Eamon sauntered into the lab, hands in his pockets and eyes tracking the two doctors. "Being famous isn't the same as having a place in history. All sorts of people have places in history, but only historians know who they are."

"I concede the point," said Moynihan, and ended there.

A clambering noise in the stairwell heralded David's arrival, and the next moment he burst into the room. He brushed past Eamon without looking at him and strode over to Moynihan. "Commander, we got a signal from NASA. They want you to stand by for a transmission."

Moynihan moved away from the microscope, pointing to it and looking at Margaret. "Doctor, if you would . . ."

She nodded.

The commander headed off across the room. "Come with me, Colonel."

As they walked by Eamon, he said, "Maybe they're launching the convoy."

David went straight up the stairwell, but Moynihan stopped long enough to answer. "One can hope. At least you can." Then he, too, vanished up the stairs.

Margaret went over to the microscope to finish Moynihan's testing. Eamon wandered closer to her, shaking his head. "Think he's a born pessimist or a made one?"

Margaret had definite opinions on that, but she didn't want to discuss them. "In a scientist, skepticism is a virtue."

Eamon sighed and sat on one of the lab tables. "I always knew we'd have to bring a scientist with us. But I never imagined they'd put him in charge. Why?"

Margaret considered the question rhetorical and didn't answer.

"What do you think, Meg? Wouldn't you be happier if your brother was the commander?"

She shot him a censorious look. "That's an unfair way to frame the argument."

He grinned at her.

Margaret sighed. "I think you're just upset that they put a civilian in command."

"Nah, I don't mind that he's a civilian. I just mind that he never had to go through boot camp."

Margaret reached out and traced the cold surface of the microscope with her finger. "I think he's been through life's boot camp."

"Haven't we all?"

David stepped into Moynihan's cabin. The commander settled into the chair before his desk and stared at the computer screen—black, awaiting the signal from Earth.

David, staying on his feet, loomed over the commander. They waited in silence for a minute or two, and then David said, "Sir, our water storage levels are registering low. Austerity measures or no, someone needs to go out and harvest water."

"You can go, Colonel."

"Alone?" It was, technically, a violation of policy for anyone to venture out of the habitat alone, but Moynihan had shown himself willing to set aside certain regulations.

"No. It's not safe to go out alone."

And some regulations he kept. David thrust away his disappointment. "I'll take Meg. We'll stop by and check out the greenhouse, too."

Moynihan, staring at the screen, said, "We've had some progress with that. Not enough."

David didn't know who was measuring, nor did he care enough to ask. He itched with the desire to get out on the plains—the sky large above him, the land stretching farther than he could see—but he held himself still. He peered again at the black screen. If the message would come, he could go.

The computer trilled its reception of the signal, and Moynihan said softly, "Colonel, let me prophesy. The convoy will not be sent. We will be lucky—"

White letters began to appear on the dark screen, one by one, as if being typed. David leaned in, reading as the letters strung into words:

> DECISION LAID DOWN BY STEERING COMMITTEE. CONVOY CANCELED. SUPPLY CAPSULE TO BE LAUNCHED INSTEAD WITH FIVE YEARS' RATIONS. YOU WILL BE NOTIFIED WHEN IT LAUNCHES.
>
> REGRET CHANGE, BUT SITUATION ON EARTH HARD.
>
> SEMPER FI.

David's pulse began to pound in his neck. "Five years? Is that how much longer they want us to be here? How long have I been promising myself—" Emotion roiled in his chest, and he paced to the doorway—it took him three strides—and then paced back to the desk.

Moynihan sat unmoved, the muscles of his neck and shoulders relaxed. David stared at the back of his head, astonished by his stillness. "Commander . . ." Then he remembered what Moynihan had been saying just before the transmission began. "How did you know?"

"I know what's happening on Earth."

"So do I." Suspicion slithered into his mind; had Moynihan been receiving secret transmissions?

Moynihan slowly turned the chair until he faced him. "I was one of the First Names, once."

David had heard, but suspicion still stalked him. From the beginning, Moynihan had always kept much to himself, stored away in great vaults beyond anyone's guessing.

Reality crashed on David with all the bracing force of an ocean wave, and he shook off his thoughts like bad dreams. He rubbed his forehead, returning to the trouble before them. "We need to tell Meg. And Eamon. We've got a long five years ahead of us." His hand dropped down to his side as he made a calculation with disgust. "Do you know how old I'll be in five years?"

"About how old I am now."

David opened his mouth, but then decided not to apologize. "Everything is narrow on Mars, Commander. It's pressing in on me from every side. I don't want to be five years older before I can breathe again."

Moynihan stood up. "Colonel, if there was anything I could do on this planet, or back on Earth, I would. But there is nothing we can do except take it and try to take it well." He pointed toward the door. "Let's go tell them."

David turned and marched out the door. He was quickly upon the stairwell, and he descended to the level below.

Margaret stood at the computer, and Eamon leaned against the stand-up desk. Ire burned in David at Eamon's proximity to his sister, and he quickly went over to join them.

Moynihan emerged from the stairwell, came to within several feet of them, and stopped. "Earth canceled the convoy. They say they will send a supply capsule instead, with five years worth of rations. But it has not yet been launched."

Eamon stared at him, his expression shifting through surprise and dismay to what looked, oddly, like calculation.

As David began to grow angry at whatever the engineer was contemplating, Margaret asked, "Why?"

Moynihan looked at the floor, his expression quiet and serious, as if he were organizing his words against its blank surface.

But he didn't speak, until David felt compelled to answer, "The situation on Earth. All sorts of promises have been broken in the last two years. I suppose it's finally our turn to share in the joy. Other people are suffering worse." His spirit lifted a little, finding encouragement with perspective, and he added, "At least we know we are going to eat."

Moynihan looked up then, and for just a moment, something—some tide of great feeling—flashed through the colossal calm he wore like armor.

Then that moment was over. Placidity closed over the commander once again, and he said, "Promises have gone the way of the dollar. They aren't worth anything—even when signed 'Semper Fi.'"

Margaret looked a question at David, and he said, "That was how they ended this last transmission."

'Semper Fi?' Eamon repeated. "They let a marine write the message? I didn't know marines knew that many words."

Moynihan raised his eyebrows. "What's wrong with marines?"

David and Eamon looked at each other. David saw, for the first time since they'd talked Moynihan out of sending them to Tharsis together, that they agreed on something. "Marines think they're so tough."

"Especially," Eamon added, "in contrast to people who do all their fighting from thirty thousand feet up."

The moment of accord died. "And if you can't stand to be thirty thousand feet up, going Mach twenty in a combat jet, they give you a boat and let you float on the water. At least the marines are the men's department of the navy."

Margaret put her hands on her hips. "Maybe we could talk about something important."

"Doctor," Moynihan said, "there is not much we can say."

"There's always something to say." Eamon took one step closer to Margaret, pushing every nerve in David's body to the edge, and unfortunately kept talking. "Since we're stuck on this rock waiting for our ride for the next few years, I think the obvious thing to do is for me and the doctor to get married."

David seized the back of Eamon's collar and dragged him away from Margaret. "Make your play some other time. Actually, make it on some other planet."

Eamon yanked out of his grasp. "A marriage proposal is deadly serious."

"Oh, it'll be deadly for you."

"And who are you to decree what your sister and I will or will not do?"

David's hand jerked up again, by the same instinct that sent words scalding onto his tongue—

"The colonel has no need to decree," Moynihan said. "Higher authorities already have. The policy of the mission forbids marriage. You know that."

Margaret looked archly at David and Eamon. "Not that it matters in the least."

David, eyes on Eamon, lowered his upraised hand and knew the fight was over. Until they resumed it again.

"Colonel," said Moynihan, "go out and drill for the ice. Dr. Killiam, I want you to go with him and check on our plants."

"Certainly, Commander." Margaret turned away from the men and headed toward the mudroom.

David nodded to Moynihan, ignored Eamon, and followed Margaret.

At his back, Eamon said, "You mentioned the policy of the mission,

Commander. Well, the mission has changed. And when the game changes, so do the rules."

"And what rules are we talking about, Mr. Eamon?" Moynihan asked.

David reached the hatchway and moved through slowly, wanting to hear. Fainter now, but still clear, Eamon's voice followed: "All of them. Nine years is a long time to live on Mars."

David took a few steps and then lingered just within the med bay. A moment later, he was rewarded with Moynihan's answer: "Nine years is a long time. But we have only lived here four."

Then the stairwell rang with a man's footsteps, and David did not doubt they were Moynihan's.

David hefted his end of the container as high as Margaret, struggling behind him, could tolerate. He carried most of the weight, and it imbalanced the container, making it slide against his palms. Again and again he shifted his grasp, seeking a firm grip.

Having Eamon or Moynihan here would have made the work go easier, but David preferred the relief to his mind over the relief to his body.

They finally reached the open back of the rover, and they shoved the container atop another just like it. David stepped away. "That's the last." The words bounced off the faceplate of his helmet, coming back at him.

Margaret didn't answer, just slid the remote out of her pocket.

As she closed the hatch, David turned around. The excavation site lay like a gray wound in the plain, plunging down to the vein of frozen water. Moynihan had discovered the ice channel and studied it with rare enthusiasm. Once, in a burst of talkativeness, he explained to David the true significance of the ice buried in the plain. All David could think, as scientific terms flowed past him, was that it was a more accessible source of water than the glaciers on the volcano, and that he missed living on a planet where water was not considered a phenomenon.

"Ready to go back?" Margaret asked, her voice reduced but clear through the transceiver.

"Not really." David looked up at the sky, yellow-brown and hazy with dust, and wanted to conquer its heights, its pristine silence. He brought his hands close to each other, barely noticing as his fingers twitched after the patterns engrained on him in a cockpit long ago.

Margaret pointed. "Look, David."

He lowered his gaze to see a gust of wind swirling dust down the plain. "It's been nearly five years since I felt the wind."

"And it will be another five years more." He shook his head. "It's too long."

"For what?"

David thought it was obvious. "To wait to go home."

"If any of us had had much on Earth, we wouldn't be here now."

"Maybe so," he allowed. "But whatever we were missing on Earth, we aren't finding it here. On Mars we can't even have a family. Policy of the mission and all."

"Do you want a family?"

He shrugged. "For the first time in my life, I'm dreaming the American dream. I wonder what it would be like to live in a suburban house, behind a white picket fence, coming home every evening to a wife and a couple kids. But maybe I'm just fooling myself. Maybe, if I can ever get off this wasteland, I'll be happy with just my old freedom again." His eyes wandered up to the sky. The ragged, icy clouds of Mars yielded no rain, and the sky was as desolate as the desert—but he knew that if he could fling himself through it, he would love it. "Maybe," he added softly, "all I really want is to fly."

"I dread the next few years as much as you—"

"Not quite as much," David muttered. "I hate Eamon."

"No, you don't."

But David worried that he did.

"Regardless, David, the last four years have passed, and so will the next five. It won't be the worst thing that ever happened to us."

David nodded, thinking of the worst thing, and stared out at the plains. The desert spread out before them like a shoreless sea, coated with coppery dust that tarnished the beaten rocks with red, like rust. It was thirsty and ravaged, covered with open scars of radiation and scouring winds. The universe had crafted it into a testament to endless endurance.

And, maybe, to survival.

He turned to Margaret. "Come on, Meg. Let's go back and start the next five years."

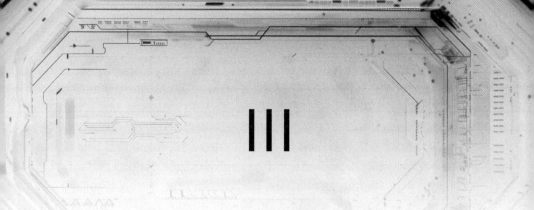

III

Manasseh Cruz lounged in the office chair. It was white leather, expansive, exceedingly comfortable, and not his own. An empty black leather chair faced him, a brazen reminder, but he saved his irritation for a living target. In the meantime, he relaxed.

The lock hummed its release behind him, and the door swung on its hinges. Cruz listened as footsteps tread the carpeted floor heavily. When he judged them to have come halfway to him, he said, "You know I hate it when you waste my time."

The answering voice carried large and strong: "Of course I know. You've told me often enough."

Cruz waited until the man came into sight around the desk to speak again. "I don't like you."

Dr. Karl lowered himself into the black chair. "I can live with that."

"Fortunately for you, so can I. We have work to do, Karl. We've passed a peaceful week, what with Reuben Jackson down in Florida, but tomorrow we enter the hardest phase. This afternoon the mechanics at Cape Canaveral declared the capsule space-worthy; tonight NASA sent in the final funding request to the committee. We're running out of excuses."

Karl shifted back in his chair. "We don't need excuses, Congressman. Just a few good tactics." He pulled a ring of keys from his pocket, then unlocked one of the desk drawers. He brought out a sealed bottle, its glass thick and stout, and set it on the desk. Then he produced two shot glasses that clinked like silver music. The light slid and settled on them, a beckon and a promise.

Cruz blinked.

Karl filled both glasses with an amber liquid, smooth as honey, and set one in front of Cruz. The other he half downed with one swallow.

Slowly, but with unspeakable deliberation, Manasseh Cruz stood .

He picked up the shot glass, gripping its cool sides with painful firmness, and walked to the window. He keyed it open, and cold gusted at him from the winter night.

And he tossed the cup out the open window.

Cruz turned and marched back to the desk. He leaned on it and, looking down on Karl, poured out words like concrete. "I don't like you, but maybe you can understand me. I am not here to have a drink, to socialize, or to shoot the breeze. I am here to do business. If you're not interested, I'll clear out." Cold air drifted from the window and washed over his back, but no muscle in his body twitched. He and Karl stared at each other, a silent contest.

Karl drained the rest of his shot. "Very well, Congressman. Business. At Cape Canaveral, they're waiting for your word, and you, obviously, can't give it. Unless blocking the funding request in the committee is an option—"

"It isn't."

"—we need a sideshow. The president is trying to get his budget passed. Throw a wrench in the works, and you'll have a diversion to last us weeks."

Cruz sidestepped the draft, letting the cold roll past him—to Karl, but he didn't truly mind that. "I already promised the president my support."

"And you care?"

"I do." He hardened his voice. "And I will never turn America's financial troubles into a sideshow. I draw a red line there the size of the Mississippi."

Karl filled his shot glass again. "I suppose we all need some sort of principles. I have my own."

Cruz didn't know what those were, and he didn't want to discuss it. "It's not only a matter of principle. I have my own interests to tend to, and the political price of gumming up the budget process is too high. The public needs to see my moderate, agreeable side. Do you have any ideas that don't damage America or my career?"

"I do. Leave town, Congressman. Your family is still down south, aren't they? Say that one of your children—"

"Leave them out of this."

Karl shrugged. "Three strikes, and I'm out. What are your ideas?"

Cruz circled back to the white leather chair and dropped into it.

He regretted the cold meandering through the room but not enough to close the window. "I have a plan. It starts with you."

"And what do I do?"

"You can figure that out. Lie, stall, put up red tape, manufacture a crisis—whatever strikes your fancy. When you've become such an irritant that Jep Baines summons Jackson back and sics him on you, your work will be done. It will be my turn then."

"And what will you do?"

"Depends on what sort of opening you leave me." Cruz set his gaze on Karl, on his sharp and watchful eyes. "Give me a few days to find an opportunity or to create one. I will find our next excuse."

"I trust you for that." Karl downed another gulp of the liquid honey. "But we need a month more; that's a long string of excuses."

"You don't know the half of it."

Karl narrowed his eyes. "What?"

Cruz opened his mouth, but a rap on the door cut him off. Karl reached and pressed down on his intercom.

The door opened, and a tall young woman wafted into the room. She moved across the floor soundlessly and set a thick folder on Karl's desk. "Will there be anything more tonight, Doctor?"

Karl pointed to the open window. "Close it, and then you can go home."

She looked at the window streaming cold air into the room as though just noticing it. Her expression casual, she walked over, shut the window, and for good measure, drew the drapes.

"Thank you, Willow," Karl said, but not like he meant it. "Good night."

Willow left the room as silently as she entered.

Karl looked at Cruz, his eyes demanding an answer.

"Not one month," Cruz said, his voice low but implacable. "With Jackson on our backs, we'll need two."

Karl shook his head. "How can he double the time we need? He has no power, no influence, no one in his contacts that would cost you or me a moment of worry. The president himself is marginal. How much more ineffectual is Jackson?"

"When it comes to the policy of the space missions, he is ineffectual. I'll even go the extra mile and call him whiny and annoying. But . . ." Cruz trailed off, staring past Karl's shoulder to the wall, covered with mementos of glory. A degree from Harvard, a degree from Dartmouth, a degree from Cambridge, awards and letters signed by names weighty with prestige.

Cruz trusted far more his own education of hard knocks, where people were his major and life gave the tests. "Jackson is persistent, Karl. For some reason, he's made it his business to care. Any man who really cares about anything has it in him to be dangerous. Two months, Doctor—that's how much we have to have in us. I have no taste to be caught."

"I can play the game and not be caught. Can't you?"

Cruz stood, his spirit stirring with dim visions of danger—the sheer drop-off of a cliff, the cold barrel of a gun. "No man can play the game and know for certain he'll win. You and I can always lose. That's what makes the game so exhilarating."

Karl stood up to face him eye to eye. "Let your philosophy of the game be what it is. Only keep your determination to win absolute. You and I can buy this time, day by day. Hour by hour, if necessary."

Cruz stepped away from the chair. "Tag. You're it."

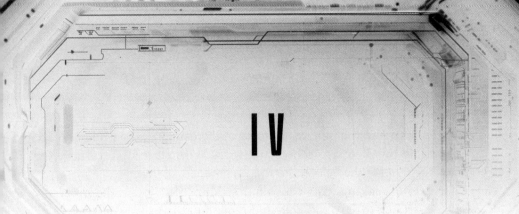

I V

Except for the dismal light of the computer screen, the room was dark. Donegan Moynihan had turned off the lights when he tried to sleep, and he had no reason compelling enough to get up out of the chair and turn them on again.

The screen stared at him unwaveringly—blank still, and maybe blank forever. They might never send another word.

Moynihan blinked, feeling the ache of the dim blue light pressing against his eyes. He put his head in his hands and sighed. "It's not coming," he whispered to himself, because he had no one else to say it to. "I know it's not coming. So, why do I sit here and wait?"

Images of the lab winked through his mind—his microscope, the glove box, shelves of specimens he could analyze. If he had any sense . . .

He dismissed the thought, sagging more deeply into the chair. He had sense. He didn't have the heart.

Margaret Killiam was in the lab, he guessed, storing up data that NASA would retrieve someday. Years into the future—maybe a decade, maybe two—they would revive the mission. A new team would take up residence in their habitat, take up the abandoned work.

And all the information he had collected with such care and so many pains, his finest analysis, would be no more than dull, sturdy facts living on a screen. The scientists who succeeded him would never know their cost, the price Moynihan and his team had paid.

The greatest payment was still to come. And it was coming. Every day brought it marginally, relentlessly closer.

Moynihan lifted his head, looking at the computer screen with bleary eyes. A conviction whispered through his soul, became words in his heart: *Tell them, you must tell them . . .*

David sprawled on the bunk, staring up at the ceiling and wishing the rover would break down so he could fix it. With austerity measures grounding them at the habitat, he saw no prospect of that.

He heard creaking from Moynihan's cabin—for though the outer walls were thick to stave off cold and radiation, the inside walls were thin. As David listened, the noise went on like a well-worn song. Footsteps marching away from David—Moynihan pacing to his door. Footsteps marching back toward David—Moynihan pacing to his desk. More creaking.

Moynihan sitting again.

David brought his fist down on the yielding mattress. Then, in a burst of energy or perhaps only exasperation, he swung his boots off the bunk and dropped to the floor. Moynihan had scarcely left his cabin in three days, and David could feel his blue funk through the walls. He didn't want to picture the commander alone in his cramped box of a cabin, waiting for the good word that wouldn't come.

But it was hard not to while listening to Moynihan pace.

David stepped out of his cabin, and though he meant to go right by Moynihan's door, he stopped. A minute dragged past as he loitered, indecisive.

Then he walked on. With all his own gloom, it wasn't in him to share the commander's.

As David descended the stairwell, Eamon's voice met him and set his teeth on edge. He stepped into the lab and saw Margaret at her microscope, Eamon lounging on a table much too close to her.

David stopped and folded his arms.

Margaret looked at him, reading his eyes, and frowned a little.

"So," Eamon said, his voice brash in the quiet, "any news of the capsule?"

David shook his head.

"And our commander—still trying out life as a hermit?"

"He's watching," David growled.

Eamon shrugged. "Hey, I did some math. We have five months of rations, and it takes six months to fly anything from Earth to Mars. Taking five from six, we have one month left. Now—"

David sighed. "I am not—"

"—the tricky part of the calculations. We have at least one more month of time than food, which means that we are at least one month short of food." Eamon spread out his hands. "Sound right to you?"

David turned away. "Don't bother me." He made toward the engineering bay, irritation eating at him.

Eamon's voice drifted after him. "Like I said, Meg—"

David threw words over his shoulder, clipped short and each as heavy as a brick: "Don't get familiar with my sister."

He stalked into the engineering bay, staring at it without seeing anything. Frustration welled in his chest like thick, hot tar, climbing up into his throat.

He sensed the shadow behind him, and he turned to see Eamon darkening the doorway. "Mars getting to you, Killiam?"

David looked away, the tar hot and choking.

"Or maybe you were like this on Earth, too. Whatever is wrong with you—"

David spun to face him, jabbing his finger toward the door. "Get out, Eamon."

"Gladly. But to make the next few years slightly less miserable, there's something you need to get clear. You don't own your sister, Killiam, and you certainly don't own me."

Every fiber of his being taut, David approached Eamon until he was close enough to flaunt his three inches of superior height. He made his voice low, calm, and as cold as a river of ice. "I don't own my sister, but when it comes to you, *Lieutenant Commander . . .*" He indicated the silver eagle on his arm, the emblem of his superiority, and finished, "Don't speak to me any more." And he shouldered past Eamon.

Eamon grabbed his arm, and David twisted back, wrenching himself free, then swung his fist into Eamon's face.

Eamon spun around, collided with his workbench, and fell to the floor with a crash, sweeping tools down with him.

David watched, his heart beating hard, his body numb—except for his hand, which stung with incriminating fierceness.

Eamon pushed himself up from the floor. Blood streamed from his mouth, but his eyes blazed. He advanced swiftly, cocking his fist and throwing it.

David raised his forearm and blocked the punch. He took no account of Eamon's left hand, until Eamon rammed it into his gut.

Pain nearly bent him, but adrenaline and instinct roared through him now. He swung again.

Eamon stumbled backward, avoiding it easily. Then he raised his fists and circled forward.

David marked his proximity and pulled his arm so far back his fist was nearly level with his shoulder. But just as he began to let it fly, a hand caught his wrist and gripped hard.

He whirled to the interloper and met the still, unfaltering eyes of Donegan Moynihan.

David yanked back his hand, and Moynihan let it go. But that second quenched all his fire. He cast a look at Eamon, who was dropping his fists and easing back.

For a long moment, Moynihan watched them, his gaze shifting from one to the other. Then he asked quietly, "Do either of you have anything to say for yourselves?"

Eamon—his mouth already visibly swollen, even past the blood—jerked his head toward David. "He threw the first punch."

Moynihan looked at him, and David nodded. "I did."

"Why?"

David looked over at Eamon, trying to build an answer, trying to summon reason from those moments hot with viscera.

Eamon looked back at him, his blue eyes still dangerously bright, then he turned to Moynihan. "He did it because he is as sick of me as I am of him. He hit first, but I enjoyed hitting back."

Moynihan's eyes rested on Eamon for a moment, then returned to David. But David couldn't speak.

Moynihan turned back to Eamon. "Go wait for me in the common room."

Eamon brushed past David and vanished into the lab. Seconds later, the stairwell rattled with his footsteps.

Moynihan went and leaned against the cutting machine. He loosely folded his arms and looked friendly, but his eyes were keen. "Is what he said true?"

David's eyes dropped to his hand, to the drying streaks of blood that speckled his knuckles—was it Eamon's blood or his? "More or less."

"And you hit first, Colonel."

Colonel. The title, his title, poured out condemnation. Shame flooded him—because he had been wrong, because he was second-in-command and he should have been more than Eamon, and instead he was less.

David slid his right hand behind his back. "I hit first, Commander. You had the right to expect better from me, and I'm sorry."

Moynihan nodded. "Colonel . . ." Then he stopped.

David watched the commander stare at the floor for a minute. Then he dropped his hands and looked up. "Colonel, go get the last of the rations out of storage."

"Yes, sir." Relieved to be ending the scene, David walked to the doorway before the obvious question hit him. He turned back. "Alone?"

"Alone."

"Yes, sir." David walked out, new enthusiasm in his step.

When they'd traversed the tens of millions of miles from Earth to Mars, they'd brought with them years' worth of food rations. The habitat—so closely compacted—did not have room to store it all.

So the spaceship had become their storage shed. It was good for nothing else. It had not been built to fly again.

David suited up and drove the rover to the old spaceship. Corrosion had set in, the hull darkening and bending beneath the brutal elements of Mars. The day when Mars would strip off the great plates of metal and bury them in the red dust was far away.

But it was coming.

David climbed out of the rover and stared up at the spaceship, the metal finger of a giant pointing to the bleak skies. He remembered those adrenaline-charged minutes when he had landed it—down from cold space, through the atmosphere, plummeting in the fire of their rockets. The moment he knew he had brought the ship safely to ground was the greatest of his life.

Clear but removed, like the scene of a movie, he remembered the exhilaration that had thrilled through him—at being on Mars, at being alive. He tried to grasp that joy again, but it slipped away.

David walked toward the ship, kicking up plumes of dust. He climbed the metal rungs to the hatchway and, tugging on the release, let himself in.

His wristlight flashed over the dirt-caked floor, over the dim and mottled steel of equipment racks, and finally settled on a wide door. David walked to it, the bright shaft of his light throwing shadows all around.

The door's mechanical system had been dead four long years, and David ran his gloved hand down the jamb. When his fingers found the manual release, he pulled.

The door groaned open, and David propped it with a metal rod and ducked inside. He raised his wristlight and focused it on the metal crates at the back of the room.

Three, all piled into one stack that grazed the ceiling. He nudged the topmost crate away from the wall, getting a grip with his right hand and pushing the other side into his left hand. But the metal crate slid against his gloves, and it toppled off the stack and crashed to the floor. Ration packs spilled from the broken lid and skidded across the cold floor.

David sighed. He reached down, righted the crate, then got onto his knees to collect the rations. The wristlight overshot them for the most part, sideswiping a few with its beam. So David went mostly by feel, finding the ration packs and tossing them back toward the crate.

He picked one up, the light and his eyes grazing it for a second. He almost pitched it after the others, but a sense of something unusual impressed him, and a casual curiosity made him stop to look. He held out the ration pack and aimed the wristlight at it.

Then, instinctively, he hurled the pack away as hard as he could.

V

Reuben Jackson swiveled in the chair, staring up at the water stain in the ceiling. He thought it had, perhaps, gotten bigger since the afternoon before.

He lowered his gaze to the black computer screen that faced him. In all his wanderings to the comm room, he had never seen it lit up, never seen anyone at this station. "Hey, Rogers," he called.

After a moment, Rogers answered, sounding somewhat resigned. "Yes, sir?"

"Could I turn this computer on?"

"Yes, but then I would have to report to the colonel that you are making unauthorized use of a NASA computer."

"That doesn't sound too bad. But Manasseh Cruz would probably fly down from Washington to yell at me for wasting resources during the Great Collapse."

Rogers didn't answer, and Reuben swiveled around. Six stations lined the walls, but only Rogers held a post there—a mousy-haired young man sitting before a blue screen, a thin wire connecting his mouthpiece to the earpiece almost invisible in his ear. "I'm bored, Rogers."

"I suspected, sir."

"Tell me, why does NASA forbid the Mars team from making regular communications to Earth?"

"NASA does not forbid regular communications; it simply discourages them."

"And why?"

"I cannot explain NASA policies, sir."

"Neither can I, and I represent NASA for the president."

Rogers only gazed at the unflickering screen, stoically unmoved.

"Rogers, you sit here hour after hour, day after day, month after month, to receive communications from the four human beings

NASA put on Mars but doesn't want to hear from. Wouldn't you like to understand who is writing the rules of this game and what they mean by them?"

Rogers cut his eyes sideways to Reuben, but that was the only part of him that moved. "I'm only a lieutenant, sir."

Reuben stood. "Well, Lieutenant, give me a call whenever you get a word from Mars."

"Sir, I relay all messages to Washington, and they distribute them."

"I should get you a job in the bureaucracy, Lieutenant." Reuben walked out of the room. After wandering through hallways, he took the elevator down. He stepped out into a broad, quiet lobby. A few people worked industriously at high reception desks, their soft typing and even softer voices floating in the air. Light shone down from the ceiling and brightened the floor, showing so clearly the blue-gray tiles, and the white streaks where the blue-gray had been scuffed away.

Reuben exited the glass doors. Outside, he nodded to the airmen standing vigilantly on either side and descended the steps.

For the next quarter of an hour, he wandered the grounds of the complex, until finally he ended at the airfield. The vast asphalt pavement stretched gray and absolutely level before him. On every side of the airfield, the grass grew wild—two or three feet high, tangled with clinging weeds. The green plants nosed up to the asphalt, which cut them off with dull, but unshakeable completeness.

Reuben sat on the ground at the edge of the field, his boots on the asphalt. He lay back, and the grass rubbed his back and shoulders, as he stared up at the blue sky.

So unchanging were the grass and asphalt and sky, and so quiet was his heart among them, that he didn't mark the minutes going by. At length he heard someone treading through the grass behind him, and then a voice above his head. "So, here you are, Jackson."

Reuben stood. "Here I am, Colonel Nelson. All I need is a plane."

The tall officer passed sober eyes over the airfield. "That is why I came looking for you. Get ready to leave, Jackson. They got into trouble in Tampa, but they'll be back soon."

Wisps of old newscasts fluttered uneasily in Reuben's mind, and he asked, "Is the trouble serious?"

"Until we have to use our guns, nothing is serious."

Reuben suddenly noticed the gun the colonel carried, in a holster at his side, and he wondered how often he used it.

Nelson turned to face the airfield, clasping his hands behind his back. "What will you do in Washington?"

"I'll get a meeting with Dr. Karl and work out whatever issues he has."

"What issues are those?"

Reuben glanced at the afternoon sun. "It doesn't matter."

"It matters to me. When I am forced to scrub a launch, particularly of a relief capsule that's weeks overdue, I would like to know why."

Reuben studied a bird swooping toward the sea, measuring the price of honesty.

"Do you believe I shouldn't know?"

"Of course you should know. That's why you don't."

The colonel waited a moment, then asked with steel in his voice, "Jackson?"

Reuben turned and looked him up and down—from the gray in his hair, to the medals on his shoulder, down his blue uniform to his boots, still showing what polish had survived the tramp through the grass. "Where I come from, I'm the odd one out of the information loop. But they've cut you out even further than they cut me."

"Care to cut me in, Jackson?"

Reuben shrugged. "Sure. You want to know what issues Karl has been raising? Here's your answer: regulations, specifications, space worthiness, budget processes, something about the Space Exploration Act." And then Reuben edged his own voice with steel. "I tell you, it doesn't matter. All Karl's issues and objections are smoke and mirrors. I am going to Washington to try to see past them; when I try too hard, it will all vanish. Karl will withdraw his objections. And then something else will come up."

Nelson narrowed his eyes, deepening the wrinkles around them. "If you're predictions are true, then Dr. Karl doesn't want to help our people on Mars."

Reuben lifted his own eyes again to the sky, to the white haze of a distant cloud. The colonel's conclusion echoed thoughts that had traveled behind him for a long time, no matter how he tried to reject them.

"But why?" he whispered. The question painted itself large on the sky, as it had hung over him for many a dreary month in Washington.

Why did Karl act as if all he wanted to do with the Mars team was rid his hands of them?

The colonel wandered a few feet onto the airfield and kicked a small, dirty rock into the grass. "Do you know them? Any of the Mars team?"

Reuben shook his head. "I never even met them." He had pored over their personnel files, had watched government footage of their training, of their launch from Cape Canaveral the day they left Earth. He still didn't know what they looked like when they smiled.

"I was one of the officers in their training program, Jackson. The program moved too fast to give me the time to know them. Yet I cannot forget their faces. They're on Mars now, making mankind's next giant leap, and nobody seems to care."

"Mankind has its own problems." Reuben stepped onto the airfield, more solid and more warm than the shaggy grass, and found relief in confession. "At the meetings in Washington, I stand up for the Mars team. Congressman Cruz stands up for everybody else. I speak for four people, and he speaks for three hundred and sixty million. You can guess who wins."

"And who does the steering committee stand up for?"

"Dr. Karl."

Nelson raised his brows. "And Dr. Karl . . . ?"

"How would I know?"

They looked at each other—Reuben and the colonel, their words riding the air between them. The breeze whispered cool around them, carrying salt from the sea.

Then a droning rumbled the air. Reuben looked up and saw the plane, black against the blue sky.

Both men backed onto the grass. They watched the plane, growing lower and nearer with the passing seconds.

The colonel took a step. "You'll be back in Washington tonight," he said. "Do what you can."

He walked away, and Reuben stood alone, the roar of the plane growing louder and louder in his ears.

VI

Donegan Moynihan, assured of peace by dispatching David Killiam to the spaceship and Gulliver Eamon to the engineering bay, returned to his thoughts. It was a dark harbor, but a quiet one.

He sat on a couch in the common area, left to himself even there. He felt relief at being away from the computer, and it held him still. Black depths plunged beneath him, but he did not let his mind venture into them. The moment was peace; he took it.

And then the moment ended. A *bang* sounded from the lower level, followed by David's yell: "Meg!"

Moynihan jumped to his feet. He hurried to the stairwell and then down, coming out to see Margaret and David beside one of the glove boxes. Margaret was just sliding her hands into the gloves that hung, limp, inside the box.

Moynihan, who had thought he would see blood, halted in the confusion of his expectation. David threw a look at him. "Sir."

Moynihan paused, taking note of the colonel's pallor. "Colonel . . . ?"

David nodded toward the box.

Moynihan drew forward. When he peered into the transparent box, he saw one of their ration packs. But its silver wrapping had been corrupted, and a strange, dead gray crawled over it.

He recoiled.

"It looks like mold," David said, and for the first time in all the years Moynihan had known him, there was fear in his voice.

"Mold? What?" The voice caused him to turn.

"Come here," he ordered.

Eamon readily obeyed, his eyes fixed on the glove box.

Margaret had taken up the laser, but she waited until Eamon joined them. Then she flicked it on and traced its red beam across the ration pack.

The corrupted wrapping split, the edges curling back. Margaret set down the laser and peeled open the wrapping, exposing the contents. It looked like it had been meat and vegetables once, but now the sick gray covered it. Patches radiated out from bull's-eye centers, overlapping each other and warping the food.

Eamon made a sound in his throat and stepped back.

Moynihan looked to David. "Report, Colonel."

David scrubbed his hair with his hand. "I accidentally broke open one of the crates on the ship. A few of the rations fell out, and they looked like that. Every *one* looked like that."

"But," Eamon said, "maybe the other crates—"

"No," David said, his voice the abrupt force of a gunshot. "I opened all the crates. I took out every ration pack. I examined each one. To the last, each looked like that." He pointed to the food, deformed with the crawling, pestilent gray.

They all stared at it.

Margaret pulled her hands from the gloves, with an all-too-justified finality. "Two months of food. All gone."

"And doing the math . . ." Eamon cut a sideways look at David. "Three months of food and six months until relief comes. That puts us on half rations."

"Survivable," David muttered, still staring at the ruined ration. "And your math is wrong; you're forgetting factors. The plants in the greenhouse, what Meg's got stashed away, from vitamins to nutrients—"

Anger shot from the dark clouds that had so long brooded in Moynihan's mind, with all the suddenness and fierceness of lightning, and he slammed his hand down on the glove box. "It doesn't matter."

David lifted his eyes, and Moynihan saw darkness in them. "Why not, Commander?"

The air grew thick and heavy. Moynihan felt Eamon's open scrutiny, a sharp-edged curiosity, and even Margaret's mild, clear-eyed study weighed on him. His anger was sinking fast, beneath old habits and old resignation, leaving him with the stares of his team and a truth he had been hiding for six years.

But it was time to speak it. Moynihan gestured toward the spoiled ration. "You think that matters, but it doesn't. This story is going to end the same way it was always going to; now it's just going to end a little sooner."

"How does the story end?" asked Margaret in a quiet voice.

The truth, an old, intimate companion, so constant a presence that Moynihan had almost grown comfortable with it, suddenly swelled to monstrous proportions. But he released it. "It ends with our deaths here on Mars. They will not send the supply capsule, just like they would not send the convoy. They never meant to. And they never will."

A few heartbeats of time elongated in frozen stillness. Then the colonel narrowed his eyes. "Have you been receiving secret communiqués from Earth?"

It was rational enough, but some elusive quality, as if the question were brought out aged from a mental cellar, startled Moynihan. He wiped the emotion, all emotion, from his voice and face, leaving nothing but a sureness too great to be emphatic. "No, Colonel. You have read every word from Earth that I have."

"Got ESP?" Eamon pointed his forefingers at his temples. "Over forty million miles?"

David rubbed his forehead. "Don't dignify that with a denial, Commander."

"I don't care what his answer is." Eamon turned to Moynihan. "The point is, I don't believe you."

"You will," Moynihan said, and the words sounded, in his own ears, like a threat.

Eamon folded his arms across his chest, and a gleam entered his eyes.

The colonel stirred, looking between Eamon and Moynihan—perhaps measuring the need for intervention, perhaps only deciding at which to target his hostility.

"Dr. Moynihan," Margaret said, "you've told us how the story ends; tell us the story itself."

Moynihan glanced at her, but her mildness was hard to bear. He looked down at the laboratory's bland white floor, sullied by chemicals and long use and the corrosive dust of Mars. In that space of stained quiet, he admitted to himself that they deserved to be told. He measured out what truth he would tell, put aside the rest, and raised his head. "You know the beginning. You were there—back when we were humanity's great hope."

They watched him, seeming reluctant to make the journey back in memory. Then Eamon said, "You know, I never believed our own press. I never thought we were going to turn Mars into the new Western frontier."

"But other people did," Margaret reminded him. "'Save Earth, Colonize Mars'—remember that slogan?"

David lightly beat his knuckles against his palm. "That was when space was still fun." And his eyes wandered the floor, as if he were looking for it, looking for the fun.

"It was," Moynihan agreed. Even for him, though he had no intention of sharing that. "So much fun that you didn't even have to try all that hard to ignore the warning signs."

Eamon made a derisive sound. "We didn't need space for that. We'd been ignoring warning signs of the Great Collapse for three generations, and it got real easy."

"But for the government, the warning signs were blazing like fire alarms. Just after they launched *Artemis*, Congress issued a report stating that in less than five years, without fail, without any more delay, the nation would default. No more money, no more loans; bills a century old were finally going to come due."

The colonel looked up again. "I never heard that."

"Of course not." The sarcasm rolled bitter off Moynihan's tongue, and he didn't bother to restrain it. "You were only an air force major. I was one of the First Names, and even I would never have known if not for Dr. Karl. He had decided that we would cancel Project Adam, put it off to another decade, when it might have the money and the spotlight it deserved. He knew that the Great Collapse, when it finally came, would knock the Mars mission off its pedestal and out of everyone's mind. So he told the rest of the First Names about the report, to arm us for the fight. None of the politicians had the courage to burst the bubble they had blown. Certainly they weren't going to deal with the bills until they had to. But we, the First Names, could force them to give up Project Adam."

"But you couldn't," Eamon protested. "You didn't."

Moynihan, considering it best to pass over that failure of logic, simply said, "We never tried. Karl gave us our fighting orders, but we didn't march. Instead of forcing the politicians to give up Project Adam, we forced him to accept it. He never actually forgave us."

"Perhaps," David observed, "he was right."

"Perhaps." Moynihan, in the solitude of his own thoughts, had debated that more times than he could count. "But as long as the government was wasting trillions, it might as well have spent billions on the Mars mission." He glanced at Eamon. "And who knows? We might be opening the new Western frontier. The first pioneers never know if anyone is going to follow them, if whatever foundations they lay will be built on or will molder into nothingness."

"If," said David, "I can be macabre for a moment—"

"Please," Eamon muttered.

"I am more concerned with whether our bones are going to molder here. So, you beat Dr. Karl. Commander, what does that mean?"

"At first, I didn't think it meant much," Moynihan admitted. "Everything went ahead. NASA vetted candidates and submitted dossiers to the First Names. And we began sorting through them."

"So," Eamon said brightly, "what made me more impressive than the other engineers?"

The question tripped over the buried truth, and its cheer rang morbid in Moynihan's ears. Eamon's own brightness mocked him, but he didn't know it. Moynihan tried to put the words together gently. "NASA culled the best of the best. Our task, on the committee, was to choose four out of a host of bright, rising stars. You decide whom to reject by discernment, but also by being arbitrary. Dr. Karl had a fine talent for discernment and an exemplary talent for arbitrariness. He struck down many candidates with an endless diversity of reasons. You never saw such a thorough parsing of every jot and tittle in a candidate's résumé. But eventually I saw a strange pattern. Karl would approve only those candidates who had no families."

Eamon thrust out a hand. "NASA wouldn't even consider anyone with a spouse or children." The light shone white on his wedding band.

Moynihan fixed his eyes on him and asked, "Are your parents still alive?"

Eamon frowned, but he didn't answer.

Moynihan pressed on. "Do you have any siblings? Are your grandparents living? Do you have aunts or uncles or cousins? Do you, Lieutenant Commander, have any family at all?"

Eamon's frown melted into paleness.

Moynihan turned to David and Margaret. "And you two?"

David's eyes flared bright with fierceness. "We have family. We have each other."

"All right. But do you have family on Earth?"

He hesitated, looking at Margaret, and she said, "No."

"You three were chosen because you were expendable." Moynihan spoke the words softly, but that made them no less hard. Pity for them—the team he had never allowed himself to know, and whom he had never allowed to know him—stung him, but he drove on with the ruthless truth. "Karl chose you because he knew that when the whole house came crashing down, there would be no one on Earth to fight for you, because there is no one who cares."

David rubbed his jaw with agitated vigor. "That's ridiculous, Sir. I mean, it doesn't—" He stopped to collect himself, while Eamon watched with what appeared to be morbid interest.

David looked at Moynihan. "Sir, it doesn't make any sense. Why would Dr. Karl want us expendable?"

"So that he can get rid of you, Colonel."

"But why?"

"Because, knowing Karl . . ." This time, Moynihan did sigh. "Actually, nobody knows Karl. But from what I have seen of Karl, only three things mean anything to him: the space missions, getting his way, and his personal domain, the First Names. And our presence here is crossing him on all three counts."

"And because he's upset," Eamon asked, "America is going to starve us to death?"

"Because he's angry," Moynihan clarified, "he's going to see to it that America does nothing. It's not usually hard to convince people who don't care about something to do nothing about it. When it comes down to conflict between those who do care and those who don't, those who do win."

Eamon gazed at him, thoughts shifting across his blue eyes. "You really believe all this. And you've believed it forever."

Moynihan half smiled, feeling an amusement with no mirth. "Five or six years. So, close enough, Lieutenant Commander."

"Close enough," Margaret echoed. "So why are you here, Commander?"

His heart plunged. "That's another story, Doctor," he said, its old humiliation on his tongue. "But it's mine, and I won't tell it now."

"Meg's right, though," said Eamon. "Signing up for a mission you think is a death trap takes some kind of . . ."

Moynihan turned away from the glove box. "I told you the truth. Do with it whatever you want. It will still be the same." Without another look at them, he walked away, went up the stairwell, and closed himself inside his cabin.

Margaret sat on one of the infirmary beds. David sat on the other. Eamon had claimed the medical bay's only chair, built to collapse into a third bed if ever it was needed. There was no provision for a fourth bed, possibly on the logic that if all of them needed to be confined to the medical bay at the same time, they were done for, anyway.

The common room would, no doubt, have been a more natural place to talk. But Moynihan was in his cabin, and each of them knew from personal experience that voices in the common room carried easily into the cabins.

Eamon, his foot planted on the floor, swiveled back and forth. "Twenty-four hours. I thought they would have answered by now."

"Did you?" David asked, staring at the wall. "I didn't."

Eamon leaned forward abruptly. "How do you know he's right? If it comes to it, how does he know he's right?"

"I don't know." David spoke the words slowly, his eyes never flickering from the wall. "But I can believe. It fits, don't you see?"

Margaret nodded, glad she was not the only one who saw it. "How they chose people like us, how they limited communications, how they wouldn't send the convoy, the commander's attitude—they're all like signs we couldn't read. And now they're refusing to answer our SOS."

Eamon leaned back again, kicking his heel against the floor. "It's incredible, though."

Margaret glanced at the clock, glaring the time from the wall, and knew that it was night outside. She thought of the dark, desolate surface far above their heads—beaten down by the universe, hostile to all life. Only the walls of the habitat kept the cold and the radiation from sweeping them after the way of red Mars. And it was a thin barrier, measured in inches.

Though Eamon found it incredible that Earth would abandon them, Margaret did not. "I think," she said, "we're pretty well friendless. Earth doesn't care, which leaves us alone to confront Mars. And Mars has always won."

"Come on, Meg," Eamon said. "We can't be that alone."

Margaret thought they could, but she took pity on him and didn't say so.

"Eamon," David said suddenly, "is it possible to launch the *Enyalius* again?"

Margaret glanced at him, wondering when the last time was he had called the ship by its christening name.

Eamon shrugged. "It depends on what you mean by 'launch.' The *Enyalius* can launch in the sense that she can get off the ground. But when she hits the atmosphere, the rockets will burn out, and the ship will fall back and crash in a giant fireball." Eamon flung out his arms to demonstrate such a thing. "That's the sense in which she can launch."

"Suppose you cannibalized the reactor, the fuel cells, the generator—every source of energy we have. Would that get us clear to space?"

Eamon plucked at the chair, his face thoughtful. "I could rejuvenate the engines—even boost them. But I will not be able to replenish the rockets. All we have is the auxiliary rockets, and those will be burned out in the launch into the atmosphere. But running the engines while the rockets blaze—yes, we should make space."

David sat a little straighter. "And the engines—would they have the juice to carry us home?"

"I won't guarantee anything, but it's possible. But we'll have no rockets for the landing, Killiam, and hardly any engine left, either."

David smiled. "You're the engineer, but I'm the pilot. It wouldn't be my first crash landing."

Eamon's shoulders eased a little, and Margaret considered the whole proposal with trepidation, but not as much trepidation as she considered starving on Mars.

A voice broke in on their quiet. "What about the hull?"

Moynihan appeared in the entranceway. When he had come down from his cabin, and how much he had heard, was anyone's guess.

"What about the hull?" he repeated. "Four years of abuse in the Martian elements—do you think it can endure the atmosphere?"

Margaret remembered the ship as she had last seen it. Its hull twisted and darkening, the once-bright metal frowning impotently on the Red Planet.

Eamon and David, to judge by the fall of their expressions, were drawing up similar images. Eamon kicked the floor. "It used to be a good idea."

"It's been fairly and soundly killed." David looked to Moynihan. "So, what ideas do you have?"

"If you mean ideas for escape, I have none."

"Then you're out of place here," Eamon declared. "This is the meeting of the Flee the Sinking Ship Committee. We may be sunk like the *Titanic*, but even the *Titanic* had a few lifeboats."

Moynihan looked at him with a kind of abstract pity. "The *Titanic* was on Earth."

Eamon waved his hand, somewhat erratically. "Oh, well . . ."

Moynihan regarded him a moment more, darkness encroaching the edges of his expression. "Many people died on the *Titanic*, too. But they died with courage and dignity. That was a gift; not everyone can meet a terrible end well. But you have to say, they had it easier than most others. They only drowned. When it's not over that quickly, when people end up camping in the valley of death, then it's hard to stay human. Starvation has spawned horrors that make death look like a mercy."

Scraps of history, dirty and frigid, swirled unwanted through Margaret's mind. The siege of Jerusalem; the duress of Nazi camps; poor, starving Korea—

She curled her hands against the bed, her palms pressing into the soft padding and her fingers wrapping around the cold steel beneath.

Eamon smirked—or tried to. The expression went awry, and he looked like he wanted to be sarcastic and couldn't.

"Commander," said David, "are you saying we might commit those horrors? Against each other?"

Moynihan took a few seconds too long to reply, and by then his silence had already answered the question. "What do you think we might do to each other?"

Margaret waited for David to answer, or for Eamon to be disagreeable, but David only stared at his swollen knuckles, and Eamon raised his hand to the right side of his mouth, puffed up and just a little black and blue.

So Margaret said, "No."

The men looked at her. "No, what?" Eamon asked, but there was a note of relief in his voice.

"No to what you're thinking. No to where this conversation has gone. While we have time, we have a chance."

"So far," Eamon pointed out, "our best chance is firing up the *Enyalius* again. That's most likely to end in us crashing fatally on one planet or another. It's second-most likely to end with the *Enyalius* floating dead in space—and us with it."

Margaret shuddered to think of that cold, everlasting drift.

"Still, it might be worth it—if we can fly for a little while." David's eyes wandered as he spoke, and his fingers twitched.

Eamon's eyes widened. "For the record, I don't think—" Then his expression changed, and he turned to Moynihan. "There are worse ways to go."

Margaret shook her head and slid off the bed. "No one is going that way. But since we shouldn't just sit in the habitat and wait, we should take a risk that means something. We should do something I've wanted to do for years."

David stood, as well. "What is that, Meg?" he asked, surprise in his voice because he didn't know.

Margaret looked at him, then at Moynihan. "I want to see how deep Jeanne is."

Moynihan cocked his head, studying her.

"If that's what you want, Meg, I'm for it." David's eyes were bright on her.

"If we go into Jeanne, we'll probably follow her down forever and meet a miserable end." Eamon slapped his hands against the armrests and stood up. "Dying like explorers in that cave is better than dying like victims here. I'm game."

Margaret looked at Moynihan, for his was the last word.

His eyes met hers—quiet eyes, sad eyes. "What do you expect to find in Jeanne, Doctor?"

"Only a little bit of redemption."

"Redemption," Moynihan repeated, a slow richness in his voice, as if the word was foreign and precious.

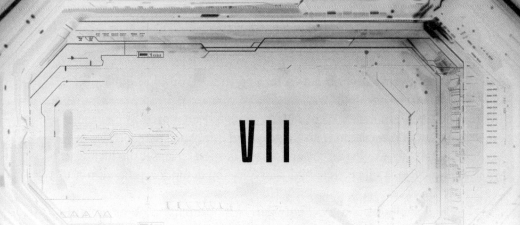

VII

No fresh snow had fallen on Washington in over a week. Lumps of snow endured against buildings, by curbs, and in ragged patches. Stale now, hard and dirty.

The wind arced down over the city, stiff and frigid. It flew out of an iron sky—gloomy, brooding with clouds, giving no more light than dusk.

But Reuben knew it was still early morning.

He jogged lightly, eyes on the sidewalk, hoping to discern any blotches of snow or ice before they flattened him on the concrete. His breath steamed out in white clouds ahead of him, and Jack Frost nipped his face.

At last the sidewalk ran past the building with the gold-handled doors, and Reuben stopped. He fumbled his ID stick from his pocket, then slid it into the key slot. Silently, and of its own power, the doors opened.

He rushed inside, only to pause a few paces in. For a moment, he savored the warmth against his face. Then he headed down the hall, his footsteps cushioned by the deep carpet.

Two turns, and he came to the large cherrywood door, and the small desk in front of it. A woman sat there already, an electronic notebook in her hand.

"Good morning, Willow," he said cheerfully. And he really did feel cheerful, for he was warm again. "Can you schedule me in to see Dr. Karl today?"

Willow looked up from the notebook, but she did not lower it. "Dr. Karl is not seeing anyone today."

"Ah." So they were in usual form. "I suppose I'll have to see him, then."

Once there had been a couch in the hall, but Karl had had it removed to discourage people, and especially Reuben, from waiting to see him. Reuben had long since gotten over it. He sat down on the carpet by the cherrywood door, his back against the wall.

Willow turned her head to look at him. "You look quite pitiful, Mr. Jackson."

Reuben grinned. Karl had often enough been moved by his beggar-like pose into seeing him just to get rid of him. Such pathetic displays—like something in the streets, poor and desperate—upset the high-class mien of Karl's office. The high-class was by definition refined, not to mention exclusive.

Willow looked away. "Dr. Karl will probably not be in until late morning."

She was a good executive assistant "I hope you can tolerate my company until then." He knew he could tolerate hers.

Willow stood and crossed her arms. "Mr. Jackson, when was the last time you talked business with anyone?"

It felt weird to stare up at her as she stood there, so he pushed himself to his feet. "I spoke to Jep Baines early yesterday."

"I think you should speak to him today—this morning, Mr. Jackson."

Reuben frowned. "What happened?"

"You should speak to Mr. Baines."

Reuben tried to read her face but couldn't. He had never seen Willow act like this before, and he wasn't sure what to do with it.

He decided, after a moment, to listen to her. "All right, Willow. I'll ask him." Thrusting his hands into his pockets, he went back the way he had come.

Reuben let himself out into the freezing day. He hurried down sidewalks, the sharp wind drawing tears from his eyes and frosting his cheeks with them.

When he arrived, shivering, at the White House gates, the guards put him through their usual security routine and finally admitted him. At the doors of the White House, another layer of Secret Service agents administered another layer of precautions. Finally they released Reuben into the West Wing.

He wound down halls, honeycombs of offices—important people doing important work. Young as the morning was, still he saw lights beneath many of the doors he passed. He had always prided himself on his early rising, but he had never yet beaten the White House staff. He doubted anyone in Washington did. In the White House, unnatural hours were a normality.

And this, Reuben had sometimes reflected, might have been why those at the White House lived so perpetually on the borders of reality.

Light seeped out from beneath Jep Baines's door, and Reuben rapped on it. A called-out permission, and he went in.

Baines's eyes flicked up, down, then up again. He sat back in his chair. "It's early, Jackson. What brings you here?"

Reuben walked up to the desk. "I'm looking for someone to tell me. I went to see Dr. Karl, and his assistant gave me the impression that something is up."

Baines gave him an odd look and, leaning forward, fished a paper from one of the lower stacks on his desk. He held it out.

Reuben took the paper, watched Baines turn back to his work, then looked down. He saw first the NASA emblem riding the top of the page. And lower . . .

Military Communiqué
Transcribed at Cape Canaveral, FL
Received from Mars Mission, Deep Space Network

SOS

DISCOVERED BACTERIA INFECTING ENYALIUS STORAGE. CALCULATE 2/3RDS OF REMAINING FOOD SUPPLY DESTROYED.

IMMEDIATE EARTH SUPPORT NEEDED. ADVISE REGARDING RESPONSE.

SOS

Reuben looked up, a numbing like he had never felt spreading over him.

Baines watched him, the strange look on his face again. "Two-thirds destroyed works out to seven weeks of rations left. And it would take about twenty-five weeks to send them food. Do the math, Jackson."

He had a smart answer, but it stuck in his throat, for looking at Baines's eyes, he suddenly realized what the strangeness was. Pity.

"What else?"

Baines leaned back again, and though pity softened his eyes, his face was hard. "The First Names officially recommended that we classify the mission a failure. Close the book, close the doors, change the status from live to dead. The Mars Appropriations Committee backed the recommendation. And the president accepted it."

Reuben's heart pounded. "They'll die. And it'll take so long."

"And there's no changing it."

Reuben crumpled the communiqué. "If we had sent the relief convoy when we were supposed to—a *month* ago—it would have made all the difference."

Baines only looked at him, and that futile *would* hung in the cold gap between them.

"I resign," he told Baines.

"I accept," the chief of staff answered.

Without one more word, without one more look, Reuben turned and left the office. Halfway down the hall, he realized he was still holding the communiqué.

He looked toward Baines's door, but he was unwilling to go back—intending, with ever-strengthening resolve, never to go back. He stuffed the paper into his coat and hurried on.

When he came out onto the lawn, snowflakes swirled down from the heavens, beautiful and glistening, but cold, so cold. The gray skies loosed themselves on the earth, heaping winter on the weary city.

That spurned cry from Mars fell through the glowering clouds, echoed in his mind and in his heart: *SOS. Save our souls . . .*

And through the tears that blurred his eyesight, the somber day was as dark as night.

VIII

Margaret sat on her bunk, looking without reason at her hands resting on the blankets, pale against the gray. She had come to soak in the perfect privacy of her cabin, maybe for the last time, and her heart was quiet and just a little sad.

Sad for what, she could not have said.

She heard banging below her—David coming in from the rover. She waited for the noise of him going out again, but it didn't come. Then a hum died in the walls around her, and she knew Eamon had shut down the reactor.

The heat went with it. Now the cold would seep into the habitat, but before it grew quite cold, they would be gone.

Margaret raised her head, lifting her eyes to take in the whole room. The cabin was small and sparse and cold—only a chair and a narrow desk facing her, and a blank wall imprinted with the lines of the storage bins.

It looked as it had when she'd first set foot in it. It looked as it would when, in some future year, another explorer came from Earth and lived in it.

Margaret rose from the bunk, walked the two paces to the door, and crossed the threshold. She shut the door behind her and walked away. Not as if leaving home, but as if ending a long sojourn in a strange hotel.

As she reached the stairwell, she heard music swirling in the quiet below, curling up to her. The style of it was old and sweet, pipes singing with violins.

Margaret descended into the lab and found Donegan Moynihan leaning against the tall computer desk, and David and Eamon facing the commander side by side. Their faces were creased as if they did not understand what was happening.

Margaret approached the commander and stopped near him, her head tilted to his music. The bright notes danced in living contradiction to the darkness that roosted deep in his eyes.

"The rover's ready, Meg," David said. "We're ready."

Moynihan gestured to the computer. "I've enabled its battery. Two weeks from now, it will send out deep-space radio waves, broadcasting all the data we've collected. I'm sure NASA will intercept it." He surveyed them. "Do any of you want to add a message? I won't read it."

The three looked at each other, but no one spoke.

Moynihan watched them a moment, then stepped away from the computer. "Then let's go." He passed Eamon and David and walked into the med bay, leaving his team behind.

They looked at the computer, still playing the sweet music, then at each other again.

Margaret moved first. She followed Moynihan into the medical bay and then into the mudroom, sidestepping a box that sat near the hatchway.

Eamon tripped over it. Recovering, he turned back and kicked it. "What is this, Killiam?"

"Rations. Couldn't fit it into the rover."

Eamon looked at him, then down again. "So, how much food do we have?"

"Enough to last us until we run out of oxygen."

The air sank beneath the words.

Margaret took her suit down from the hooks and pulled it over her jumpsuit. The men suited up, too, and the rustling of the heavy suits shuffled together with the snaps of all their fastenings. From the open hatchway, wisps of music slipped in among the other sounds—a stray note of happiness.

Moynihan lifted his helmet off the wall, and like they had received a cue, the others did the same. Margaret locked her helmet in place and turned on the transceiver in time to hear Moynihan say, "The doors, gentlemen."

She turned on her oxygen, and it gusted softly, coolly against her neck.

Eamon closed the hatch, cutting the medical bay off from the mudroom. David unsealed the outer door and opened it wide.

Moynihan tapped the computer screen mounted in the wall, and the habitat sighed—air puffing out of its ventilation ports, then ceasing altogether. All the lights winked out with one accord. The computer screen reduced itself to a ghostlike glow as the computer went into deep hibernation.

Light sprang from David's hand, filling the doorway with a stark patch of brightness. "I've got the door."

Moynihan walked out first, with Eamon right behind. Margaret left third, and then lingered while David shut and sealed the door. Then, as he stepped away from it, she turned toward the rover.

It hummed, its headlights mixing crazy shadows on the cavern walls. Eamon had already climbed in, but Moynihan stood beside it.

Margaret and David walked together until they reached the rover. Then he hurried around to the driver's side, and she got in by Eamon.

In a minute they were all situated as they had been the day they arrived on Mars—and had not been since: David in the driver's seat, Moynihan riding shotgun, and Margaret and Eamon behind them.

"So," Eamon said, "I hope we didn't forget anything. It only took us fifteen days to pack."

No one answered, but the truth shot through Margaret's mind like the sound of breaking glass. It hadn't taken them fifteen days to pack. It had taken them fifteen days to give up hope. Earth hadn't given them a word, and the days of silence finally forced them into the admission that Earth would never give them anything.

"We planned well," Moynihan said. "And so we should have. This is the last expedition of the first Mars mission. Take us out, Colonel."

"Yes, sir." The rover shifted forward and began rolling. "And we are on our way." David angled them toward the turn that led upward into the tunnel, up through Annie and onto the icy slopes of Arsia Mons. Then, suddenly, he added, "You never found it, Eamon."

"Never found what?"

"The Home Sweet Home sign."

Eamon was silent so long that Margaret began to think that he had, for once, no response. Then he said softly, "Maybe the next Mars team will bring it."

Margaret looked back at the habitat. Its silver lines caught the light that trailed behind the rover, but inside it, blackness and emptiness took up residence. And within that darkness—impervious to the absence of oxygen, oblivious to the cold—one computer was awake still, playing merry, old music to the blank rooms.

They emerged from Annie into the daylight of Mars. For a long while, they rode over the slopes of the volcano, until they came to the mouth of Jeanne. Then David put the sun to their backs and steered them in.

They were for the darkness now.

Moynihan watched the radar, the gauges, the time. He balanced his helmet on his knee, the atmospheric controls keeping the air oxygenated but too cool, and he marked milestones.

When they had gone deeper into Jeanne than they had ever gone into Annie, he began, "I think, Colonel—"

The colonel started, and the rover swerved for just a second.

Moynihan eyed him. "Anything wrong?"

David pushed his shoulders back against the seat. "No. What is it?"

"I think you and Eamon will have to take shifts driving."

David frowned, still looking straight ahead. "Now?"

That had been very nearly Moynihan's plan, but the colonel looked so unhappy he changed his mind. "Eventually."

David relaxed.

"I could go for now," Eamon said.

"I can last for a while yet," murmured David.

"Just like Dad on vacation trips. He could go on for hours." There was something odd in Eamon's voice, some undertone that ate at his words. Then it suddenly washed away. "Does anybody want to hear my imitation of a whiny kid in the back seat?"

"No," Moynihan said, mainly to forestall a longer response from David.

And they went on. The cave walls were very near, hardly three feet from them on either side. The dark, gritty rock turned white beneath the headlights, and the blackness danced just beyond reach of the light.

The rover bumped softly over the floor, all stone and sand, while shadows and light ran on ahead of them down the tunnel. So ceaseless was the movement that it seemed, after a while, hardly to be movement at all. It sank and flowed into one hum—light and darkness and the cruising rover keeping one unchanging rhythm.

Moynihan relaxed deeper into his seat. The sense of time deserted him, and he drifted into sleep.

A sharp swerve jerked him back into consciousness. His eyes shot open just in time to see the rock wall flying at them.

Then they veered away, spinning at the opposite wall. Again the rock leaped at them. Again the rover threw itself to the other side. They slowed and straightened, and in no more than ten seconds, the rover idled in the middle of the tunnel, stock-still.

Moynihan's heart, meanwhile, galloped in his chest. He looked at David.

The colonel slumped forward at the controls, staring out the windshield with wide, bright eyes.

Words like *stroke* and *heart attack* jumbled incoherently in his mind, and Moynihan reached over and grabbed the colonel's shoulder. "Are you all right?"

David shook his hand off. "Fine."

"Did you fall asleep?" Margaret asked, concerned.

"No. No, I—" He dropped the sentence abruptly and turned his head, tilting it up to see behind him.

At first, Moynihan thought he was looking back at Margaret. Then he realized the colonel was looking out the rear windshield.

"I'm okay, too," Eamon mumbled. "Can I drive now, Killiam?" Then he yelped as the rover began moving in reverse.

David taxied them backward, staring into the darkness behind the rover. Moynihan didn't understand, but he gave David a chance, and waited.

The others also were silent, but tension rode the air. Moynihan studied the cave wall as it slowly slid by, but he saw nothing—only drab stone whose every crevice and cranny was filled with blackness.

A human figure, wrapped in shadows, loomed up in the cave, and his heart jumped. Then, as David brought them alongside it, he saw it was only a stalagmite. Taller and narrower than a human being, it tapered and thickened in all the right places to suggest the human form.

"When I first saw it, it looked to me like a person standing in the tunnel," the colonel said.

Fascination surged through Moynihan. He reached for the dashboard and tapped the outside camera's touchscreen, focusing it on the stalagmite. As he racketed up photographs, Eamon said, "It's human."

It was the tone, not the words, that froze Moynihan's hand. He looked back at Eamon, who stared at the stalagmite as though receiving a revelation.

He probably thought he was. "It's not human, Lieutenant Commander," Moynihan told him. "It's not even humanoid. It's a chance formation, created by lava when the volcano was still active."

Eamon did not spare him a glance. "But it looks human."

Moynihan recalled, from those dossiers of long ago, that Eamon had graduated with highest honors from the Naval Academy, and he wondered how a man so intelligent could fix on so superficial a point.

"So does the Washer Woman in the Canyonlands, from a certain angle, and with a certain point of view." He passed his eyes over the formation, and for a moment he saw it as David had, felt a gleam of the shocked dread that could make a man lose control. Then he looked again, and he did not see a human form rising out of the darkness. He didn't even see a crumbling token of a lost alien race. He saw only a stalagmite, the unmeaning debris of a volcanic eruption.

Satisfied that he saw true, Moynihan turned away. "It's all your fancy, Lieutenant Commander. The resemblance to us in that stalagmite is only one of God's good-natured tricks."

Silence dropped like a falling blade, and Moynihan looked around. Eamon watched him, one eyebrow cocked, and David and Margaret were looking at each other in that mode of wordless communication they had mastered so well.

He sensed that the silence pointed at him, but he could not guess how he had provoked it. So he set his eyes resolutely ahead and ordered, "Drive on, Colonel."

The colonel did. The journey resumed its monotone of shadows and headlights, but the taut silence remained.

Moynihan took stock of the dashboard again. "We're deeper into Jeanne than our deepest soundings," he told his team. "And the radar still shows no end to the tunnel."

They didn't answer.

He heard stirring behind him, one of their suits crinkling, and then Eamon said, "Can I make a wish? I want to see something amazing."

Moynihan thought of those things he had most outlandishly dreamed of finding—above-freezing temperatures; liquid water; bacteria or mildew or anything that, in any way, lived. And he knew that none of those were what Eamon wanted. He wanted—well, a human statue in a place no human had ever been, something wonderful for the imagination and not only the intellect.

A noise rose in the tunnel, and just as Moynihan recognized it as the wind, he felt it rushing past them, shaking the rover, moaning at the windows.

David cut their speed, wrestling the joystick against the wind and still not keeping them steady. "Where did—"

The wind keened to a musical pitch, overriding his voice. Louder and louder it grew, until—in a revelation instant and horrible—Donegan Moynihan knew that the wind was not the music. It carried the music.

Up from the subterranean depths of Mars, up from ages and ages of darkness, music came—chimes and cymbals and bells clamoring together. The fractured music roared like the ocean and swept them under its waves. Its cold, furious clarity pierced him through and left him frozen, from his feet to his fingertips to the roots of his hair.

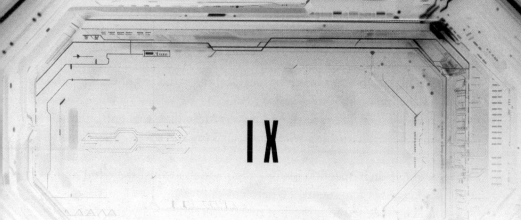

IX

Manasseh Cruz entered his office hastily, and wholly unaffected by the morning quiet and the golden sunbeams long and soft on the faded red-and-yellow carpet, he hurried to his desk.

With one swipe, he scooped up the notes his assistant had left. He riffled through the stack, but his eyes barely grazed the words. Today he left Washington to join his family, and his heart quivered with anticipation that was nine-tenths happiness and one-tenth fear.

Cruz shoved the papers into his pocket. Then he hesitated, his head cocked toward the computer and his posture tilted toward the door. It wasn't likely that any truly important reports or messages had come in.

But it wouldn't take long to check.

He rounded the desk and pulled out his chair, but before he sat down, he noticed a piece of paper, folded double and propped against the screen. It had an off-white color and looked thick.

Curious, he plucked the paper up and weighed it in his hand, rubbed his fingers against it. Good stock. Official paper?

He sat down as he flipped it open, then took note of the NASA emblem. Then he read the text.

And he shot to his feet again.

"So." Reuben hadn't meant to stop there, but he did. He tucked his hands into his pockets to keep himself from looking too foolish, and he finished, "I'll be down in Florida again." He watched Willow's face, willing the hope in his heart not to show in his eyes.

She smiled at him. "And just after the snow finally melted."

He nodded—vaguely disappointed, but what did he want her to say?

They only saw each other when he showed up to wrangle a meeting from her boss. He had no right to hope she would miss him.

He would miss her, though. "Willow–" His courage dropped down to his stomach as she lifted her dark green eyes to him, and he had to clear his throat. "Willow, I'm leaving tomorrow. But I would like–"

"Jackson!"

Reuben turned, too relieved and disappointed at being interrupted to mind that Manasseh Cruz was yelling his name.

Cruz strode up to him, his dark eyes on fire. Abruptly he stopped, and when he spoke, his voice was quiet, but filled with the perilous tension of a bowstring drawn to its farthest limits. "May I speak to you for a moment, Jackson?"

Never, since their first meeting, had Cruz spoken with such politeness, and never at all had Cruz looked at him with such black intensity. Reuben had already lost to the congressman, so now he could feel nothing more than idle interest. "I can give you a minute, Congressman. I could use a little excitement."

The congressman narrowed his eyes and walked away.

Reuben looked over at Willow, shrugged his regret, and followed Cruz.

Cruz had gone right down the hall, heading deeper into the building. As they reached the elevators, Reuben caught up to him. "I thought our relationship had ended with the Mars mission two weeks ago. If you have a problem, or want a fight, surely you have more relevant antagonists to–"

"Cork it," Cruz said, the command as absolute and impersonal as a lightning strike. He pressed on the elevator panel, and as the elevator doors slid open, he said, "Step on, Jackson." He did so himself, and held the doors open.

Reuben edged up to the elevator and peered inside. Save for the congressman, it was empty, and wholly unworthy of any particular notice. Holding that vision of normalcy against the unaccountable sense that he was going into somebody's trunk or basement, Reuben stepped into the elevator.

The doors clicked shut, the floor began to rise beneath his feet, and before Reuben knew what was happening, Cruz's hand was against his chest, and his back was against the wall.

Cruz yanked something from his pocket, and for a second, Reuben thought a gun flashed before his eyes.

Then he blinked. The congressman held only a piece of paper, and Reuben's adrenaline wilted.

Cruz rattled the paper in the air. "Is this your idea of a threat?"

"It's my idea of a piece of paper." Keeping eye contact with the congressman, Reuben gripped the hand pressed into his chest and forced it away.

Cruz pulled his hand back, but he stood as close as ever. "What do you mean by this, Jackson?"

Reuben looked at the paper, but it was bent along a half-dozen different creases, and all he could see was a NASA emblem, half the bolded heading of a military communiqué, and a few scattered words of the text.

He looked back at Cruz, at his dark, unflinching eyes. And he gathered the distinct impression that the congressman was staring him down. He just didn't know what Cruz was trying to stare him down about. Reuben spread his hands in a conciliatory gesture, but it was hampered by the little space he had between Cruz and the wall. "Congressman, I have no idea what you're talking about."

Cruz crushed the paper in his fist.

The elevator settled, and Reuben watched his escape route open. Then Cruz walked over and jabbed the control panel.

Reuben looked on wistfully as the doors closed again. Then he turned his eyes to Cruz.

The congressman tucked the mysterious paper away in his coat, scrutinizing Reuben with cold-blooded measurement. "You play this like an amateur. I could own you in two moves. But I've got better things to do with my time, so I'll give you a chance to just go away. I'll even give you a warning. Jackson, I rule in this town. I'm smarter than anyone who's tougher than me, and I'm tougher than anyone who's smarter than me. Presidents negotiate with me, senators jerk when I pull their strings, congressmen follow my tunes. A little third-rate functionary like you, I take apart for practice."

Reuben stared, feeling that he had somehow wandered into somebody else's delusions. "All right. That sounds true. You could take me apart. I still don't know what you're talking about."

Cruz eyed him. "Just get off the field. Somebody could run over you by accident."

In one second, anger dried up Reuben's bewilderment. As he drew it up into words, the elevator doors slid open, and Cruz walked out into the hall.

Reuben scrambled after him and called to the congressman's back, "You know, they founded the Betty Ford Clinic for people with problems like yours."

Somewhat to Reuben's surprise, the insult stopped Cruz in his tracks. And somewhat to his dismay, Cruz turned around and walked back.

The congressman stopped just short of Reuben and looked down on him. "What are you doing here, Jackson?"

Reuben thought of Willow and said nothing.

"Do you have business with Dr. Karl? I can't imagine what it might be."

Reuben no longer had anything to do with Karl, and that was no secret to be guarded. But Cruz had put him out of any mood to share. "I can't imagine what you've been raging about."

Cruz studied him, and a calmness more disconcerting than his anger settled in his face. "One final question, and I don't need your answer. Do you want to keep your new job at Cape Canaveral? And here's the answer: Of course you do. With thirty percent unemployment right now, any job is a good job." Cruz pivoted on his heel and strode off.

Reuben remained where he stood, left alone in a swamp of confusion. Of all that had just happened, the only thing he clearly understood was Cruz's threat to take away his job.

Could the congressman actually do it? It was likely enough. Would he? That was likely enough, too.

Images crowded into Reuben's mind—camps of dirty tents, legions of decaying suburbs, both upon which soldiers descended at intervals to bring order and law by the power of their weaponry. The lines at the exchanges were long and pathetic, ragged people standing for hours with their arms, bags, or boxes overflowing with cash.

He wished he knew what Cruz wanted; he would very seriously consider giving it to him.

X

The wind dropped to nothing, and the clanging music died with it. But David's ears still rang.

He realized, after a long moment, that his foot was pressing the emergency brake into the floor. Slowly he eased his foot off it, feeling the tension on the rover slacken. They began moving down the tunnel again, but his hands shook a little as he steered.

Moynihan retrieved something from the satchel by his feet, then David heard him speak: "Commander's log, oh-three-oh-two-forty-three. After passing the farthest mapped point in Jeanne, we encountered a strange phenomenon. An unexplained wind blew from deeper in the tunnel, its ultimate origin unknown."

Eamon said, "I think–"

"Be quiet until I'm done dictating." Then Moynihan resumed, "The wind carried a sound like bells and cymbals, without any rhythm or melody. The sound ended when the wind did. Possibly it came from an unknown subsurface source. Possibly the wind entered the cave from above surface, simulating the sound of music as it passed through vents and shafts."

David did not shift his eyes from the tunnel ahead, but he sensed movement from Moynihan, and he knew the commander had finished.

After a circumspect moment, Eamon said, "You didn't mention aliens."

"That, Lieutenant Commander, is because no one will need my help to think of that hypothesis. They might need my help to remember that there are other hypotheses."

"Nothing's been proven to you yet?"

"I'm a scientist."

Moynihan's quiet tone made David's muscles tighten, but he could not have said why.

Eamon barreled over the warning. "You saw the statue."

"I saw a stalagmite."

"You heard the music."

"And what, Mr. Eamon?" Moynihan snapped. "The aliens are at the end of the tunnel banging cymbals and chimes?"

The words sliced the air, sliced Eamon, and left them in a jagged silence.

Finally, David commented, "Sounds like one of my lines, Commander." And why, from Moynihan, did it sound so much worse?

Moynihan didn't reply.

The headlights jounced over cave walls, skimmed the earthy, stony floor. At length they shone off something large and lightly colored in the tunnel ahead.

David braked again. As they idled in the cave, the bright headlights lit up a massive heap of stones. It filled up the way before them, piling halfway to the ceiling and from one wall to the other. The stones were of a dead tannish color, dusted with chalky powder.

"That's interesting," Margaret said. "What are we going to do?"

"I count three options," Moynihan said. "First, we could put the rover into reverse and drive back to the habitat." No one spoke in favor of that, and Moynihan continued, "Second, we could try to clear a way through the rubble."

"I wouldn't," Eamon said. "And not only because I'm lazy. We'd have to move nearly all of it. We could leave—how much, Killiam?"

"Two feet by either wall," David said, then hoped that would give him enough clearance.

"And where would we put it all? Scatter rocks against the walls for a kilometer up and down the tunnel?"

"We could pile the rocks in the cave behind us," Margaret suggested.

They could. But David stared at the rubble. "Another thing to think of. Those rocks have sharp edges, and a bad tear in the wrong place could ruin our suits. And then—well, why do we wear them?"

"So that we do not asphyxiate," Moynihan answered. "The third option is to proceed on foot."

"We couldn't proceed long," Margaret said. "We can't eat with our helmets on, and we can't breathe with them off."

"We should clear a way through it, Commander," said David.

"Agreed. Suit up."

David picked up the helmet from by his feet and fastened it into place. He flipped on the transceiver and said, "Ready."

A moment later, Eamon announced, "I'm a go."

"As am I," Margaret said, more or less at the same second the commander said, "I'm ready."

David powered down the rover's environmental system. Then he twisted the hatch release, and the hatch at his side swung open and bumped the wall. He slid out.

Shutting the hatch, he walked around the rover to the stone heap. It looked taller when he stood in front of it, and he sighed.

Eamon tromped up beside him. "I'm always glad to know I'm not the only lazy one in the group." He reached toward a large stone, but his fingers froze inches from it. Then, jerking back into action, he brushed off the white, clinging dust and snapped on his wristlight.

David watched him study the rock and then, shaking his head, he grabbed a stone. "I'm always glad to know I'm not the laziest one in the group." He hefted the stone to his shoulder and waited for Eamon's comeback.

Eamon stared at the rock, apparently too entranced with it to respond.

He turned away as Margaret and the commander arrived. Despite the glaring headlights, Margaret swept her wristlight ahead of her.

David trekked around the rover, into the deep gloom behind it. He couldn't see the floor, so he threw down the rock from his shoulder without any care.

When he rounded the rover again, he saw Margaret shining her light past the rubble into the tunnel beyond. Then her voice carried over the transceiver: "The darkness might be fooling me, Dr. Moynihan, but I think the tunnel narrows."

Moynihan climbed unsteadily onto the rock heap and then slid down it to the other side. Margaret followed him. In a moment, their wristlights scoured cave walls that looked, to David, as wide apart as ever.

David glanced at Eamon. The lieutenant commander was kneeling now, sifting the dusty stones. And though the sight should have been tinder to David's smoldering irritation, it checked him. He saw the deliberation of Eamon's movements, a focused smoothness that convinced him that whatever Eamon was doing, it was real.

Suddenly Eamon stopped and stood up. "It's a wall."

David looked down at the stones. "A—"

Eamon raised his voice, though the transceiver piped everything he said directly into their helmets. "It's a wall, Moynihan. Somebody built this, and maybe somebody destroyed it, too. You may be a scientist, but I'm an engineer. I know a designed thing when I see it, even in pieces."

David saw Moynihan, a still, shadowy figure between the rover's light and his own wristlight. Yet Moynihan gave no sign he'd heard.

Neither did Margaret. David focused on her standing near Moynihan and, like him, unmoving in the shadows.

Eamon scrambled up the rubble and jumped to the other side.

David clambered after him and, getting dangerously close to the ceiling, skidded down the loose, broken stones. Ahead of him, Eamon reached Moynihan and Margaret.

David hurried to them. They shone their wristlights on the cave wall, and when he finally looked at it, he froze.

The rock was black, but unnaturally smooth, and covered with white and silver stars. They circled in patterns of solar systems, spiraled out in great constellations. David's eyes traced the form of a bear, written in stars among a field of stars, and his soul quivered.

A silence like he had never known fell on them as they found, far beneath the surface of Mars, a painted mirror of the sky.

Moynihan stared at the rock, his mind comparing the map of stars against the astronomy charts he had so thoroughly studied. And the longer he compared, the more he reeled.

Almost dizzy, he had to turn away. "They were astronomers."

"What?" David asked.

He motioned to the cave wall, jerking the beam of light. "They charted the stars." On the surface of Mars, they charted stars, and then they came down, down . . .

Moynihan blinked, feeling the universe slipping away from him in pieces.

Eamon began to move away. "Let's go. Now."

"Go where?" Moynihan asked.

"On. On, on!" He started off down the tunnel, swinging his wristlight at the darkness.

Moynihan kept his voice mild. "Lieutenant Commander . . ."

"What?"

Moynihan drew in a breath—angry at Eamon's carelessness and oddly pleased by it. It brought him back to the safe, sure ground of logic. "You are an officer, Lieutenant Commander, and an intelligent man. You don't need me to tell you."

"You're right, Commander." Eamon turned around. "I know what you want. But try to understand what I want. For years we have lived the routine written out for us by experts and approved for us by NASA. Whenever we wanted to deviate from the routine, we cross-checked the idea against a book of regulations. You want to think and calculate and analyze and probably haul away the rubble so we can take the rover. But that will ruin the moment. Commander, I don't want to ruin it. I want to run in it."

Moynihan tapped his helmet. "How thick is this faceplate?" He grasped his suit in his fingers and tugged. "How thick is this material? That's how far each of us is from death. All those routines and regulations were written to keep us on the right side of that very thin line. Every breath we take is in defiance of this entire planet. We cannot simply run off on a lark."

"Yes, we can," the colonel intervened. "Life is more than taking one breath after another. Let's have a lark, an adventure, a holiday. Let's play hooky from regulations. We can't wait for Earth to have any of those things again. You know we are never making it back. We don't even have much more time here."

"Please, Commander," Margaret spoke up.

"You, too?" Moynihan asked, more struck by her appeal than by Eamon's or even David's. She had always been so cautious and sensible.

"Yes, Commander."

The colonel lowered his light until it illuminated only the cave floor. "You've had our advice, Commander. Now we'll take your decision."

Moynihan looked back at the rover, blazing fat beams of light over the rock heap. Then he looked ahead, where the narrow beams of the wristlights exposed patches of rock and dust.

And the painted stars.

The universe slid around him again, and he decided. "All right. Let's go."

"I'll need my kit." Margaret headed back toward the rover.

Moynihan smiled to himself. She was, indeed, sensible.

Eamon turned after her. "And I'll need some water and rations."

And Eamon, he understood more and more, wasn't sensible. "Really, Lieutenant Commander."

"I live in hope."

The engineer hurried away. Moynihan, unmoved in every sense, stayed behind.

"I need to shut down the rover," David said. "Commander, do you think—" He paused.

Moynihan, guessing what he wanted to ask, said, "I think you should do whatever you want. This is apparently a lark, after all."

"Do you want anything from the rover?"

"No." Moynihan pulled his recorder out of his suit's pouch and displayed it to the colonel. "I have all I need."

"I'll be back in a moment." David followed the others, leaving Moynihan alone.

Moynihan did not, as a matter of fact, mind. He woke up the recorder, switched it over to video setting, and began shooting footage of the wall.

So content was he in the task that he almost regretted it when his team returned. The rover's great lights went out behind him, then he heard them scramble over the stone heap, come down the tunnel. He continued to shoot another minute, but conscious of their attention on him, he reluctantly slipped away the recorder.

"All ready?" he asked, flashing his wristlight over them.

"All ready," the colonel affirmed. He had a satchel slung over his shoulder; Moynihan did not inquire about its contents. He skipped the light to Eamon—and stopped.

"Mr. Eamon . . ." Moynihan, feeling his patience strained, spoke tautly.

Eamon patted the gun in his belt. "When you go on an adventure, you ought to have a weapon. Haven't you read the stories?"

Moynihan motioned to the blaster tucked at the other side of Eamon's belt. "You need two?"

"If I had a bow and arrow, I'd bring that, too."

Moynihan flicked the light to Eamon's face, but Eamon squinted, and his expression provided no enlightenment.

"I'll explain him to you later, Commander," David said.

"Very well. It's a lark, after all, and if weapons complete it for you, why should I criticize?" Moynihan turned from the team, shining his light down the tunnel. "Let's go." But even as he led them away, he calculated how many hours he could permit them to walk before they had to go back.

Margaret tilted her light up at the ceiling, down at the floor, from side to side. "The tunnel is narrowing."

"And the floor is much smoother," said Eamon. "Like people were figuring on walking here."

Moynihan focused his light on the wall, on the field of charted stars, and he marveled.

"Do you see that, Commander?" the colonel asked suddenly. He surged past Moynihan, Margaret and Eamon at his heels. They stopped a short distance ahead, and Moynihan trained his wristlight on the spot.

A recess opened a black mouth in the wall. White stones jutted brokenly from its edges like teeth, and more lay piled on the ground before it. "Another collapsed wall," David said. "Do you want to see what's behind it, Commander?"

Moynihan walked slowly to them as his eyes measured the black opening. If it had been walled, it had been walled for a reason—possibly an exceedingly good reason. He didn't relish crossing the wisdom of the unknown builders.

But he felt the stars at his back, upending his old, sad, sure expectations and remaking their mission. Deep in his spirit, something he couldn't put a name to stirred as if in slumber. "Colonel," he answered, "let's take the adventure."

David stepped into the recess, and Margaret slipped in after him. Then Eamon, too, vanished into the darkness.

Moynihan tread over the rocks that cluttered the opening of the recess. On the other side, he felt the cave walls close in. Fixing his eyes on his team—ghost-white figures behind their lights—he ventured deeper in. The ground felt strange to him. Loose, almost as if it was shifting beneath his weight. He stopped, focusing his wristlight down.

Shale covered the floor of the cave, a thousand small, flat stones. Moynihan kicked lightly at the shale, and it skittered away from him with disturbing uniformity, all gravitating in the same direction.

Then David said sharply, "Don't anyone move."

Moynihan obeyed, his sight filled with shale.

"We are not in a cave," the colonel informed them. "We are standing on the edge of a slope, and we're about one step from falling down it."

Moynihan mustered himself to his position. "So then, just . . ."

A gravelly crunch interrupted him, followed at once by an abrupt cry. And by a noise like dry bones rattling together, he knew someone had fallen. The shale slid beneath his feet, and he turned, quickly grasping at the wall. But his gloved fingers scratched futilely at the rock, and he slipped.

Another shout sounded over the transceiver, and then another, and to the cries of his team he plunged downward. He flailed, but his arms swished in the loose stones and sped his fall. So he went still, surrendering to the inexorable slide.

Words muttered in his ear, overwhelmed once or twice by a yell, but he couldn't tell one voice from another. The whole mountain of shale rustled and rumbled. And there seemed to be a million pieces now—tumbling down, sweeping him along, slapping and jabbing him. The rocky current gained speed, rushing toward some unknown landfall.

Abruptly he hit solid ground, with force that threw him to his knees, slamming his back into a rock wall.

He felt the rending, the rock tearing through every layer of clothing and into his flesh. Cold air poured onto his back; warm blood streamed down his skin.

He groped over his shoulder, pressing his palm against the tear—not to staunch the blood, but to staunch the flow of air. Yet he knew that it was already too late.

A groan—not his own—sounded in his ears, and then Eamon's voice: "I think I've broken every bone in my body."

"I take it you're all right, then," David said, though Moynihan could not see him at all. "Meg?"

"I'm fine," she answered. "David—"

They could not have been more than feet from him, but he felt as if their voices carried from unpassable distances, and the words melted together into indistinction. He wondered if he should say anything to them, wondered what his last words should be.

He breathed in and tasted a musty, vaguely sulfurous scent—the Martian air polluting his oxygen supply. It wouldn't be long—not till he died, even less until he couldn't think.

What, then, should he say? *I love you* was the favored phrase for moments like this, but he had no one to say it to. And those who were with him, the team he had led to Mars, to this—

Moynihan took another breath, traced with metallic hints as well as sulfur. And amid his wandering thoughts, and the Martian air filling his lungs, and the voices of his team, he found what he wanted to say.

I'm sorry.

He opened his mouth, breathed the air of Mars once more. And a realization crashed down on him, like the whole sky falling.

XI

Reuben leaned back against the wall, loosely grasping the strap of the duffel bag at his feet. He kept one interested eye on the street through the window, one disinterested eye on the screen in the wall. On the screen he saw the president's press conference; on the street he hoped to see the bus come lumbering to a stop.

As his gaze wandered back to the president, motion flashed in the corner of his vision. He turned to see a black sedan rolling to a stop by the curb. A man got out and headed toward the very apartment building in which Reuben waited.

Reuben watched the man, trying to be subtle in his curiosity. The income bracket of those with personal transportation didn't often mix with the income bracket of those who lived in his apartment building.

The man walked in and straight over to Reuben. "Mr. Jackson?"

Reuben scanned the man's features and recognized nothing. "What?"

He answered only with a gesture toward the door, making it so deferential it startled Reuben into complying. He followed the man outside and to the car.

He stopped when the man did and found himself staring at the darkly tinted window above the passenger door. His guide moved toward him. "I'll take your bag, sir."

Reuben reflexively pulled the duffel bag close to his body and leaned away.

The passenger door opened, and a man emerged from the car—and stood, his dark suit making the pockmarked sidewalk and its casually dressed passersby look dingy.

Jephthah Baines. The chief of staff leaned his arm on the top of the car door and turned bemused eyes on Reuben. "You should let him take it, Jackson. Otherwise it will be on our feet the whole way."

Reuben stepped back. "I have to catch a bus so I can catch a plane."

"Don't you think the airport is where we're going?" Baines ducked back into the car without waiting for an answer.

And that was, to Reuben, all for the best. He found the question unanswerable. He felt the driver—so he now knew him to be—right at his elbow, and he grudgingly gave over the duffel bag. The driver hefted the bag and then grasped the top of the door. And he just stood there, holding it.

Reuben got in, and the driver shut the door. He glanced over at Baines, by the opposite window with the middle seat empty between them. "Yesterday," Reuben remarked, "Congressman Cruz pulled me into an elevator for a private chat. Today the White House chief of staff gives me a lift in his car. I've never been so important, and I don't even have a job here anymore."

Behind them, the trunk slammed shut, and Baines's eyebrows tilted. "What did the congressman say to you?"

"He told me to stay out of his way, or else. Which is odd because I'm not in his way."

"You truly have no idea why he thinks you are?"

Reuben shrugged, eyes wandering from the chief of staff. "Truly, no idea. I'm probably guilty of understatement when I say that Cruz carried on like a raging lunatic."

The driver pulled open his door and climbed in. As he started the engine, Baines said, "Take us to Reagan."

Reuben pressed his fingers against the upholstery, feeling the smooth thrum of the car. They pulled away from the curb and into traffic, and in the quiet privacy, in the power to go where one chose, Reuben missed his own car.

"So you cleaned out your desk two days ago."

Reuben nodded, not bothering to look at Baines. The sight of the world moving past through a car window tugged him toward memories from better years.

"And you officially turned in your office keys."

Reuben nodded again, the bright memories still drawing his heart away.

"Mail came for you at your old office yesterday. I read it."

Reuben finally looked at the chief of staff, knowing that this conversation was the price he had to pay for the car ride. He put his daydreams aside until the plane flight and asked, "Isn't that a federal offense?"

"As a lawyer, I can tell you that before opening mail can be a federal offense, it must first have been in the hands of the post office." Baines held out an envelope.

Reuben took it and scanned its front. There was no postage, no return address, nothing but his name in dark, stamped letters. He flipped the envelope and shook its contents out into his hand.

Two pieces of paper slid out—one thin and cheap, the other thick. He read first the sparse, printed type on the cheap paper:

> Patrick AFB
> Cape Canaveral, FL
> DSN Monitoring
>
> To: Dr. Karl, Mars Discovery Steering Committee
>
> Attached: Military communiqué from Mars mission
>
> cc: Marked for general distribution to Mars Appropriations Congressional Committee, Steering Committee principals, the White House

Reuben looked at the second paper, but he didn't need to read it. He recognized too quickly the communiqué that had ended the Mars mission.

He felt Baines's eyes on him, and he tossed the envelope and the papers onto the seat between them. Then he looked directly at the chief of staff and asked, "So?"

"So, who sent you this and why?"

"I can't begin to guess."

Baines sorted the heap, separating the papers from each other and laying them over the envelope. "Then try a guess at this question. What do these papers mean, and why does it matter?"

Reuben didn't feel like guessing. "I don't know. Didn't we seal the end of the Mars mission two weeks ago?" He looked at the communiqué again, and as his eyes rested idly on it, two images flashed through his mind.

Jep Baines holding out the communiqué in his office on that cold, early morning.

Manasseh Cruz rattling the crumpled NASA document as he cornered Reuben in the elevator.

A third memory shot after the others, and Reuben shoved his hand into his coat pocket. At the bottom, his fingers brushed paper. He latched onto it and pulled.

He brought out the mashed wad of the communiqué and unfolded it crease by wild crease. Then he laid the wrinkled paper beside its crisp twin and looked at them. "You see, Baines—"

And then he saw. Reuben started so badly he nearly swept the papers off the seat. Snatching up both communiqués, he held them out again. His eyes darted from one to the other half a dozen times before he believed what he saw.

"They're different!" he exclaimed. "The first one"—the battered paper drooped rather sadly when he shook it—"says that two-thirds of the food supply was destroyed. The second one"—the new paper warbled with his swift shake—"says that nearly one-half was destroyed." The scene with Manasseh Cruz stood in his eye again, the bent NASA communiqué the congressman clenched. "Maybe the reason why Cruz was so angry . . ." He let the words go, falling into his thoughts.

"Do tell."

At Baines's voice, Reuben looked at him. "The congressman waved a paper in my face and asked if it was my idea of a threat. I couldn't read it, but I saw the NASA emblem and the Cape Canaveral heading. I thought Cruz was acting crazy. But if he got this altered communiqué, as I did . . ." And Reuben stopped, not liking where the idea was leading him.

Baines sighed. "You need to learn to finish your sentences, Jackson. If Cruz got this communiqué, then someone is accusing him of, at best, shutting down the Mars mission on a lie, and at worst, of forging a military document in order to shut it down. Of course he was angry. But who forged the second version of the communiqué, and who is distributing it around Washington?"

Reuben traced the questions in his mind and scraped against their unspoken assumption. He lifted the papers, offering them up for viewing. "And which is the forgery?"

Baines returned him nothing but a flat gaze.

Reuben hardly cared. He had torn out the assumption at the very base of the matter, and it had the effect all such tearing did: it shifted mountains. "Maybe the second communiqué is the authentic one. Maybe the decision to end the Mars mission was based on a lie, and maybe Cruz knows it." The most extraordinary possibility rose in his mind, brought something to life in his heart, and burst from his lips. "Maybe it's not too late for the Mars team."

"Jackson, even calculating by the second version, they have less than three months of rations left. And when you consider how Congress and Karl fought against sending relief when the team had five months left—well, you know their fate is still sealed."

Reuben grasped at the new hope, afraid it would melt away as quickly as it had appeared. "But—"

"Give me facts, Jackson, or nothing at all."

Reuben groped for any facts that supported his hope.

After a long, fruitless half minute, Baines said, "Somebody has created false versions of a classified military communiqué. Do you think that's a prank? And that communiqué in your hand—that's a crime, no matter how you cut it. If it's not a forgery, it's a stolen classified document. The other paper in that envelope with your name on it is apparently a cover letter sent to Dr. Karl. And, Jackson, you have no business having it. This whole thing reeks of scandal, but it will not be our scandal. Don't get involved. Stay out of it. Go down to Florida and start a better life."

Reuben dropped the communiqués onto the envelope and cover letter. "Do nothing, you mean."

Baines nodded.

Reuben drew in a breath and felt he drew sadness in with it. The car gently rolled to a stop. And he took a distracted look out the window and saw the soaring white columns of the airport.

"Get Mr. Jackson's bag," Baines ordered, and the driver pushed open his door and got out. At the *click* of the door shutting again, Baines leaned back in the seat and fixed intent eyes on Reuben. "This is the town where what is whispered in the ear will be shouted from the rooftops. If our secret sender persists, then this is a scandal breaking wide open. You don't want a special prosecutor knocking on your door, Jackson. But if he does and if you're ignorant and honest, he'll let you live. You're already honest. Now stay ignorant."

Reuben glanced down at the communiqué, at its plaintive *SOS*. "And the Mars team?"

Baines collected the papers and slipped them into the envelope. "There's no hope for them. So don't hurt anyone for their sake. The country doesn't deserve it. The president doesn't deserve it." The chief of staff stretched out the envelope.

Reuben took it, but he couldn't find words in the clutter of his thoughts and feelings. Then he heard a sound like oiled metal turning, a cool breeze gusted over his face, and the driver held open his door.

He slid to the seat's edge and stepped out onto the sidewalk. The driver ceremoniously offered the duffel bag to him.

As Reuben slung the strap over his shoulder, Jep Baines leaned over to look at him from within the car. "Nothing in Washington is forever," he said. "Someday I'll get out of this town, and like you, I'll be done with Washington once and for all. Be happy in sunny Florida, Jackson." He sat back.

The driver shut the door and, with a nod to Reuben, took his own seat.

They drove off, and Reuben stared after the vanishing black car, gripping the strap of his bag in one hand and the envelope in the other, with a hundred thoughts fluttering in his mind.

Small houses sprinkled the highway on either side—one-story affairs, without fences or driveways. Stubborn grass grew out of the sandy soil, unmowed around every house.

Reuben Jackson stood at the front door of one of the houses, watching a middle-aged woman open it up. She tugged the key card out of the slot and pushed on the door.

It swung open, and they walked inside.

"Your boxes came," the woman said. "I had them stacked up by the wall."

Reuben nodded, then let his duffel bag slide off his shoulder and *thump* to the floor. He saw the boxes against the living room wall, high as his shoulder, but he saw nothing else. "What about the furniture?"

Her eyebrows lowered. "You didn't send any furniture."

"I rented the house with furniture."

She pointed, and he turned to see, in the kitchen, one plastic-and-metal chair. "There's more in the bedroom," she told him.

An acerbic remark sprang to his mind, but he was too tired for sharp words. He stretched out his hand and asked, "A bed, I hope?"

She placed the key card in his palm. "Yes, the most important piece of furniture. I'll take the rent the last day of every month." She walked out, shutting the door behind her.

Reuben looked all around—the kitchen on his left and the living room on his right, all faux-wood floors and white plaster walls. He sighed but tried to be grateful. Not everyone had a bed to sleep on, or even a floor.

He pulled the envelope stamped with his name from his coat pocket. Placing the envelope between his teeth, he shed the coat, letting it fall to the floor beside his bag. Then he took the envelope in hand again and went over to the window. It faced west, and the lowering sun filled it with brilliant, momentary light.

Reuben sat with his back against the wall and spread out the papers on the floor, in the fragile brightness.

Two communiqués, one genuine and one a forgery. And the cover letter.

He studied the cover letter, trying to understand why it was sent to him. At first and second glances, it showed nothing he didn't already know. He knew that transmissions from the Mars team were received by NASA at Cape Canaveral and sent on to Washington. He knew they were distributed to the White House and the Four First Names and Manasseh Cruz's committee.

Reuben pictured Rogers in the water-stained room, sitting at his solitary computer: *Sir, I relay all messages to Washington, and they distribute them.*

The word lingered in his mind, linked with the same word on the paper before him.

Marked for distribution to . . .

They distribute them . . .

Dr. Karl distributed them.

Reuben traced his finger over the cover letter, imagining the line between NASA and the decision-makers in Washington, imagining Karl as the silent halfway point. It would be easy, so easy, for him to alter the message before passing it on.

He wondered if Jep Baines knew the White House received the Mars communiqués through Karl. The next moment he decided it didn't matter. If Baines knew, he didn't care, and if he didn't know, he didn't want to know. He didn't want the truth.

Stay out of it, the chief of staff had told him. *Don't get involved.*

But he was already involved, because he knew the truth.

Did Manasseh Cruz know the truth? It would explain his anger. It would explain his threats. And understanding them, Reuben feared the threats far more.

He wanted, in that moment, to heed them, to take Baines's advice and try to build a better life, just try to be happy. The chief of staff's warnings and the congressman's threats flowed in and out of each other and became one current, pulling Reuben in the same direction.

He heard one more voice, rising in lonely opposition, as distant as the others were near. The SOS blazed on the communiqués. It cried out to him.

Save our souls.

Reuben knew they hadn't made the plea to him. They had made it to NASA, to the president, to Congress and the First Names. To everyone who had the power to help them.

Reuben had no power. Yet he stood alone with the plea as those who had power turned away.

The sun set, drawing its golden light from the little house. Shadows layered the papers on the floor beneath the window, but still Reuben stared at them. The voices chorused in his head, but one grew stronger than the others—high and clear—with the piercing sweetness and irresistible danger of a siren song.

Save our souls.

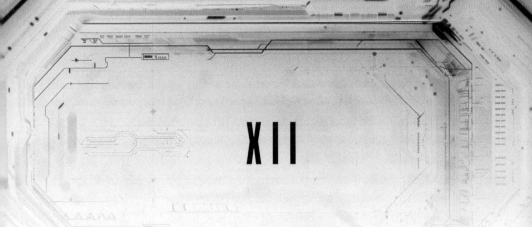

XII

Margaret flexed her fingers, then wiggled her toes. She ran her hands over her arms and down her legs, searching for any gash in the fabric.

In the middle of her self-inventory, she heard Eamon groan and say, "I think I've broken every bone in my body."

David scraped the small rocks and loose stones scattered over the ground as he stood up. "I take it you're all right, then. Meg?"

"I'm fine. David, are you all right?"

"Sure." A beam of light shot from his wrist into the darkness.

Margaret blinked. David stepped nearer and offered his hand, and she let him help her up. Then she retrieved her kit from the mess of stones and dirt and brushed it off. "What is your condition, Eamon?"

"Like I said, all my bones are broken."

"I'm asking as a doctor who can give you a shot and put you in traction."

More scraping against rocks. David swung the light toward the noise. It shone on Eamon, scrambling up from the cave floor. "I'm peachy."

Margaret nodded, though she knew he couldn't see. "Commander?"

No answer came, and David turned from Eamon, sweeping the light over the area. It flashed past the hill of shale and hit a sheer rock wall, like a cliff. Then it caught a white figure.

David pulled down the beam of light and focused it on Moynihan, who sat propped against the cave wall. The commander was lowering his arm, and blood ran down from his glove, tracing crimson lines to his elbow.

Margaret started forward, but the ground was treacherous with shale and slowed her. David, more reckless, got ahead.

Moynihan stood, steadily but very slowly. Then he put his hands to his helmet and began to twist it loose.

David lunged and knocked his hands away, wrapping the commander in a restraining grip. Eamon ran and skidded over the shale toward them.

Margaret stopped, knowing she would have to let the men apply brute force before she could apply medical expertise.

Moynihan, with startling strength, threw off David. His hands went straight back to his helmet, and—as David leapt at him again—he wrenched it off.

David brought himself up short, stumbling against his own speed. Margaret let the medical kit drop from her fingers to the ground. Half her mind struggled to grasp the horror of what was happening; the rest of her just waited for Moynihan to die.

David backed away from the commander as Eamon halted beside Margaret with a scuffing of stones. The three drew together by some indefinable instinct to watch the triumph of the commander's death wish play out before them.

Moynihan tossed his helmet down and undid the fastenings at his wrists. He yanked off his gloves and then—with more vigor than Margaret thought possible by this time—he stripped off his suit.

Her eyes riveted on every motion, expecting them to betray clumsiness or weakness as the commander suffocated on the air of Mars. Yet he moved fast and with precision until he drew himself up straight and tall.

And he faced them, dressed only in a gray jumpsuit, still and steady and strong.

Margaret no longer knew what she expected, what she felt. Horror shifted half to confusion and half to amazement; Moynihan wasn't dying, but she didn't see how he could live.

Eamon's voice broke through. "Shouldn't he be keeling over?"

Margaret twitched her light, focusing on the commander's face. He smiled at them, a smile she had never seen him wear before. It held no wry amusement, no inscrutable edge, no bitter tincture.

It held only happiness.

"Meg?" David prodded.

She shook her head at him. "You don't need me to tell you that he should be keeling over, if he can't breathe." That if—that small word—thundered in her mind. Looking at Moynihan's smile, she snapped loose her gloves and pulled them off. Cool, dry air engulfed her hands.

David's voice rose with alarm. "Meg?"

"It's all right, David." And with that promise and a deep breath, she took her helmet off. The cool air touched her face, and she breathed in the smell of sulfur and rust and iron. She drew in a lungful of the strange air, exhaled it, and knew the incredible truth: it was breathable.

"I wondered when one of you would believe what you saw," Moynihan said to her. "When do you think they will come around?"

Margaret tossed a smile at David and Eamon as she began to remove her suit. "Directly, I'm sure."

The words no sooner left her mouth than David began stripping off his suit. After another beat, Eamon did the same, and their wristlights winked into darkness.

"Commander," Margaret asked in the blackness, "how did you know?"

"My suit got torn during the fall, Martian air leaked into the circulation system, and I discovered I could breathe it. But my back is bleeding. You have a little mending to do, Doctor."

Margaret remembered the blood on his suit but thought the injury could not be too serious. "David?"

"I heard," he said, and his voice, no longer carried by the transceiver, sounded near and warm. "What do you need?"

"Light, to begin with."

"I got it." Light followed Eamon's voice, and he lifted the wristlight, detached from his suit.

"Good. Time to play my assistant, David." She moved toward Moynihan, who knelt on the ground.

David retrieved her kit and followed. "Assistant? A gopher, you mean."

Eamon came over, too. "And let no one say you aren't qualified. You can fetch and everything."

"But are you qualified to hold the light?"

Margaret stationed herself behind Moynihan, ignoring them. The smell of blood was strong, and a spreading stain darkened the gray of his jumpsuit to black.

She heard Moynihan pull on his zipper, and together they tugged down the clothing to reveal an open gash streaming blood. Margaret held out her hand. "Gauze."

David gave her a long strip, and she pressed it against the wound. In a minute, blood soaked it, and she tossed it to the ground. "Another."

That one, too, was soon damp beneath her fingers. But it grew wet less quickly than the first, and within a few minutes, she thought the bleeding had stopped.

When she felt it had been long enough, she threw aside the bloody gauze and said, "Sterilizing pads."

David passed them to her, one after another, while she cleaned out the wound. The muscles in Moynihan's neck and shoulder twitched, and though he made no sound, she knew the cleaning stung badly. But it was all only for his good, and she devoted her concentration to doing the job thoroughly.

She dropped the last soiled pad and opened her hand. "Antibiotic."

Margaret spread the gel over the wound, then bandaged it. Finished, she raised her hands and stepped back, ready for a cleansing of her own. That was when she realized that as far as she knew, they had no water. Even if they did, they couldn't spare a drop to wash the blood off her hands.

David stretched out a couple more sterilizing pads to her. "Here, Meg."

As she began to wipe her hands, the commander pulled his jumpsuit back over his shoulders and zipped it again. "Thank you, Doctor."

Eamon turned away, swinging their light with him. David, still putting the kit back together, muttered.

"Look at this!" Eamon called over his shoulder.

Moynihan pushed up from the ground, Margaret tossed away the dirtied sterilizing pads, and they went to him. David muttered again and then followed.

Eamon stood at the foot of the slope they had slid down, shining his light on it. A few heavy rocks poked frowning heads out of the rubble, but mostly it was shale—countless numbers of small stones, a massive and precarious heap. He raised the light, until it climbed the rickety hill far above their heads. The beam lost itself in the darkness, still not reaching the top of the shale.

"We'll never get back up," David said.

Eamon kicked at the shale and watched pieces clatter down. "We only have what food and water I brought."

"I brought a little, too," David said.

"How much?"

"A little."

Eamon took a few long steps up the shale. It gave way beneath him, and he rode it down. "We fell out of the frying pan and into the fire."

"I think we're still in the frying pan," Moynihan commented. "A sizzling hot frying pan, I grant you, but we're not in the fire yet."

Margaret looked at him, and she felt David turn, too. "What's up with you?" Eamon asked. "Why are you, Commander Doom and Gloom, putting a ray of sunshine on this?"

"I'm not trying to be sunshiny, Lieutenant Commander. But I've been learning how much I don't know. We have lived in this volcano four years, and all the time this was beneath our feet. We didn't know. We would never have known if we hadn't been willing to lose ourselves in Jeanne. And now we are lost, but we've found the edges of a great civilization. We've found a place on Mars where we can breathe the air. Yesterday we knew both of those things were impossible. Now we don't know anything. Now anything can happen."

Margaret looked up into the fathomless blackness above them and drew hope from what they didn't know.

Moynihan turned from the shale-slope, loose stones crunching beneath his boots. "Salvage what you can from the suits. It's time for us to march forward and see what is here for us to find."

"What direction are we heading, Commander?" David asked.

"North, Colonel."

Eamon flashed the light past the shale, past the sheer rock, into unpierceable darkness. With the slope to their backs, nothing of the vast black underground could be seen. "Why north?" he asked.

"There's no *why*, Lieutenant Commander, just *why not*."

The scuffing of heavy boots against rough ground filled Moynihan's ears. Little else reached his senses through the darkness. For hours they had trekked, nothing in all the universe for them but the stony ground beneath their heels and the light beams going ahead of them. They followed those white fingers stretching out into the blackness, and nothing changed.

Moynihan felt the march sapping away all his comfort. He shored up his conviction that anything—even something good—might happen, but it did not encourage him.

"Who thinks," Eamon said, "we're really moving?"

"I do," said David. "And it just makes me want to cry." Margaret stilled. "Did you notice that?"

"Notice what?" Moynihan glanced her way.

"When we talk, there are no echoes."

"Yes, I noticed. This cavern could be the size of half a continent. How would we ever know?" He halted abruptly. "Let's make camp. Gather in a circle." He kicked aside a rock and sat down.

The others sat down around him. Margaret extinguished her light, but Eamon and David pointed theirs upward. White light fell over their circle, showing Moynihan his team's pale faces, smudged with dirt, marked with scratches and scrapes.

"Let's inventory our equipment," Moynihan said, and laid down his recorder and chronometer.

The others followed suit—Margaret putting forward her kit, Eamon his weapons, David a knife and a multipurpose tool.

It was pitiful, but not nearly as sad as what would follow. "Now the food," Moynihan ordered.

Eamon grabbed his satchel and emptied out fourteen field rations—each a nutrient bar attached to a tube of water. David then took out seven more.

Two days of rations.

For a minute they all stared at the pile. Moynihan ran the calculations in his mind. The rations, even stingily doled out, would run out in four or five days. After that, their physical condition—already weakened by days of hunger—would deteriorate without any halt. Death would come by dehydration, most likely in another four or five days.

One or two of them might eke out a few more miserable days. But even for the hardiest, death would not long be deferred.

Moynihan, his mouth dry, glanced at his team. They wore the grim sentence on their faces, with no need for him to tell them anything.

He reclaimed his recorder and chrono and dropped them into his jumpsuit's expansive breast pocket. "Let's eat."

David grabbed a ration and tore off the wrapping. He broke the nutrient bar and gave what Moynihan judged to be the larger half to Margaret.

Eamon opened another ration, pulling free the water. "You got a thing about germs, Commander?"

"I generally object to them."

"So do I. But I don't see them. That's a scientist phobia." Eamon held out the water. "You drink first."

They made a dismal meal. As they finished, David turned off his wristlight, and then so did Eamon.

And the blackness was complete. Moynihan pulled his legs up and wrapped his arms around them, seeking warmth. It was all right while they moved, but when they rested, it grew cold.

"When the Eurasian war broke out," David's voice came through the darkness, "I was deployed to the front. I flew combat missions in Mongolia when the whole country was in anarchy. Sometimes it felt like all the land was no-man's-land. There were gaps between military lines hundreds of miles wide. The only territory any side really controlled was the ground their army happened to be standing on at the moment. I patrolled the sky above the American lines and made air strikes on things that got too close. But I refueled on a base outside the country. That was when it was most dangerous, on the flight west out of Mongolia. An enemy or a confused ally who had a missile launcher and a bit of luck would have been the end of me."

Moynihan knew all this; he had read all the colonel's files, and he had always followed current events closely, to the depreciation of his optimism. But he had never before heard the colonel speak of it, and David's voice brought the war near to them once more.

"I made the resolution," David went on, "that although I didn't want to die for my country, I wouldn't particularly mind it. I'm not going to revisit that resolution now. But I never thought that if I died for my country, it would be their choice."

Someone sighed, either Margaret or Eamon. Then Eamon said, "It wasn't blind fate or bad luck that landed us here. We're not random victims. We are here, each one of us, because we made a mistake."

Moynihan pictured the wedding band the lieutenant commander always wore, and he guessed, "Like a failed marriage that, if it had lasted, would have saved you from this."

"Yeah," Eamon said, his voice suddenly subdued. "Like that." He cleared his throat and said more loudly, "And you, Commander?"

His own mistake wasn't hard to find. "I said yes."

"To going on the mission?"

"No. To joining the Four First Names." He turned his head in the direction he believed David to be and asked, "Colonel?"

Silence followed, so long Moynihan began to think about going to sleep. Then Margaret said, "We're too much like our parents."

And they sat together in the dark, their half-shrouded secrets between them.

Moynihan heard the noise of someone starting up, and Eamon asked, "Do you see that?"

David had a testy edge to his voice. "Eamon, I couldn't see my hand if I held it an inch from my nose."

"No, look, over there!"

Another sigh, and this time Moynihan knew it was from David. "Eamon, if you're pointing, we can't see it."

"You couldn't see it with the light on," Eamon said. "But I'll point the light toward it, and then I'll turn it off."

A beam of light stabbed the darkness and left Moynihan blinking. He looked in the direction it shot, craning his neck to do so. Then, with abruptness, the beam vanished.

Moynihan stared into the blackness, and for a moment he thought he saw afterimages—two or three tiny spots of light. Yet they didn't fade, and it finally dawned on him that they were really there.

He stood up, eyes locked on the lights. They were smudges on the darkness, whitish and vague, and hardly bigger than a firefly.

He heard the others getting up—scraping the ground, kicking aside pebbles. They stepped close around him. All seeing the pale, blurry lights, all wanting the same thing.

And because they had really nothing else, Moynihan gave in to the tug of the ghostly lights on his spirit. "Let's go," he said. "Stay close."

They shuffled over the rocky terrain invisible to their eyes, so near to each other Moynihan heard his team's breathing, felt the warmth of their bodies.

Many minutes rolled silently past, and the lights slowly changed. They grew brighter, larger, more solid. New lights, fainter than the earlier ones, emerged from the darkness until a line like the horizon cut across the blackness.

When the lights looked about the size of his hand, Moynihan felt a perception of their true largeness pressing on him. He began to doubt, too, that they were exactly lights.

He snapped on his wristlight, shining it on the path ahead, and found that the distant lights were now too strong to be washed out. Without a word, the team spread out and increased their pace.

Gradually, but surely, the lights grew greater and greater. Moynihan came to see that there was not one line of lights, but two lines, close beside each other. The lines were sinuous, curving and undulating into a serpentine figure.

As they finally came near, Moynihan extinguished his wristlight and stopped. The others halted with him, and they stared at the twisting double row. Moynihan could judge now that many of the lights were taller than he, and most of them were nearly as broad. All glowed white out of the blackness. None flickered with the endless vicissitudes of flames.

A ledge raised itself between the two lines and linked them—a dim shadow between the pale lights. Moynihan could not guess its purpose, a narrow, half-lit platform coiling through this waste of a cavern. Nor did he understand what the tall things were that emanated the white, motionless light. The strangeness, all wrapped in darkness and pallid light, pulled the breath from his chest.

"Commander?" the colonel asked.

He brought his mind back to his team and ordered, "Forward."

They crossed the remaining yards quickly. As the rest scrambled up onto the platform, Moynihan lingered by one of the light things. He felt no warmth from it, and—fear clutching at his arm and slowing his movement—he touched it.

It was cold, with no crackle or sting of energy. Moynihan stroked his fingertips on the cool surface, and recognition ignited in him and flamed into a laugh.

A yard above, the figures of his team turned toward him. "What's funny?" Eamon asked.

"I thought it would be . . ." But he didn't know what he had thought it would be. He began to have trouble recalling what he had felt it would be. "It's merely rock—phosphorescent rock. No great wonder."

The colonel stepped back, his head tilting up. "No disrespect meant, sir, but that depends on your point of view. These are not just phosphorescent rocks. These are phosphorescent rocks carved into pillars and set up by aliens."

Margaret nodded agreement with her brother. "Some of them have been broken. The taller ones are smooth at the top, but the short ones are jagged. Once, these pillars were all very much the same."

Moynihan climbed onto the platform. Its width was enough for six people to stand side by side; its length was beyond knowing, stretching out past their sight on either side. The light of the rock pillars made everything plain to see, yet also pallid, as if the phosphorescence leached away half the color.

Eamon walked forward a few paces, his head swiveling right and left. Then he turned around. "Do you see what this is?"

"The Great Wall of China, only three feet tall and with glowing rocks by it." David threw up his arms. "Eamon, how are we supposed to know what this thing is?"

"Because you've walked on something just like it a thousand times. Stop thinking of it as some bizarre architecture left by aliens. Think of Earth." He shot David a look. "But not the Great Wall of China. Remember being out in the city on a warm night in America."

Moynihan held those memories so distant and so familiar in his mind while he looked at the ledge and the phosphorescent columns again. And this time, he saw.

"It's a road," Margaret breathed. She gestured to the glowing rocks. "Those are streetlamps."

"Then, here's the question that matters," David said. "Where does it go?"

Eamon looked at Moynihan. "Maybe we can learn."

Moynihan nodded assent, and it took all his willpower not to point out that their true obstacle was time, running out with the rations they carried.

XIII

"And do you miss Washington, Mr. Jackson?"

Reuben smiled at the woman, sitting at the end of the row of chairs that faced the desk. "I was there yesterday. I haven't had time to miss it."

One of the men in the row shifted, drawing Reuben's eyes to him. "But you must have left on bad terms."

A few feet to his left, Colonel Nelson stirred, but Reuben didn't hesitate before answering. "The end of the Mars mission was disappointing for all of us." *Except Karl*, he grumbled in his mind, while he plastered pleasantness over his face for the reporters. "We've lost four good people, members of our military who served this nation. All Americans feel the pain of that."

The woman leaned forward, seeking his attention again. "So you resent the decision."

Reuben shook his head at the word. "The *Enyalius* storage was infected, and the Mars Appropriations Committee made a recommendation in keeping with that fact. The president accepted their recommendation, and I know the good of the American people is always his highest concern."

Behind the reporters, the door opened, and Colonel Nelson's aide walked in. He crossed the room to the desk, and silence fell at his intrusion. With a deferential air, he said to the colonel, "It is nearly time for your next appointment, sir."

Nelson nodded, and his aide turned to the reporters. "Ladies and gentlemen . . ."

Reuben, still hiding behind a pleasant expression, watched the aide sweep the reporters from the office with a flow of friendly remarks. When the man disappeared with the whole gaggle, Reuben exhaled. He grabbed the edge of the desk and leveraged himself up from his chair. It didn't feel soft anymore.

"You did well," Nelson said. "You answered all their questions, and you never really told them anything."

Reuben nodded without looking toward the colonel. His thoughts distracted him, worried him, and he said distantly, "It's why you hired me." Then he sighed. "They want drama. Bad feelings. Why isn't intellectual argument ever enough for reporters? Why does everything have to be sensational?"

"Which do you think makes more money, intellectual argument or sensationalism?"

"You have me there." Reuben turned to the colonel, still seated behind his desk, and edged toward his troublesome thoughts. "Did you ever read the communiqué from Mars—the last one?"

Nelson shook his head. "You know the business of this command is not overseeing or directing the Mars mission. The communiqués are for Washington alone to deal with, so to Washington alone they go."

"But you must have a copy of the communiqué in one of your computers. It was received and transcribed here. Computers never delete anything."

Nelson studied him.

Reuben imagined what he would say to the special prosecutor. *Jackson asked about the communiqué, but I had no idea why. He never said.*

Reuben was determined not to say, nor to draw the colonel into the trap in which he himself was caught. Yet he needed advice. He gazed back at the colonel, respectable from his gray hair to his crisp uniform to the burnished insignia on his collar. His eyes, webbed with wrinkles, were sharp with intelligence and wakefulness.

"Colonel Nelson, I've got a dilemma on my mind." Stepping through his words carefully, Reuben asked, "What do you do with a truth no one wants to hear?"

"That depends on how important it is."

Reuben thought of the Mars team, growing ever nearer to starvation. "Life or death."

"Then speak it."

"To whom?"

"To those who can help."

Reuben paused, reckoning that up in his mind. Only the White House, the First Names, and Manasseh Cruz had any kind of ability to send aid to Mars, any kind of authority to make that decision. And they didn't want to.

His shoulders slumped a little. "And what if they don't want the truth?"

"Is that anyone's responsibility but their own, Jackson? Attend to your own duty, and let them do or fail theirs."

Reuben clasped his hands together to keep himself from fidgeting. He didn't relish the idea of appealing to the powers in Washington, and he tried to think of someone else to whom he could bring the truth. The reporters he had just talked with would surely be interested. If he leaked the two communiqués to the media, they would faithfully turn it into a scandal.

Then would come the endless spinning wheel of accusations and defenses, lies and truth, who knew what and when. All of Washington would go on the warpath or else make for the hills, and what good would they be to the Mars team then? If the powers that be were so caught up in helping themselves, how could they help anyone else?

Then would come the special prosecutor, with whom Reuben did not want to meet.

Then would come a political crisis, which America did not need. Too much had been knocked down already, and the house quivered on its foundation.

So he rejected the idea of dragging the media into the fight, and that brought him full circle. Back to Cruz and the First Names and the White House.

"It's strange, you know."

Reuben focused on Nelson again, needing a moment to bring his mind to bear. "What?"

Nelson leaned forward, his leather chair creaking. "It's strange how much time we can spend with others, how much we can do with them, only to learn in the end how shallow those relationships always were. After two years in Washington, is there anyone in the whole city you can call?"

"Dr. Francis might pick up the phone. Jep Baines might. But just because they would hear me out doesn't mean they would listen." Jephthah Baines surely wouldn't, not on this; he had closed that door. Dr. Francis, like the other First Names, always listened to Dr. Karl. Worse, he might carry tales to Karl—the man Reuben distrusted most.

Nelson swiveled a little in his chair, a casualness in his movements that didn't touch his eyes. "And there is no one who would listen?"

"No one . . ." The words faltered, and Reuben veered into a new thought, a new sentence: "Except . . ."

He sighed. Manasseh Cruz would listen. The congressman might be roused to carry out his threats, but he would at least listen first. He had a chance with Cruz, however small. That was the terrible thing.

Nelson turned back to the work on his desk. "Make sure you study all the files on that info-chip. If you're going to represent us to the media, you should know more about us than they do. Studying that data is your first assignment. In fact, you don't even need to come in for the next few days."

Reuben nodded, some part of him trembling at the release the colonel gave him. "Yes, sir."

He left the colonel's office and walked the halls, conducting an argument in his head over whether he should speak the truth to Manasseh Cruz. He wasn't sure which side of the argument the congressman was on.

At length he came to his office. It was somewhat larger than his old office in Washington and more drab. The info-chip rested still on the cold metal desk, and so now did something else—a bulky envelope, almost a package.

He picked it up and read his name, typed above the base's address. Then he ripped the envelope open, slipped his fingers into the tear, and pulled.

A single piece of paper slid out. Reuben felt the weight of the envelope's other contents, but for a moment he fixed his attention on the paper. He read MEMORANDUM in the top-left corner, but there was no indication as to the sender or receiver. The page was also blank of any date or subject or location.

One line of text stated, *Final list of candidates to be voted on in May 9th meeting.* Below that line scrolled a list of ten or so names. Three had been underlined—Margaret Killiam, David Killiam, and Gulliver Eamon.

Reuben read the page again and, divining no great meaning, laid it on the desk. He tore the rip in the envelope wider and, tilting it over the desk, shook it hard.

Four dossiers spilled out. Reuben dropped the envelope to the floor and spread out the dossiers on the desk before him. Names marked the covers—Donegan Moynihan, David Killiam, Margaret Killiam, Gulliver Eamon.

That was predictable enough. the large photographs clipped to the covers were not. Reuben went slowly, studying each one before looking at the next, knowing he was seeing something he had never before seen.

In the first picture, he saw Donegan Moynihan with an old, broad, handsome stone building for a backdrop. The scientist looked a decade younger than in his government photos, though the difference was not only physical, but also something more elusive—more softness in the set of his mouth, more warmth in his eyes.

The next photo showed David Killiam perched on a combat jet, one hand held aloft with two fingers pointing into an insouciant victory sign. Reuben read cockiness in every line of his posture, in how his lips bent as if equally halfway to a smile and a smirk. But he thought a shadow lurked at the edges of the pilot's expression.

Margaret and David Killiam were both in the third photo. They were casually dressed and relaxed, a gleaming skyscraper to their backs. The wind mussed David's hair, lifted up Margaret's hair, deep brown against the skyscraper's shining gray.

Gulliver Eamon, in his photo, sat on a couch with a pretty woman. His arm wrapped around her, held her close, and her red hair spilled over his shoulder, his chest.

Reuben took a step back, the better to hold all four pictures in his vision at once. They stirred his spirit, bore up his resolve with power.

Now he knew what the Mars team looked like when they smiled.

Spring stirred in the yard. It swelled the buds on the stark tree branches, revived the grass, coaxed pale-green shoots from the dark soil of the flower beds. Reuben's eyes wandered all around him as he walked the stone pathway. He could only imagine the beauty of the place in one more month.

He stopped when he reached eight redbrick steps, framed by a white railing on both sides. His eyes traveled up to the porch, overhung by a roof and spanned by wooden columns and more white railing.

Behind the railing, the house was also white. The black front door took center stage, its glass panels veined with gold-silver filigree and reflecting pure sunlight.

Reuben took it all in—the freshness of the paint, the sparkling transparency of the glass windows, the mere size of the house. Tens of millions had been broken by the Great Collapse, and tens of millions more left wounded. Manasseh Cruz, evidently, was not among them.

Liking the congressman no better for that, Reuben climbed the brick steps. He hesitated before the front door, and a feeling of intimidation shamed him. It was one thing, and a rational thing, to be intimidated by the congressman. But to be intimidated by the congressman's house?

With venomous abruptness, Reuben rang the doorbell.

Behind the brilliantly clear outer door, the magnificently black inner door cracked open. And stayed that way.

Reuben eyed the slit of darkness between the door and its jamb. He saw nothing, sensed no movement, but he was fairly sure he heard breathing.

If that was the congressman behind the door, the congressman was plotting murder.

Reuben waited, still but very conscious of the bulky envelope he balanced between his arm and his side, concealed beneath his jacket.

Then the door slowly swung open, and Reuben found himself staring down at a small child, no more than eight. The little one looked up at him with dark eyes startlingly like Manasseh Cruz's. An image of the congressman, his eyes burning with anger and will, came to Reuben's mind. He saw both for an instant—the eyes of the man, the eyes of the child.

The child put his mouth against the glass door's keyhole and called, "Who are you?"

"Reuben Jackson."

"What?" the boy asked, the glass muffling his voice.

Reuben tapped the door. "Can you open the door?"

The little face scrunched up. "I'm not allowed to. Who are you?"

Reuben had anticipated many travails in his trip to the congressman's home. This was not one of them. He spoke slowly and a little loudly. "Could you ask your—"

A woman appeared behind the child, and Reuben dropped his question—still more his tone—quickly. She shooed the child away and opened the door. "Yes?"

"Good afternoon, ma'am. I'm here to see—" He cut himself off just before saying *your husband*. For all he knew, she was the maid. "I'm here to see Congressman Cruz."

She looked him up and down, and wariness came into her blue eyes like a shield. "Who are you?"

"Reuben Jackson. Until a few days ago, I was the White House's liaison to Congress and the Mars Steering Committee. I represented the president at the meetings Congressman Cruz held with the steering committee."

The woman looked at him intently but said nothing. All Reuben saw now in her face was the shield. She stepped back, opening the door wide, and said, "Come with me."

Relieved, Reuben stepped into a foyer, bright in cream and light-yellow tones, and followed the woman to a broad door of some rich, dark wood he didn't know. She walked right in.

Not the maid, then.

Reuben went in on her heels and found himself in a much darker room. Whether the light was dimmer, he could not say. But every color glowered at him—from the red carpet, of such a brooding hue there was no brightness in it, to the grainy wood paneling, to the black walnut of the bookcases that spanned an entire wall.

Manasseh Cruz sat at an expansive desk, marking papers before him with a pen. He didn't look up.

"Manasseh"—the woman's voice, in that one word, proved beyond doubt who she was—"you have a visitor."

Cruz lifted his gaze, and it locked onto Reuben. Surprise flickered across the congressman's eyes like lightning, then storm clouds gathered there. He glanced toward his wife, but she was already sweeping out of the room. With a very distinct *click*, she pulled the door shut behind her.

Pen still in hand, Cruz leaned back in his leather chair and gazed at Reuben.

Reuben walked over to the congressman. He did not sit down, because Cruz did not invite him to, and because he felt at less of a disadvantage while he looked down on the man. "I want to say first of all, Congressman, that I am sorry for that shot about the Betty Ford Clinic. It was in poor taste."

Cruz did not accept the apology. It even looked as if the storm clouds in his eyes intensified.

Reuben talked on. "But I wasn't entirely without excuse. Do you realize what your behavior looked like to me? But now I think I understand."

Reuben moved nearer, and as Cruz's eyes bored into him, he brought the envelope from beneath his jacket. He dug his hand into the tear and pulled out the two communiqués. Earnestly hoping he was not measuring out the rope that would hang himself, he placed the communiqués in front of Cruz. "This is why you were so angry, isn't it?"

Cruz barely looked at them before returning to Reuben his implacable stare.

Reuben had set out in his mind all the things he wanted to say, yet it unnerved him that Cruz was giving him the opportunity to say them. "I received one of those communiqués from Jep Baines. I think you know which one. The other was anonymously sent to my office the day before I left Washington. I think several other things. I think that communiqué is what you waved in my face that day in the elevator. I think that it's the genuine article, the true message from Mars, and the decision to end the Mars mission was based on a lie. And I think that someone sent you the original communiqué, and you believe that someone was me."

He stopped there, for he had nothing more to say.

Cruz picked up the communiqués and, extending his hand, dropped them in front of Reuben. "Are you stupid, Jackson, or do you think I am?"

This return to familiarity heartened Reuben, and he said, "I know you're not stupid, Congressman, and that's not flattery. I hope you know that I'm not stupid, either."

"I'll admit that there's a kind of covert cleverness about this. I can't figure out what dumb game you're playing."

"I'm not playing any game, Congressman Cruz. All I've said to you is the truth."

Cruz stood up and asked in a voice of dangerous quiet, "Don't you think I can put you in the exchange lines?"

Reuben had, while traveling to see the congressman, formed his own threats. He had read the communiqués, and in their secrets laid hold of a weapon. Yet every hint of exposing those secrets froze in his mouth. He looked at the congressman, at the thunderclouds brewing in the darkness of his eyes, and said, "Yes. I think you can."

Something in Cruz's face yielded, just a little. "What do you want, Jackson?"

"I want to help the Mars team. I want them not to starve. Send them food, Congressman, and I'll go away forever."

"It's too late for them."

Reuben pushed the second communiqué back toward the congressman. "It isn't. At least it's close enough that we have to try." He sought the congressman's eyes. "Or do you think this piece of paper is a lie?"

Cruz shrugged. "It doesn't matter."

"The truth always matters."

Cruz pointed a finger at him. "If you honestly believe that, then all the more reason why you should not be playing this game. Why don't you go away now, Jackson?"

Reuben blinked and, having no answer, retaliated with a question of his own. "Why do you have it in for the Mars team, Congressman?"

Cruz shook his head. "I don't have it in for them. I don't know them, and they certainly never did anything to me."

Reuben scooped up the communiqués and placed them back into the envelope. "Every attempt I've made to help them, you thwarted. You and Dr. Karl, working in tandem."

"Politics makes for strange bedfellows."

Reuben glanced at Cruz, and though he never made much of any politician's appearance of sincerity, he thought the congressman really believed that. "I never thought you and Dr. Karl a mismatched pair."

Cruz sat down again. "Neither did you ever know me."

"No more than you know who I am." Reuben pulled the dossiers out of the envelope and set them in front of the congressman. "The doomed Mars team, Congressman."

Cruz looked at the cover photograph on the topmost dossier—David and Margaret Killiam. His expression wholly unaffected, he lazily flicked open the dossier. He turned a few pages with an air of boredom, then looked up at Reuben. "So you've been in Karl's filing cabinets."

"Is that where the dossiers came from? I didn't know."

They gazed at each other. Yielding nothing, showing nothing. Then Reuben leaned forward and took back the dossiers, his heart sinking. He should have known better than to try a sentimental ploy with Manasseh Cruz.

"They're in the wrong place at the wrong time. That's all."

The soft tone startled Reuben, and he looked at Cruz. Then he stuffed the dossiers into his envelope. "You can write that on their gravestones."

"It's not cruel, not when taken in sum."

Anger flared in Reuben's blood, burning away all regard for the earnestness in the congressman's voice. "Tell me why it isn't cruel to let them starve."

"I'll show you."

Skepticism narrowed Reuben's mouth. "I doubt I'll see it. But I'm game."

"Good. We can leave in an hour." Cruz picked up his pen.

"Leave?"

Cruz smiled, probably enjoying his surprise. "Where would you go to see the Great Collapse?"

Reuben had thought they were talking about the Mars team. He should have remembered that for Cruz, everything was about the Great Collapse. "That's on the other side of the country."

"I'll give you a ride in my plane."

Many people went all their lives without saying or hearing those words, and the novelty alone made Reuben nod.

Manasseh Cruz dropped his gaze back down to his work, but it caught for a moment on Reuben's envelope, and some unreadable thought or emotion obscured his eyes.

XIV

A wall cut off the highway, rising higher than the pallid rock lamps could show. They had been walking toward it for some time, and Moynihan thought they were finally getting close. In the strange pale twilight, caught eternally between a sunset and a dusk that never fell, it was hard to judge.

Moynihan gave little thought to what they would find, or do, at the wall. He was distracted by the pang of emptiness in his stomach, by the dryness in his mouth.

He was distracted by David stalking down the road in front of him, and by Eamon fidgeting to his right. For nearly two full days, they had walked the alien highway. In that time, they had consumed half their rations and found not even the shadow of a hope. Like a cord drawn unrelentingly tighter, the tension grew with every passing hour. And so Moynihan watched David and Eamon. He felt that when the cord snapped, so would they.

"Can we stop for lunch?" Eamon asked, his voice sudden in the dead quiet.

"It is hours ahead of our time to eat again," Moynihan said.

"I know. I want to eat anyway."

Moynihan set his eyes ahead. "No."

"But—"

"Shut up, Eamon." The colonel, several feet in the lead, didn't so much as turn his head, but the command came, forceful and clear.

Eamon's eyes shifted to him. "So the aliens died and made you king?"

David stopped and turned, but Moynihan headed him off. "Mr. Eamon, I suggest you obey the colonel's order."

Eamon glanced between the two men, frowning. "Why?"

"Because he is my second-in-command and your superior."

Eamon's eyes darkened, even as his face flushed. "I know. They slapped that silver eagle on him five minutes before we lifted off, just so he could outrank me. But what good is his silver eagle now?"

The challenge struck something elemental, and Moynihan's insides turned cold. David walked over to stand with him, but he felt a stillness in the colonel now. All the pettiness and irritation of the interminable quarrels vanished in the face of something serious and darkly earnest.

"That eagle," Moynihan said, "makes the colonel your superior and gives him authority over you, Lieutenant Commander. That has not changed."

Eamon raised his chin. "The people who made Killiam my superior and gave him his authority abandoned us to die here. The mission is over. We're just chasing hope, and you would be the first to say we won't find it. We're wasting time until we die. What do ranks matter now?"

Moynihan refused to wade into the deep, horizonless sea of theory. He gripped hard facts like rocks. "If the colonel has no authority, neither do I, and I am not commander of this team."

The air clotted around them. Eamon stared at Moynihan—neither taking up the gauntlet nor yielding. Moynihan stared back.

Seconds slipped past, each one unfurling breadths. Then Eamon stepped back, his jaw and shoulders loosening from their defiance.

Moynihan looked at him one moment longer, and finally turned away. He didn't glance at David or Margaret. Moynihan, with resolve, marched on, and soon Margaret and David walked at his side, but Eamon's footsteps lagged behind them.

They continued down the highway, toward the wall. An empty doorway became visible in the wall, an oblong shadow interrupting the near-white stone. The wall was not, then, a dead end.

At last Moynihan reached the wall, and he silently passed into the yawning doorway. Darkness leaned in on every side, but he felt the change of the air. They were in a building, even if a large one.

The rest of the team filed in after him, snapping on wristlights. Moynihan turned on his own, and it illuminated a wall covered with two-dimensional reliefs. A river flowed down from a mountain, spilling recklessly over boulders and stones into a canyon.

In the corner of his eye, Moynihan saw yellow light shooting across the floor. He swung toward it, but darkness swallowed the light as soon as he moved.

Moynihan switched off his wristlight, but all he saw was more darkness. Heart racing, he turned deliberately toward the others. They were exploring a little distance away from him, flashing their lights over decorated stone walls and the shining obsidian floor. One of them had caused the yellow light, he told himself—the reflection of a wristlight.

Someone turned around, a shadow behind a narrow beam of light, and David's voice came to him. "What's behind you, Commander?"

Moynihan looked in the direction David shone his light. The beam split on a wild shape, more than a dozen strange arms raised upward, and mixed white shafts of light with black shadows.

For a second he thought it was another relief, but his eyes knew better. Light and darkness didn't fall that way over a two-dimensional thing.

"It's a sculpture," Margaret realized. "Of a tree."

Moynihan blinked, and the alien vision of those wild, reaching arms melted into one of the oldest sights of his life. A tree. Branches. Star-shaped leaves.

He drew closer, and so did the rest of his team. They gathered around the tree sculpture, and Moynihan marveled at its perfection.

Eamon lost interest in the sculpture first, shifting his light and drifting away. After a moment, he called, "Look, a door!"

Moynihan turned toward the engineer. He stood a few paces away, by the far wall, pointing his wristlight at another empty doorway.

"I see stairs going down," Eamon reported. "And I feel a draft of air. I think this leads out of the building."

"The next turn in our journey, Commander?" David asked.

Before he had time to answer, Margaret said, "I don't think that door was there earlier. I didn't see it."

David shrugged. "It's dark in here, Meg."

"I know, David. And I don't think that door was there earlier."

The rare irritation in her voice silenced the men. Moynihan walked over to the doorway and, peering through, saw glowing stones lighting up a wide flight of steps. The light blurred into haze in the distance, without revealing where the steps ended. "I think it goes to a deeper underground level, beneath the road."

"We didn't see anything there." Eamon gestured toward the doorway that opened out to the road, bouncing his beam of light all over it. "Let's try this other door."

"Colonel?" Moynihan asked.

He heard the colonel's footsteps as he came to join them, but it was a minute before David spoke. "Either we go back the way we came, or we choose a door in this building to go through. There's more hope in choosing a new door. Why not this one?"

"Dr. Killiam?"

She spoke from close at hand, though he hadn't heard her draw near. "My intuition is that something opened that door after we arrived. Maybe it was only a mechanical response."

Moynihan did not dismiss that, and he did not dismiss the light he had seen flash over the black floor. Yet other facts were too plain. "The colonel is right. We have more hope going into the unknown here than going back the way we came."

He stepped over the threshold, onto a broad stone step. The world was lighter here, the phosphorous rocks transforming the blackness to a cold, twilit dimness. He ventured down, hearing the others coming after him.

And then he heard something else, a light, sharp scraping. Moynihan spun and saw, in moving shadows, something swinging down into the doorway behind them.

He brought his light to bear just as a stone slab fixed firmly in the doorway. It fit seamlessly, with no line to betray it, and masked the way up and out of this lower cavern.

Shock held them silent, staring at the barred way behind them. "Perhaps," Margaret said finally, "a mechanical response."

"No one who goes in comes out?" Eamon's quip was more of a mutter.

Moynihan flicked his wristlight up and down the smooth wall. It gave way to gray jutting rocks on either side, natural walls with no breaches. He pointed the wristlight straight upward, and its beam glared against a black, rocky ceiling not far above their heads.

"Trapped." The word fell from David's lips, the word that rattled in all their minds.

Eamon surged back up the steps. He ran his hands over the wall, and his movements grew faster until he abruptly pulled back. "I can't feel it. Not a crack. Not the shallowest line. We don't have a prayer of opening it up again."

Moynihan switched off his wristlight. The pallid light of the phosphorescent rocks was, for their needs, enough. "A prayer is the one thing we've always got."

David turned from the closed way back, flashing his wristlight on the steps marching away below them. "Keep talking like that, Commander, and someone is going to mistake you for a religious man."

Moynihan blinked. *Mistake?*

"We're another degree trapped," the colonel continued, "but I doubt we're any worse off."

"Logically, we'll never know." But the words passed Moynihan's lips almost by reflex, while his mind ranged elsewhere. Then he shook himself out of those hazy regions and turned away from the stone wall. "Let's keep going."

The steps were ill-defined in the weak light, and Moynihan walked them cautiously. He had little attention to spare the shadows beyond the glowing stones on either side of the steps. But he caught, at the edge of his vision, a muted gleam of a light, like a large red eye.

He whirled, and it was gone.

Margaret, descending the steps, stopped and looked at him. "Commander?"

He shook his head, turning back. "It's nothing." And he told himself it really was nothing, but the skin on his neck tingled and wouldn't stop, as if strange eyes watched him.

The steps ended at last at another road, this one rough and scattered over with pebbles. The road's other side plunged down into a drop-off, as abrupt and jagged as a cliff.

David stopped when he set foot on the road, looking to his right and left. Blackness waited beyond the glow of the phosphorescent rocks. That glow fell faintly on the road, and on the slopes into which the steps had been hewn. They rolled upward, bare and steep, and though David thought he could climb them, he knew he would need to use his hands as well as his feet.

Margaret came up beside him. "Let's see what's over the edge, David."

He looked toward the lip of the rock and nodded his assent, but she was already past him. When he caught up, Margaret said, "You should go easier on Eamon. He's wrong, but you don't help."

David's surprise halted him in his tracks, and Margaret left him behind again. He scrambled after her. "Meg—"

Margaret reached the drop-off and peered down. "David, if you just think . . ." Her voice trailed away, and her body went still.

David reached her side and looked over the edge. He saw a vast sprawl of shadowy buildings, spreading beyond his sight. Faint lights rose up from the unseen ground and hung like strips of luminous clouds, thinning the darkness. Minarets pierced up through the gloom; long, wide buildings with flat roofs squatted under the dusky light. Smaller buildings shrank down, the darkness deepening into blackness around them. Much was lost in shadows, but David knew he looked at something great. Mighty even in its ancient decay.

At his back, Moynihan asked, "What is it?"

David struggled to find a reply, and it was Margaret who answered, "It's a city, Commander. The city of the aliens."

Moynihan and Eamon joined them at the edge, and they stared down at the dead city. "Do you suppose," Eamon wondered, "that there's anything still alive down there?"

David looked at Moynihan, waiting for him to shoot down the idea, but the commander stayed silent.

"I don't suppose," David said.

Moynihan pulled out his recorder and aimed it at the city below.

Eamon folded his arms. "What are you doing?"

"Shooting overhead footage of the city. I'll get more detailed shots when—"

"What for?" Eamon interrupted.

David's muscles tightened, but Moynihan looked away from his recording to bestow a calm gaze on Eamon. "I set up an interlink between this recorder and the habitat's main computer. All the data I record will make its way back to Earth."

"I always figured that. But why are you recording it?"

Moynihan turned back to the alien city. "For posterity."

"I have no posterity."

David knew Moynihan wasn't going to respond and so put in, "None of us has posterity. But most everyone else does."

"Right," Eamon snapped, turning on him with savage agreement. "Everyone else has kids, including idiots who don't take care of them. Why not me?"

David stared at him, an extraordinary thought rising like the sun. "You mean you want kids?"

For a moment, Eamon looked at him, his jaw twitching. Then the engineer's eyes darted to Margaret, to Moynihan, and he turned and stormed away.

Moynihan stepped back from the edge, lowering his recorder, and called, "Mr. Eamon! Come back!"

But Eamon strode on, vanishing into the blackness.

David stared after him. "I can't believe he wants kids. It makes me feel like I don't know anything about him."

"Colonel," Moynihan said, "I don't think any of us knows much of anything about the rest of us."

"And that was intentional, wasn't it?" Without waiting for an answer, Margaret turned from Moynihan to David. "Why should you be so surprised that Eamon wants children?"

"Because I never wanted children."

"What has that got to do with it?"

David took three seconds to make it clear in his mind, and when he did, he knew he couldn't say it. They wouldn't approve if he said wanting children was a sign of maturity and he was more mature than Eamon.

"We shouldn't be separated," Moynihan said to them. "Certainly none of us should be alone. Colonel, go bring the lieutenant commander back."

David swallowed his protest and went after Eamon. When he passed out of the tentative phosphorescent light, he snapped on his wristlight. On his right, the ground fell away to the city below. On his left, the rocky slope ascended to touch the cavern ceiling. Ahead of him, the darkness rolled on and on.

He made his strides long, sweeping the light back and forth. The motions flowed into a steady pattern, uninterrupted by anything new, and his mind wandered into daydreams. He hazily mused on images and thoughts, without purpose and without conclusions.

Time slipped away from him. At last he shook himself out of the daydreams and looked over his shoulder, expecting to see the blurred glow where Margaret and Moynihan waited. He saw total blackness.

Unease slithered over his skin, and David stopped and called out, "Eamon!"

His voice rang loud, faded slowly away. David resumed walking and picked up his pace, trying to think. The city. The slopes. Dead ahead. Where else could Eamon have gone?

He journeyed on into the darkness, and his suspicion grew with his frustration. He combed the slopes with his wristlight, as if he might see Eamon ducking behind a hump of earth. And then, swinging the light forward, he saw the end.

Several paces in front of him, the light shone on a dirty cave wall, filling its depressions and fissures with shadows. The cavern went no further.

As David stood still, pondering again Eamon's elusiveness, he heard a faint sound. He stiffened and bent all his concentration to listening.

He heard it again, softer this time, and then again, softer yet. The sound came from his right, and it was moving away from him.

David hurried to the edge and looked down, pointing his light. A building stood directly below him, much nearer than the buildings he had seen from his last vantage point. In fact, he thought he could safely jump down to its flat roof.

That realization ignited his anger and he shouted, "Eamon! Eamon, get back here!"

His words came back to him, bouncing off the endless stone of the infernal cavern. David angled the wristlight in the direction into which the noise had faded. "Eamon, do you think I want to find you? Do you think this was my idea? The commander wants you back. So come on, let's go. We don't have time left to waste."

He listened to his voice carry and finally die. He saw nothing and heard nothing. The ghost city swallowed his shouts in its thick silence, in its interminable shadows.

A pang of doubt dug into him. He hadn't seen Eamon. Maybe the engineer wasn't sneaking into the city.

Then again, if he wasn't, where had he gone, and what had David heard moving away from him? Shoving away doubt, he yelled again. "Eamon, come here, and we'll go back to Meg and the commander. I don't want to be here." Then his voice dropped lower as his appeal lost its anger. "It's—it's about time to eat again."

Silence returned. David found he didn't like staring down at the city, and he backed away. As he stepped backward, he put his foot down on nothing. One split second of terror, and then he fell.

He plummeted through empty air, wrapping his arms over his head, trying to kick his feet to point straight downward. He was still fighting his body into a good position when he made impact.

Shock stabbed through him. The shock of wet, of cold, of his whole body being horribly jarred and then submerged. His conscious mind did not, in that moment, understand what had happened to him. But a training deeper than consciousness rose up in his muscles and took hold. He held his breath, even as his lungs heaved for air, and he kicked and swept his arms in sure strokes.

If he was moving, he could not tell, nor did he know up from down. Water encased him, crushing his breath.

Then his head broke the surface, and he released the air from his burning lungs. He drew in a breath, blinking moisture out of his eyes and still seeing nothing.

David fumbled his wristlight on. He sank a little into the water as he did it and then came up again. Treading water, he flashed the light into the pitch-black darkness.

Smooth stone walls enclosed the water on every side and towered above his head. When he tried to crane his neck and light to see the edge he had fallen over, he slipped beneath the water.

Water sloshed into his mouth, so cold it made his teeth ache. He fought his way into the air and spat it out. But a chill, not only physical, seeped through his whole being. He couldn't stay in the water. He couldn't climb out of the water.

He drew in all the breath his lungs would hold and shouted as loudly as he could, "Eamon! Eamon, help!"

The name echoed on the high, featureless walls that made him a prisoner of the water. Despair cascaded through his heart, and David called out, "Meg! Commander!"

And the cry, like all his cries, went unanswered.

XV

Manasseh Cruz trod the blackened earth, occasionally crunching charred bits of rubble beneath his boots. He cut around the debris heaps, not trusting their steadiness, and the tallest he gave the widest berth. Mounds that rose higher than his head and cast expansive shadows marked the sites of great buildings. Wood and plaster had vanished into smoke and ashes, but blocks of concrete endured. Steel endured, bent and scarred. Plastic and glass poked out of the mounds, out of the ash heaps—melted in the blasting heat of the inferno, now solidified again into ugly slabs.

"Why did you have them drop us off here?"

Surprised at how far behind Reuben's voice was, Cruz turned around. The younger man had stopped, and he stood awkwardly, his left arm clenched against his side. Through his jacket, Cruz could make out the contours of the oversized envelope.

Jackson had clung to it throughout their trip with an admirable suspicion but with a careless lack of subtlety. Cruz could have taught him a thing or two. He would have, if Jackson hadn't already driven his stakes into hostile ground.

"Is the walk too hard for you?" he asked.

Jackson frowned and began trudging over the rubble-strewn ground. "No, but what's the use of it?"

"Jackson, you are looking at the Great Collapse."

"With all due respect, Congressman, I didn't need you to show me that the Collapse is ugly. I see it every day."

His tone was a trifle brusque, and Cruz nearly smiled. "Have some faith. I didn't get where I am by wasting time."

Reuben looked him over, and Cruz saw the grudging concession in his eyes. Then the younger man stated, "It's going to rain."

Cruz looked upward at the clouds stooping low in the sky and smiled. "You haven't often been to California, have you?" He led on, and Jackson followed.

Soon they approached a bank of interlacing steel beams, almost two stories high. The steel buckled toward the ground, thrusting out jagged edges over the ruins, and the light slid dully over the disfigured metal. Hills of scorched debris piled up around the patchwork steel wall.

Reuben stopped again to stare at it. Then he looked at Cruz. "I suppose that used to be a skyscraper."

Cruz nodded and pointed to the mountains that, themselves enduring and unscarred, stood back and looked down on the disaster. "Those are the San Gabriel Mountains. You're walking on what used to be Los Angeles." He turned, surveying the wreckage that spread without relief in every direction. "An entire American city leveled."

"By Americans."

Cruz looked at Jackson. "And then the president ordered the National Guard to put down all riots. It was one of the best decisions he's ever made."

Jackson grimaced and looked away.

He was probably thinking of the dead rioters. The rioting had quickly ended, after mobs had a few losing confrontations with the shooting National Guardsmen, but the complaints went on and on. Cruz heard people lamenting still that Americans had died by the orders of their own government.

As if it would have been somehow better for them to die in fires started by their rioting fellow citizens.

Cruz began walking again, listening to Jackson's footsteps scuff the ground behind him. He skirted a chunk of concrete and sidestepped the drifts of ashes, half-melded by the rains and concealing who-knew-what wicked shards of debris. And he wondered if he smelled fire or only imagined he did. When he'd first visited Los Angeles after the riots, it was still burning.

The memories stirred his anger, and he spoke without looking behind him. "For a century, America's fiscal policy was, 'We'll pay for it tomorrow.'" He gestured to the burned city. "Tomorrow came. All debts have to be paid, Jackson. It's the law of the universe. Even in canceled debts, someone has to stand the loss. All things have their cost, and the price is always paid. Not always in money. There are other currencies."

"Like human misery?"

Cruz circled past a warped lump of glass. "You could look at it that way." He saw the vague figures of buildings ahead and quickened his pace.

The shapes grew larger, clearer, and finally resolved into a motley collection of tents and lean-tos surrounding a broken stump of a building. A truck idled nearby, a jumbled line of people meandering away from it. Children dodged among them, dashing back and forth. Shouts carried over to them—the high-pitched yelling of children, the stronger yelling of adults.

"Why do people live here?" Jackson asked.

Cruz pointed to the one true, if splintered, building—its brick walls singed, its windows knocked out, black tarps stretched over it for a roof. "I suspect it began with that. There's enough left of it for a shelter." Then he gestured to the truck. "They got on our radar a while ago. An exchange truck comes once every month."

He walked to the house and sat down, his back against the blackened brick. Jackson came and sat by him, and for a few minutes, they watched the transactions around the truck. The slipshod people of the slipshod village brought cash by the armload, heaping it into the back of the truck. One of the guards shoveled the dollar bills deep into the vehicle's interior. The second leaned against its side, his machine gun slung over his shoulder. The third man handed out the food.

Cruz turned his argument around in his mind, looking for a good angle. He had tailored it for his constituents, for his colleagues, for the broad American public, for the president. He wondered how to frame it for the last man in America who cared about Mars.

At length, he asked, "Do you ever think about how to solve America's problems, Jackson?"

"No, and for the same reason I don't think about solving Bangladesh's problems. I wouldn't know where to start."

"I think about it."

"Well, they pay you to."

Cruz glanced at Reuben. He made his tone soft. "When we paid off the debt, we destroyed our currency and the economy with it. Our dollar bills are worth more as paper than as legal tender. But they have just an iota of value because of these exchanges. It's not only that it gets Americans to treat our money like money. All the cash the government collects this way, it destroys. We have eradicated close to a trillion dollars through the exchanges. It's less than five percent of the money we printed up, but it does help. When the government gives people food in exchange for cash, it's not only keeping our people eating, it's also salvaging our nation's currency."

He paused to gauge Reuben's reaction, but Jackson only fidgeted with his envelope, looking away.

Was it too abstract? It was an unhappy truth, and a leading cause of trouble in the world, that most people did not like to think abstractly. Cruz motioned toward the shabby people clustering around the truck. "One of the primary sources for the food is military warehouses. Jackson, all the food you wanted to send to Mars will now feed people in places like this. It will be used to gather cash and make the American dollar worth something again. All the expense you want to put into launching and flying a capsule to Mars will go to restoring our society, of which we are, every one of us, a part. It's a zero-sum game. Either we spend the resources on America or we spend them on Mars. And Jackson, there are only four people on Mars. There are three-hundred sixty million in America."

Jackson raised his head and gazed at the black field of ruin that used to be Los Angeles. He watched the people drifting away from the truck, their meager food supplies in their arms.

He stood up from the scarred earth and turned to look at Cruz. "Almost thou persuadest me to be a Christian."

Cruz took those words—absorbed them deep, understood them well—and he also stood. They began walking to the truck together, with a silent understanding that they were finished. Already Cruz felt their paths dividing again, felt their tentative experiments at confederation dying. Each of them carried the empty-handed, the no-good *almost*.

Manasseh Cruz sat in the chair, swiveled so that he could prop his feet up on the bed. He leaned his elbow on the desk, staring at the window in the wall. All he could see was a snatch of blue, unchanging and yet never the same, second by second. He felt the plane thrum, deep and smooth, as it shot like a bullet above the clouds. The sky streamed past his eyes, and he watched without ever entirely noticing, his mind thick with thoughts.

Someone rapped lightly, and he called permission to enter automatically. Reuben Jackson stepped inside and lingered by the door. He put his hands in his pockets, but his posture was rigid.

Cruz looked at him and then back at the window. He did not want to leave his thoughts; Jackson would have to do more than just walk in to bring him out of them.

"Congressman Cruz, what do you think of Dr. Karl?"

Cruz went on staring at the sky and answered out of his preoccupation. "When the Rapture comes, he'll be one of the last to go."

A few beats passed. Cruz felt Jackson's eyes on him, sensed his consternation, and suddenly realized what he had said. He kept still, his posture casual, but irritation at his slip roiled through him. Hadn't he taught himself long ago not to say such things without calculating it first?

"Doesn't Karl share your principles?" Jackson asked.

"No."

"So why did he shut down the Mars mission?"

Still turned away from Jackson, and with no inclination to admit his ignorance, Cruz said, "Ask him yourself."

"And what do you know about Donegan Moynihan?"

Cruz looked at Reuben this time. "Why are you asking about him?"

Reuben's eyes shifted back and forth before settling on Cruz again. "Moynihan was on the steering committee for a year. He helped set the goals and policy of the mission, and he voted on the selection of all the candidates, including himself. He was one of the First Names. And now Karl and the other First Names are letting him die. It's a kind of fratricide."

Cruz had always known that Moynihan left the First Names to take command of the Mars team, but never had he brought that fact into the present. "And what does it matter?"

"I want to understand."

"That's no kind of answer."

Jackson tried to straighten and only looked stiff. Awkward but resolved.

So Cruz gave up the idea of pressing him. "I would guess," he told Jackson, "that there's no love lost between Karl and Moynihan."

Jackson studied him. After a minute, he shrugged and turned back to the door.

"Jackson," Cruz interrupted his departure, "this, this—" He snapped his fingers as though trying to summon the word, then said, "This informant of yours—"

"Whistleblower," Jackson corrected.

"Whistleblower. Informant. It's criminal either way. I suspect these documents are stolen. Even if they aren't, this unauthorized distribution is illegal. Best to stop before somebody catches you."

Jackson frowned. "Congressman, I am not the whistleblower. And I don't know who is."

Cruz believed him, though some part of his nature didn't want to accept Jackson's word so easily. Jackson played no game, or if he did, he played it straight. That accounted for his foolish moves. "That's a pity, NASA Man. Your whistleblower could use a friendly warning."

"Against you?"

Cruz met Jackson's eyes and their challenge. "You shouldn't have tried to persuade me, Jackson."

The challenge strangely faded out of Jackson's eyes, displaced by thoughtfulness. "I suppose not. But my attempt to persuade you was no less successful than your attempt to persuade me."

Cruz shrugged, though his decision even to try bothered him as much as his failure. What did he have to prove to Jackson? "I tried the easy way to win."

"So did I." With that, Jackson ducked out of the plane's cabin.

Cruz rubbed his eyes with his palms. Jackson had been uncomfortable. Did he come to Cruz's cabin to talk about Karl—and Donegan Moynihan?

Cruz summoned what facts he knew about the Mars commander, trying to see the reason for Jackson's sudden attention to him. Old rumors about Moynihan and Karl swirled in his memory, just below the surface, and eluded his grasp when he tried to fish them out.

Had Jackson been poring through his envelope? Maybe the informant was prodding him in this direction.

The informant. Cruz contemplated this new factor, this anonymous player whose identity he did not know, whose loyalties and intentions he could not guess. Was Reuben Jackson, after all, the second-to-last person in America who still cared about Mars?

Or was he genuinely the last, and the informant had a different purpose? Many people might desire a scandal in Washington.

Would Karl be so subtle?

He sorted out possibilities in his mind and tried to calculate the dangers of each one. And he tried to see a path that threaded safely past all of them.

There was no such thing. With Jackson on a quest, and the informant bent on stirring trouble, there was no entirely safe way. But there was a shrewd one.

Cruz worked the keyboard swiftly, putting in the call, sending a transmission across two thousand miles. A minute passed, and then a voice issued in answer from the computer: "Good afternoon, Congressman Cruz. What can I do for you?"

"I'd like a private meeting with the president, and soon."

"Of course. May I ask what it's about?"

"I think we have a leak, Jep. Possibly in Dr. Karl's office."

"What information is getting out?"

"I've heard little with clarity," Cruz answered. "But what's coming out seems to revolve around the Mars mission."

Baines paused, a rare thing in Cruz's dealings with him, and in that brief silence Cruz felt the seriousness of what he had just put into irrevocable motion. "You'll see the president soon," the chief of staff said.

XVI

Donegan Moynihan scanned the cave wall with his wristlight, though he didn't really doubt it was the end of the cavern. He just wanted that fact, the fact that he had come to the end and still not found his missing team members, to sink in.

Into his mind, and down into the pit of his stomach.

Moynihan shifted his wristlight to the drop-off in front of him. Margaret knelt there, and he knew he had to look, too. He lay on his stomach and peered over the abrupt edge to a pool of water.

He estimated it was perhaps twenty feet down to it. The stone on every side was too smooth to be nature's work. A small tunnel opened in the far right wall, barely above the water.

It looked like an aqueduct, and that was a hopeful thought. But he didn't feel hopeful. He felt sick. "The good news," he said to Margaret, "is that it is possible we will not die of dehydration. The bad news . . ."

"The bad news," Margaret took up his thought, a slight tremor in her voice, "is that David may have drowned in there."

Moynihan stared down at the black water. "Or Eamon," he said, taking refuge in analysis. "Or neither, even if one fell in. No one could climb out of that water. But the tunnel may let out at a good place."

"It leads . . ." Margaret rose and walked to where the plateau overlooked the city.

Moynihan didn't stir. He filled his eyes with the water, his thoughts combing blacker depths than it possessed. They had searched for David and Eamon to the cavern's end and found nothing. The two men had left somehow—fallen into the water or climbed down to the city—and those facts cast the shadow of a terrible reality he could not yet see.

Eamon was, maybe, venting his anger in wandering from the mission. But the colonel would never wander. He was too loyal to the mission, and far more to his sister. Either he was unable to return or he was still pursuing Eamon. The thought of the colonel and the engineer meeting each other alone, once so casual, now twisted ominously in his mind. He had seen them fighting in the engineering bay, had seen the anger and the blinding fire in their eyes. What might they have done to each other had he not intervened? What might they do now?

"Dr. Moynihan?"

Margaret's voice lighted among his thoughts, and he pulled back from the water. After getting to his feet, he went to her.

She pointed at the city. "We can get down from here, Commander. They might be in the city since they're no longer up here."

"We'll go down into the city, Doctor. But not for them. We'll go for us. We need to find food and water quickly, and the city is our best chance. Our goal now is our own survival, not finding the colonel and the lieutenant commander."

She didn't answer, and he wondered if it sounded as cold to her as it did to him. But the logic was perfect, and it could not be disputed.

He stepped up to the edge and looked down on the city. Then he focused his wristlight on the long emptiness between the nearest rooftop and where he stood.

Then he looked at Margaret. "There's no way to climb down."

She raised her eyebrows at him. "Climb? Commander, we'll jump." Margaret flipped off her wristlight, stepped forward, and jumped.

He watched her fall, her body poised, and then hit the rooftop. She stayed on her feet, to all appearances unhurt by the landing, and she backed away, looking up at him.

So now it was his turn. Moynihan ran the best method through his mind, took a breath, and jumped.

For a moment he was caught in the strange sensation of a free fall: moving yet motionless. Then he made impact.

It hurt, jarring his bones. But he, too, kept his feet as Margaret watched him.

"Getting off the building should be easier," she said. "Flat roofs like this are usually used as a patio. There ought to be either an outdoor staircase or a way down into the house."

The words stirred up a discordant memory, and he murmured to himself.

"What?"

"Nothing. I just thought of the Middle East and their flat roofs. When

I was a doctoral student at Cambridge, I . . ." The residue of humiliation brought his sentence to a halt. But she couldn't know. The stories had never escaped Washington's back rooms. Dr. Karl had been true that far. "I went," he said, "to the Middle East with an archaeologist friend of mine."

He felt sure she took note of the strange pause, but Margaret only said, "We should start looking."

Moynihan turned, shining his light, and saw a metal rod curling over a stone post and then plunging over the edge of the roof. He hurried over and, looking down, saw a flight of steps cut into the side of the building. The rod, a handrail, ran down beside the steps.

"Here is the way down, Dr. Killiam," he called. His eyes flitted over what lay below—an open pavement like a plaza, dominated by a statue whose form he could not comprehend. Other buildings stood along the edges of the pavement, brooding and elusive in the half darkness.

And then, in the gloom that pervaded the plaza, he saw a red flicker.

Margaret passed by him and began down the steps, and he was almost too fixed on the strange light to notice. Then he hastened after her, wondering what might be waiting for them.

There was a little more light at street level, and Margaret began walking toward the statue, but Moynihan forestalled her. "Just a minute, Dr. Killiam."

He flashed his wristlight on the ground and scooped up a rock about the size of a baseball. Snapping off the light, he weighed the rock in his palm. "Dr. Killiam, what would you think if I told you I kept seeing red lights?"

"Is this a medical question?"

A gleam of red slid into the edge of his vision, and he said quietly, "Not yet. Hold still, Doctor." He took two, three steps forward, watching the red light follow in the corner of his eye. He tried to fix a sense of its position in his mind, then he spun around, hurling the rock.

His eyes registered a floating red sphere shining out of the gloom, and the next second the rock smashed into it. With an explosion of light and a high-pitched keening noise, the thing burst into pieces.

Moynihan just had time to wonder what he had destroyed before Margaret gripped his forearm. "Commander!"

He turned and saw spheres gliding out of the shadows, their red luminescence like embers among ashes. The spheres—he counted six—arranged themselves into two even columns and advanced.

He backed away, and Margaret moved with him. Something snapped beneath his heel, and a strange jolt shot through the sole of his boot and pierced his leg muscles.

Moynihan stumbled. Shards on the ground, with a lingering red glow, caught his eye. He had stepped on remains of the shattered sphere. Could that act of destruction have been to the spheres or whatever controlled them the first shot fired?

Margaret tugged at him, drawing him onward. "There's an open doorway across the plaza, Commander. I think we should make for it."

He did not find anything appealing in that idea. As he searched for an idea of his own, the spheres swooped at them. "Go, Doctor!" he barked.

Margaret sprang away, and he followed. They raced across the plaza, heedless of what might be hidden in the half darkness, and the spheres flew after them.

Margaret made the doorway first. Moynihan, seeing that she was safe, sped faster over the pavement. He was so nearly there.

A slab of stone began lowering itself down over the doorway. In a final burst of energy, Moynihan dove into the shrinking space.

He ended up full-length on the ground, hands scraped and jaw nicked, listening to the stone *click* into place behind him.

Total darkness. He pushed himself up, marveling that he had made it, and then he heard Margaret say, "Nice slide into home, Commander."

She sounded amused, and he did not truly understand why. Moynihan touched his palms, feeling a warm ooze of blood.

A piercing musical noise froze him. From outside, muffled by the stone walls, came a series of high-pitched notes. Much like the sound that sphere had made when he smashed it.

He could have turned on his wristlight and explored the building they were locked inside, but he didn't. Neither did Margaret. They only listened in the darkness to the strange notes, signaling things they did not know to an audience they could not guess.

Consciousness came slowly and painfully. At length, he dimly connected the ache in his head to the hardness pressed against it. Planting his hands against something rough and warm and unyielding, David pushed himself up.

He looked down at a knobbly rock formation. He glanced at his hands, spread on the rocky surface, and felt warmth pulsing against his fingers and palms. A thought penetrated the fog in his brain. Rock ought to be cold. Why was it warm?

He cast his eyes around and saw a rugged incline leading away from the rock formation, as well as scattered clumps of phosphorescent stones. The place was wholly unfamiliar to him.

Yet here he was.

David massaged his temples, trying to gather memories. They came to him in fragments of unpleasantness. Treading the frigid water, spotting the tunnel in one stony wall. Crawling and sliding down the slanted tunnel, banging against its enclosing sides. Falling into a chilly stream. Dragging himself out of the water and wandering over unforgiving ground that made him stumble.

Drawn by warmth. He remembered that, too. He remembered lying down, nothing in his mind but relief to feel heat.

Now he was mostly dry, and pain throbbed in various degrees over all his body. He thought of his irreversible way to this strange place and knew that in searching for Eamon, he had gotten lost himself. He was separated from his team and from his sister, and he didn't know how to get back.

David, realizing these things, slammed his fist against the rock. Wincing, he put his smarting hand to his mouth.

His mind continued to clear. After a time he unzipped one of his jumpsuit's voluminous pockets and found a soggy half ration. He ate it, and the whole universe became better.

So he picked himself up from the rock and struck out.

He toiled up the incline, finding it was all lumpy rock. It stretched on, longer and longer, a gradual and relentless slope.

At long last, he crested the incline. A building like a giant-king's hall confronted him, a single story wide and tall beyond all human proportions. Massive pillars five times his height upheld the roof and glowed faintly. In that pale light, he could see a gaping entranceway quite as high as the pillars.

It looked as if it had been made for something far different from him, and a strange reluctance crept over him. David pushed it aside and drew closer. Walking between the pillars, he passed into the building.

The walls were paneled at intervals with sheets of a metal David had never seen the likes of before. It shone with its own native radiance, so soft and strong it suffused the building with silvery light.

That light revealed a scene of ruin. From within, the building looked as if it had been picked up, shaken violently, and set down again. Smaller, ornate pillars lay toppled, with what looked like crystal shattered around them. Stone benches lolled on the cracked floor, overturned. Many other things, which he could not name or understand, were scattered about—metal, stone, and crystal, wrought into shapes beyond definition.

David made his way through the wreckage, not bothering with his wristlight. He had worked his way well into it when a gunshot split the air.

He dropped to the ground. Another shot exploded in his ears, and instinctive fear thundered through him.

Suddenly perplexity burst through his fear. Who on Mars had guns?

Then he remembered who did, and now fury swallowed his perplexity. "Eamon!" he yelled. "Eamon, you idiot!"

A few silent, frozen seconds. Then he heard running, and David cautiously got up from the floor.

Eamon hastened toward him with a gun in his right hand, darting around the wreckage. Curses and threats rose so thick in David's throat they nearly choked him.

The engineer skidded to a halt, his eyes wide. "I had no idea it was you, Killiam."

David only glared at him.

Eamon waved his hands vaguely, the gun, too. "I keep hearing noises. It has me spooked, I'm not ashamed to tell you." He shoved the gun into its holster. "What are you doing here, anyway? I thought you would have gone reporting back to Moynihan by now."

"That's another thing," David snapped. "When I was looking for you, I—" Then Eamon's words finally worked all the way through his brain. "Reporting *back*? You knew I was looking for you?"

"I heard you yelling. It was hard to turn down an invitation like that, but I decided to go on anyway."

The cavalier tone set David's teeth on edge. "Eamon, you sound like a kid who needs the concepts of authority and discipline beaten into his skull by a drill sergeant. You don't decide whether or not to obey orders. And you shouldn't even need orders to keep you from wandering far afield of the team in an unknown situation."

"Don't lecture me, Killiam. That silver eagle didn't teach you anything I don't know. I understand perfectly, but you don't. So let me lay out the situation for you, Killiam. I've gone AWOL."

"So, that's the end of your professionalism?" David scrutinized Eamon, feeling another end, a greater one.

"I'm free again. For the first time in years, I'm free. No regulations, no procedures, no routines, no Moynihan. I get to do what I choose to do."

David wondered if, as second-in-command, he ought to restore Eamon to the team. A restoration to be begun by knocking Eamon down. But he had no energy for it. The end he felt encroaching was his end, and it was their end. Death would close the book on their mission.

The team's breakdown was only a faint precursor of that bitter conclusion, and David no longer cared enough to stop it. He walked past Eamon. "Enjoy your freedom. I'm going to find my sister."

David picked his way over a scattering of glassy shards. Once he cleared them, he struck forward with determination.

"Killiam?"

He turned his head.

Eamon watched him, his expression unreadable. "You came from the opposite way. How do you know where you're going?"

"I don't."

Eamon tramped over to him. "I'll point you in the right direction."

The two men continued through the building, finally reaching another line of colossal pillars. They walked between the monoliths and emerged into cool, open darkness.

A beam of light shot from Eamon's hand. "This way," he called, with a cheerfulness David found wholly unjustified.

The engineer led the way to a white stone bridge, an easy confidence in his gait. David added his wristlight to Eamon's and followed him across the bridge.

On the other side, he paused. The aliens' streetlamps glowed ahead, and he caught the form of a road, pressed by towering buildings on either side.

Eamon beckoned him on into the street. When they had gone half a block between dim buildings, Eamon stopped and pointed. "Do you see that?"

David looked ahead and saw only pallid light and gray shapes. "No."

Eamon's hand dropped. "Whatever. Just go straight ahead until you reach the big road. Then go up."

"Up?"

"The main road slopes up. You'll see. Anyway, it'll take you back to where we left Meg and Moynihan."

But would they still be there? Moynihan could not wait very long before continuing, not with the mission in such hard straits. David's heart sank, and he wondered suddenly how long he had slept. "Eamon, how long ago did you leave the team?"

"A few hours, I guess. There's no way to know. No sun or moon or stars down here, and only Moynihan has any kind of clock. Good person for it, too."

"There's nothing wrong with Moynihan," snapped David.

"Except for one or two things."

"You've already left, Eamon. Why are you still criticizing?"

"Why do you care? There's no reason for Moynihan to be anything to you. You're not anything to him. He's more interested in his ice specimens than he is in us."

David sighed because he couldn't argue that fact. "Don't be so personal. Moynihan is our commander; nobody hired him to be our friend. He's been a good commander, and there's no reason to put him down."

"Is that why you're going back to march to his tune until you die?"

"I'm going back because that's where my sister is."

Something fell like a shadow over Eamon's eyes, and he turned around, heading back the way they had come.

David looked in the direction Eamon had pointed him, ready to continue his journey alone. Then a resounding *crack*, like stone splitting apart, turned him back.

Eamon had halted, his back to David, and for a handful of seconds, the whole street was still. Then a large building, where the street dead-ended by the bridge, teetered and collapsed.

With a crashing that buffeted David's ears, large stones slid and tumbled into the street. Soon the building lay in a mound of rubble, obstructing the way to the bridge.

David's breath stopped, the oddity of the sudden, perfect collapse digging uneasily into him.

Ahead of him, Eamon stood unmoving in the street. Then he looked back at David before facing the bridge. Squaring his shoulders, he marched resolutely on.

Another *crack* pierced the air, and Eamon scurried back a few steps.

The building opposite the one that had just fallen wobbled and pitched at the street. Chunks of the building rained down, heaping onto the debris already there.

The cascade of stone ebbed and finally stopped, but its scraping and striking still rang in David's ears. He stared at the wreckage, now piling more than a story high and effectively sealing off the way to the bridge. The two buildings had crumbled into a barricade.

David switched his gaze to Eamon, curious to see what he would do now. The engineer loitered a long minute, and then turned and walked back.

He reached David and passed by without a word. David kept pace with him, and they headed toward the main street of the city. Not together, but just, for the time, going in the same direction.

XVII

Manasseh Cruz slouched down in the easy chair, staring at the enormous abstract painting directly across from him. The painting was quite as long as the couch it hung above. It nearly grazed the ceiling, too, and its whole impressive expanse was a swirl of blues, grays, and blacks. But Cruz could not now judge Dr. Karl's artistic taste. He was too busy talking himself out of the alarm that Karl had invited him to his home. Never in all their years of conspiracy had Karl done so. Cruz could only wonder, and worry, what had led the doctor to do it now.

He heard footsteps, ice clinking, and then Karl entered his line of vision. The doctor sat on the couch opposite Cruz, a tumbler in his hand.

"So?" Cruz asked.

Karl took a drink of the liquor, his eyes smoldering. "Jephthah Baines summoned me, Cruz. *Summoned*. He's staff, and I'll remind him of it someday."

Cruz didn't have time for Karl's offended ego. "But you went?"

"Yes. He told me there were rumors of a leak of classified documents from my office. Documents concerning the Mars mission."

Cruz wanted badly to know if Baines had mentioned him, but it was too dangerous to ask. So he relaxed into the cushions, scanning the painting and contriving to look careless. "I know. I was at the White House this morning too."

"What did you tell them?"

"I told them Reuben Jackson is mixed up in this somehow. He came to my home down south, you know, and advocated for the Mars team. He's on the warpath again, and I think someone is deliberately setting him off. There is a leaker, Karl." Cruz met Karl's sharp eyes. "So, who is it?"

"You think I know?"

Cruz leaned forward. "I think you could know. It's not for nothing that the White House pinpointed your office as the source of the leak. Something led them to you. Jackson is only a liaison. He couldn't steal files from you if he wanted. But your people have access. And people they know could get access through them."

Karl swallowed more liquor. "I'll handle my people, Congressman. What do you think we should do about the White House nosing around?"

"Let them go for it. I want them to find the leaker."

"You don't know where that might lead, Cruz. And you don't know what they might find as they look."

"I've done nothing wrong."

Karl studied him, his expression interested and yet cold, as if he were analyzing something beneath a microscope. "You may think that, Congressman. Will your constituents agree, though, if they ever learn what we've done?"

Cruz shrugged, though that was a story he wanted no one to know.

Karl raised his cup, his face thoughtful, and took a long, deliberate drink, and suddenly Cruz longed for a drink too. He looked away, forcing his mind to business. "We succeeded, anyway. Helped along by the mold that infected the Mars food, I'll admit. But you lost one of your own."

"What are you talking about?"

Cruz affected surprise. "Donegan Moynihan, of course. He was one of yours, and now he's going to die on Mars."

Karl gazed at Cruz, a half smile on his lips. "Would you believe I never much cared for Moynihan?"

"Have you ever much cared for anyone?"

"You would be surprised."

Cruz wasn't sure what to make of that, so he moved on. "I met David Killiam once at a dinner in honor of America's decorated veterans, and I questioned Gul Eamon at a congressional hearing. But many people in Washington have had contacts like that. I have no real connection with anyone on the doomed Mars team. You, on the other hand, sent your fifth man to Mars, and it has as good as killed him. You're not a politician, so you don't have to worry about appearing appropriately sentimental over a dead former colleague. But what if someone connects what we've done to your history with Moynihan?"

Karl shook his head. "There's no reason they should. We were not enemies."

Cruz absently slid his fingers into his pocket, wondering if that was a lie.

"Besides, that was all finished with five years ago. No one has brought it up since, and nothing has happened that they should bring it up now."

Cruz pulled his fingers from his pocket and looked at Karl. "That depends on what the leaker has dug up in your office."

For a split second, rigidity froze Karl's face. Then it fled. "No, it doesn't."

This time Cruz knew he was lying. He had been probing for weakness, and finding it, he felt suddenly vulnerable himself. Karl's secrets might bring him down, even though he had nothing to do with them.

Cruz shifted, ready to check the last item on his list and then go. "One more thing. I got a call from the Speaker. He's been hearing rumblings; House members have begun talking about killing my Mars appropriations committee in six months, and your steering committee with it."

Karl glared at him. "They won't do it."

Cruz eyed him. "The Mars mission is over. We killed it. And now they're going to kill our committees, and I don't care. I'll finagle a new chairmanship out of it, maybe on Foreign Affairs. The Speaker will owe me, and I'll collect. Just decide what you want from them, Karl, and play your cards right."

"I want to run the exploration of Mars."

By an act of restraint, Cruz did not roll his eyes. "Karl, we ended it."

"We ended this one mission. But the Mars project is still alive. Mars will be explored, and it will be conquered, and I will control it."

Cruz heard the iron resolve in the scientist's voice, and he didn't know whether to marvel at the grand ambition or scorn it. He etched the words into his memory and then dismissed them from present consideration. "I won't give you advice on getting what you want. It's your business and, if they take away the committee, your loss."

"Congress will not abolish the steering committee," Karl stated. "They know the Red Planet is our future. They will allow me to plan the next stage in taking Mars and, when the time comes, to execute it. They didn't listen to me when I told them that sending Moynihan's team was a mistake. They'll listen to me now."

Cruz didn't care. He stood up. "We won, Karl. Now, watch out for Jackson, and watch out for the leaker, his informant. The White House isn't aiming for you, they're aiming for Jackson's informant, so let them have a clear shot." He strode toward the door.

"Congressman?"

Cruz turned back. Karl studied him with dark, gleaming eyes. "Do you know something about all this I don't?"

Cruz felt something disquieting but elusive in the doctor, like a rip current lashing beneath the pleasant surf. He was cautious as he replied, "Dr. Karl, I have told you everything you ought to know."

Karl looked hard at him as though he did not accept the assurance. And he had little reason to. Cruz left before Karl could speak again.

Reuben searched out the quietest nook of the library. Up to the second floor, down the main halls into the narrow ones, through neglected aisles of books to a smattering of study areas. He picked the farthest of them all, in a corner without windows. It smelled as if it was not often used.

Two lines of bookshelves, smudged with dust, framed the small space of the study area. A tatty easy chair was shoved into the corner, a coffee table in front of it. There Reuben set up shop.

He sat down on the chair and laid his envelope on the splotchy surface of the table. From that envelope he pulled one piece of paper— the memo listing the candidates to be voted on at the May 9th meeting. Then he drew his notebook from his pocket and opened the files he had received during his flight to Washington with Cruz.

The first file was a memo listing the tallies of the May 9th vote. Gulliver Eamon, Margaret Killiam, and David Killiam had carried that day, the only Mars candidates approved by the First Names—as the whole world had learned years ago. The exact reckoning of *ayes* and *nays* meant nothing to Reuben, but one strange pattern emerged from them. Donegan Moynihan had voted against every candidate.

The second memo reported the vote on Moynihan's own candidacy to become commander of the team. The First Names, including Moynihan, had unanimously approved it.

These curious facts before him, Reuben began to delve. He had earlier read the whistleblower's dossier on Moynihan, and it revealed nothing to him. But perhaps it held only pieces, and the rest of the puzzle was somewhere else.

Reuben logged onto the library's database and ran a search of Donegan Moynihan's name. The results piled on top of each other until they scrolled down his screen. Slowly, patiently, he sifted them. Articles written about Moynihan, articles written by him and published in academic journals, references in books . . .

A noise, soft but distinct, rustled in the quiet, and Reuben froze. He heard it again. Footfalls, getting nearer.

Reuben snatched the memo off the table and stuffed it into the envelope. Leaning down, he slid the envelope beneath the easy chair. A backward kick with his heel sent it *thump*ing into the wall.

Then Reuben fastened his gaze on his notebook and tried to appear relaxed.

The footsteps reached Reuben's nook. He didn't look up, waiting for whoever it was to pass on.

"Mr. Jackson?"

Reuben looked up and saw two men watching him. Their clothes were nice enough and casual enough, nothing to be noticed in offices across America. But there was a straightness to their posture and an edge in their eyes that turned Reuben's spirit cold.

He had an urge to stand up, but he didn't. "Yes?" he asked.

One of the men stepped forward, taking a wallet out of his pocket. He flipped it open and displayed an ID card dominated by a shimmering three-dimensional symbol. "FBI," the man said. "I must make clear, Mr. Jackson, that you are not under arrest, so this is a request, not an order. Would you come with us?"

Reuben looked at him and then at his silent partner. "Where?"

"To the White House. The Justice Department has opened a probe into an alleged leak of classified documents. Our lead investigator would like to interview you in the presence of the White House counsel. You can call your personal attorney to come also, of course."

Reuben didn't have a personal attorney, and it occurred to him that this created a perfect opportunity to retreat from the interview. But by another instinct, he stood up. "I can talk to the investigator without a lawyer."

The FBI agent nodded. "Let's go, then."

Reuben remembered, as he stepped around the coffee table, the envelope he had shoved beneath the chair. He didn't want to leave it there. He wanted even less to root it out before the eyes of the G-men, so he followed the agents without a backward glance.

They led him through the maze of the library and finally out of the building. A black car brooded at the curb, its plates marking it as government property.

The agent who had not yet spoken climbed into the driver's seat. The other ushered Reuben into the back and got in after him.

Reuben listened to the engine rev, felt the car slide into motion. He sat quietly, thinking idly of his last car ride with Jep Baines. The chief of staff had been wiser than Reuben had then supposed. His prophecies were coming true.

The car clipped along the streets of Washington and soon glided through the White House gates. It swung up the drive and stopped.

Reuben eyed the White House, bathed in the light of the midday sun, and knew they expected him to get out. But the volition seemed to have left his limbs, driven out by the prospect of the investigator awaiting him.

"Go ahead, Mr. Jackson," the FBI agent said.

Reuben mustered his will and got out. He straightened, looking up at the president's house, the people's house. The cool, whitewashed stone whispering of history was impressive, but he wasn't impressed. Those feelings had slipped away, and he couldn't remember when.

The agent came alongside him. "This way, Mr. Jackson."

Reuben followed him on the familiar path to Jep Baines's office. They entered and found the chief of staff alone, seated behind his desk.

The FBI agent gestured to Reuben with both hands, as though presenting him. "Here he is."

"So I see," Baines answered. "The others went to the counsel's office. Go get them."

The man's eyes went to the phone. "Sir, you could . . ." Then he looked at the chief of staff, stopped talking, and left the room.

Baines turned his eyes on Reuben, sharp with the glint the FBI man had not wanted to challenge. "You didn't listen to me."

Reuben, guilty as charged, shrugged feebly.

"And you would go and confront Manasseh Cruz, of all people. What am I to do with you, Jackson?"

Reuben shrugged again. "Cruz didn't know what to do with me, either."

"Yes, he did. He tattled on you to the president. Now you're my problem, and the Justice Department investigation is yours."

Reuben gnawed on that thought and found it unpalatable. "He's kind of fiendishly clever, isn't he?" he suggested meekly.

Baines's eyebrows bent down. "Jackson, you know Cruz is dangerous. You didn't need me to tell you that. You could have told yourself."

"I did tell myself."

"So, why didn't you listen?"

"Because the Mars team had been abandoned, and he was my only chance of changing something." A little defiance crept into Reuben. "I did succeed in breaking the status quo."

"Yes, and now you're at the center of a criminal probe. Congratulations."

Reuben walked forward, drew out the chair opposite Baines, and sat down. "You were a lawyer in another life, weren't you? Do you have any legal advice for me?"

"Retain a lawyer. Remember your sacred, constitutional right to remain silent. And if you do talk, tell the truth." Baines cocked his head, studying Reuben. "Is it incriminating?"

"It's incriminating of something, but not a crime. More like stupidity, but stupidity with a purpose. Now someone has to care which communiqué is a forgery." Reuben felt a grim satisfaction in that.

"But not for the sake of the Mars team. No one cares for the sake of the Mars team. They care for the sake of finding whoever forged the document. They care for the sake of finding the leaker. Reporters will care for the sake of the delicious scandal of forged documents and stolen documents and a secret informant. They'll play one of Washington's oldest games: What did he know, and when did he know it? Congress may hold hearings and investigations, but they won't send food to Mars. You've hurt a lot of people by lighting a fuse to explode this situation into a scandal. But you haven't helped anyone."

Reuben's stomach soured, and he tried to fight away the words. "You don't know yet whom I've hurt or whom I haven't helped. And isn't the truth worth knowing, despite the consequences?"

Baines closed his eyes and, sighing, gave a sharp shake of his head. "I don't know why you can't see. You're so concerned with the Mars team, millions of miles away, but you can't see the people in front of you in the streets. The country is barely keeping body and soul together."

"But . . ." Reuben struggled to capture, in his own mind, what had been troubling him since Cruz had told him, in the ashes of Los Angeles, that the few had to be sacrificed to the needs of the many. "But that's not enough, is it? It's not enough just to keep body and soul together. You have to do right, and be right, to make it worthwhile."

Baines opened his eyes to stare at Reuben. His eyebrows slowly drew upward.

A rap on the door, and then people were coming in. Baines stood and went over to them.

Reuben didn't turn his head to look, but he listened. Portentous words rolled to him—*questioning* and *crime* and *waived his right to counsel*.

Reuben slouched in his seat, dreading the moment they would come to him. The voices and the footsteps began to close the brief distance. Ice thrust through Reuben's chest, and it felt thicker with every second of their approach.

XVIII

David knew they had nearly reached the main road by the light ahead, welcoming and beckoning, at the end of the street.

At last he and Eamon emerged from the gray rows of buildings to a broad avenue. It was the brightest place he had been since they'd trundled into Jeanne, leaving sunlight behind for the secrets of the tunnel. The light revealed many strange and beautiful buildings. Some were many-pillared, like Greek temples. Others were crowned with pinnacles that pricked the darkness above, and still others with towers as narrow and graceful as church steeples. He saw buildings that soared upward, buildings that spread wide, and a few that swelled into circular shapes.

David looked up and down the street, gradually noticing that it did slant, ever so slightly, down. He thought he caught the form of a large tower, some distance down the avenue. It was vague, and he had the sudden sense that it was vaguer than it should be.

That was when he realized that the light, bright as he found it, was yet dim. It was not white, like the glowing stones, nor golden, like the sun, but silver.

Eamon clapped his hand on David's shoulder, startling him. "I'll see you, Killiam. Maybe."

He walked away, his boots clomping softly on the avenue. David watched him head downward, deeper into the city. Then he turned, setting his own direction upward. Back to the ledge of rock that looked over the city, back to where he had last seen his sister and Moynihan.

Suddenly a wind swept up from behind him, hitting his back and nearly knocking him off his feet. Then a musical clamor, as powerful as the wind, shattered the silence of the dead city.

The wind and the clamor drove him to his knees. David clapped his hands over his ears and pressed as hard as he could. He stole looks upward and saw, in the minarets and towers and reaching pinnacles, chimes swinging violently. They were of every description—bulky and dainty, obelisk and straight like a ruler—and they banged into each other with great fury.

He dropped his eyes and bowed his head. The wind whipped him and tore at his clothes, but it was small discomfort compared to the chaos of musical notes that battered his ears and into his brain.

It seemed to go on and on, seconds ticking by in slow agony. Then it ended. The wind died around him, and the clanging of the chimes vanished.

David managed to get to his feet, his ears ringing. He squinted up at the towers and minarets, remembering the wind that had carried music up to them in Jeanne. He hadn't dreamed of an explanation like this.

He sought Eamon and found him in the avenue. The engineer pointed upward and said something. David saw his mouth moving, and even thought he faintly heard his voice, but he couldn't make out anything.

Eamon was probably just saying he had been right about the music when they first heard it. David returned his attention to the buildings. The ringing in his ears subsided, and as it did so, one sound grew louder and clearer. It was like a high tinkling, and David began looking for its source.

Looking upward, he spotted two small chimes shaped like teardrops, swaying and shaking. They hung in a dim recess in the wall of one slender tower that loomed directly above the avenue. The wind did not blow or sigh, and the other chimes neither moved nor sang. The teardrop chimes alone vibrated in the stillness of the great stone city, and their sweet trill sent chills skittering over David's flesh.

The chimes dropped from the recess in their tower, ending their music. David watched them fall until they hit the avenue only a few feet from where he stood.

For a moment all was so still that David could hear the beating of his heart. Then the chimes raised themselves from the ground and stood erect, perhaps four inches high. They glided toward David.

In shock, he stood rigid as the chimes wove around his feet. They skated past him, spun a pretty half circle around Eamon, and continued down the avenue.

David watched until they disappeared beyond his sight. Then his eyes went to Eamon. The chills had changed to a tingling over all his skin, and he wasn't sure his voice would be steady. So he picked calm words. "There is only one rational explanation for this."

Eamon nodded. "The city is haunted."

"No," David said, his tone snappish from habit more than real feeling. "There is something in this place besides us. Something alive, or at least awake."

"And how is that incompatible with what I said?"

"I don't believe in ghosts."

Eamon thrust a finger to the chimes. "You believe in that?"

"Only because I saw it."

"Fair enough," Eamon conceded. "I have no idea what this—presence—is, but whatever it is, I think it wants something."

"Well, I know that I want to find my sister." David took a step back, and as he did so, the light behind him died into blackness and the light before him blazed to gold.

David blinked and shaded his eyes, staring at the brightness. Then he glanced over his shoulder at the darkness.

Eamon gestured down the avenue. "It wants us to go that way."

David huffed. "Well, whatever *it* wants, I need to find Meg. I need to find Moynihan. I'm still part of our team."

"Then go. And tell Moynihan that I told him so about the music."

Making no promise for that, David turned away from Eamon and walked into the darkness.

"Killiam!"

David ignored him, going up the slanting avenue and finding it smooth beneath his feet. But his conscience stirred, then scratched, until he spun around and went back.

Eamon waited where the light met the darkness, just on the side of the light. David stopped at the border, barely within the darkness, and they faced each other.

"Look," Eamon said, "I want to know what's down there. I want to know if whatever's here is friendly, because it might save us if it is. But I know that it might not be friendly. Those chimes, these lights going on and off is kind of a creepy invitation. I want to go, but I want someone watching my back."

"Sounds like you want a teammate."

"Not a teammate. An ally." Eamon pulled the gun from his holster and stretched it out toward David. "If you'll watch my back with this for the next few hours, I'll let you keep it when you leave to join Meg and Moynihan."

David eyed the gun. He longed for a weapon, for that power against whatever power lived still in the alien city. He held out his hand, and Eamon placed the gun in it. David closed his hand around it and felt bolder, more dressed.

Eamon began striding down the avenue into the golden light. David flipped the gun to point upward and followed, watching the buildings that lined their way. Side by side they ventured into the heart of the city.

The stone wall was hard and cold against Margaret's back, and no doubt dirty as well. But it did not give her any motivation to move. The only other thing to do was to pace the small building as Moynihan was doing, on another fruitless inspection. The building was one single room, and not even a large one. They had already scoured it completely and gained nothing.

Margaret watched the commander, a silhouette trailing the beam of his wristlight, and wondered what he was really doing.

Her lips felt dry, and she licked them. But her tongue felt dry, too, as dry as her mouth. Every once in a while, hunger stabbed her, but her thirst gnawed constantly. The pool of water they had discovered earlier stood in her mind, like a tantalizing vision, but they could not get to it, and they had no way to draw the water out if they did.

That led her thoughts to the image of Donegan Moynihan staring into the stony pool, a terrible light in his eyes as he looked for death in the water.

She stirred and sat forward. "I think David is somewhere in the city, searching for us."

Moynihan stopped pacing. "I can't find a way out," he said. "The door we entered practically melded with the wall. But the aliens had a way to open it. If only we could imagine the design . . ."

He was avoiding her remark, so she waited until he trailed off and then repeated, "I think David is looking for us."

"He may well be, Doctor."

May. Donegan Moynihan could not give false comfort, and she admired him for it. He could not lie, nor would he be unrealistic even when reality was a cold, dark night. Nor was he much good at offering true comfort. He couldn't comfort others, and he couldn't comfort himself, and that tugged her heart toward him.

Margaret stood up from the cold floor and joined Moynihan in examining the room, pointless though it was. Turning on her wristlight, she combed the walls again with its beam.

"I wonder," Moynihan speculated, "if I should have sent the colonel after Eamon. I wonder if I should have done something about them years ago. I knew, since our journey on the *Enyalius*, that there was something wrong between them. But I told myself that I was not their psychologist; I am their commander. Their personal issues were not my business, and beyond my fixing anyway. Now the team has splintered because of those problems. I should have tried to broker peace between them."

Margaret had never heard him reflect in so personal a way. "You probably couldn't have made peace."

"*Probably* is the word," he said. "But whether I would probably have succeeded or probably have failed, shouldn't I have tried?"

There was a distance and deep regret in his voice that made Margaret understand he was talking about more than his failure to intervene between Eamon and David. "You know, Commander, they made their choices, too. You can't take responsibility for their decisions."

"My own are enough," he said heavily.

"Surely you haven't done anything that bad."

Moynihan didn't answer, and she thought he either wouldn't speak or would change the subject entirely. But then he said, "What I have done, taken in the chronicle of human behavior, isn't that bad. What I haven't done is inexcusable. And I didn't do it because I lacked the courage. It's a terrible thing for a man to know about himself."

Margaret felt a crack in the walls the commander had built around himself, making her first real acquaintance with the man who was their scientist and the commander. What she had sought in vain in the bright lab of the habitat, she found here in the fusty dark of the cold alien city. She keenly regretted that they would be dead before this moment could grow beyond itself and lead them into something more.

"So, it was inexcusable," she said, looking at him. "That doesn't make it unforgivable."

"At the risk of being *mistaken* for a religious man, I believe that. I always have," he answered. "And my soul is still as dry as a bone."

Margaret had no comfort for that. She wished she could discern his expression through the gloom.

Then she felt something brush her booted foot oddly. She jerked her foot and found herself splashing in a puddle.

Margaret swung her wristlight down and gazed at the water covering the floor. It rose even as she looked at it, lapping against the cold, hard walls.

She looked at those walls, and at the rising water, and the conclusion was simple.

Moynihan gazed also. "I wonder where it's coming from." He took some steps, stirring up the water with his feet.

Margaret stayed where she was, keeping her wristlight on the water. She noticed bubbles beneath it, saw movement like a minor current within, and tracked its source to the wall. She knelt and thrust her hand into the water.

The current tugged against her skin, and she followed it to a narrow fissure where the floor met the wall. Margaret could feel water rushing up into the building through the gap. "Commander," she called, "the water is coming from here."

"And here." His voice carried from across the room. "It's coming up through the floor."

Margaret ran her fingertips along the gap, feeling the smoothness of the edges even as her fingers numbed with the cold. "And notice how very neat and straight the crack is." She tried to push her fingers deeper in and only scraped them against the stone.

Margaret stood. The water came up to her knees now.

Moynihan struck the wall with his fist and then came over to her, sloshing through the water. "They're going to drown us."

In wristlight illumination, Margaret saw his eyes were ablaze. "Who is 'they'?"

"Whoever controls the city. Whatever is here."

Margaret felt something warm on her hand and looked down to see blood trickling over two of her fingers. She pressed them against her left sleeve. "Where is the door we came in through?"

He pointed, and together they forded through the rising water.

They stopped before the door, its existence betrayed only by faint lines in the wall.

"It cannot be pushed open." The familiar detachment returned to Moynihan's voice. "It cannot be pulled open. There's no knob to turn, no lock, no latch, no buttons or control panel."

Margaret, the water nearly to her waist, joined the analysis. "No hinges. It doesn't swing. It slides up and down."

Moynihan ducked beneath the water, and for a long minute, she heard him scrabble at the door. Then he came up, scattering droplets in every direction. "Nothing," he sputtered. "Can't wedge anything under it, can't push it up, can't find—"

"Anything," she said soberly.

The water crept higher up their bodies, and for a moment, they neither moved nor spoke.

Margaret felt the water's strength now, trying to buoy her up. She fought it to stay on her feet but knew she would not be able to fight it long.

Moynihan placed his hands lightly on her shoulders and gently turned her to face him. "Margaret," he said, "I'm sorry."

Margaret looked at him, tenderness and resistance mingling within her. "Are those your last words?"

"The best I have."

Margaret felt the water lift her hair and spread it floating around her. She instinctively kicked her feet up and swam.

She went to the door again, her only clear thought being that she wasn't ready for last words. The water lifted her near to the ceiling, and she ran her hands over places she had not been able to reach before. But her fingers found only smooth stone and the door's shallow lines.

Moynihan plunged into the water and came up beside her, but he didn't join the search. He knew there was no point. Margaret felt his silent resignation.

Moynihan put a hand up to the ceiling, to keep his head from knocking against it. They were running out of space and out of air, and Margaret suddenly thought of her parents. They'd been hardly older than she was now when they'd died. Strange, that they should all die young and on doomed missions.

The walls rattled a little, as if pummeled on the outside by a strong wind, and a tumult of wild musical notes roared on the gale. Margaret's heart spun with the riotous music. Images of her parents, faded from the many years, raced through her mind. Memories of David, brighter and clearer, joined those of their parents. Was he searching for her even now?

Margaret blinked water out of her eyes and grasped at the door again.

In the midst of her desperate splashings, Moynihan said softly, "Margaret."

She heard in his voice what she knew she would see in his eyes, if she looked—fatalistic acceptance, a quiet and bitter peace. It ignited her stubbornness to full life, and she dove into the water.

Margaret found the door and pressed her hands against it. With all her strength, she willed it to open.

And, to her great amazement, it did. She heard grinding, the door scraped her skin as it moved, and then the water was breaking out of the building. It dragged her down in its rush, and she barely avoided bashing her head against the door.

The water carried her out in a mighty wave and crashed onto the street. Margaret made jarring contact with the pavement and struggled up, half-stunned.

When her senses became fully clear, she found herself on her hands and knees in a puddle. The dim plaza surrounded her, and she heard water running.

Margaret looked behind her. Water streamed out of the open doorway of the building, coursing over the pavement and spreading out on every side.

Moynihan sat in the middle of it. He was sopping wet, clothes bedraggled and hair a wild mess. He swiped at the wetness on his face. For a man sitting in a puddle, hopelessly wiping his face, he looked surprisingly thoughtful. "How did you do that?"

"I pushed against the door and willed it to open."

He looked at her, with intrigued eyes, and she thought he was about to flee back to the safe and scientific theorizing that was so far from the emotions their near-drowning had unshuttered.

He stood up hesitantly. "Two things," he said, "are immediate and important. One, there is sentience at work in this city. And two, it is hostile to us."

Margaret didn't answer him. She looked away, to the cold city and its thick shadows, and took a moment to be glad she was alive and to believe that, somewhere in the shadows, David was alive, too.

She heard Moynihan walk toward her, splashing through puddles, and it wasn't until he stopped right beside her that she looked up at him.

He held out his hand to her.

Margaret considered the offer, then finally placed her hand in his, and he helped her to her feet. At that moment, the pale light around them was suddenly snuffed out, and they stood in darkness so deep it was black.

Moynihan's fingers tightened around hers.

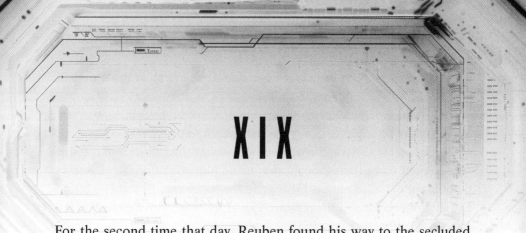

XIX

For the second time that day, Reuben found his way to the secluded nook. The library was even quieter now. He felt the emptiness of the great building, felt the night that surrounded it, a heavy sheet of darkness. It grimly echoed the dismal tenor of his own spirit.

Reuben knelt beside the shabby easy chair he had sat on earlier that day. Shoving his hand beneath it, he found the envelope and pulled it out. He lifted it up, relieved to have it.

And then he just went on sitting on the floor.

After a minute or two, he mustered the will to stand up. He dropped into the easy chair and gazed forlornly at the envelope. He knew he ought to get up and go to his hotel, but he couldn't find the energy. His body was tired enough, but that he could bear. It was soul weariness he could not overcome.

The last few hours passed before him—the relentless questions, the answers he fumbled, the investigator's hawkish eyes and long, pale fingers as he made entries into his notebook. Baines had watched him, too. The chief of staff's eyes never missed anything.

Baines's words looped endlessly in Reuben's mind: *No one cares for the sake of the Mars team.* And no one did. Whatever family they had surely cared, but they had no part or place in these decisions.

Reuben ran his fingers lightly on the edge of the envelope. He had seen no news reports about the relatives of the abandoned team, and that was strange. Surely someone in all the media would have sought the interview, asked for the story. And surely someone among all the relatives would have given it.

Surely more of them would have lobbied the government to save their loved one. Yet Reuben had seen no trace of that, either. Neither Cruz nor Baines had raised even the possibility of having to deal with distressed relatives. They were politically acute, both of them. They knew the power of one visceral image, and what was more visceral than a father or mother grieving for a lost child?

Yet, as far as he had seen, these political men had never been worried, and as far as he could tell, they had no reason to be.

Reuben sat up straight. He sensed something enormous, and it was instinct more than thought that made him yank Gulliver Eamon's dossier out of the envelope. He flipped the pages rapidly until he found the engineer's vital information. The next-of-kin provision—labeled *Casualty Notification Information*, a typical military phrase—was blank.

Gulliver Eamon had listed no next of kin.

One beat, and then Reuben was racing through the pages again. He knew he had seen a record of Eamon's parents, though he had skimmed past it as an unnecessary detail.

He found it shortly, two names with the same parenthetical note: *Deceased*.

Reuben tossed the dossier down on the table and seized the next one. Swiftly he ran through them, gathering the facts. Margaret Killiam had listed only David, and David Killiam only Margaret, as a relative to be notified. Their parents were long dead. Moynihan's file mirrored Eamon's in this one respect. No next of kin, no living parents.

Dropping the last dossier, Reuben stared at it and tried to understand. The military *Casualty Notification* caught his eyes and intensified his uneasiness. It was no idle paperwork, no perfunctory question. They had all known that there was on the perilous Mars mission a multitude of ways to die. And every day another chance of it. Each member of the team had to reckon seriously with the question so formally put to them by the government, dry as dust and earnest as life. Who to tell, who should know, who would inherit their property or arrange their funerals?

And they had all answered the same: no one. They had left no one behind when they departed into cold space toward the Red Planet.

The First Names could not have picked such a team by chance. It would be hard to do even on purpose. Not many people had no family at all, especially those with enough status to contend for a place on the spaceship to Mars.

"So then," Reuben whispered to the empty quiet, "the First Names sent to Mars only people who wouldn't be mourned or missed when they died. But why?"

Reuben closed his eyes, his bewilderment breaking into dreadful clarity. He remembered the fevered enthusiasm when they'd first launched the Mars mission, all the foolish hopes. Nobody had anticipated, in those gone and forgotten days, that the mission would end a perfect tragedy.

Except the First Names.

"How?" he asked aloud. "And why, anticipating that everyone who left would die, did they . . ." His voice faded into thought. *Why did they make sure to send only people whom, when they died, no one would care about?*

Years earlier, when Reuben was newly appointed the president's liaison and before he had established himself as the thorn in Cruz's side, Manasseh Cruz invited him to one of his Christmas parties. Reuben went and found himself surrounded by people more powerful than he was. They ignored him, and he could not bring himself to engage them. After an hour of affecting interest in Cruz's potted plants, Reuben decided that going to the party was the worst mistake he had ever made.

But this night, Reuben revised his old estimation. He was glad he had gone to that miserable party. It had taught him a fact not publicly available, a fact he had entirely discounted and now needed.

It had taught him where Manasseh Cruz lived in Washington, D.C.

Reuben walked the shadowed streets beneath a pale, distant moon. He kept his pace brisk.

It was midnight when he arrived at the house with its redbrick and black trim peeping out of the darkness. Reuben climbed the front steps then stopped before the door and rang the silver bell. Even outside the house, he heard it tolling faintly, but he didn't worry about whom it disturbed. Manasseh Cruz lived alone in this fine brick D.C. house. Wagging Beltway tongues had spread the word that his family had stayed in the south when he returned to Washington to begin the new session of Congress.

The door swung backward, and Reuben found himself staring at Manasseh Cruz. The congressman looked him over, disapproving. "Get in, Jackson."

Reuben stepped inside, and the congressman swiftly closed and locked the door behind him. Then Cruz walked into a room that opened up on their left, and Reuben followed.

He instantly saw money in the room, in the richness of the furniture and drapes and the starkness of its immaculate order. But he was not impressed.

Cruz settled onto a couch and propped his boots on the glass surface of the coffee table. "I don't like you standing on my front porch at midnight. What might my neighbors think?"

"You care, Cruz?"

"I don't think I like you standing on my porch during the daytime, either. I find your sudden habit of showing up at my house annoying. Didn't your mother teach you not to turn up at people's homes without an invitation?"

"Yes. She also taught me never to visit anyone after eight at night. But she never taught me what to do when I find myself in the middle of a political scandal."

Cruz rubbed his face. "I hope you're not here to whine."

Reuben moved closer but didn't sit. He didn't feel friendly enough for that. "I feel more like yelling, Congressman. But I won't do that, either. What I have to say can be said quietly." Cruz glanced at him, eyes deep. "Congressman, when you said that the Mars team was just in the wrong place at the wrong time, I believed you. But now I know you lied."

"That was the truth," came the response. "It doesn't matter if you don't believe it."

Reuben studied the congressman, wishing he could somehow unsnarl all the man's words and actions and attitudes to find his core. "Really? Then why did you tell it to me?"

Cruz's expression was dismissive and his eyes preoccupied. "I'm tired of this conversation. Get to the point, or get out of my house."

"As you want it." Reuben stood at his greatest dignity. "Congressman, I know about the setup."

"What setup?"

"Your setup—and Dr. Karl's setup—of the Mars team."

Cruz froze.

Reuben, gathering new confidence, stepped forward. His foot knocked against something half-concealed against the darkened side of an easy chair, and it clattered to the floor.

He bent down to grab it up, and realized only after he straightened that he held a dark liquor bottle. Gold stenciling glinted faintly on its alluringly smooth surface.

Reuben held it up to Cruz. "Drinking to the fact that the Mars team was in the wrong place at the wrong time?"

Cruz pulled his feet off the table and abruptly stood, his dark eyes flashing.

Reuben felt an impulse to shy away and instead stayed. "I looked at their dossiers, Cruz. Not one of them has any next of kin. That's why you have no trouble abandoning them to die. Nobody cares. But wasn't it hard to find four people who were both qualified to explore Mars and also completely unattached to everyone on Earth?"

Shadows deepened in Cruz's eyes. "Where are you getting these ideas, Jackson?"

"They're not ideas. They're facts. And I told you, the dossiers. Go and look it up. I'd love for you to try to prove me wrong."

"Your *idea* is that I planned to abandon the Mars team years before the Great Collapse. I hate conspiracy theories, Jackson. It's not because they're ugly or despicable—I could get past that. It's because they're so illogical."

"And what is the logical explanation of why the First Names sent only people with no living relatives to Mars?"

"Am I a First Name? Why are you asking me?"

"Because you worked with the First Names to maroon the Mars team, and now I know the team was chosen for it." Reuben held out the liquor bottle.

For a moment, Cruz gazed at it without stirring. Then he slowly reached and grasped the bottle. "You've proven nothing, Jackson."

"I'm not here to persuade you of anything, Cruz," Reuben declared. "I can't win a debate against you, but that doesn't make me wrong. The Mars team was chosen to die. And it's not that you and Karl saw this disaster coming. You created it. I don't know why I ever hoped you might help."

"What I did to the Mars team, I did for America, for all Americans. Even for you. I'm not ashamed of it. But I had no part in choosing them."

The congressman looked sincere, but Reuben didn't care. "Maybe that's true. Maybe it isn't. It doesn't matter. Whether they were unlucky when they were first chosen or unlucky only after the Great Collapse, doesn't make a difference. They're still unlucky. And they're still going to die."

Cruz opened his mouth to speak, but Reuben cut him off. "So, here's a question for you, Congressman. When a man dies, does it matter why? He's still dead. And if he survives, does it matter how? He's alive, after all."

Reuben turned on his heel and walked out, but near the doorway he turned back. "By the way, those tales you carried to the president did their work. They're investigating me, and they're looking for the whistleblower. I don't know how interested they were when I told them you had the second communiqué before I did, but we'll see. From here on in, it's every man for himself."

Cruz didn't answer. He only watched Reuben with eyes smoldering like coals, still gripping the liquor.

Reuben let himself out into the cold night.

XX

David, the gun in his right hand, watched the city all around. He held his attention to it very sternly, because he felt his wariness slipping. Softened by the uneventful hours, eaten away by his own irritation. They had stopped for rations, a half meal that left him hungrier than before. He thought, as he ate, of how Margaret had no food.

Ever since, he'd been angry.

Eamon still went ahead, and David didn't look at him more than duty required. He felt the rage climbing up again, clawing at him and wishing to claw at Eamon. One part of him wanted to give it release; another was weary, and almost ashamed, to let it go again.

So he walked on, struggling in his silence. A voice in the darker recesses of his mind muttered that this was all Eamon's fault, and he tried to ignore it.

"An archway!" Eamon exclaimed. "Do you think it matters?"

David looked up just in time to see Eamon step through a large, freestanding arch that spanned the avenue. And perhaps it did matter, because Eamon halted on the other side.

David passed through, too, and he stopped beside Eamon at the head of an expansive stairway. An equally enormous stairway faced him, and two others converged on the sides—east and west, north and south, all meeting here.

The stairways marched down to a deep gray platform that shimmered with streaks of blue and green. David detected patterns in the stone, but he was too far above to fully discern them. A yellow light glistened on the steps and spun slow circles on the platform below.

"That's it," Eamon proclaimed. "That's where we're supposed to go." He began the descent, stepping down onto the stairway.

David reached down, grabbed the back of Eamon's collar, and

swiftly yanked him back up. "Don't you think this is something to think twice about?"

Eamon rubbed his throat and glared. "So, what's your plan? We came, we saw, we left?"

"Try thinking like a military man, even if you are an AWOL one. What does our escape route from down there look like? There's no way to run but up. Up at least fifty stairs. We would be easy pickings for anything above us or below us."

"I ask again, Killiam: What is your plan?"

David pivoted and pointed to the soaring black tower a short walk behind them. "That has the look of a command center."

"Why didn't you say so when we passed it?"

"Because I didn't want to prolong this little jaunt. But if we're going to explore something, it should be the tower."

Eamon shook his head, but set off toward it. "If you want. But we'll be back. The city will see to it."

David ignored him.

They trekked to the tower and paused in front of it. David scrutinized its smooth, black surface, shining in a way no stone ever did. He saw no break in it, not the shallowest line. He tilted his head back until it strained his neck, and still he saw only the glassy, featureless exterior.

"I think it's an elevator."

Eamon stood, gazing at a circle of stone that abutted the side of the tower. It was colored darker than the surrounding pavement and dominated by a kind of pillar, waist-high and as stark as the tower.

"Where are the buttons?" David asked, sarcasm lacing his tone.

Eamon, his expression intent, stepped onto the circle and stared at it.

David watched him a moment and then began to walk around the tower. He kept an eagle eye fixed on it, but he saw not even the suggestion of a window or a door.

A sudden shout rang distantly, followed by a crash. David raced back to Eamon. He rounded the front of the tower and saw Eamon sprawled on the ground. David instantly slid off his gun's safety and raised the weapon into the air, scanning the avenue and all the buildings close by.

"Relax, Killiam." Eamon scrambled up. "I was a little stunned from the fall, but it's nothing. The thing is, I've discovered it."

David looked at him, then the ground. "Gravity?"

Eamon pressed his hand flat against the top of the pillar. The circle of stone rose a yard into the air, sliding up against the tower's sheer wall, and hovered there. Eamon bestowed a smug look on David. "It's an elevator."

After a quick intake of breath, David leaped on with Eamon, and they rose upward with greater and greater speed. Strong currents of air twisted past them—tousling their hair, rubbing their skin, tugging at their clothes.

David closed his eyes and lifted his face to the wind, luxuriating in the sensation. It was so close to the feeling of flying and yet fell so short that it filled him with a painful sweetness.

"There are no buttons, you know," Eamon said with a slight smirk. "But if you place your hand on the right part of it, the whole thing will do what you will it to do. If you will it to go up, or down, or be still—"

The elevator slammed to a jarring halt that flung David to the floor. He found himself staring over the edge at the ground far, far beneath.

His heart surged with great fear, then he saw that the elevator had stopped at a kind of walkway that encircled the tower. It fit precisely into a half circle, carved out of the walkway, so that the two were now continuous.

David crawled onto the walkway. When he reached the wall of the tower, he stood up.

Eamon, his hand still planted on the pillar, watched him. "I'd like to join you, Killiam. But I've got this thought that if I take off my hand, the elevator will just plummet."

David regarded him a moment, a snarky retort lurking on his tongue. Moving forward, he seized Eamon and pulled him onto the walkway.

The elevator plunged back down, obeying some ancient programming. They observed its departure and then looked around themselves. An absolute bareness gripped everything they saw: the tower, with its surface one glossy uniformity and the walkway nothing more than a platform extending briefly from the tower. It hadn't even a railing.

A breeze brushed past them, probably eternal to these exposed heights. David cast a glance toward the edge of the walkway and calculated how far they were from a long fall and instant death.

Six feet. It had to be enough.

"Come on," he said to Eamon. "Let's find out why they built this walkway."

He had hardly taken two steps when a deep, low rumbling rolled over them and a tremor shook the tower. David dropped to his knees and hugged the wall, sharply aware that it had no handholds.

The tremor passed, the rumbling died away, and silence returned to the city. Then Eamon said, "I told you it wanted us to go down that stairway."

David got to his feet and walked on, keeping as close to the wall as he could. He followed the walkway to where it curved out of sight. For a time they pursued that path.

Then, as they rounded the endless curve, a midair plaza opened up before them, extending from the walkway and the tower. Ten or so machines squatted on the plaza, which David apprehended as vehicles.

The height instantly vanished from his mind, and he ran to one of the smaller vehicles. The craft had no wheels or wings, though its shape tapered, nose to tail, like fins. It was airily constructed—no roof, low sides, and nothing resembling a windshield. Its front bench faced a flat, featureless console and was wide enough for only one. From there the craft flared outward, and the second and third benches were long enough to seat two.

David gripped the side. It felt hard and cool, like an alloy or an unknown metal, and he swung himself into the front seat. The light reflected languidly on the console, making its jet-blackness seem alive. From that, and from Eamon's accomplishment with the elevator, David gathered hope. What was it Eamon had done—touched and willed?

David placed his hand on the console and mentally commanded, *Turn on. Wake up. Come to life.*

He felt a vibration, rising from deep within the craft, and something flickered in front of him. When he glanced up, he saw thin, hazy gray beams cutting a rectangle in the air.

David quested with his left hand and pushed against a strong, invisible resistance. Not wishing to challenge it, he lowered his hand. At any rate, he understood it to be a kind of windshield. The prospect of speed he saw in that lifted his spirits even higher, and he commenced experimenting.

Up—the craft lifted. *Down*—it descended. *Up* again. *Forward*—the craft glided. *Reverse*—so it did. *Stop*—it hovered. He willed it to swerve to one side—then another—

"Killiam!"

The shout jolted David, and the craft pitched wildly. He righted it and looked over at Eamon.

Eamon eyed the craft, idling several feet above the ground. "What are you doing?"

"Learning how to fly this thing."

Eamon's expression twitched, and conflict showed in his eyes. Then boyish pleasure changed his face. He grabbed hold of the craft and pulled himself aboard. He settled himself on the bench directly behind David. "This is sweet, Killiam. Not only will it spare our feet from walking so much, we can get down the tower without killing ourselves."

David goosed the craft upward until it floated above everything else on the plaza. "Now that we have this, Eamon, the only thing to do is search for Meg and Moynihan."

Before Eamon could finish the first syllable of his protest, David sent the craft shooting out over the city. Their flight was uneven, and he knew it, but all he cared about was that he was flying. It sang through him, all of him—an intense song with the brightness of the sun and the pristine freedom of the boundless sky. He yelled his exhilaration to the alien city, all its shadows and silences and gloom-shrouded mysteries now nothing to him.

Eamon also yelled, not wholly without terror.

Moynihan knelt on the cracked pavement, his shoulder against the rough wall of a building. He watched the sooty darkness above him, and a red, shining globe ghosted across it.

When it passed from sight, Margaret whispered, "Another one."

"And going the same way," Moynihan said. "I wonder if there's trouble somewhere in the city."

"I wonder if David and Eamon are causing it."

It was plausible, more plausible than he liked. It pained him to think of his fractured team scattered and striving against the same enemies, weaker apart.

"Let's go." Unwilling to turn on his wristlight with the spheres flying overhead, but equally unwilling to wait any longer, he moved forward blind. He groped along the wall, hearing Margaret follow behind him.

Suddenly his hand slipped, scraping on broken edges and plunging into open air. Thrown off-balance, he pitched forward.

And then he was tumbling down a slope, and he clawed for traction. A moment later, he hit level ground. Jolted and a little out of breath, but unhurt, Moynihan stood up.

A narrow light beam flashed down on him, and Margaret called softly, "Commander!"

He gestured her to come down and, their stealth already broken, turned on his own wristlight. It lit up the black ground, frozen into coils like rope beneath his feet.

Margaret skidded down the slope, catching herself beside him. "What is this?"

"Let's have a look." Moynihan turned, shining the light first on the ropy ground and then outward. The land grew lumpier, black humps and flat, splintered ridges rising up. His beam found the charred, broken pieces of a building, and he lingered there a moment.

Margaret stepped away from him, sweeping the ground with her light. "Is this lava? Hardened lava?"

"That's exactly what it is." A sense of familiarity coated the scene around him, discordant in so strange a place. He had walked on ground like this, in a time and in places so far away. "Do you know I once wrote a book about volcanoes?"

"It was called *Vulcānus*, a scientific history."

Startled that she really did know, he added, "I've seen destruction like this. I've written about towns and cities ravaged by volcano fire." He turned, lifting his wristlight to illuminate the alien city, mighty buildings towering up in darkness. And he wondered if the aliens, strong as they surely had been, had been too weak for the volcano. They built their home in Arsia Mons. Did Arsia Mons expel them?

"What an appendix this would be." He spoke the words to himself, something like a daydream wafting in his mind for the first time in years.

Then he shook his head at his foolishness and turned to Margaret. She was kneeling now, running her fingers over the lava-encrusted earth. When he stepped closer, she looked up at him and said, "It's warm."

"Arsia Mons is dead," he answered, but the words were automatic, as if she had touched some spring that launched them. He knelt and touched the ground.

Warm. "Arsia Mons is *dead*," he repeated, standing up. Anger sparked through him, but he didn't know what he was angry at or why.

A small sound scuttled ominously in the dark, and Moynihan swung his light toward it. Steam, or something that looked like it, issued up from a rift in the lava. It thinned and vanished, but his anger burned hotter. "We need to get out of here."

Margaret was on her feet. "Will the volcano erupt again?"

"It might. If the pressure doesn't boil off quickly, it will." Despite every scientific verdict about cold, lifeless Mars.

They toiled up the slope, their boots slipping too easily on it. When they reached the street again, Moynihan turned and ran his light over the land below. As far as it reached, the beam showed old lava and blackened, toppled buildings.

And wisps of vapor, rising from the ground. "We have to leave the city," he said.

"But not without David and Eamon."

"I couldn't begin to guess where they've wandered. And with the city awake and hostile, and the volcano active . . ."

"And no food," she added to his reckoning of troubles. "I'm not sure our odds of survival are better if we leave the city than if we stay. But I don't care if they are. Eamon and David are part of our team. And David is my brother. If you had a brother, wouldn't you go looking instead of leaving?"

Moynihan would. If he had a brother, or anyone else he simply and unquestionably loved. He sighed, but not at Margaret. "We'll look for them." He switched off his wristlight, trying to think of a logical place to start the search.

Margaret extinguished her light, and he watched for another glowing sphere, and by the time it glided through the high blackness, he was resolved. "We'll follow the spheres, Margaret. Maybe they will lead us to something besides trouble."

"As long as I find my brother, I'll take any trouble with it."

"I suppose that's love."

XXI

The morning was new when Reuben walked out of his hotel. He sat down on the cold steps, their stone chipped and cracked, and rested his arms on his knees. Cradling his notebook in his hands, he eyed the empty street and looked up and down the sidewalk.

All was quiet. Reuben tapped on his notebook, connecting it to the satellite network. Then he put in the call, hoping the colonel was in his office so early.

The steps felt colder and colder as he waited, and finally he stood up and began walking. The air was cool, and it refreshed him, lifting some of the heaviness from his mind.

The notebook pinged, and Colonel Nelson's voice emanated small from it: "Jackson?"

"Yes, sir." Reuben lifted the notebook closer to his face and continued to walk. "I've studied the information you gave me, and I am ready for an assignment, except . . ." He grimaced. This would sound so bad. "I've gotten into some hot water. The Justice Department is investigating a leak in the government, and I'm pretty prominent in their sights."

For a few long seconds, there was quiet. "Yes," Nelson said eventually. "I know."

The colonel's tone made Reuben's muscles tense. "And?"

"A lot of pressure has come down on us from Washington. You're on unpaid administrative leave, Jackson. I'm sorry."

Reuben stopped. The words slowly soaked in, and he briefly closed his eyes. "Who?"

"Who what?"

"Who got me fired?"

"You're not fired yet."

Did Nelson expect him to believe the false comfort the words offered, or was he only evading the question? "Good as fired," he countered.

"Right now you're just dotting the i's and crossing the t's of my pink slip. Who did it?"

"I can't tell you."

"Covering their tracks, are they?"

Another pause. "When the decision is finalized, Jackson, I'll tell you."

Thank you was by no means appropriate, and before Reuben could decide what was, Nelson cut off. Absently, Reuben slipped his notebook away into a pocket.

A metallic rattle drew his eyes down the street, to where a man opened a store, and he watched with a feeling of great distance. The man vanished inside, and it was another minute before Reuben got his feet moving again. He walked down the sidewalk, his mind beginning to whir.

Fired.

No job.

No more money.

What now?

He picked up his pace, thoughts coming fast and furious, and not one of them happy. A woman came toward him, and he distractedly stepped out of her path. It wasn't until she was passing him that he caught a glimpse of her face. That glimpse burst through his thoughts, and he turned, catching her arm. "Willow?"

She pulled her arm away, but stopped, lifting her green eyes to him.

His heart flipped, and his unemployment suddenly seemed a little less important. "It's good to see you again, Willow."

Willow studied him, and her eyes were filled with carefulness. "You're back in Washington, Mr. Jackson. And in trouble."

There was no reason to deny it. "How do you know?"

"I am Dr. Karl's assistant. And he is looking for trouble in his office. With your name on it. The Justice Department arrived yesterday."

A new uneasiness clenched him at this consequence he had not anticipated— Willow and all Karl's staff pulled down into chaos. "How bad is it?"

"No one in the office will be sleeping well for a while, if that gives you a picture. Justice is eying each of us in turn, and that's bad. So is Dr. Karl, and that's worse. Today I am on probation."

"What does that mean?"

"It means that today Dr. Karl is going to decide if I am part of the trouble you have been causing, and so I've been told not to come in. Tomorrow I'll go back to work—if I still have a job."

"Willow, I—" But before he could apologize, she was gone, hurrying away from him down the sidewalk. When she had disappeared from sight, he resumed walking, slower than before.

A black car drove by on the road—probably a high-ranking official on the way to some government building. Reuben thought of Jep Baines, serving his president with steely devotion and trying so hard to ward off trouble. Reuben had very neatly sabotaged those efforts.

His mind drifted to Manasseh Cruz as he had last seen him—liquor in his hand, anger in his eyes. Reuben had burned the bridge he had been trying to build, but the loss felt very small. The hope of help from the congressman was a chimera, a pipe dream he had played to himself. Now he was awake. Yet a shade of sadness followed along behind him. He didn't even know what he regretted, only that it had something to do with his discarded hope and the memory of Manasseh Cruz alone and awake at midnight.

A *snap* and *crackle* of fire suddenly ignited Reuben's awareness of where he was. He saw a woman near the mouth of an alleyway, stirring up a fire. Something shifted behind her, and a small child came into view.

Jep Baines's voice whispered in his thoughts: *the people in the streets.* And who knew? Maybe Reuben would join them soon. He didn't have a job anymore.

He sat down on the curb and took in the area surrounding him. He had wandered into a degenerate neighborhood—flimsy dwellings erected beside run-down buildings, garbage in the road and on the sidewalks. A few people were straggling back to what passed for home, not all steady on their feet. Those who were steady, returning to this shameful district after nighttime errands, he tracked warily. He guessed too well the nature of what they had probably been doing.

But most of the neighborhood was just rousing. He listened to the sounds of life, caught whiffs of breakfasts that could not raise his hunger, and watched the luckier ones leave the tumbledown buildings and head for work.

And he mused. He thought of Cruz, of Baines, of Willow, of the scandal he had heated to boiling, and of his own darkening future.

The harm of his efforts to help the Mars team spread all around him. The good was more elusive. So he sat, with nothing in all the world to do, and his mind trod through gloomy forests.

XXII

"You know, Killiam, we could use a new plan."

Eamon's voice came muffled, but still too clear. David tried to ignore him, fixing his eyes on the dark way ahead and bending his will against the craft.

"Maybe we need a strategy. We should set down and think this—"

"Don't distract me, Eamon. I'm trying to fly this thing."

That gained David silence, and he inhaled deeply, exhaled, and focused his energy on his task. Above the city, they flew through an empty twilight, yet all his concentration seemed hardly enough.

Red lights flickered ahead, and David blinked. And then he saw them again, wavering but growing stronger.

He had one moment to be puzzled. Then a glowing orb came shooting at them with incredible speed, and he banked hard to dodge it.

Behind him came a *thud*, followed instantly by Eamon's shout. "Killiam!"

David turned the craft back again, steadying it, and saw a whole array of red orbs spreading out before them. They shone in a vast and precise formation, turning the twilight into a bloodred sunset.

David willed the craft to be still. The curtain of spheres brushed the buildings below and soared into the vault overhead. Perhaps the shadows and ruby light confused him, but he thought he caught glimpses of the ceiling of this massive cavern.

"They want us to go back," Eamon told him. "Back to the stairways."

"*You* want us to go back," David muttered. He swung the craft ninety degrees and raced parallel to the spheres, hoping to find a gap in the formation.

A sphere swooped down at his head, and David awkwardly spun the craft to evade it.

"Killiam, just turn around!"

David gritted his teeth. "You give up easily." He held the craft motionless and studied the red orbs. "Eamon, I have the gun in my belt. Pull it out and shoot one of those things."

"What? Why?"

"Because I want to ram through that blockade, but first I need to know what happens when an orb is smashed. So shoot one."

"No."

David breathed deeply. "*No?*"

"I won't. You're not my commanding officer anymore, and I don't think we should destroy anything."

Bitter insults about deserters rolled in David's mind, but he was beyond words. He flew the craft at the spheres. One shot forward to meet him, and David corkscrewed to collide with it.

It exploded in a blast of light and shards and a keening wail. Blinded, David flew by memory, hoping he was drawing the craft up and away from the spheres.

In what could only have been seconds, his vision cleared, and he found that they were flying in an uneven slant downward.

David pulled up. Movement danced in the corner of his eye, and he looked to see all the spheres descending on him.

"Give up, Killiam," Eamon warned. "They can't be beat."

Anger singed David's blood, but he had no time for Eamon. He twisted the craft around and raced for clear space as the orbs spread and fell like a net.

The net fell too fast. David's eyes bore sharp on the orbs' trajectories and speed, and he chose the last direction left open.

Straight down.

He dropped the craft and skimmed the tops of the buildings for a span of seconds. Then, as the orbs closed in, he dove between two roofs spiked with minarets.

And into thick shadows. Blind again, David fought to slow the craft but sensed the wrongness of the descent. "Hang tight!" he shouted, wrestling against the craft's momentum.

Then they crashed. The force threw David out of his seat, onto the nose of the craft, and he tumbled over it to hit the ground.

David found himself, after a hazy moment, flat on his back, staring into darkness. He pushed up to sitting, his body protesting, and called, "Eamon!"

"Yeah?" Eamon's voice was tight and irritated.

For once, David didn't care. Relieved not to have killed Eamon, he stood up and pulled free the gun. His fingers worked it by feel—checking the cartridge, sliding the safety off and then on again.

A heavy shuffling and scraping, then Eamon's voice again: "What are you doing?"

"Getting ready. Those things must have marked where we came down." David paused, listening to the noise from Eamon's direction, as if he were clumsily scrambling out of the craft. "Be quiet. And don't turn on your wristlight."

A beam of light sliced the darkness, and David rounded on Eamon. "What is the matter with you?"

"Why should I listen to you, Killiam? You don't listen to me. And you're wrong."

David heard a strange timbre in Eamon's voice, some tension that felt new. "And what is right, in your opinion?"

"Going into the center of the city and finding out what it wants."

As David wavered between cold dismissal and yelling, a sudden noise of running came from behind him.

He spun around, snapping the gun up, and looked vainly into the dark beyond the short reach of Eamon's wristlight. The running grew closer.

Then two voices at once.

"Colonel!"

"David!"

He nearly dropped the gun. He hurriedly jammed it into his belt, and the next second Margaret burst into the light. David caught her exuberantly into a hug, with relief so great it was joy. Then he stepped back, trying to see her face in the dimness. "Are you okay?"

"Yes," she assured him. "You look worse for the wear, though."

The light behind snuffed out; apparently Eamon didn't need to see anymore. A new light sprang up in front of them, shining from the tall, straight figure of Donegan Moynihan.

Moynihan scanned his wristlight over them, and then flashed it toward Eamon. It froze on the craft. "Did you come here in that derelict?" was the commander's greeting.

"I flew it," David said, pride warming him.

"Crashed it," Eamon added under his breath.

David's anger flared. "Those things hounded us out of the sky. But you're so understanding, you would like to sit down to tea and ask what's bothering them."

"I told you, Killiam," Eamon answered, his voice raised. "I said—"

Moynihan interrupted him, "I think we came in late, Doctor. And they don't know, do they?"

Eamon gave him a look. "Know what?"

"We found you by following the stalkers." Moynihan stopped there, and then seemed to be looking at Margaret.

Curious at that as much as at the commander's words, David repeated, "Stalkers?"

Margaret gestured. "Look up, David."

David did, and he saw a cluster of orbs floating silently overhead. More spheres spiraled out from that—a long, undulating chain, weaving a luminous way through the darkness. They did not dispel the deep shadows, but they did mark an unmistakable path.

"They're guiding us back," said Eamon. "Back to the center of the city."

Margaret switched on her wristlight. "We need to leave the city. The volcano is still active."

"The volcano—this volcano?" David jerked his head around. "We are inside an active volcano?"

Before anyone could answer, the spheres dropped into a half circle around the team, surrounding them on every side except that which opened to the shining line of the other spheres.

Moynihan gestured his wristlight in that direction. "Let's walk for a little while. The spheres may let us alone if we do, and then we can talk and hope they—or whatever controls them—can't understand our speech."

Moynihan walked point, following the spiraling orbs and shining his wristlight on the path. He kept his head cocked, listening to the voices behind him.

Margaret had begun the conversation, telling David about the volcano and their entire journey. Then the colonel related his encounter with the spheres and, telling his story backward, described the black tower and the converging stairways.

As Moynihan walked ahead, Eamon trailed behind, and he kept quieter than Moynihan would have guessed. The colonel went on to his separation from the team—his fall into the water, crawling through the tunnel, and coming out near the city.

He had barely finished speaking the last word when Eamon cut in, "What now?"

Moynihan glanced back at him, surprised at the abruptness of the question, and took a moment to review the colonel's scattered narrative. David had left a sizable gap between when he emerged from the water and his exploration of the city with Eamon. "Is there anything else I should know about, Colonel?" he asked.

A tremor passed through the ground, a faint shaking far beneath their feet, and the city seemed to moan around them.

"That depends, Commander," David responded. "If we survive, I have news we will have to do a lot of talking about. But if we need to run for our lives, it can probably wait."

Moynihan acceded to the point. "We need to get out of the city," he said. "But we will have to evade the—"

"I dispute that, Moynihan," Eamon interrupted. "We can't leave the city and shouldn't."

He was irritated to be interrupted and to be addressed by his surname alone. "The *can't*, Mr. Eamon, is a whole different matter from the *shouldn't*, but let us take first issues first. It doesn't matter whether or not we can until we have settled whether or not we should. I say we should leave the city because something in it is trying to kill us and because the volcano is active. Why do you say we shouldn't?"

Eamon's voice was testy. "All the answers we need are in the city, and any hope we have is here, too. You may see the bright side of wandering lost and starving on the highway, but—"

Moynihan stopped him. "I'll take your opinions, Mr. Eamon, but I won't take your sarcasm."

The others stopped when he did, and Moynihan faced them. "You have only a guess or a feeling that staying in the city will give us answers and some kind of hope. All the evidence is that the city is against us. And even if it were not, there is still the danger that the volcano will erupt again."

Eamon kicked a rock that threw shadows. "The *can't* is part of the *shouldn't*. We can't defy the city, and we shouldn't try. We shouldn't fight this power."

David refocused his light on the engineer. "You were on that submarine, Eamon, the one that sank the flotilla during the war. You weren't a pacifist when it came to fighting people. Why did you become one about fighting aliens?"

"Killiam—"

Eamon was nearly shouting, and Moynihan felt no reluctance in curtly interrupting him. "The decision is mine to make. And we will try to get out of the city."

David nodded and pulled a gun from his belt.

"How, Commander?" Margaret asked.

Moynihan looked up at the spheres hovering in the gloom. Not knowing what they were, understanding neither their abilities nor their intentions, it was hard to plot any strategy. "We'll just go. If there's pursuit, Colonel, your gun will be effective. Your blaster, Lieutenant Commander—"

"I don't think so. It's a bad idea, Moynihan."

"You don't think so?" Moynihan repeated slowly, astonished at the flat rejection and the insolent casualness of Eamon's tone.

Eamon fell silent. David and Margaret watched the confrontation with equal stillness, and the air thickened.

Moynihan looked hard at Eamon. "It's time for you to stop talking and do what I tell you."

Eamon shook his head jerkily. "You're only going to hurt yourselves."

Margaret's eyes widened slightly. "'You'?"

"Eamon," the colonel's voice strained with impatience, "are you going to be man enough to say it, or are you going to force me to?"

"I'll say it." Eamon looked at Moynihan. "Commander, I went AWOL. I deserted the team. Killiam and I ended up together again by accident. I haven't obeyed him, and I won't obey you, either."

Moynihan swung his light to the colonel. "This was your news that you thought could wait?"

"I thought the survival instinct would keep us together for a while."

"Sometimes the survival instinct does keep people together. And sometimes it separates them—every man for himself, the survival of the fittest, the law of the jungle." Moynihan made his voice even, his analysis cool, hoping that he could build enough distance not to feel the stinging indictment of his failure. His team was broken, and it was too late for repair.

He shifted the light from the colonel to Eamon. "I won't force you into obedience. So I suggest you be on your way. If you want to leave, you should leave, and not hang around until it ceases to be convenient for you." Not waiting to see if Eamon would rebel against this, too, Moynihan turned to Margaret and David. "And where do you stand? Do you leave the team, or do you stay?"

"Stay," Margaret said immediately.

David saluted with his gun. "Stay, Commander."

Moynihan nodded to them, surprised by the gratitude he felt, though they should have done no different. "Then be ready with your gun, Colonel. I'll lead the way, the doctor will come behind me, and you, Colonel, will come last and cover our retreat. If we're separated, make for the highway above the city, and don't stop until you reach it."

Eamon still stood there, hanging at the back of the group. Moynihan ignored him and turned, flashing his wristlight along the path of the shining orbs. To his right, a building like a temple gave way to a kind of courtyard, strewn with wild statues.

He motioned to it once and then snapped off his light. David and Margaret drew beside him, and he led them off the designated path.

They crept into the courtyard, going slowly in the gloom. The black shape of the nearest statue rose silently and balefully, and Moynihan veered toward it, reaching out questing hands. As his fingers brushed the glassy stone, a shrill cry tore through the dark city.

Moynihan reflexively pulled his hand away. He glanced up, saw one distant red gleam, and began to turn around.

"Don't look back." The colonel's voice was solid behind him. "Keep going. And don't get separated."

Moynihan, heart sinking with the certainty that they would not all make it, circled to the other side of the statue, his ears sensitive to every small sound of Margaret following.

A gunshot exploded behind them, and then a shattering and a high-pitched wail. Even with his back to it, he saw the flash of light, momentarily scattering the relentless shadows.

He half turned, reaching out, catching Margaret's hand. And then he began to run, while the first, solitary shot turned to gunfire and the orbs shattered. The clangor drowned the beat of their footfalls, the bursts of light throwing crazy snatches of illumination on the courtyard.

A human shout seemed to slip in amidst the gunfire and the keening of the spheres. And then, more impressive than any noise, perfect silence fell.

Moynihan halted and looked back. The orbs stooped down over two black figures, limned with the red glow. Both were frozen in that stillness born of the extremity of vigilance.

With a gasp, Margaret pulled away from him and swiftly headed back. Doubting the wisdom of it, but having no confidence in any other decision, he followed her.

Spheres swept down as they walked, clustering around in ever-greater numbers. Moynihan perceived, in the growing ruby light, that the nearer figure was David, his silver eagle bloodred with the light. Three steps more revealed the second figure was Eamon. The men faced each other, weapons drawn and pointed—Eamon with his blaster, David with his gun.

Moynihan changed his course, aiming at Eamon. Without twitching in his direction, Eamon ordered, "No closer, Moynihan. You, too, Meg."

Out of respect for his blaster, Moynihan halted and looked over at Margaret.

She stood close to David, her feet spread as if ready for action. "What are you doing, Eamon?"

"Settling a difference of opinion." Eamon lifted his chin, the blaster in his hands not wavering in its focus on David. "Wouldn't you say, Killiam?"

The colonel's voice was like a glacier—with a coldness completely its own, smooth for very hardness. "I thought you were just a deserter, Eamon. If I'd known you were a traitor, I would have taken care of you first."

"Lost opportunities, Killiam." Eamon took a brief glance at Margaret and Moynihan, his eyes reflecting the glowering light of the spheres. "Now this can end without anyone getting hurt. It should end without anyone getting hurt. Put down your gun, Killiam, and all of us will follow the spheres to the center of the city."

Margaret shook her head. "That ends with no one getting hurt? The commander and I were nearly drowned, and you and David might have died in that crash."

"But think about it. Only when you fight do things like that happen. In fact, both incidents happened right after someone destroyed one of the orbs. What do you think they'll do when you run and Killiam shoots up the place? But go quietly and you'll be safe."

"Including from you?" Margaret challenged.

One beat passed. Then Eamon said, "I won't shoot him."

"Eamon," the colonel said, "whatever cards you hold, I have an ace. The ace of spades, and I can play it for death. You say you won't shoot me. How will you convince me not to shoot you?"

"Gentlemen," Moynihan interjected, "the situation is easy to judge. If either one of you shoots, both of you will shoot, and how can you miss?"

Neither man flinched. They stood like statues, their drawn weapons gleaming in the red light. Death in pulsing potentiality, one hairsbreadth leap from the real.

They were shadows of his last nightmare, the team not only broken but devouring each other. The spheres increased on every side, haunting the clash with their dark, inscrutable presence. And Moynihan, seeing it all, decided to grasp for just enough light to chase away the shadows and keep the nightmare at bay. "Colonel," he said, "holster your gun."

"Commander . . ." David sounded as if he spoke through clenched teeth.

"We've lost, Colonel. The only question left is who will get shot before these orbs march us into the heart of the city. My answer is no one."

Seconds slowly unfurled, and then David lowered his gun. "Not because you're right," he said, "but because you are my commander, and it doesn't matter."

"Thank you." Moynihan turned to Eamon. "Would you go first?"

The engineer nodded tautly and walked from the courtyard, his blaster slung loosely in his hand. Moynihan followed, Margaret and David after him.

Like a cloud, the swarm of orbs lifted and accompanied their journey—flocking above, behind, and before them.

XXIII

Reuben Jackson sat on the curb of a dirty street and thumbed his notebook's screen, idly flipping through pages of research. His eyes grazed words that flashed through his mind without import, with hardly any meaning at all. After some time of this, he gave up the pretense. The notebook drooped in his hands, and he stared at the street. His thoughts skittered, never settling on anything, worthless.

People passed by, and Reuben watched their feet. At length someone came walking toward him—fine shoes, sturdy and well-formed and unscratched, deftly skirting all the litter.

The man stopped right in front of him, and at first Reuben still looked only at his shoes. Then, with something like a sigh, he looked up.

Manasseh Cruz gazed down on him, the sun lighting up his black hair like a halo. "What are you doing here, Jackson?"

Reuben looked up and down the street, at all the grime and poverty, the sordid decay. He hadn't paid enough attention to notice what he was doing there, but now that he tried, it was easy to see. "Moping," he said.

Cruz surprised him by sitting down by him. "You've picked a good place for it."

Reuben didn't respond, nor did he glance over at Cruz. He waited for the congressman to say something, probably about the Great Collapse.

"I heard," Cruz said, "that you got fired. Would you believe me if I said I didn't do it?"

"I might," Reuben conceded. "But then I would ask who spared you the trouble."

"Dr. Karl, NASA Man. Not that it was hard. You're a leper. Nobody wants to catch scandal from you." Cruz apparently held himself immune.

"How do you know he got me fired?"

Cruz leaned forward to rub smudges of dirt from his black shoes.

When he straightened again, he said, "Karl spreads his complaints in high places. And I walk in high places."

Reuben lifted his eyes to the blighted neighborhood around them, wearing its filth and degradation like sores. "This isn't one of them, Congressman." And yet he had walked with Cruz in a place much like this. Cruz had said there that he didn't waste time, and Reuben had believed him.

He still believed him. Reuben put away his notebook, a rousing curiosity in his mind. "What are you doing here, Cruz? I thought we were done trying to talk to each other. I burned my bridges last night."

"I know you did. You found me guilty. And early this morning, I found you innocent. I guessed you were, earlier, but my suspicions die hard. Karl finally killed them by orchestrating your professional demise. So now it's my turn to build a bridge."

Reuben looked out on the garbage-strewn road. "Go on."

Cruz didn't answer at once. Odors wafted on the air, suggesting spoiled food and worse things. The squalid neighborhood sprawled left and right as far as Reuben could see, and he felt in it the eternal pathos of the human condition.

"The liquor bottle you found in my house last night," Cruz said.

"What of it?"

"Karl sent it to me. Not to toast our victory or to drink to the end of the Mars team, Jackson. He sent it as a threat. Now I know what will happen if I break ranks during this investigation."

Reuben glanced at Cruz, but nothing in his expression threw illumination on his words. "A bottle of liquor is usually a sign of celebration. What does it mean to you?"

"It means—" The congressman stopped and mingled a sigh with a dry laugh. "There's no reason to put it delicately. Until a year and a half ago, I was a drunk."

Reuben stared at him. "A year and a half? But I knew you then. And I knew you years before that. I never saw . . ." He didn't know what words to use and decided it was easier not to use any.

"Never even saw me take a drink." Cruz's tone was wry. Wry to a razor-sharp edge, and only he knew how deeply it cut. "Nobody did. I only drank alone, and I could go weeks without drinking at all. The secret is easier to keep than you might think."

"How did Karl find out?"

"I don't know, though I've suspected for a long time that he knew. And now he's blackmailing me with it. If I do anything to undercut him, if I try to fight him, he'll let the whole world know what I really am. I'm a politician, so it will be a crisis for my career. I'm a great politician, so I can handle it. But what will I tell my children when they hear about it?"

Reuben had to look away, his old image of the congressman shattering. Words bubbled up from his confusion: "I don't understand."

"Don't understand what?"

"I don't understand what all this means. Do you mean that you can't fight Karl because of his blackmail? Why would you fight him, anyway? Haven't you two been partners in all this? Have you changed your mind, or are you and Karl running scared and ready to sell each other out?"

Cruz held up his palm. "Stop before you hurt yourself. More questions, and you'll addle your brain." He lowered his hand and studied Reuben. "Jackson, Karl and I were partners in preventing the convoy and the capsule from being sent to Mars; we were partners in shutting down the Mars mission, and in such a way that we didn't have to explain ourselves. We slow-rolled and stopped up the gears with sand and made sure it never came to an open fight. But I had nothing to do with choosing the Mars team, and I had nothing to do with the fake communiqué."

"And which communiqué is that?" Reuben asked, his eyes fixed on Cruz's face. No one, not even Jep Baines, had owned the communiqué on which they decided the fate of Mars a forgery and a lie.

"Do you know," Cruz remarked, "that at first I thought the second communiqué was the forgery, and you had done it? When I realized that wasn't true, I pretended to myself that I couldn't guess which communiqué was false, or who was behind it, and it wasn't my business to find out."

Reuben shook his head. "I didn't know you were so good at pretending, Congressman."

"Jackson"—the congressman's voice was suddenly weary—"I pretended to myself for years that my binges weren't a problem because I had an intact family, a brilliant career, and everyone who met me said, 'He's in control.' I am very good at pretending, but let me pretend no more. I can't understand the second communiqué as a lie. I understand the first as a lie perfectly. It achieved my goal in the way I wanted to achieve it: efficiently and without fingerprints. And no one would or could do that but Karl."

Reuben searched the congressman's face for truth, trying to see what lay behind the bright, knife-edged gleam in his dark eyes. He thought he saw the congressman more truly than he ever had before, and belief of the whole tale grew in his mind.

Still he asked the question: "And not you?"

He was prepared for Cruz's thunder, but the congressman only shook his head. "Not me. Karl lied to me, too. My sins are, of course, vile, but I have never conned the president, the Congress, and all the American people. But Karl did, on behalf of our cause, and I might have let it go. I might have pretended I didn't know and then gone safely on my way. But last night you came and told me that Karl had planned six years ago for these people to die on Mars. I had no idea. I don't know anymore why they're dying. I don't know what I'm a part of, but I won't be a part of it any longer."

Reuben looked at the congressman, a tremulous hope stirring in his heart. "Karl's blackmail won't stop you?"

Cruz's mouth flattened into a straight line, and his eyes sparked. "It will drive me. I won't be a hostage to Karl, and I won't be a hostage to my own shame. I'll pay the price, but I'll be free."

Reuben remembered the little boy with Cruz's eyes. "And your children?"

Cruz looked away, and his eyes grew distant and gentle. "My children," he said, "will know the truth. They will be all right."

Reuben let his gaze rove over the degraded buildings, his spirit soaking in the words, and he suddenly felt sad. He perceived in shadowy forms the cost of this freedom from Karl, from shame—to be borne mostly by Cruz. But not only.

His eyes ranged to the sky above them, clear and bright, and stopped there. He gazed at the shining blue far beyond his reach, soaring untouchable above all the grimness of these streets, and knew it was the only beautiful thing in all the decaying district.

He turned to Cruz again. "You didn't come here because you wanted to confess. I'm not a priest. I've never even been your friend. So, why are you here?"

"To ask if you want to take on Karl with me. I'm declaring war. Are you on my side?"

Reuben thought a moment and shook his head. "No." He stood up and looked down on the congressman. "You're finally on mine."

Cruz stood also. "Either way, we're together. So, come on, Jackson. Karl won't know what hit him until it's too late."

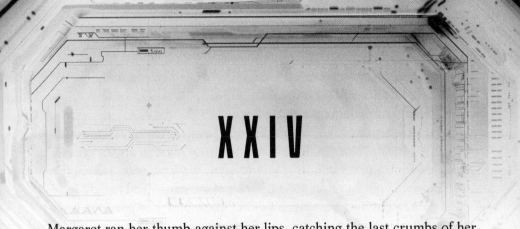

XXIV

Margaret ran her thumb against her lips, catching the last crumbs of her rations bar. Moynihan had ordered them back to full rations for reasons she understood but didn't want to think about. So she ate, quietly and slowly, and finished long after the men with her did.

David stayed beside her, his hand twitching toward his gun every once in a while. Anger rolled off him like heat, and it dried the air and imbued it with a suggestion of danger.

Moynihan walked in front of them, his recorder in his hand and raised to his mouth. The commander softly dictated their story, pausing every so often to shoot footage of the city on either side.

Eamon walked first of all, with the red spheres spinning their path before him and all the team following in his wake. He had won.

The orbs flew in thick droves and hemmed them in on every side. Their smoldering glow stained the gray shadows of the city red.

Margaret took little interest in the city until a sheer black tower rose powerfully amid the gray. She tugged at David and pointed. "Is that your tower?"

He looked at it, and his eyes flashed to Eamon and then back to the tower. "That's it." His hand wrapped around the butt of his gun.

Eamon turned back, his gaze going to the tower and then to David. "Don't even think of it, Killiam."

David's fingers tightened around the black gun. "Since when do you give me orders?"

Eamon drew out his blaster, his gaze never wavering from David's face.

Moynihan, standing between the two men, lowered the recorder and fixed his eyes on Eamon. "Move on."

Eamon looked at him for a long moment, his expression unreadable. Then he swung the blaster uselessly down and continued forward. Moynihan cast a pointed look David's way and followed.

Margaret felt David bristle even as he marched on.

They passed the tower, and the street spilled out into an avenue that spanned with the might and purpose of a highway. Light filled the avenue, and Margaret blinked several times as she stepped onto it.

The orbs swept after them, crowding in on every side, keeping them to the path. An archway loomed ahead, and its whiteness was so pure, and the light of the road so bright, that Margaret momentarily shut her eyes.

They passed beneath it, and Eamon stopped at the head of a stairway. Margaret, curious, pressed forward and wove around Moynihan to peer down.

There were at least fifty steps, all sculpted out of gray stone with a great and delicate precision. They gleamed with a soft yellow light, a yellow light that also swirled on the platform below. The platform at the foot of the stairs was also gray and glimmering with rays of green and blue.

So this was the heart of the city. David had told her of the four long stairways marching down to a bare platform, but he had given her no notion of its beauty.

"This is it, Meg," Eamon declared. "This is what your brother wanted to run from."

His voice carried something his words did not, something lighter and almost happy, and Margaret looked at him. He didn't smile, but his blue eyes were finally unburdened. "I don't see anything to fear," he said. "Do you?"

Margaret looked down and knew that this place was beautiful, and beauty was not to be trusted. She glanced behind her.

David and Moynihan watched—David, his whole body rigid, and Moynihan, his face reposed and thoughtful and his eyes keen.

A breeze lifted from somewhere in the city. It brushed her face with cool, light fingers and carried faint, discordant music. David clenched his jaw. Moynihan's eyes flicked away in the direction of the music.

But Eamon watched her steadily. "What do you think?"

Margaret, for her answer, stepped down onto the first step and began her descent.

Eamon followed, and a minute later, David brushed past Eamon to join her. "I don't like this, Meg."

"I know." She gazed at the red spheres, ringing the four stairways like heedful sentinels. "But we can't fight, and we can't run."

The wind rose, and the music rose with it, a clamor of beautiful notes at war with each other. The yellow light slipped and shifted beneath their feet, and the radiant blue and green beckoned them onward.

When there were more steps behind them than before them, a tremor rumbled through the city. The stairway wobbled, and Margaret, frightened of being thrown headlong down the stairs, froze.

The city stilled once more, and Margaret took another step down, her pulse throbbing.

The entire world jolted with sudden, terrifying violence. Margaret's feet slipped, and she twisted to fall backward. Her knee slammed into one stair, and her elbow onto another, and she tried to grip the cold, hard steps.

The stone vibrated against her fingers, against her whole body, and fear rose from it and filled her mind like a haze. She saw, as if from another place, Eamon tumble off a shaking stair.

He collided with David and knocked him over. Through Margaret's haze, she reached out to grab David to stop his fall.

And so they all fell.

It seemed to last a long time, as the stairs buffeted her and fear spun in her mind. Then, all too soon, it ended.

Her hands rammed into the platform, and she felt the skin tear. She let herself drop into a roll and, following through the movement, sat up. As the wild music sang and shouted, she looked around the trembling platform.

Eamon was crawling off David, who was already struggling to get up. He managed to rise to sitting and, wiping blood off his face, snapped, "Eamon!"

Margaret said softly, "David."

He looked at her, and she saw the anger and fear spinning together like a whirlwind in his eyes.

Then a *boom* washed over them, a sound that could be felt. Margaret lifted her eyes and saw a wall of lava shooting above the dim roofs of the city and spitting out flaming chunks. A shadow billowed and curled out of the inferno, as though gaining life and substance.

She stood up, forgetting all her aches.

Then the light that filled the city's great avenue withered to a heavy, gray dusk. A sudden smell of sulfur overcame Margaret, and she wondered what other gases were pouring down on them.

Ash showered down out of the baleful dusk, like the rain of a cursed world. It fell warm on her skin, and Margaret glanced down to see the ash running with the blood on her hand.

David stumbled to her side, and she could hear the slight rasp in his breathing, either from inhaling the volcano's gases or its ash. "Meg, we've got—"

He broke off as the city shook all around them. Margaret looked up at the towering eruption of lava. It was obscured by the shadow, which she perceived now as sallow, churning clouds, but its light still burned a fierce and morbid red through the veil.

She had the desire to flee, but it was too late to run.

"It's a horrible majesty."

Margaret turned toward the calm voice. Moynihan stood on the last stair, regarding his team.

She felt David turn, saw Eamon shift toward the commander. And they looked at him, and he at them, while the ash rained down and the city rumbled.

Eamon coughed once and swiped at the ashes on his face, leaving dark smears across his cheek. "Never surprised by a disaster, are you?"

"There's no sense in being Irish unless you know that sooner or later, the world is going to break your heart." Moynihan stepped down onto the platform.

Beams of blue and green light shot from beneath his boots. And then the bright rays flashed from Margaret's feet, and David's, and Eamon's. Yellow light surged up like a wave from the stone and engulfed them.

Margaret's senses swam in that light, yellow shot through with green and blue. When it swirled away from her, she stood in a dark, quaking cavern, in which one pure, white light shone like a too-near star.

She stared and saw, in the heart of the light, two columns linked by a crystalline roof that flashed like lightning in the radiance. Six steps led up to the columns.

"A doorway?" Her voice was both small and too loud in that place.

"Yes," said Eamon. "A doorway."

David stepped closer, the light reflecting doubtfully on his eyes. "But to where?"

Moynihan's voice came out of the shadows with a strange and distant wistfulness. "If I could live long enough to write the book of this . . ."

The quaking grew more violent, shaking dirt and small stones down onto their heads. Somewhere, close enough for them to feel it, the volcano still raged.

Margaret hastened toward the shining doorway, and the men's boots pounded the cavern's hard floor after her.

Eamon dashed ahead and leapt up the stairs. There, before the burning white light, he swiveled around. "Here is a door to lead us out of this nightmare. I hope you follow."

Then he stepped into the light and vanished.

The light winked out of existence, and for a black instant Margaret thought the doorway was dead. Then it burst into radiance again.

She stopped, a few feet from the stairs, and turned. "Commander—"

Moynihan was several paces behind, kneeling and shining his wristlight on what must have been an opening in the floor, for it swallowed the narrow beam.

Then, with a noise like shattering thunder, the cavern pitched wildly. It flung Margaret to the ground, and the very rock groaned and broke. A slab of dark stone hurtled down and crashed on the cavern floor.

She tried to push herself up, desperation consuming her as the floor seemed to roll beneath her.

"Meg!" David was by her then, stretching out a hand filthy with ash and blood. She placed her own bloody hand in his, and he pulled her to her feet and didn't let go.

They reeled, in the swaying cavern, toward the doorway of light. Rocks rained down from the unseen ceiling, and the thunder of their landfall resounded.

The doorway rocked, but its light blazed in undimmed brilliance. They struggled up the steps, and David, still gripping Margaret's hand, entered the light first.

She threw one last glance behind her to Moynihan. He was on his feet now, abandoning whatever had captured his interest, and was coming toward them.

An enormous, jagged rock sliced black across her vision, and a fractured image filled her eyes—the rock, Moynihan stumbling, chaos and darkness churning.

And then the light. The light cut off everything else, and she saw it, felt it, tasted it, breathed it. Free as the wind, solid as a mountain, purer than starlight and stronger than sunlight, it caught her in its insuperable current and swept her away.

XXV

"This carpet looks new."

Manasseh Cruz looked over his shoulder to see Reuben Jackson examining the carpet at his feet. He turned back to the door and pressed the call button.

"And there was a chandelier in the lobby. And a doorman at the door."

Cruz watched the door and wondered if he should ask the purpose of this chatter or simply ignore it.

"I knew the doctor for years. I never knew he lived like this."

"Why should you have? You were just another person at a meeting." Cruz glanced back and, at Jackson's expression, made his words gentler with explanation. "It's the Washington illusion, Jackson. All the public work and the public life fool people into thinking they know more about each other than they really do." He thought of his drinking, that dark companion to whom he had been chained so many years and to whom everyone else had been blind.

The door swung inward, and Dr. Francis stood looking at them. "Well, well, gentlemen, what do you want?"

His tone was friendly and brisk, but Cruz caught the wary edge in his eyes. "To begin with, Doctor, we'd like to come in."

The briefest pause. "Of course." Francis stepped back and ushered them in.

A living room, nearly as rich as any Cruz had ever been in, opened around them. Past it, a truncated flight of steps led up to a raised floor and created a new room without walls. A dining room set was arrayed in the elevated room, brilliantly lit by sunshine blazing through crystal balcony doors.

Cruz ambled through the living room, up the steps, and around the dining table to stand before the doors. Francis followed him, but Jackson dragged his feet, his eyes darting over the opulence.

He was too far away to kick, so Cruz turned to Francis. "There's been talk in the House of what to do with your committee now that the Mars mission is over."

Francis drew a chair and sat down. "Really," he said, with hardly any inflection.

"The emerging consensus is that it should be eliminated."

"Truly, Congressman, that would be a change."

Cruz scrutinized the man's face and saw only the laxness of boredom, but he knew how to break that. "Dr. Francis, tell us about Donegan Moynihan."

Francis coughed a little, then cleared his throat. "Why do you ask about him?"

And Cruz knew he had been right to come. "It suddenly occurred to me how interesting it is that you sent your own fifth man to Mars, to run the mission, then marooned him there and doomed his mission."

Francis stared at the surface of the table. "That's interesting?" he asked.

"They'll write books about it. You know what else is interesting? That there was no fifth man before Moynihan and no fifth man after him. It was your idea to expand the committee, Dr. Francis. But I guess it wasn't a good idea for long."

Francis shook his head and looked at Cruz. "It was a mistake to involve Congress so closely. We should have taken our chances with the executive branch." He turned his head. "Don't you think, Jackson?"

Reuben, standing opposite Cruz, nodded. "I certainly do, sir."

"But what mattered," Cruz continued, "is what Dr. Karl thought. He always got his way. In the House, where we live by threatening, cajoling, and bribing, we used to marvel at the unity Karl kept."

Francis's lip twisted. "You're baiting me."

"I am."

"I can throw you out of here."

"You could. But I hope you'll tell us about Moynihan instead."

Reuben pulled out a chair and sat at the table with Francis. "We want to know because we think Dr. Karl doesn't want us to."

Francis regarded him, then Cruz. "Oh, you do live dangerously."

Cruz met his eyes and nodded. "And you can appreciate why we want to keep this whole visit a friendly secret."

"And thus you can understand why I want it a secret." Francis leaned back, and his eyes grew distant. "I didn't know him well, though I see that more clearly now than I did then. But I was impressed with him. Moynihan had real skill and real passion for the work of science. He was a very intelligent man, a man who was always watching. Most of all, he had an unbreakable composure."

"Composure?" Reuben echoed.

"It's the best word I have for it. Moynihan always seemed in control of himself—never surprised, never upset, never angry, never afraid."

"Impressive," Cruz agreed, and thought that Moynihan's control must have had its secret fractures, as surely as his own had.

"And so I chose Moynihan. I wanted to add a fifth man, to balance Karl's power in the committee so that he would not always get his way. Moynihan had everything I thought would be needed. He was young, gifted, ambitious, unintimidated, and he had no history with Karl."

"So, why didn't it work?" Cruz inquired.

"It did—at first." Francis's lips twitched a little, and the ghost of a smile passed across his face. "Karl didn't want Moynihan, but I rallied the others, and we overruled him. Then, together with Moynihan, we forced the approval of the Mars mission. How Karl kicked!"

"A bad year for him," Cruz observed. "He lost twice."

"Yes." Francis's eyes looked into the distance again, and he sighed. "But he wouldn't stop."

The scientist fell silent. Cruz counted to maintain his patience, took a breath—

"Who wouldn't?" asked Reuben first.

"Moynihan. He wouldn't stop fighting with Karl. They fought over the selection of the Mars team, over the committee's procedures, over the supplies sent to Mars, over how we reported to the White House."

Jackson smiled faintly. "You *didn't* report to the White House. You sent them general updates."

"Precisely Moynihan's point. He wanted something that held us to actual accountability. That kept us, as he used to say, firmly in the chain of command."

"And you shipped him to Mars," Cruz remarked dryly. "Very convenient."

"He chose to go." Francis's voice rose. "No one forced him to join the mission."

Cruz eyed him. "But perhaps Karl was persuasive?"

Francis set his jaw and didn't answer.

Rueben leaned forward. "Do you know why Moynihan voted against every candidate but himself?"

Francis looked at him quickly, his mouth opening and then closing. "How—" He strangled off the question.

Jackson responded to it anyway. "We've been hearing things, Dr. Francis."

Francis ran his hands lightly over the polished table, fingers skimming back and forth along the shining wood. After a long moment, he said, "He thought they were being set up to fail."

They had been set up, and for something worse than failure, and Cruz was startled at the news that Donegan Moynihan had, those long years ago, known it. And it left a grim puzzlement in his mind. If Moynihan had grasped, back in that long-dead time of optimism, the ultimate doom that lay on the Mars mission, why had he joined it?

"Karl must have been persuasive." Cruz's voice was like ice. "Moynihan knowingly signed up for failure, and that's not a thing a man does easily."

Francis stood up, abruptly scraping his chair hard against the floor. "I don't care for your tone, Congressman."

An acidic response burned Cruz's tongue, but he took a moment to reconsider. Then he said, "I'm sorry, Doctor."

Francis only watched him, staying on his feet.

Cruz decided to take the hint, largely because he sensed that a door had closed and he would get nothing more. "Thank you for your time, Dr. Francis. I'm sorry for interrupting your day."

"Have a good day, gentlemen." But Francis neither looked nor sounded like his heart was in it.

Cruz left promptly, Jackson on his heels. As he walked down the hallway, he sorted the pieces Francis had given him: how they had overcome Karl to add Moynihan to the First Names, Moynihan's fractiousness and his understanding of the failure that awaited the Mars team. And they framed the shape of the missing pieces, momentous gaps.

"He knows more," Reuben said. "But he's ashamed of it."

Cruz cast a look at him. "You think so?"

"Definitely. Ashamed, and perhaps guilty."

Cruz remembered that glimpse of vulnerability—could it have even been fear?—he had caught when he'd pressed Karl on Moynihan. He did not understand the reason for Karl's unease or for Francis's shame, but he knew it was tangled with Donegan Moynihan.

They reached the elevator and boarded it. He stood back as Reuben keyed for the ground floor, certainty coalescing from the swirl of thoughts and facts in his head. "You ever read about dragons, Jackson?"

"When I was a kid." Jackson stepped back, and the elevator walls hummed.

Cruz felt the downward motion. "Maybe you remember, then, why it was so hard to kill a dragon—they were covered with scales that no weapon could penetrate. But when one of the scales was broken, a hero could kill the dragon. He just had to strike in exactly the right place—a few square inches of opportunity to do the impossible. Jackson, we've found Karl's broken scale. We know where to strike."

Reuben darted a glance at him and, partially turning, stabbed the panel. The elevator gave the slightest hitch, and then all movement died. "Congressman, we have only one clear shot."

"I know."

"You want to gamble it on Moynihan's story, and you don't even know what it is."

"Jackson, I think this is the thread that unravels everything. Karl's setup of the Mars team and even the true workings of the First Names. Moynihan's story will lead us inside."

"What are you going to do?"

Cruz reached over and keyed the elevator out of its standstill, needing a distraction from the answer he couldn't give. "Come to my house tonight. I should have more information by then."

The Sub Rosa Court usually worked that quickly.

Reuben set his notebook on the table and looked around. Windows filled up two of the walls, now veiled with wispy white curtains that betrayed glimpses of the black night outside. The honey-wood floor and the dining table and chairs—solidly and attractively built, with no trace of fanciness—were somehow welcoming.

All in all, it was a homier room than Reuben had expected to find in Manasseh Cruz's house. He sat down, noting that the table easily fitted eight, and tried to remember how many children Cruz had.

Cruz entered the dining room and took a chair with purposeful swiftness. "Are you hungry?"

Reuben glanced over the table, bare except for their notebooks, and said, "Sure." What part of the afternoon he had not spent researching he had spent considering his own situation, and he would take what free meals he could get.

Cruz's fingers moved over his notebook's screen for a moment, and then he said, "The meal should be delivered in about half an hour."

"Delivered?"

"I don't cook, Jackson."

Of course not; he was too high up in the world for that. "A housekeeper might do well for you," he said absently, looking at the cobwebs in one corner of the room.

"I can't afford to have a housekeeper."

"Cruz, you're rolling in it."

"Your innocence moves me." A dark amusement rode the congressman's voice. "With my wife still in the South, and me alone in this house every day—I cannot afford to have any woman, even a housekeeper, in the house with me. And I also don't want a man. I cannot afford the gossip the Washington rumor mills would manufacture."

Reuben remembered what rumors were already in circulation about the congressman and his marriage, and here, in Cruz's company, he felt strangely embarrassed by them. "Do you have any news?"

"Some. It turns out that, in the days leading up the launching of the mission, Moynihan sold his car, furniture, books, and just about all his property that could be sold."

"If you expected to be off the planet for the next five years, wouldn't you?"

"Oh, I would. But I wouldn't give all my money away unless I never expected to come back to this planet."

"All? The man has no more money than a squatter?"

"Yes. Of course, on Mars you don't notice it. It would be inconvenient here on Earth, though. All Moynihan has to his name is a few cartons of papers gathering dust in some university's storage. Can't pay the rent with that."

Reuben studied the congressman, casually dealing out intimate facts of Moynihan's financial affairs. "Who told you all this?"

"No one."

"Then how do you know? Records like that are buried pretty deep in privacy laws."

Cruz's dark eyes glinted. "It only takes one court order to unbury them."

"Yes, but . . ." Reuben fumbled the sentence as he tried to compute Cruz getting ahold of Moynihan's financial records. "You only decided to go after the truth this morning. Do you just snap your fingers and judges give away private information to you?"

"I got the court order, Jackson. What more do you want?"

Reuben felt he wanted something. A slippery wrongness hung about the situation, a sense of something that should not be. Yet, if the courts had approved . . .

"Francis said Moynihan expected the team to fail. I would say he actually expected them to die. But there are no answers in that, only our first questions. How did Moynihan know, and why did he go anyway?"

Reuben pushed aside the shapeless unease that swam in his mind and refocused his thoughts. "You were in Congress when Moynihan was with the First Names, weren't you?"

"Yes, but I wasn't the powerful mover and shaker that I am now."

Reuben, knowing that was not boasting but an exact statement of truth, skipped past it. "Shouldn't you know what made Moynihan controversial?"

"What, with the First Names?"

"No, in Congress. This afternoon I found an interview with one of your colleagues, published about three years ago. This congressman, Hunter, said that you had all learned from, quote, 'the Moynihan controversy' to be more inquisitive about who you approve."

Cruz shifted, leaning farther back in his chair. "He must have meant the academic-paper kerfuffle. Scarred by it, was he?"

Reuben straightened somewhat. This was new. "What happened?"

Cruz spread his hands. "To understand the story, you have to understand that Congress approved Moynihan's addition to the First Names. Not just another scientist: him. We didn't vote the funding for his salary until he met with our committees and justified himself to us. And then, months later, we learned he had committed the worst offense known to man."

Reuben looked at the congressman doubtfully. "Murder?"

"No, Jackson, bigotry. Back when Moynihan was a doctoral student, he and an archeologist friend of his published an academic paper on Sodom and Gomorrah. They put the old story in what archeological and scientific context they could scrape up from a trip to the Middle East."

"So?"

"So the paper didn't challenge the story. You might even say it was supportive of it."

Reuben still didn't understand. "And?"

Cruz rapped the table. "Don't you know the story of Sodom and Gomorrah? A whole town of people who practice a different lifestyle get burned off the earth for being too evil to live. Burned off by brimstone from heaven, no less."

"And, years and years ago, Moynihan supported the story in a paper."

"Exactly."

Reuben's eyebrows rose as he regarded the congressman in all his self-assurance. "Sounds like a tempest in a teapot to me."

"Yes, but in politics we sail on paper boats. There was a lot of agitation about what might happen if it got out that we'd put a bigot on the Mars Steering Committee. I heard the White House was in a pother, too, though back then, they didn't let me see. Everyone agreed the best thing would be to make Moynihan go away, but no one could figure out how to do it with no questions asked. Then Moynihan resigned and left Washington, and the whole thing died away. But I don't understand why Hunter would mention that mess in public. It could only be embarrassing."

"So, it was a private tempest, government leaders only. You don't suppose Karl stirred it up?"

"I suppose it very easily, but our answer can't be found there. Moynihan didn't join a suicide mission because Congress and the White House were fretting about a paper he wrote." Cruz's eyes roved to the window, as if the answer might be found in the night beyond the curtains. "If we could imagine where to look . . ."

"Congressman, there are two people who know exactly and entirely what happened: Dr. Karl and Donegan Moynihan. Karl would never tell us. Moynihan just might. He's on Mars, but he's not dead."

Cruz looked at him with silent consideration.

Then Cruz nodded.

XXVI

David stumbled from purest light into a white haze. His feet caught on something hard and uneven—it might have been the ground—and he fell.

Someone fell beside him, and then he heard Margaret's voice, sharp and very near: "David!"

David remembered he was gripping her hand. "Sorry, Meg." He let go and, rolling onto his back, blinked at a ceiling made of rock. "Are you okay?" Because he hurt.

"You dragged her to the floor, Killiam." Eamon's boots entered David's vision. And before David could gather a response, Eamon stepped over him to help Margaret up.

David forced his aching body to stand and took a look at Margaret. Her face was dirty, and her dark hair streaked gray with ash, but he saw no obvious signs of injury. "Are you hurt?"

She looked at her hands, encrusted with bloody ash, but shook her head. "Nothing serious." She looked around. "What is this place?"

David took stock of where they were and saw an underground chamber with nothing in it but the alien doorway they had just come through. A gentle silver light suffused the chamber, seeming to seep from the stone walls.

David's brow furrowed, the sight drawing out images of memory. "Is this . . ."

"The place we left?" Margaret asked. "That's what I thought."

"But we went *somewhere*. The ceiling's not collapsing on us here." Yet when he looked at the strange columns, with the six steps mounting up to them and the rocky chamber all around, he could not help seeing what they had just fled.

"At any rate, we're alive, and now more likely to stay that way." Eamon moved to sit down on the steps, a little slow, a little stiff. "What about Moynihan? Is he not coming?"

David tried to summon up his last memory of the commander. He had seen him, hadn't he, as he scrambled to Margaret?

"He was coming," said Margaret. "I saw him following us to the doorway. And then, just before I stepped into the light, I thought I saw him fall. He may have been hit by debris. He may not be able to come now." She looked at David.

Eamon looked at David.

David looked at the doorway. Light leaked from its columns, from the graceful designs that whorled over the smooth stone, but the white blaze was gone. He wondered if anyone could cross through it again, and he hoped that practical consideration would squeeze out all else.

It didn't. Guilt soured his soul because he hadn't thought of Moynihan, just of Margaret and himself. And beneath it he felt a furtive bracing for more guilt, for he wasn't sure he was willing to go back after the commander.

"Well?" Eamon asked. "What do you think?"

David focused on the engineer, noticing that, in addition to the filth, his face was marred by a substantial scrape on his forehead and a bruise forming beneath his eye. Bloodstains discolored many of the tears in his dirty jumpsuit. "You're a disaster," David told him.

"Go wash the blood off your own face."

The retort made David want to feel his face for any open wounds, but he wouldn't give Eamon the satisfaction.

Eamon turned to Margaret. "Still equipped to take patients, Meg?"

She indicated the medical kit dangling at her hip, secured to her belt by a utility cord. "I'm sure I can do something for you, Eamon. Both of you boys need checking out. Do you have water, Eamon?"

He began burrowing in his pockets. "Not much. Just—"

"Wait." David watched them turn to him, and he stepped into Moynihan's place, took up his burden of responsibility and decision. This was why they had given him the silver eagle. "We all need some treatment, but none of us is in too bad a way. Moynihan may be dying."

"Or dead," Eamon said. "If we go back into that cataclysm, we could all die."

"That's the heart of it, isn't it?" David sought Eamon's eyes, thinking that Eamon might understand because he had also fought in the war, and knowing that every word he was about to say would hurt them both. "It's the brag, the creed of the military, that we don't leave anyone behind. But it's all lies. I could tell you the names of men we left behind. There are nights when I can't sleep for seeing their faces. We can leave Moynihan behind, too, and for just the same reason. Who knows if the chance of him living is worth the risk of us dying?"

Eamon stared down at his hand, rubbing his palm. Black, gritty flakes broke off from his skin and drifted lazily down. "You think I have no honor, Killiam?"

"You tell me how much honor you have. I don't know. But it's not only a matter of honor."

Eamon looked up. "What else is it about?"

"Life and death."

Margaret's brown eyes met David's. "What matters most, David?"

He almost said it was her—the only person he truly loved, the last family he had left to lose. But he turned away and looked again at the doorway, trying to sort his thoughts.

A sound swept somewhere beneath their feet, and David froze. It whispered through the chamber. Rustling, humming . . .

A square portion of the floor lowered and slid away. A glow of golden light brimmed up from the opening, and wherever it touched the floor, the stone was silver and gold.

The humming stopped, like a song suddenly ending, and for just a moment all was silent. Then they heard footsteps echoing in the opened passage, each louder than the last.

David breathed in deep and steeled himself for whatever was about to happen.

After a few heartbeats, a figure began to rise out of the glow. It stepped up into the chamber and, facing them, went still.

He heard Margaret stifle a cry and sensed Eamon's alertness. His heart beating in his throat, he stared at the being in front of him. It looked almost human, except for a strange burning in its eyes and its mottled skin, white and brown streaking haphazardly together.

Those eyes combed each of them in turn, and then it—he—spoke, a stream of clipped, fluid syllables that meant nothing to his hearers.

Eamon stood up from the steps. "Is this where we say, 'We come in peace'?"

David eyed the alien, who watched them with perfect equanimity. "Oh, I doubt he's worried about that."

"Well, then." Eamon turned toward the alien. "Take us to your leader."

The alien came to him, his steps swift and graceful, and it seemed like it had been the wrong thing to say. His hand darted and grabbed Eamon's jaw.

David tensed, sliding his hand toward the gun in his belt.

The alien peered intently into Eamon's face for a minute, then let him go.

And turned to David. Every muscle in David's body stiffened, but he couldn't decide what he ought to do, and so he did nothing as the alien reached forward.

The alien's fingers pressed against his jaw, stronger and far colder than David would have guessed. But he forgot his surprise when his gaze met the alien's. The alien's eyes were a rusty color, orange fired with red, and they had an unnatural brightness, like metal heated to glowing. And staring at them, David felt that they were not looking at him, but into him.

A powerful uneasiness surged against the frontiers of his mind. Yet his thoughts could not seem to form properly, and he stood there, with no notion to do anything else.

The alien released him, and David blinked, suddenly bewildered. When he focused again, he saw the alien stepping away from Margaret, and felt he had missed something. David rubbed his jaw, trying to construct the last few minutes.

The alien spread his hands, speaking again, and when he finished, the three humans glanced at each other.

Then Eamon undertoned, "At least he doesn't sound angry."

David found no comfort in that.

The alien walked forward, and Margaret and Eamon hastily cleared out of his way. David stood his ground, out of a vague sense that, being in charge, he was obligated to meet certain things with firmness.

The alien passed him and ascended the stairs. He circled to one side of the doorway and pressed his hand against the stone column. With a heavy sliding and scraping, the whorling designs shifted. One that looked like a flowing river stood on its head and became a waterfall. A meaningless curve turned into an arc like the rising sun, and two lines that met in a mountain peak shifted into straight, solitary grooves.

Light beamed out from the carvings and burst in glory from the doorway. David turned away, afterimages blotting his vision.

"See how he controls it," Eamon marveled, a ring of awe in his voice.

David's thoughts flashed back to Moynihan, and he wondered where the doorway would lead now. A sick wave of apprehension and guilt broke over him again.

It drained away when the alien swept down from the blazing doorway, gestured to them, and pointed at the passage in the floor.

That, at least, was plain. "Come on," David said to Margaret and Eamon, and led the way toward the opening and its glow of light.

When he saw they were obeying, the alien turned and vanished down into the passage. David reached the opening next, and with one look at the narrow stairway, its end concealed in golden haze, he followed.

The rock walls crowded in on either side, so close David could not have stretched out his arms, and the ceiling brushed against his hair. The footsteps of his team rang behind him, drowning out the foot treads ahead.

He emerged out of the stairway into a bright room, its walls paneled with a metal he had never seen before. Its honey color and metallic gleam combined strangely in his eyes, and he couldn't even guess what substance made the hard, milky floor.

A tree grew up out of a pool of water and spread its green-robed arms on the other side of the room—exotically out of place, vitally alive. The alien knelt beneath the branches, drawing something out of the water. He stood up, a sort of transparent flask dripping in his hand, and walked over to them.

He offered the flask up to Eamon, who took it and remarked, "He's giving us a drink! At least that's hospitable and even kind of normal."

David watched him a moment. "You're not drinking it."

"It has green specks floating in it." But Eamon raised the flask to his mouth. "Well, bottoms up."

He threw back a gulp of the water, but the alien's voice rang out so sudden and so sharp that he spat it out.

With a shake of his head, the alien extended his hand, and Eamon gave back the flask. The alien's eyes moved to David, and then to Margaret. And he held out the flask to her.

Margaret accepted it and, securing it to her belt, passed over the conundrum of what to do with it by doing nothing.

The alien caught her right hand and turned it to display the drying wound in her palm. He jerked his head toward the injury and then looked at her.

Margaret met his eyes. "I don't understand."

For a moment, the alien studied her quietly. Then he held out his hand just above her head, like a priest giving a blessing.

And three thin, copper tendrils shot out of his palm.

Margaret gasped and scrambled away so fast she tripped and fell.

David yanked free his gun and trained it on the alien. "Stop!"

The alien turned to him, but his whole face was set in the unbroken composure he had shown since he first saw them. David could see no suggestion of fear in the burning eyes.

Probably he had no idea why a gun should be feared. David aimed at the water, calculating the angle least likely to cause a ricochet, and fired.

The gunshot clapped their ears—the sort of thing the blood responded to, even if the intellect did not. No human could have failed to feel the power, or the threat. But nothing disturbed the calm of the alien's face.

David flicked the gun back to him, his hand trembling with adrenaline, not fear. Even here, a stranger in an incomprehensible world, he had power. He could kill.

The alien, staring at him, lowered his hand, and the tendrils slithered back into his flesh.

Eamon cringed, and David felt the same. He looked at Margaret, who was standing again and dividing a wary gaze between him and the alien. "Be careful, David," she told him.

Caution, in David's worldview, involved wielding a gun. He fixed his sight on the alien and recalibrated his aim.

"Killiam?" Eamon half whispered.

"Yes?"

"We're not exactly in a position of strength here. We should make nice if we possibly can. And if we can't, it would be better to wait until we know where to run, and maybe how many of him there are."

David could not deny the logic of that. He forced his hand down and slid the gun back under his belt.

A low, powerful moaning passed through the ground and rattled the chamber. The walls, shining with metal, trembled, and then the floor began to shake violently, and Eamon threw himself down with a curse and covered his head with his arms. David considered following suit, and immediately lost the choice as the chamber heaved and knocked him down.

He raised himself up against the hard, cold floor, twitching wildly in the grip of pulverizing forces, and looked around for Margaret. But his eyes landed on the alien—still on his feet, somehow keeping his balance while the planet shuddered, and watching them.

XXVII

"You know, Congressman, I was surprised by your visit."

Manasseh Cruz had heard that at least half a dozen times this morning alone, and he had responded every time with some well-constructed nicety. But now it was time for a change. He cut around the officer in blue, throwing out as he passed, "That is a symptom of bureaucracy. Twenty-four hours' notice just isn't enough." He seated himself at the colonel's desk and glanced at the empty chair facing him.

The colonel spoke from behind him. "It's not convention to make an official visit with so little notice. Especially when you imply our funding is at stake."

"I know." Cruz put his feet up on the desk.

The colonel went around his desk and took the empty chair. Cruz watched him closely. This was Colonel Nelson, whom Jackson had told him was all right. Cruz had made Jackson recite everything he knew about the colonel, though he gleaned little from it, but now he had to act on trust.

Or, at least, on hope. "So, you run the base's Mars activities."

Nelson shrugged. "Such as they are, yes."

"Now that the mission is over, what do you still have to do?"

"We monitor the DSN for any transmissions." Nelson's lips thinned. "They might send one, you know. They haven't died yet."

"But what could they have to say?"

Nelson shrugged.

Cruz dug into his jacket's breast pocket and drew out a wrinkled piece of paper—his whole purpose for coming, for which the morning's bustle of meetings and reporters had been only a cover. "Colonel, as chairman of the Mars Appropriations Committee, I have one final inquiry to send to the Mars mission."

Nelson stretched out his hand to receive the paper. "I will send it for you."

Cruz gave it over, secretly glad the man asked no questions, then resumed his tone of friendliness mixed with presumptuous confidence. "You send it. But I would like to see you do it."

"Very well." Nelson tucked away the paper into a coat pocket. With all the gold buttons and fancy insignia and medals, it still managed to have some functionality.

Nelson rose and led him through hallways and up an elevator to a dreary room, comprised of six comm stations, dead except for one young man. He glanced over his shoulder when they entered, then started up from his chair. "Sir—" His hand flew up in a rigid salute.

Nelson's hand flicked up and down, a swift and precise salute. "Sit down, Lieutenant. You've got work to do."

The lieutenant resumed his seat, adjusting his mouthpiece. "What, sir?"

Nelson laid the paper down on his console. "Transmit this message to Mars."

The lieutenant began flicking switches with what struck Cruz as pathetic eagerness. Cruz looked around at the empty chairs, the black screens, the dingy walls, and the water-stained ceiling. "I've never been here before, Nelson. It's pitiful."

"Is that an official criticism, Congressman?"

"No, it's a commendation. You're plainly not wasting our nation's precious resources here." Yet he felt sorry for the lieutenant, stuck in this room with the atmosphere of a gloomy February day, having no company and nothing to do. He himself would be driven to acute depression.

"Sir," the lieutenant said, "do you want me to wait for the return signal?"

"Defer that till the end," answered Nelson. "The congressman hasn't got time."

"What haven't I got time for?" Cruz questioned as the lieutenant began hitting keys.

"To wait for the Mars habitat to confirm that it is receiving our transmission. It takes half an hour. Fifteen minutes for our signal to travel to Mars, and fifteen for their return signal to travel back. So we will send your message, Congressman, then query the habitat computer to ensure it received it."

The lieutenant flattened the paper and, looking at it, typed its words into his computer. Vulnerability tingled beneath Cruz's skin, and he wondered what either man would make of his inquiry, if they would catch a scent of the unusual doings surrounding these few minutes.

"Sent, sir," the lieutenant declared.

Nelson nodded, eyes on the screen. "I will tell you if Mars fails to confirm, Congressman. Or would you like to wait here for it?"

Cruz did not want to trust that Nelson really would tell him. But he wanted even less to arouse curiosity about his visit to Canaveral, and a half hour was too long to be undocumented. "I need to return to Washington, Colonel." He leaned over the lieutenant's shoulder to pluck up the piece of paper, on the theory that all evidence was best minimized. "Thank you."

He let himself out into the hall and began retracing the way to the elevators. His mission was finished. Now it was for Moynihan to decide its worth. What would the commander think to receive such a request after his own SOS had gone entirely unanswered? Would he be angry or confused? Worst of all, would he be hopeful?

Cruz began digging in his pockets for his long-gone cigarettes. Since he and Jackson had joined forces, they had not discussed the fate of the Mars team. He didn't know if Jackson had set aside the matter until they were finished with Karl or simply assumed it had already been settled in his favor. Cruz hadn't asked and would not ask. Jackson, if he cared so much, could raise the painful question.

And because he did care so much, he would.

Cruz reached the elevator and keyed it for the vehicle hangar, the answer he would give Jackson hanging in his thoughts like a dark cloud. He did not like it, but he could not argue against it. All the reasons he ever had for abandoning the Mars team still stood; the logic of it was beyond debate. His feelings could not set aside the clear rationality of cutting off the mission or the paramountcy of America's needs.

The elevator doors parted, and Cruz stepped out into a large, half-lit space that felt cool and smelled like oil. Ancient fluorescent lights mingled patches of severe light with shadows and revealed an array of vehicles in precise rows.

"Congressman!"

Cruz turned to see his aide hurrying toward him. "Where's the car, Flynn?"

Flynn stopped and pointed vaguely to his right, his hand clutching a notebook. "This way, sir." He scooted off in that direction, and Cruz followed. Flynn shifted his notebook from one hand to the other, cleared his throat, and said, "Sir, we have a problem. Lynx News just broke this story." He held out the notebook.

Cruz took it and glanced over the screen. A headline glared out at him: DONEGAN MOYNIHAN, MARS COMMANDER, DECLARED DEAD.

His heart hitched, but he bestowed a cool look on Flynn. "Did my name come up?"

"Yes. They're reporting that you did it."

"Declared him dead?"

"Declared him dead, had him declared dead." Flynn waved his hands. "Does it matter?"

"In a more rational world, it would." Cruz handed back the notebook and quickened his strides.

Flynn rushed to catch up. "Sir, Tori called me. The office is being flooded with inquiries about this story that she can't answer. And it's spreading by the second. We need to say something."

Cruz listened to the earnest conviction in his voice and reflected on how widely he had missed the mark.

Ahead, headlights lit up between two military jeeps, and Cruz recognized his car. A security man got out of the front passenger seat and opened one of the sleek black doors.

Cruz gave the man a nod as he reached the car, but he lingered a moment by the open door, turning back toward his aide. "Do you trust me, Flynn?"

Flynn blinked two or three times in the dim light. "Of course, sir."

"Let's hope everybody does." Cruz turned from him, ducking into the car.

"Thank you for allowing me to come by so late, Congressman Cruz."

"It's only late for normal people. You and I, we're not even late for dinner yet."

"All too true." Jep Baines settled himself in the chair and raised his eyebrows inquiringly. "Hard day, Congressman?"

"Why do you ask?"

"You got implicated in a delicious bit of government shenanigans. That is usually a hard day, for a politician."

"Implicated? Such a nice, rounded word. No edges, sharp or hard."

"All right, Congressman." Baines shifted forward. "You've been accused, and you're looking awfully guilty."

"Silence is incriminating."

"And yet you stay silent."

"I know better than to rush into a lie—or the truth." Cruz looked directly into the chief of staff's keen gaze. "I did it, Baines, as you already know. It was entirely legal, the valid ruling of a valid court. But you know that, too."

"I'm sorry to say I do." Baines let his eyes roam to the wall, to the procession of photographs that displayed the glorious march of Cruz's career, every picture worth a thousand words. "But I do wonder, Congressman. Why did you do it?"

"Because they let you see a man's private records a lot easier when he's dead."

Baines continued to stare at the photographs, but suddenly his eyes seemed less focused on them. He sighed and looked at Cruz again. "And how are you going to explain that? Sometimes, when I look at this country, I don't see America, but it's still American enough to hate the idea of a government leader declaring a living man dead so that he can rifle through his records."

Cruz leaned so far forward he stooped across the desk. "Know what the American people cotton to even less?"

Baines mimicked Cruz's conspiratorial tone back to him. "Tell me."

Cruz almost whispered: "A secret court." He watched a flicker pass over Baines's eyes and sat back.

"You reach the heart of the matter." Baines laid his hand on the desk and straightened. "Congressman, I am here to appeal to you on behalf of the president not to reveal the existence of the court. I appeal to your patriotism. I appeal to your respect for the office of the presidency. I even appeal to your party loyalty, if that will help."

"How are you going to appeal to my self-interest?"

"By pointing out to you that although the executive branch set up the Sub Rosa Court, Congress validated it in return for the right to use it. If you expose the court, all of Washington will be caught in the fallout. And they will never forgive you."

"Yet it would be the greatest diversion tactic ever. And you know something, Baines? My constituents don't live in Washington." Cruz swiveled his chair to face the windows behind him, black with night.

"I won't argue. But you're a patriot, Congressman. For the sake of the country, do not expose the court."

"It might be good for the country, you know. The Sub Rosa Court was never a good idea."

"A useful idea, though. You know that. You used it."

Cruz swiveled back. "Have you? Has the president?"

"That's beyond the scope of this discussion."

A sarcastic line stuck in Cruz's throat. He appraised Baines, sitting as the president's emissary, and he wondered how seriously they feared the spilling of this secret. "Give me your best reason that I should stay quiet."

Baines was silent long enough for Cruz to notice the dark rings beneath his eyes. Then he raised his gaze. "America is already damaged enough."

That was all too true. Cruz briefly closed his eyes, trying to measure the consequences of precipitously unveiling the secret court.

"Congressman, the Sub Rosa Court is bound to abolition sooner or later. It will be best if it is done quietly. The president would like to work with Congress to that end. But now is not the time for a public spectacle. The president is trying to restore America's credibility in the world. They can't trust our money, and they can't trust our debts, and if our secret court is outed—well, that will be another thing they can't trust. More crucially, the president is trying to restore the hope of the American people for our future, their faith in our American experiment. Don't work against him."

"If the truth works against him, maybe the faith isn't deserved."

"Maybe. But when it's undeserved, then it is needed. We expect people to believe in us when we succeed. It's only natural. When we fail, and it is unnatural to believe, we need someone to do so."

Cruz had to look away. His greatest failure, messy and ignoble in every way, was about to be uncovered, and the faith others had once given him would vanish like steam. But what a thing it would be if someone could see his failure and believe in him anyway.

"Congressman, I know what I'm asking from you. I'm asking you to bury your best weapon. I'm asking you to take the heat alone when we both know that, if the public wants to be outraged by shenanigans with the courts, a lot of people should be burning alongside you. But the country needs it."

Cruz was unable to speak for a dawning dread that the chief of staff could be right.

Baines watched him carefully. "Do you want to see the president?"

"No." He needed no more presidential entanglement in the decisions he had to make. For his sake, and possibly even the president's.

"Then, if there is nothing further to be said . . ." Baines waited a moment, and when Cruz said nothing, he rose from his chair. "Good night, Congressman."

Cruz watched him walk all the way to the door before he spoke up. "You never asked what I wanted with Moynihan's records."

Baines turned. "I always trust you have your reasons."

Cruz read plainly his desire not to be involved any further, but he went on anyway. "Well, I'm generous. So I'll give you the reasons anyway. I know that Karl has a vendetta against Moynihan, and he has been conspiring against him for years. It was Karl who leaked the declaration of Moynihan's death to the media. He has a vendetta against me, too. And to prove all this, I will offer a prediction. When it happens, believe that I am right about everything else."

Baines remained by the door, his hand on the knob. "What is your prediction?"

"Within the next few days, the story will go out that I am secretly an alcoholic, that I've led a double life since the day I entered politics—a public life of power and a private life of addiction. Karl will be responsible for that story, too. And like the first, it will be true."

Baines studied him, his eyes intense and searching. Then, wordlessly, he turned and disappeared out the door.

Cruz watched him go, listened to the door shut. That was what came of runaway drinking and shameful secrets, wasn't it?

He stood up from his desk and turned to face the wall behind him, to the photographs that flanked the windows. He had chosen each one with care, knowing exactly what it meant. The first was a photo of him, his parents, and his brothers and sisters in front of the house in which he had grown up—its paint peeling away, the broken front window and precariously hanging gutter easily discerned. And from that beginning, it soared upward.

Election Night pictures showed him in exuberant rallies. Bright lights and happy faces all around, moments of victory frozen in time and color. He saw his swearing-in—his wife, stylish and beautiful, holding the Bible while he swore on it his allegiance to the Constitution. An American flag hung behind them, its red and white stripes bold beneath the silver sheen of its stars. He saw himself with the last president at the signing ceremony for a bill he had coauthored and onstage with the current president before he was president. In one photo he stood with a ranking senator; in another he sat with the House leaders at a State of the Union address . . .

A bittersweetness filled his throat, because everything he saw was true, and behind the glossy pictures was another truth. That hidden nook of his life, filled with the blackest shadows—no less real than the glory he broadcasted to the world.

And when, very soon now, light flooded it, the world would know.

Cruz turned from the wall of pictures that everyone who came to him saw. Leaning on the back of his chair, he stared at the pictures that, propped on his desk, faced him always and him alone. His wife and children smiled at him from the photos, and he felt far away from the happiness in their eyes.

He bowed his head beneath the weight of his longing and his distance, finding it almost more than he could bear.

XXVIII

When the floor stilled at last, Margaret got up cautiously. She looked at David and Eamon, climbing to their feet with a dour air, and then at the alien. He scrutinized them as if trying to understand these ungainly creatures who flopped across his floor. Margaret clasped her hands behind her back, self-conscious beneath the alien's study.

"Can you believe," Eamon said, "that we left an earthquake and an erupting volcano to land in another earthquake and another erupting volcano?"

"Eamon"—David's tone was contradictory—"we don't know where that thing sent us. We could just be in another part of the city. This might be the same earthquake and the same eruption."

An unintelligible command from the alien drew their focus back to him. He stood pointing at the stairs, a definite look on his face.

"Apparently he doesn't want us down here any longer. Let's be good guests and oblige him." David led the way, striding toward the stairs, and he did not seem to mind the departure in the least.

Eamon immediately followed, but then the men halted just after emerging into the chamber above, and Margaret had to skirt around them. Then she saw the spheres suspended in the air, their red raised to scarlet by the radiance of the light doorway.

The alien's footsteps sounded on the stairway behind them, and Eamon and David parted to make way for him. He walked between them and, stopping, beckoned.

An orb swooped down to him and hovered ready, putting Margaret oddly in mind of a dog obedient to its master. The alien lifted his hand to the orb, and the copper tendrils shot from his palm and anchored in the crystal sphere.

Eamon edged closer. Margaret felt a little curiosity mixed with her instinct to recoil. David, on the other hand, looked only appalled.

The tendrils pulled out of the orb and sank back into the alien's flesh. The orb flashed with a bright light. And, reflecting it as exactly as a mirror, all the other spheres flashed, too.

Eamon stepped back.

In perfect concert, the spheres swept down and closed in around them. The alien spoke, gesturing to them and then to the orbs.

"He's handing us over." Margaret spoke to David and Eamon, but she looked at the alien's tranquil, inscrutable face.

David laid his hand on the butt of his gun. "It's all right. We'll have more space away from him." He looked at the one orb that hung a little apart from the others, seeming to seek direction from it.

The orb provided it. It coasted away from them, toward the other side of the chamber, and David went after it. When Margaret and Eamon followed, the rest of the spheres flowed along with them.

As she walked, Margaret perceived a large circle subtly different from the rest of the floor. There, the gray of the stone was tinged with suggestions of yellow, blue, and green. The familiarity quickened her blood and empowered her with an understanding of what would happen next.

All three stepped into the circle, with the spheres levitating at their shoulders. Then, just as Margaret expected, rays of green, yellow, and blue light burst from the floor. The white light followed like a tidal wave, sweeping them off.

When it ebbed away, Margaret found herself standing in cold, open air. She watched the light fade back into the stone beneath her feet, then lifted her eyes.

And her heart jolted. They stood again at the feet of the four converging stairways, but this time each step of the high flights was covered with aliens. A staggering impression of unearthliness swept over her, and she could hardly pick out any details of their foreignness, could hardly see the leaves for the forest.

The aliens were all silent and motionless, their faces raised upward. Margaret looked up, too, into a sickly yellow twilight. The air, though cold, felt heavy, and oppressive, and fine ash wafted down through it. A gray coating already clung to the platform, spread across the stairs, and besmeared the unmoving aliens.

And she smelled sulfur. Burning. Destruction. And another bitter, bitter scent she could not identify.

Margaret turned toward the buildings she had last seen wreathed in lava. She saw dark, boiling clouds now, and a great crimson stain spilling over the roofs and the animate, foreboding darkness.

The city groaned and trembled. She braced herself, but the aliens perched on the stairs were frozen like statues. The stairways swayed, yet they stared above unwaveringly.

Margaret looked up again into the unnatural twilight. Was something going to come out of it?

"It's like Judgment Day," David said, a fearful reverence in his voice.

Eamon squinted in the strange light. "That can't be what they're waiting for."

"For all we know," David returned, "they're not waiting for anything." He glanced at the orbs, floating sentries around them. "Why did he send us here? And why does he get to hide from this?"

Eamon coughed and, gripping a tear in his jumpsuit, ripped off a shred of fabric. He covered his mouth and nose and began to turn in a slow circle, eyes darting over everything.

David tore a strip of cloth from his own left sleeve and cast a look at Margaret. "Not a bad idea, Meg."

Although she heard, she wasn't listening. Her mind was stretching back through memories, to the moment they'd first spied the decaying alien city, and gathering images, thoughts, flying impressions.

And she understood. "It's not Judgment Day." She faced the men, whose faces were pale, where they were not bloody or dirty. "It's the apocalypse," she told them. "The doorway took us through thousands and thousands of years of time to the aliens' apocalypse. We saw the dead city. This is the city dying."

Eamon's hand, grasping his makeshift handkerchief, fell. He stared at the aliens thronging in the heart of their city. A speck of ash drifted down into his eye, and even as he blinked jerkily, he stayed intent on the sight before him.

"But why?" asked David. "Why does the doorway lead here?"

His question hung with the ash in the sulfurous air. A sphere broke out of its formation, curved around them, and then flew toward the nearest stairway.

It was probably a hint. But Margaret felt no desire to join the aliens in their vigil, and the men didn't move, either.

One of the spheres emitted a short string of notes, too brisk to be musical, and at last one of the aliens took notice of them. She stepped off the bottommost stair and came toward them, her violet eyes piercing the shrouded twilight more brightly than a cat's.

She stopped in front of them and gestured, speaking meaningless syllables.

David sighed.

"Do we suppose," Eamon remarked, "that if we just stand here looking dumb, she'll know we can't understand?"

The alien crooked her finger, and an orb flew over to her. She stretched out her hand, and the tendrils shot out and sank into the orb. In another moment, they drew back into her palm, and she looked at the humans.

"She read it," said Eamon in a low voice.

The alien pointed to the stairway on their left, and swept to it across the platform, her movements lithe and graceful.

The orbs leaned in closer. David considered them a moment, and then the assembly of aliens, hundreds strong. With a final look at the black-and-crimson sky in the distance, he followed the alien, and Margaret and Eamon followed him.

The aliens opened a space for them on the last stair, and just as Margaret stepped onto it, she felt a powerful vibration in the air. The wind kicked up, and a deep shade fell over them, darkening the twilight almost to night.

Margaret raised her head, her hair whipping into her eyes, and saw a massive shape bearing down on them. It stopped, hovered, and she felt power thrumming from it.

Four lights blazed into existence on it, and stairways spiraled down out of them. One touched the head of each stone flight of steps, and the aliens began to ascend the hanging stairways.

Margaret watched the figures, small and distinct in the patches of bright light, vanish into the bowels of the ship. For that she now knew it to be: a ship to carry them all away.

"It's an evacuation," David realized.

"Yes," agreed Eamon. "And guys—we're in it."

The aliens near them began moving upward as the highest stairs emptied. Margaret walked up three steps and then had to stop again.

Eamon joined her. "That ship could take us anywhere in the universe. Even out of this galaxy. There's a reason we never made contact with these aliens." He began to talk faster, excitement rising in his voice. "We'll be the first human beings ever to leave our solar system, ever to interact with another species. We're going into a world—who knows how many worlds?—that nobody has ever dreamed of."

They moved up another couple steps, and Margaret's mind whirled after Eamon's and found a different landfall. "But what about *our* world? If we go up in that ship, we'll likely never get back to our time, or to Earth, or our own species—"

"Or Moynihan."

Margaret looked back at David, but away from the ship's lights, she could see nothing. "You want to go back for the commander?"

"I don't know!" David's voice rose with the wind, a desperate note clinging to it.

The aliens started moving again. Margaret held back her hair with one hand and lifted her face to the wind. She saw the ship swallowing up the yellow twilight, powerful enough to destroy them and even to save them. It would take them far away, cut them off from everything they had ever known, but they would be safe. And Moynihan . . .

Margaret closed her eyes, letting thoughts of him fill her heart for a moment, and when she opened her eyes, she felt conviction and with it, peace. "I know. We need to go back."

"He's probably already dead, Meg. And even if he isn't, wouldn't he want his team to grab this chance?" Eamon gestured upward. "Let's just go. Isn't this the miracle we've been waiting for?"

"A miracle shouldn't cost this." Margaret's eyes went to David, appealing to him. "David, we must go back for him. Everybody on Earth abandoned us, but let's not abandon each other. We four are all each of us has. Let's not fail each other."

David's face was hidden in the deep shadows, but after a moment, he said, "All right, Meg. We'll go. Eamon, you can come if you want to. If you don't, then leave Mars with the aliens. Even I won't blame you." David abruptly turned and went swiftly down the few steps they had climbed.

Margaret went down, too, but nothing happened as they stood on the platform. Then the red orbs came gliding out of the gloom, glowing like hot embers.

She dropped to her knees and, pressing her hands on the stone, willed it to work.

It didn't.

A cadence of footsteps on the stairs drew her eyes up. Aliens were flowing toward them down the stairway they had just left. Eamon stood in the aliens' path—a larger, darker figure.

He leapt down to the platform, landing with force she could feel through the stone. Stepping over, Eamon stooped down, caught her elbow, and drew her to her feet.

Margaret rounded on him, a demand on her lips, but it withered when she saw, in his right hand, a blaster reflecting the orbs' red light. At the edge of her awareness, she sensed David lunge at them.

But it didn't matter. Eamon owned the moment. He twisted the blaster, and with it pointed at the ground, he fired.

A burning bolt struck the platform, and a second flew after it. Light sparked in the stone, raced in the shallow grooves of its patterns, and then exploded.

When Margaret could finally blink the light away, she stood in the chamber with the light doorway. "We're back."

Her eyes shifted as she spoke and saw the men frozen in a fight. David—with one arm locked across Eamon's chest and one hand seizing his hair—was well on the way to winning their incipient struggle. But, with a darting glance around the chamber, David released Eamon, pushing him away.

"Let's get out of here." David ran across the room, up the steps to the shining doorway, and stood, a gun drawn in his hand.

Whether for Eamon or for any other pursuit that might be coming, Margaret didn't know, and she had no time to care. She sprinted to join David. And so did Eamon, and though he could easily have outrun her, he didn't. Perhaps it was chivalry.

Or, with David waiting at the finish line and brandishing a gun, perhaps it was wisdom.

A slight scraping noise rose up from the passageway to the chamber below and signaled the coming of the alien. Margaret gained the steps and looked over her shoulder.

Light shot up like a geyser from the transporting circle. But before it dissolved into their pursuit, Margaret stepped up to the doorway. With David beside her, and Eamon right behind, she walked into the light, and it snatched her away.

XXIX

The house, viewed from across the street, beckoned with its lighted windows and white front door, illuminated by the golden wash of the porch light. Reuben wondered if it held any secrets.

He peered down at his notebook screen, finding it hard to read as night overtook the world. The message was almost cryptic in its brevity, simply inviting him to the address below to discuss "issues and actions." Reuben read the address again; he had already memorized it, so light or no light, it made no difference. Then he looked at the house across the street.

The porch light shone on the house's number, confirming it was the same given in the message. But he had already known that, too.

Reuben slipped the notebook into his jacket pocket, knowing he had all the information he was going to get. He needed now to decide. He thought the message was from Cruz. He hoped it was from Cruz. Two full days had passed since he'd last heard from the congressman, and he was anxious for any word. Every day dwindled his money and made his situation more urgent. When it grew desperate, he would have to abandon the cause of the Mars team to contend for his own survival. Until he did what he had to do, he would do what he could.

Which would be more if Cruz would talk to him. Besides, who except Cruz had any "issues" or "actions" to discuss with him?

Reuben treated that as rhetorical, ignoring a deep and murmuring suspicion, and crossed the street. He watched the windows, but nothing stirred as he walked to the front door and pressed the call button.

A woman opened the door. Somehow her clothing, though no kind of uniform, gave away her subordinate position in the household. "Yes?" she asked.

"Ma'am, my name is Reuben Jackson, and I am here to see Congressman Cruz."

"I was told you would be coming." Her voice was toneless, her expression closed. She stepped back, with an abbreviated gesture to follow her, and walked away from the door.

Reuben entered the house hastily, crossing a spacious foyer to join the woman by a large, carved door. "Go on in," she told him.

"Thank—"

She walked away.

Reuben tried to shrug her off, as well as his own disquiet, and went through the large door. He found a living room, wealthily furnished, but his eyes were attracted at once to the most enormous painting he had ever seen, covered with swirling clouds of blue, gray, and black.

"Good evening, Mr. Jackson."

Reuben jerked toward the voice, startled to discover that he wasn't alone. Dr. Karl sat in an easy chair pushed into the corner, looking up at him with dark, hooded eyes. "I wasn't sure you would come," the doctor said.

"I thought the message was from Cruz," answered Reuben, the words lame in his own ears. "I'm stupid that way."

"I had hoped you would. I figured it would make you more likely to come. But you should appreciate, Jackson, that Cruz is far too busy to plot with you these days. Didn't you notice? His life is falling apart."

Reuben had spent the whole day hiding from the newscasts parading Cruz's humiliation, from people chattering about his diminished power, his uncertain prospects, and how his drinking explained his wounded marriage, and perhaps a few other things. He had trouble being defiant about it now. "I suppose he has you to thank for that."

"That's exactly right. I'm glad you understand that already." Karl lifted a small, rectangular black thing—like a remote of some kind—and pressed on it.

A hologram sprang onto the cream-colored wall, and Reuben saw Manasseh Cruz gripping a lectern, staring darkly at something invisible to him. He recognized the image well enough: Cruz's press conference, which even he had not been able to entirely flee.

A disembodied voice floated into the room, carried through the hologram: *"Now that we know you've been hiding this, Congressman, why should we believe that you don't have more secrets?"*

For a moment, Cruz said nothing, his eyes still focused on something beyond the margins of the image. Every second ticked by with growing agony, until finally the congressman answered. *"If you want to believe that, I can't stop you. Negatives are always hard to prove. That's why our justice system puts the burden of proof on the accuser."*

"But the point is, how can people trust you, and how can you lead without trust?"

Cruz's mouth bent down a little, and displeasure shaded his eyes too plainly. He was all out of form—his poker face cracking, his appearance suggesting he had been up all night with too-hasty attempts to smooth over the effects. His eyes looked tired, and his hair, only raggedly in place, seemed to be in sullen rebellion.

"Whatever I have done in my private life," the congressman said, *"my public record still stands. I've kept my promises. I've done exactly what I said I would. My constituents know . . ."*

Even his tone was wrong. Too clipped, too impatient. Reuben turned away from the hologram, wishing he could block out Cruz's voice, too. "He's off his game," he told Karl, and the only excuse for it was that he needed something to distract himself.

Karl only watched him, while Cruz's voice droned on: *". . . personal struggles have not affected my governing . . ."*

Reuben threw a glance over his shoulder at the holographic congressman, almost as large as life and quite as painful. Every minute of the press conference had been an elaboration of embarrassment, and all of Cruz's testiness was only his futile thrashing against it.

Reuben turned back to Karl. "Turn it off, Doctor. Why do we need to see this?"

"Is it hard to watch?"

"Only if you've got a soul."

"Unfortunately for you and Cruz, Jackson, victories aren't made by ripostes. Answer my question, and I will, as you ask, turn it off. Who has lost more—him or you?"

The words grated on behind him: *". . . know me—"*

A new voice interrupted: *"Do they really know you, Congressman Cruz?"*

"They—" But Cruz fumbled the sentence.

Eager to bail, Reuben said, "He has lost more. A job is easier to replace than a reputation."

Karl squeezed his finger down on the remote, and the hologram snapped into nothingness. He tossed aside the remote, his eyes never moving from Reuben. "He can lose more, Jackson. So can you. But it doesn't have to be that way." Karl rose from his seat, putting his hand into his pocket, and walked toward Reuben.

Reuben stood his ground.

Karl drew his hand out and displayed two stiff, narrow slips of paper. "Take it."

He took them, reading the smaller and then the larger one. And then, to be sure of his eyes, he read each again.

"The plane leaves tonight," Karl said. "The job voucher will get you the highest job you can test for. I think you'll rate a nice, middling job."

Reuben shuffled the plane ticket behind the voucher, not even feeling the insult. He scrutinized the crisscrossing blue lines beneath the words, and they looked, to him, entirely authentic.

So he accepted it—a voucher, better than gold. Reuben looked up at Karl, his fingers tightening on it. "Are you trying to bribe me?"

"If that works. I'm threatening you, too, in case it doesn't. My threats and rewards are promises I always keep, Jackson. Ask any of the First Names."

Reuben pondered that. "I used to wonder how you always got your way. Except that you didn't, did you? You've lost a few times."

"Once or twice. And I've ensured that everyone regrets it more than I do." Karl nodded to the papers in Reuben's hands. "That's your passport out of this, Jackson. The plane ticket is for tonight. The voucher will expire in a few days. And it must be used in the employment center in the city listed on it. Remember that."

Reuben felt he ought to hand the ticket and voucher right back, but his fingers seemed frozen. So he fell back on words. "It's just an invitation to give up."

"You will have to give up eventually. You know that. The Mars team is almost beyond help, and you yourself are fast running out of time. You won't be able to worry about whether the Mars team can eat when you can't eat, either. I'm only making the retreat easy for you. Go think about it, Jackson. I'll learn what you decide in the morning."

Reuben obeyed the dismissal, moving off toward the door. Some part of his mind urged him to throw the ticket and the voucher on the floor and stalk out, but his muscles did not respond. Gold was hard to throw away.

"You will miss Manasseh Cruz at the airport," Karl called after him.

Reuben looked back. "What do you mean by that?"

"He's getting out of town, Jackson—flying out this very night. He needs to go back home and start picking up the pieces so he can reconstruct his life. You will probably miss him at the airport."

Reuben walked out, deciding he didn't owe Karl a reply. Out in the night, growing cold with the departure of the sun, he stuffed the voucher and ticket into his pocket and hurried away from Karl's house. He wandered down the dark streets, under the scattered streetlights that still functioned, and tried to decide which direction he ought to go.

XXX

The light faded, and David found himself again on the stone steps leading up to the doorway. Two aliens waited at the bottom of the steps—the male with the rust-colored eyes, the female with the violet eyes. A host of orbs hung behind them.

The male alien pointed, almost languidly, in their direction, and the orbs streamed through the air and surrounded them.

"How is it," Margaret said, "that we didn't go anywhere?"

Eamon answered, "Probably they manipulated the doorway to—"

The alien cut him off with a brief order, and the spheres pressed in until they forced David, Margaret, and Eamon off the steps to stand in front of the two aliens.

The female alien spoke, but not to them. David had the impression the aliens were done speaking to them; they were hardly looking at them now.

As the male alien replied, Eamon whispered, "How committed are you to going back for Moynihan, Killiam? You need to decide now."

David glanced down at the gun in his hand, and he sensed the spheres close in. One came up against his shoulder, hard and cold.

He looked up to see the male alien walking away toward the passageway in the floor, and he stepped forward. "Wait!"

The alien turned back and looked at him, and David holstered the gun. He spread his empty hands and approached the alien carefully. "You seem to be some sort of guardian of this doorway, and we need a favor. We need you to send us back to our own time."

"Killiam," Eamon hissed at his back, "what are you doing? He doesn't understand."

But the alien watched him steadily, and David went on. "We need to look for our commander." Commander—could that be translated into the alien's mind, and if it could, would it carry the importance David needed? "We need to look for our—our friend."

Was Moynihan a friend? David had never thought of him as one. Yet he believed now that given what he was about to do for Moynihan, he must be something near to a friend.

David stopped two feet from the alien. He held up his right hand and tapped three fingers against his palm. Then he raised his hand to his own forehead in imitation of how the alien had raised his hand above Margaret's head.

No understanding dawned on the alien's face, but neither did any confusion cloud it. So, David, in hope and partial dread, knelt before the alien.

The alien lifted his hand, and the skin of his palm quivered just before the tendrils burst out.

David closed his eyes, fighting down revulsion. He felt something like pinpricks—a cool sensation—and just as his nerves recoiled, it all fled away from him.

His consciousness was all at once submerged in grayness. Awareness lingered, in some abated form, and he felt suspended—unable to lose his waking self, unable to return to it. No real feelings, no solid thoughts existed in him, just that grayness that simply but truly was . . .

Suddenly sounds, colors, and physical sensations he could not sort out blurred together in his consciousness. Then he realized, with a certain dimness, that he was being pulled to his feet, that a strong grip pressured his arm and shoulder, and people talked beside him.

Finally he understood, like someone just waking up, that Eamon stood at his right, supporting him, and Margaret stood on the other side, calling his name.

David looked at his sister, then at Eamon. Then he noticed the alien, right in front of him with his tranquil face and keen eyes.

He rubbed his forehead, feeling rather vague. "Did he do it?"

"You bet, Killiam." Eamon began to draw away. "Are you all right?"

"Sure." David lowered his hand. His fingers were dirty, but it was the grime of his adventures. He saw no blood.

As Eamon moved back, the alien strode forward and passed them by. The orbs parted, then closed after him like a curtain, and he climbed the steps to the light doorway.

David could see him well, now higher than the orbs. The alien laid his hand on one of the columns, and a curved, shining line twisted in the stone. It alone moved, and then the alien withdrew his hand.

A wave seemed to roll through the light of the doorway, though its brightness neither increased nor decreased. The alien, haloed by that light, gestured, and the orbs divided into two crimson walls on each side of the stone steps. They formed an aisle, leading up to the doorway, and David stood in the center of it.

He looked down at Margaret, her skin ruby with the glow of the spheres. "Shall we try again?"

"I vote yes."

"I thought this was a dictatorship," Eamon said. "But if it's a democracy, I vote yes, too."

David led the way between the orbs, the whole makeshift corridor red with their light. He glanced at the alien, who stood to the side and made no sound or movement. Something in the subterranean of his mind stirred and settled again before he could grasp it—a memory, a recognition starting out of grayness and disappearing back into it.

He set his gaze ahead and walked into the light. It carried him in its current, deposited him on the same steps, and he, growing used to this, decided to just stand there until . . .

Someone walked into him, and David slipped, but he didn't fall. He skidded down the stairs and, hands stretched blindly, caught himself on cold, rough stone that nearly knocked the breath from his lungs.

"Whoops," said Eamon from above. "You okay, Killiam?"

David did not answer the question, feeling that it lacked sincerity, and he steadied himself, kicking away unseen shards that crunched beneath his boots. The haze had gone from his eyes, but the white radiance of the doorway left much to the shadows.

A wristlight beam shot from the stairs and swept the room, laying bare a shambles of splintered rocks and collapsed stone. Dirt was thick all over the place, and the air smelled of musty soil.

David looked to see what he had grabbed and found a slab of rock even huger than he had imagined, fully the size of a car. He raised his eyes upward, wondering how much more was where that had come from, but darkness concealed the roof.

"This looks right," Margaret said, lowering her wristlight.

"Great." Eamon came briskly down the steps. "Let's grab Moynihan and see if we can still catch that ride."

"There's the thing, Eamon." David turned on his own wristlight and raised its beam to the torn chamber. "Where is Moynihan?"

"Not here, evidently, though we should do a sweep to be sure. Then—well, where might he go from here?"

David's brain clicked rapidly along those lines, and it comforted him to confront a problem he could take charge of so easily. "Where could he? First, the—"

"Wait."

The men turned to Margaret. She descended the steps while they waited. "When I last saw him," she said, "he was around here, and he had just been looking at . . ." She scanned her wristlight over the floor, and its beam exposed a black, plunging emptiness.

"The stairs down into the lower chamber." She angled her wristlight and, without another word, entered the passageway in the floor, and the men hastened after her.

David found the stairs treacherous, littered with gray, broken debris and cracking under the weight of innumerable years. He stepped down cautiously, shining light on each stair and kicking out of his path rubbish too caked with dirt to confidently identify.

As he kept his eyes and his light fixed downward, he heard Margaret breathe in sharply and then rush ahead.

David made the last few steps with heedless rapidity and, on flat ground again, sought Margaret with the beam of his wristlight. She was kneeling—

His breath went cold in his throat. Margaret knelt beside Moynihan, who was curled awkwardly against a wall of metal tarnished to ruin. His face was obscured, buried in his bent arm. Patches of blood dried all over his clothing, but the stains looked light to David, and he didn't worry about them.

He worried about Moynihan's stillness. He sensed immediately its wrongness, that it was too perfect to be natural.

Eamon joined them with a clattering of stones, bumping against David and then freezing.

"Oh," he said, in the dead air of that dark place.

Margaret laid her fingers on the side of Moynihan's neck, and after a thick moment she pulled her hand away and sat back.

"Is he dead?" asked Eamon.

"No," Margaret answered. "But something is wrong. Lay him flat. I need to examine him."

David meant to comply, but Eamon pushed past him and got to it first.

"Gently," Margaret admonished as he began to move Moynihan. "David, keep your light steady over here."

He held it up and watched her. Margaret quickly unhooked the alien's flask from her belt and set it aside, against the wall. Then she unhooked her med kit and, springing it open, selected a med patch and her penlight.

"Meg," Eamon said, in such a tone that David and Margaret both instantly swiveled to him.

He had settled Moynihan on the ground, pulling back his arm, and now they could see that blood coated the left side of the commander's face and ran down onto his neck. All coming from an open wound in his forehead.

"Switch places," Margaret ordered the men, scooting to Moynihan's side.

Eamon stood and stepped back, and David moved into his place on Moynihan's other side. They had all been drilled in emergency medicine, back in that long-ago life of training in Cape Canaveral. But David had been chosen for special instruction, chosen to be Margaret's assistant and, should anything happen to her, the next best thing to a doctor they had. He had pitied, even then, anyone who would ever have to take him as a substitute for a doctor, and he doubted he could contribute much to Margaret's work now.

Yet he obeyed the training without a beat of hesitation. In the light that Eamon shone over them, David took a closer look at Moynihan. He was pale and unresponsive, and David felt that he was in some way absent.

Margaret, busy applying the med patch to the commander's neck, spoke over her shoulder. "Cut his sleeve over the elbow. Get his vitals."

David reached for the kit. It was a moment's work to slit the gray fabric, another moment to fasten the vitals cuff to Moynihan's wrist. He noticed Moynihan gripped his recorder in his hand.

With curiosity, and a faint sense of pathos, David gently pried away Moynihan's fingers and freed the recorder from his grasp. He lifted it to the white beam of light, trying to read the screen.

And he made out the words, gray in the paucity of light: TRANSMISSION CONFIGURED. READY FOR SENDING.

"Look, Meg," David said. "He was using this. After he was hurt and before . . ."

"Before he got so he won't even wake up," Eamon finished for him.

Margaret knew better than either of them what such a decline might mean, but she didn't bother with any commentary. She examined

Moynihan's head wound, not glancing up, and said, "Put a plasma patch on his arm, David."

David, pressed with the gravity of the commander's condition, still didn't move. He stared at those dim words, wondering what sort of transmission Moynihan had been preparing. Alone in this black chamber, injured and perhaps guessing how badly—whom had he been trying to reach, and what had he wanted to say?

And did David, for the decision he had to make, really need to know?

He moved his thumb over the TRANSMIT key, and it hovered there. Vestiges of his old suspicion drifted through his mind, his dark fancy that the commander had all along been in secret contact with someone on Earth . . .

"David."

There was an edge of warning to Margaret's voice, and David knew he had no more time to think about it. For reasons he could not distill in that moment, David sent the commander's transmission. Then, dropping the recorder into his pocket, he stretched for the kit again.

As he grabbed the plasma patch, the vitals cuff beeped. Margaret leaned over to scan the readings and shone the penlight into Moynihan's eyes.

David hurriedly peeled back the protective layer and affixed the patch to the commander's arm, right over the artery. He straightened a little, looking at Margaret and waiting for more orders.

She was checking Moynihan's ears, probably for blood. Moving with terse efficiency, she shone the light in his eyes again, stooping even closer.

Margaret curtly extinguished the penlight, but she sat back onto her heels slowly. She looked at David, and he poised himself to swoop for the bandages and sterilizing pads.

"He's dying," she said, in a clear voice that echoed off the walls, echoed in the darkness. "And there's nothing we can do about it."

XXXI

The jet idled at the end of the long runway, its silver lines gleaming under the huge, bright lights that flanked it on either side. The rest of the runway was left dark, and at the far edges, Reuben lurked in thick shadows. He had slipped past the Restricted Area signs to get within sight of the plane. It looked like Manasseh Cruz's private jet.

He couldn't be sure, though. This venture was beginning to remind him of his unwitting visit to Dr. Karl, and part of him wanted to slink back to those areas of the airport where he could not be arrested for trespassing. But his bolder, more reckless self was ascendant, strong with desperation. He continued on in the shadows, across the long span of runway.

When he finally walked into the light, his heartbeat picked up. He saw no one else on the runway, but as he approached the jet, two men stepped out onto the air stairs. They descended rapidly with a clatter of footsteps.

The men came arrow-straight toward him, and Reuben quickened his step to meet them. He held up both hands in an attitude of concession and said, "Take me to your boss."

The men exchanged a look. "If you want to see our boss," one of them said, "spread your arms."

Reuben obeyed, and the man frisked him. Then, with a nod to his partner, he led them back to the jet. The second man trailed behind Reuben the whole way up the air stairs, into the plane, and finally to a door marked with platinum letters.

A brisk knock on the door, a muffled answer from within, and the man walked in. "Sir, we found a man out on the runway. He says he wants to see you. Have you got time for him?"

Reuben, his view blocked by the man's back, could not see the man he spoke to inside the room, but he heard the answering voice very clearly: "That depends on who he is."

He smiled to himself as the man stepped to the side and revealed Manasseh Cruz. The congressman sat on a short, black leather couch, one arm draped on the couch's back and his legs stretched out in front of him. His face registered no response to the sight of Reuben, and he said, "Glad you made it. Sit down."

Reuben took another abbreviated couch, perpendicular to Cruz's, and the other two men withdrew.

The brimming concerns that had driven Reuben to this place went suddenly mute as he looked at Cruz. The congressman appeared more tired in person, and in his flesh-and-blood presence Reuben sensed a wornness more elemental than the hologram could convey.

"So," Cruz said. "How was your day?"

"Not so good." Reuben paused. He couldn't gauge Cruz's mood, but added anyway, "Of course, it was better than yours."

"That's nothing to brag about, Jackson. Why, the day I've had is enough to drive a man to drink."

"That's not very funny."

"Funny," Cruz repeated, but with an odd distance, and he wasn't looking at Reuben. "Would it be funny if I said I converted back to Catholicism and it got out of hand? I'm thinking of using that joke when I get back home."

"I think that would be in poor taste."

"Yes," the congressman agreed easily. "But that isn't the question. Would it be funny—not flippant, you know, but appropriately self-deprecating?"

Reuben tried to figure out why they were talking about this.

"Ah well. I'll think of something to say. I always do. Glibness is a great gift, especially for a politician."

Reuben decided it was time to change the subject to something relevant and asked, "So you are going back?"

"Of course. I have a lot of rebuilding to do."

"I know how important that is, Congressman. But how urgent is it?"

Cruz's eyes went past Reuben but didn't seem to see anything. "My wife and I talked today. She made it very clear that I need to come home, be a man, and get to work putting this right with our children. My wife is a patient woman, Jackson; I know because I've tested her patience before. But I am afraid not to go home."

"I appreciate that you have troubles, Congressman. I'm sorry that you have troubles. But . . ." Reuben hesitated for a second at what was boiling up inside him.

Then it overflowed. "But I have troubles, too, Cruz. Look at this." Reuben yanked the plane ticket and voucher from his pocket and rattled them in the air. "Karl tried to talk me into a Faustian bargain, and I'm not even sure it didn't work. I'm out of work and heading straight to the exchange lines and squatter buildings. I don't have time to wait to do what needs to be done. The Mars team doesn't have time to wait. Our window to save them is slamming shut, and if we don't seize it, they're going to starve on that worthless planet. *That's* trouble. So, I believe, Cruz, that you should delay your rebuilding back home to destroy Karl right here."

"Oh, well said, NASA Man. As extemporaneous speeches go, that was very good. It doesn't change my mind, though. I will be back home tomorrow. But tonight we can go hunting."

Reuben caught a glint in his eyes, and though the congressman was still to him a half-solved enigma, he understood it well enough. "What do you have in mind?"

Cruz smiled. "I got a message from Colonel Nelson just in the past hour. The Deep Space Network intercepted a transmission from Mars—a complex one, with images and audio recordings and even some footage."

A tingle washed over Reuben's body. "Moynihan answered us."

"So it appears. Nelson said I should receive a copy tonight, but I just don't trust Karl. So we will go and get it, you and I."

"Go where?" Reuben asked warily.

"To Karl's office, of course."

Reuben supposed he had a way of getting in, and he equally supposed it was ethically challenged. "This is going to involve committing a crime, isn't it?"

"Is it a crime," Cruz proposed, "to enter a colleague's office without permission? Some overeager people might construe it as one, but I call it a quick visit to pick up some papers he meant to give me. As chairman of the Mars Appropriations Committee, I have a right to that transmission, and no one can deny it. But the question will probably never come up. Likely no one will see us there, and even if they do, they're used to both of us going into Karl's office."

Reuben just looked at Cruz, the easy picture he painted clashing with the dire scenarios Reuben's own imagination cooked up.

Then he laughed. "Congressman, I know I am being snowed by a politician, and yet I let myself be."

"How very American of you." Cruz stood up. "Let's get moving, Jackson. The night's wasting."

The dim light of the hallway spread little illumination into the reception area, and that nearly faded before it reached the heavy door. But Manasseh Cruz did not, for his present business, want much light. He slid the master key into the door's slot and hoped the unsanctioned programming would hold.

Jackson shifted closer and whispered, "Isn't this how Watergate started?"

"Bite your tongue." A *click* sounded, and Cruz pulled out the key. Then he pushed at the door, and when it opened, they slipped quickly inside.

Cruz reached blindly, found the light, braced for the sting of its sudden brightness, and turned to survey Karl's office.

Jackson was already ambling toward the large, polished desk. A strange noise like sizzling hissed in the quiet room, and at the same moment Jackson recoiled, stumbling backward and reaching groping hands toward his face.

Cruz eyed where he had just been and saw nothing at all—only empty air and bare carpet. Then he focused on Reuben and detected a slight clumsiness to his movements.

He moved swiftly forward and grabbed Reuben's shoulder to keep him stationary. "What's wrong?"

"I don't know," Jackson mumbled, rubbing his face. "I didn't see anything, but I felt like I hit something, and then I got this jolt . . ."

Cruz nodded, more to himself than to Reuben. "Must be a force-shield." He dragged Reuben back a few steps and then let him go. "Don't walk into it again."

"Thanks," Jackson answered, the sarcasm in his voice assuring Cruz of his recovery. He turned and looked toward the desk. To all appearances nothing stood between them and it except clear, empty space. "A force-shield? I didn't know those had gotten beyond the military."

"Other parts of the government have begun using them for security. I guess Karl got himself on the list. I'm impressed."

"You're also blocked from getting that transmission. I can't believe Karl set up a force-shield in front of his desk. What a paranoiac."

Cruz looked sideways at him. "You realize, don't you, that the only reason we're not ransacking his desk is because he set up a force-shield?"

"Even paranoiacs have real enemies." Jackson gestured toward the invisible force-shield. "Do you know how to get past that?"

"No. But we can think around this. This office is not the source of the transmission, you know. It comes here from somewhere else."

"Cape Canaveral."

"Yes," Cruz said, hearing the irritated note in his voice. "But to think—"

At their backs, the electronic lock beeped. Cruz lunged for the light, vaguely noticing that Jackson dove in the opposite direction.

His fingers brushed the switch, and as darkness plunged, he made for the easy chair in the corner. He knocked against it, scrambled to the far side, and dropped down between the chair and the wall.

With a gentle *whoosh*, the door opened.

Cruz froze, bracing for the exposing light. But the blackness remained, and after a moment he discerned footsteps falling softly on the floor.

Far too softly, really, to be Karl's.

Cruz eased himself deeper into his hiding place, but he peered out at the room even as he did so. Curiosity had displaced some of his fear. He wanted to know who the interloper was.

A few noises, faint and indistinct, whispered in the silence. Then the force-shield became visible for one moment, shining blue and highlighting a dark shape in front of it.

The blue light died with a small hum, and Cruz blinked at afterimages. But he had already seen that the shape was a woman's.

More footsteps, and he knew she had brought down the force-shield and was walking to the desk. A *creak*, a *click*, and the desk lamp flared to life. Its light shone gently on a woman seated in front of the computer. Her face was turned away, veiled with a sweep of blond hair, painted silver by the light. Cruz heard her fingers tapping on the keys—a swift cadence, with the very beat of efficiency.

She raised her head, looking quickly over the room, and Cruz saw her face.

Willow.

He slid back, as close to the wall as he could get, and watched Willow turn back to the computer. A few minutes crawled by, then Willow stood and flicked off the light. Cruz heard, a moment later, the force-shield power back up, and his disappointment at that was allayed by his relief when she walked out the door.

He gripped the side of the easy chair and leveraged himself stiffly to his feet. His knee cracked painfully—a reminder, periodically given him, that his fortieth birthday was behind him.

"Cruz!" Jackson's voice carried, an unrestrained whisper. "I nearly got up and declared myself!"

"Is that so," Cruz said, heading for the door in the dark. "Thanks for not being an idiot."

"She's the whistleblower."

"You're just saying that because she's pretty." Cruz found the door, and he paused, letting Willow get farther away.

"Cruz, I can list to you ten good reasons why she is the whistleblower."

"And I can list ten good reasons why she is really in with Karl to the bottom of this. You believe your list because of hormones."

Reuben's answer came through gritted teeth. "Look, Congressman . . ."

"Jackson," Cruz interrupted, "I don't mind if you tell me off, but let's get out of here first." He opened the door a couple inches and listened. There were no sounds in the room behind him except Jackson's breathing, and in the dead stillness, he heard nothing at all beyond the door.

Cruz edged out, watching over his shoulder to see Jackson follow him and close the door after them. Exhaling the tension of their trespass of Karl's office, he looked ahead.

And froze in his tracks. Willow blocked his path, her arms crossed over her chest.

Reuben approached her. "We were, uh, trying to pick up some documents from Dr. Karl."

Willow raised her fine eyebrows. "Then come, gentlemen."

She retraced her steps back into Karl's office. The light sprang up, beckoning them on.

Reuben looked at Cruz, shrugged, and hurried after her. With a shake of his head, Cruz entered the office again.

He arrived just in time to see the force-shield flicker off. Willow circled around the desk and surveyed the men. "Now, what do you need?"

Cruz sensed the jest underlying her words, but he did not know what the joke was and regarded her warily.

Jackson smiled at her slowly—a smile that irritated Cruz, and then alarmed him. Before he could intervene, Jackson said, "You are the whistleblower."

Willow's green eyes almost seemed to glitter beneath the light as she fixed them solely on him. "I am, Mr. Jackson. And I'd hoped you would do more with what I gave you."

"Maybe we have done more."

Cruz perceived the tenor of subdued eagerness in Jackson's voice. "Jackson—"

Jackson talked over him. "Mars sent us a transmission, Willow. We came here to get it from Karl—unchanged."

Cruz gritted his teeth, holding back a tongue-lashing.

"Dr. Karl doesn't have the transmission. Are you sure it was sent?"

Worried that Reuben would out Colonel Nelson as their source, Cruz interjected, "Are you sure Karl hasn't got it?"

Jackson frowned at him. "She said he hasn't. What kind of proof do you need?"

"Hard," Cruz shot back, more for Jackson's benefit than Willow's.

"Very well, Congressman." Willow leaned over to Karl's computer, and her fingers sped over its screen. Cruz recognized the government's communication system before the shifting images stilled on one bland icon imposed over a background of solid green. "This contact," Willow said, "is labeled 'Local Source.' Do you know what that means?"

"A local call," said Reuben. "Data hidden by privacy shields."

Willow tapped the icon, and a scroll of data displaced it on the screen. "This log goes back four years; the 'Local Source' has been sending regular, if infrequent, messages for that long. All the dates correspond exactly to when new Mars transmissions were received in Washington. The last date, you'll notice, is when Mars broadcasted its SOS. The 'Local Source' sent two messages on that day."

Jackson leaned closer. "The real and the forgery?" Then he pointed. "Look, there were two on that day, too!"

Cruz raised his hand. "Wait." He stared at the screen to let the truth fly to the fullness of its meaning, and they waited for him. "This 'Local Source' is somewhere in the city. So we track him down and get the transmission from him, and maybe a lot more."

"Him?" Willow echoed. "What sort of *him* could get messages from Mars for four years, invisible to everyone and completely silent? I think it's a *what*, not a *who*."

"A *what* couldn't doctor the messages," Cruz pointed out, but a doubt nagged at him. He couldn't imagine, any more than Willow could, an unknown person secretly passing on the Mars transmissions all these years.

"Look," Reuben said. "These messages from Mars are classified military communiqués, and NASA has been sending them to the 'Local Source' since the beginning of the mission. Who finagles a privilege like that? The 'Local Source' is probably an office in some government agency, some bureaucratic . . ." His voice dwindled, and he left the sentence dangling. Then he slammed his hand down on the desk. "The old offices!"

"What are you talking about?" asked Cruz.

Jackson gestured emphatically. "You know the structure of the Mars venture. NASA carried it out, Congress had a funding veto on everything, and the First Names ran it. We never even knew what branch of government they belonged to. You know what an unholy mess it was. You manipulated it all the way from Capitol Hill to the White House."

Cruz gave a brief nod. Those were all unvarnished facts.

"Remember the interbranch office they set up to help smooth it out? We had people from Congress, NASA, the White House, and the First Names all working the Mars issue together. After the Great Collapse, you insisted that we shut it down."

It began to take nebulous shape in his memory, and even without exactly remembering victory, Cruz was certain of it. "And it was."

Jackson regarded him. "It wasn't. While we were arguing about it, the Hungry March fell on Washington. Those offices were in one of the neighborhoods the Marchers tore apart. The workers all fled. They never went back. Neither did anyone else. But the interbranch office was never officially shut down."

Cruz rummaged in his memories and recalled going over lists of damaged and destroyed federal buildings with colleagues—funding restoration with private selectivity, leaving as rubble what they wanted to see gone . . .

He thrust the memory away. "If the shutdown was never worked through official channels, then no one ever went to the abandoned offices to collect the computers or anything else."

"And no one ever told NASA to scratch the offices off their distribution list, either." Jackson rubbed his hands together. "Well, let's go."

"Tonight?" Willow asked, her tone like ice water on his excitement.

Cruz glanced at her. "Tonight is all I have."

She slid her finger over the screen, closing everything. "The offices aren't actually abandoned. Someone is secretly active there; meddling might be dangerous. Even worse, all those neighborhoods the Hungry March ruined are now squatter districts, and you know that with whatever happens in a squatter district, you are on your own until daylight."

Cruz knew. "That will just make things interesting."

XXXII

David sat with his back against the metal wall. Margaret sat only a few feet away, keeping vigil by Moynihan.

The commander lay still, unresponsive to everything, unable to return to consciousness. David heard his breathing, a low rasp that sounded as if it should hurt. But Margaret had said he was beyond pain.

David looked at his sister. She had her medical kit set out by her right hand, and he had watched her bandage the commander's wound and administer medicine to him out of sheer principle. But she was as motionless as a statue now, gazing at Moynihan with what David could only understand as sadness.

He wondered what she was thinking, what she was mourning. Was it regret for a death like this, or grief all and only for Moynihan?

A tremor passed through the wall, vibrating gently against his back. It was so faint David wondered if the others had felt it, but he didn't ask. It didn't matter. Despite the volcano and the earthquake and Mars itself, they would go on waiting.

He leaned his head back against the wall, impossibly trying to calculate how long it had been since he slept, wondering if he would ever truly, deeply sleep again.

Boots heavily scuffed the floor beside him, and he did not need to look to know Eamon now towered over him. "Get up, Killiam," the engineer said. "There's something I need to show you."

David felt little impetus to go, but even less desire to stay, so he pushed himself up from his hard resting place. "We'll be a minute, Meg."

She barely nodded.

They circled around her and Moynihan somewhat gingerly, then mounted the stairs. When they emerged into the upper chamber, David faced Eamon. "What is it?"

Eamon walked up the steps to the light doorway. "Did you notice what the alien did to send us back?"

David motioned to the patterns, bright with radiance, that were ingrained into the stone columns. "Moved one of those symbols."

Eamon nodded and tapped the left-hand column. "This one. It turned clockwise. And see, it's turned back again."

David reached the steps, but he had neither enough interest nor enough energy to impel himself up them. So he sat on the steps instead. "And?"

"And I think it means the doorway is set to bring us back to the aliens' apocalypse. I also think we might be able to shift these patterns ourselves and open the doorway to a different time—maybe when the alien city still prospered, or maybe into the future, when human beings have settled Mars. Do you want me to experiment with moving these designs? We might not be able to get back to the aliens' settings."

It sounded as if he was asking for permission. Something that, in four years of David outranking him, he had shown a remarkable capacity to avoid. "Why are you asking me?"

Eamon leaned against the stone column. "Because we need to be practical. We have all our old problems back, and if we don't get it from the volcano, like Moynihan did, we're going to get it from starvation."

"And you don't intend to get it from anything."

"My point is that we need an exit plan. There's nothing good for us here. The only thing that's keeping us here is Moynihan."

David looked at him sharply, but Eamon, standing beside the doorway, was cloaked in the wash of its light. "You're not suggesting we leave him?"

"Killiam, I can't think of one rational argument in favor of risking our lives to stay with a man who is going to die without ever waking up. But I never thought rationality was all of life. I don't even think it's the best part. I know we need to stay with Moynihan until the very end, and then give him the best burial we can, before we save our own necks. And I can't explain why except to say that it's the only human thing to do."

So he had honor after all.

The chamber trembled, shaking dirt and rock splinters from the ceiling. David watched them fall in the white brilliance of the doorway, felt them dust his hands and face, his hair. And he still could not worry. He pondered what Eamon had said.

"And to think," David said softly, "you always disliked him."

"I didn't dislike him."

"You talked—"

"I know how I talked." Eamon's voice was suddenly loud.

David didn't answer, too tired to enjoy arguing.

Eamon plodded down the steps, then sat by David. David did not look at him. "I suppose you won't believe me unless I tell you that the only thing I ever really held against him was that Meg was interested in him and not me. I thought she might accept my attention when she realized Moynihan wouldn't give her his. I know how to appreciate a woman, and I would have appreciated her whether she took me first or second. But she never took me at all. And I took out my disappointment on Moynihan." Eamon shifted on the steps and spoke in an altered tone. "Tell me, Killiam. Do you think Meg would have me if I were the last man on Mars?"

The words were light, but David heard the sadness beneath. He shook his head, wanting to shrug off the whole pathetic conversation. "We should live so long." He looked behind him, at the light doorway, and returned to an easier topic. "Don't experiment with the doorway. As soon as we can, we will go straight through. Back to the aliens, and then away with them. Shake the red dust of this planet off our feet forever."

"And Earth, too."

"We lost that a long time ago." The chamber shivered with another tremor, and David fancied it was stronger than before.

"There's the burial, too. I say we build a cairn. We have more rocks than dirt, and anyway, he's Irish."

"That sounds right." David's mind went further along that track. "As commanding officer, I'll have to preside. I wish I had a Bible to read from. I suppose I'll just have to make something up."

"Don't worry about it. Just say what you know, and don't think too hard about how. Meg and I already understand."

The chamber shuddered, sprinkling them with dirt. David tried to wipe the dirt, cool and dry, from his hand, and only smeared it. He looked, unconcernedly, at the brown streaks on his skin, then let his hands drop again. "I wonder, Eamon. When did we begin to understand?" He gazed into the sooty corners of the chamber, lost beyond the light, and felt a sadness without definition, as if he were losing something he had never known he had.

A thunderous sound reverberated in the rock all around them, so that they felt it as much as heard it. Eamon sat up sharply, but David didn't stir.

Then the entire chamber began to rattle. The unseen ceiling groaned as though buckling beneath a great strain, and shards of rock rained down out of the darkness above.

And the sudden, close peril killed David's torpor with one stroke. He bolted to his feet and ran. He dodged around wreckage, almost slipping again and again, pelted with the falling stones. Crashes resounded behind him, but he didn't look.

At the lip of the downward passage, he remembered Eamon. He glanced over his shoulder.

Eamon was sprinting toward him, but the floor spasmed just as he tried to evade a jagged chunk of rock, and he pitched headlong.

David dashed back. As he reached Eamon, the engineer struggled up to his hands and knees. "Go!" he shouted. "I'm right behind."

David pivoted and fled back to the passageway. He bounded down the stairs and came upon Margaret, standing in front of Moynihan as if guarding him. "The chamber's coming down up there." David grabbed her hand. "We need to get—"

Margaret tore away from him and instead sat down beside Moynihan, who was still sunk too deep for anything in the universe to reach.

David divined her choice instantly, divined all its heights and depths, for in his heart he had known the same choice. He did not dispute it, a choice of the soul beyond disputing, and he knelt by her. "All right, Meg," he said, his voice soft amid the clangor of rock battering rock. "Cover him."

Margaret stretched across the commander's chest, shielding his head with her arms. And David shielded her, interposing his body between her and whatever happened next.

In the corner of his vision not obscured by Margaret's hair, David saw Eamon kneel down on the ground at Moynihan's other side. He stooped close over them, and the team of four huddled together.

The rocks fell with furious tumult. Tremendous crashes shook the ceiling above them, and stones tumbled down the stairs. One flew into David's leg with stinging force sure to leave a bruise—if he lived long enough.

David shut his eyes, his ears filled with the uproar, and every beat of his heart became a cry for life. His own life, and the lives of those whose warm, breathing presence pressed into him.

Then a noise struck him—a noise of power and wrath such as he had not heard since the shrieking bombs and rending explosions of Mongolia. It wrenched him, body and soul, jarring his teeth and freezing his heart. The floor bounced beneath them, and he waited for the worst.

The cascade of stone that beat the ceiling ebbed, then ceased. Sound died with it, and David pushed gently away from Margaret. His heart drummed, and only one thought took form in his head: *We're alive.* But he didn't speak it. He felt, in that deathly stillness, that it would be premature to say.

Eamon straightened, too, and the beam of his wristlight cut a shaft in the darkness. He swept it to the stairs, covered with rocks large and small, and then upward. The white light exposed a smooth-faced stone cutting off the passageway at the very head of the stairs.

Margaret shifted, rising onto her knees. "Is that all one rock?"

In response, Eamon slowly, thoroughly scanned his light over it. There was no gap, not even one as wide as a hair. A single stone covered the opening up to the higher chamber—and who knew how much more?

David leapt up and made for the stairs. He stumbled over the debris but persevered until he could reach the stone that blocked their way out. With his bare hands he scrabbled at it, yearning for the slightest give, the barest shift.

"David," said Margaret, "your hands."

He looked at them and saw that they were smeared with fresh blood; he had torn his old cuts and somehow not felt it.

"It won't move," Eamon stated. "You know enough about physics to know that."

"Maybe there's another way out." Margaret angled her wristlight and meticulously combed every wall in the chamber.

David tracked the beam of light, his eyes burning with the effort to see everything it revealed. But by the time Margaret came back to where she had begun, all he saw was the seamless metal that armored the walls, floor to ceiling.

Horror broke in David's mind, spawning a close and suffocating fear.

Eamon extinguished his wristlight. "You remember how we were talking about a cairn, Killiam?" His voice was subdued. "It looks like we have ourselves a crypt."

XXXIII

Once the building had faced the world with large, crystal-clear doors framed by transparent walls. But all that remained of that bank of glass in this humbler time was a line of clear, razor-edged shards standing upright.

To Reuben Jackson, they looked like malevolent pickets. He walked between two of the shards and ignited his flashlight. The beam blazed on what had been a lobby and was now an urban ruin. Splintered furniture rotted on the floor, and fragments of the walls and doors made the whole place a peril. Garbage, much of it past the point of recognition, lay scattered everywhere. Two years of exposure had driven in dirt—in some places so thickly that pale, thin plants grew up in it.

Reuben spotted two black cavities in the molding wall opposite them and focused his light there. "See?" he said, and his voice sounded all wrong in the ruin. "A way into the building."

Reuben began picking his way to it, and he heard Willow and Cruz following. When they were within a couple of yards of the black gap of a doorway, a sharp *hiss* turned Reuben around. The beam of his flashlight caught Cruz squatting amid the garbage and rubble, clutching his ankle.

The congressman looked up and scowled, though the effect was mostly lost as he blinked into the light. "Go on. I'm all right."

"What happened?"

Cruz stood again, a bit hesitantly. "A piece of glass nicked my foot."

Reuben noted well that it did it through Cruz's shoe, and he shined his light on the ground around his own feet.

"It's a force-shield."

He looked up to see Willow training her flashlight on the doorway. "There is a force-shield there," she repeated. "This way into the building is sealed off."

Reuben strained his eyes but couldn't see whatever she did. "Are you sure?"

Willow picked up a shapeless piece of junk and hurled it at the black gap. They heard a faint sizzle, and at that same second, the piece of junk flew back out of the darkness.

Cruz began to walk away, declaring, "I'm going to wring Karl's neck."

Reuben and Willow traced their way back more gingerly, finally emerging from between the glassy pickets to join Cruz out on the street. He faced the alley that ran against the side of the building, studying it in the glare of his flashlight. As they came up to him, he gestured with the flashlight. "Do you see that?"

The light illuminated ground coated with filth, and in that filth were imprints of a man's footsteps. Cruz struck out, tracking the path left in the grime.

Reuben, trailing after him, flicked his light to the wall on their left. Unlike the front, the side of the building was brick and had not been smashed. But it was chipped, cracking in places, and despoiled by graffiti.

They had nearly reached the back of the alley when Cruz stopped. "It ends here." He focused his light, showing how the footprints turned toward the wall and then ceased. Raising the beam, he swept it over the brick wall.

"If the front way was guarded by force-shields, should the back way be easy?" asked Willow. "Perhaps it's a chameleon skin."

"Perhaps." Reuben knelt in the grime, sliding his flashlight under his belt, and ran his hands over the wall. The brick lightly scraped his skin, and a few motes broke loose onto his hands. He brushed them off. "It feels real. But that's not the gold-standard test, is it?" Reaching as far to his right as he could, Reuben rapped the wall at short intervals.

At first, the knocks sounded as if they were made on brick. But the tone changed, and when Reuben finished his brief canvass, he was sure. "Right on the money, Willow." He pointed to the wall, right where the footprints ended. "Here, it's wood, not brick. Probably a door, not a wall."

"Good," Cruz declared. "Stand aside."

Reuben barely cleared the space before Cruz kicked the supposed wall with ramming force. Two, three times more Cruz kicked, and there was a jarring dissonance between the brick they saw and the noise of splintering wood, which they heard.

With a final *crack* and loud tearing, the camouflaged door gave way.

It swung inward, and portions of the illusion failed, so that strips of broken wood and peeling white paint winked among the reddish brick.

They were inside the door, which hung limply on its hinges. By the beams of the others' lights, Reuben caught glimpses of the cold walls of a blank, sizable corridor.

"Hold it right there!"

Reuben whirled toward the shout. A man walked slowly out of the dark corridor, sweeping a narrow beam of light before him.

A beam whose source, Reuben saw in the next moment, was a light mounted on an assault rifle.

He froze, and so did Willow, but Cruz strode forward. "Who are you?" he demanded. "Do you work here?"

The man jerked, concentrating the light—and rifle—squarely on Cruz's chest. "Stop!"

Cruz obeyed, and the man's posture relaxed a little. "Yes," he said. "Yes, I work here. My job is to keep everyone out, or else get them out. That's what you three need to do. Get out."

"'Get out'?" echoed Cruz, as if there were something incredible in the concept. "Who do you work for? What is his name?"

"Don't know." The words were brief, clipped.

"You swing a gun for a man, and you don't know his name?"

Reuben twitched a little at the belligerence of Cruz's tone, and the gunman hiked up the rifle's muzzle. "He pays me food and board."

"This being the board, no doubt." Cruz gestured derisively up at the ceiling. "But this is federal property, and unless your boss is the president of the United States, he's outside his rights."

"I eat well."

Reuben guessed that summed up all the man's loyalty, and an idea blazed into his mind. He took a step forward. "I have a deal for you." The man shifted the light-mounted rifle to aim at him, but Reuben continued to walk until he stood in the center of the corridor. "I have something to show you," he told the gunman. "I'm going to take it out from my pocket."

Reuben slid his hand into his jacket's breast pocket, and the man, tracking the movement with his rifle, pinpointed his light right over Reuben's heart. Reuben very gradually drew out the plane ticket and the job voucher, and he stretched them out to the gunman. "I have a plane ticket and a job voucher, and I'll give them both to you if you let us search the building and take what we want."

"How do I know they're not fake?"

Reuben shrugged. "How can you risk losing them if they're real?" And he held them out.

The gunman didn't answer, and no one could see his face behind his light. Thick silence wrapped around them like a cocoon, and Reuben didn't dare to breach it.

The man lowered his rifle. "I used to be an accountant," he said. "I owned a home. I bought my own food."

"I have that life in my hand," Reuben told him. "Take it."

The man abruptly swung his rifle down to his side and plucked the ticket and voucher from Reuben's hand. "I'm going to see if these are real. And if they're not, I'll be back." The corridor rang with his rapid footsteps until he vanished out the door.

Reuben exhaled and suddenly felt his heart skipping. "I hope they are real."

"Where did you get them?" Willow asked as Cruz began to wander down the corridor.

"From Karl. He offered them to me as a bribe."

"Then you have nothing to worry about. Dr. Karl's bribes are as real as his revenge."

Ahead, Cruz opened a door, leaned in with his flashlight, and exclaimed, "Aha!" He straightened and called to them, "Here is our first stop."

"What is it?" asked Willow.

Cruz's voice was barely audible as he ducked through the door. "The basement."

"I suppose," Willow remarked, "he has an idea."

"I suppose." Reuben snapped on his flashlight, and they followed Cruz into the basement. The door had opened onto a flight of wooden steps, and they descended to find Cruz scouring the nearest wall with his light.

Reuben flashed his light over the large, cold room and saw nothing worth a second's notice. "What are you looking for?"

"The fuse box. I am going to throw every breaker on it."

"Okay." Reuben aimed his flashlight at Cruz. "Why?"

"Because after being ransacked by a mob, and then boarded up for two years, a lot of this building has gone dark. But I guarantee you that in whatever office Karl uses, the lights still come on. So when we make the search, we can eliminate out of hand any offices that stay dark."

"Reasonable." Willow pointed her flashlight's beam at the wall opposite the one Cruz examined. "The fuse box is there."

The congressman turned around. "Ah," he said. "Thank you."

Reuben drifted over to stand by Willow, and they watched the congressman throw the breakers. "So," Reuben said above the clatter. "What made you turn whistleblower?"

"An accident. Dr. Karl's accident, to be exact. He left the real version of that first communiqué on his desk, and I found it."

"And you sent it to me."

"And to Congressman Cruz. I hoped—"

The lights of the basement flared on, and Reuben squinted at swaths of dismal gray. Then, with a burst of blue light, the light panels overhead exploded.

As blobs floated over Reuben's vision, a harsh, burning smell filled his nostrils. And the breakers clacked on.

"Take a hint?" Reuben called to Cruz.

"Never." But the next moment, the clacking stopped, and the congressman turned from the fuse box, swinging his flashlight toward the stairs. "Let's hunt."

The first floor was mostly darkness, defying their attempts to activate lights, and soon they climbed the metal stairwell to the floor above. At Cruz's urging, they divided to search more quickly.

Reuben, alone in a dark hallway, hurried from one office to another, eager to find what Karl had tried so valiantly to protect. Light leaked from beneath one door, and he cracked it open and eased himself inside.

His wariness dissipated when he saw that no one was in the office. He began to search it, then stopped. Suddenly he took in the destruction—the walls scrawled over with vile words and crude insults, the floor littered with broken glass, dirty shreds of paper, and splinters of wood. The furniture had been smashed to a thousand pieces, and Reuben shivered to imagine what frenetic, senseless rage had done it.

The secret computer with the transmissions from Mars could not be in here.

"Jackson!"

Reuben left the room to see Cruz standing at the other end of the hallway, his flashlight blazing in his hand. "Come on," the congressman beckoned. "We've found it."

Reuben joined him quickly, and Cruz led him down two halls to a wooden door with a defaced plaque. Light seeped out of that door, too.

They entered a larger room, fully lit and swept clean. Willow sat at a computer console, her chair the first intact piece of furniture Reuben had seen in the building.

Without looking up, Willow said, "It's no good. The computer is locked down."

Cruz clicked off his flashlight and moved toward the computer. "Let me try a couple of passwords."

"I'm afraid, Congressman, that you can't even get to the point of entering passwords without knowing what command key to enter first. And any computer protected with a special command key will also be protected with specialized passwords. Your congressional passwords may work on the computers on Capitol Hill, but they won't work here."

When Cruz didn't argue, Reuben decided that option was truly dead. "Congressman," he said, "am I right in assuming that among your resources are people who could cut through all that protection?"

"You are," Cruz acknowledged. "But it would take a few hours to round them up and get them here. By that time, Karl will have done his dirty deed. I'm surprised he hasn't done it already. And the computer is a post-Snowden model, which means we can't remove the hardware and take it with us. So . . ." Cruz stopped, staring at the computer.

And then his eyes narrowed, as strong a signal of coming trouble as Reuben knew. "Willow," said Cruz, "why do you think Karl hasn't come to doctor the transmission?"

"Probably he doesn't know about it yet. NASA sent it late, after most people are in bed."

"Can you get ahold of him at this hour?"

"I have a number for that purpose, during a crisis. But what is the crisis?"

"A newly disgraced congressman is pestering you for help in getting the latest transmission from Mars."

Willow shook her head but smiled. "Completely accurate and yet totally misleading."

"He's had practice," Reuben put in. "But let me see if I understand this craziness. We are fortunate enough to be in the lion's den while the lion is out, and you want to lure him back in?"

Cruz clapped his hands together. "Precisely. He will open the computer for us."

"How can I put this?" Reuben pretended to consider, then said, "Cruz, he won't open it for us."

Cruz looked at him a moment, and then startled Reuben by flinging his arm around Reuben's shoulders. "You don't appreciate me, Jackson. But you will. I have this whole plan and all our parts in it worked out. Willow will put out the bait, I will provide the sneakiness, and you will be the thing that goes bump in the night."

Excitement and dread both spiked Reuben's blood. "I might live to regret this, but—what's your plan?"

XXXIV

Margaret tallied up the contents of her med kit, sorting them into rough order and tossing out pebbles. When she finished, she set it aside, pulled her knees up to her chest, wrapped her arms around her knees, and admitted to herself that what she really wanted to do was cry.

David, crunching through rubble behind her, suddenly stopped. "Look at this."

Margaret twisted half-around and saw he pointed his wristlight at the wall that buttressed the stairs. The metal had warped, looking as if it were crumpling beneath the immense stone that blocked the passage. "What do you think it means?" David asked.

Eamon's voice carried over the chamber. "It means you shouldn't stand there."

"You think it will collapse?"

Eamon crossed the room, noisily kicking his way past debris, apparently to carry on the argument more conveniently. "Killiam, I'm not enough of a prophet—"

Margaret turned away, scooting closer to Moynihan. She raised her wristlight and studied his face. His skin had turned ashen, and the bruises around his eyes had darkened. Dried blood still covered much of his face, and she felt a pang of sadness at that, but she could not reduce any more their meager supply of water or of sterilizing pads.

By rote, she checked the commander's vitals, then peeled back the bandage on his forehead. Her professional judgment was that his wound should be cleaned again—it was so open, and so deep, and the underground chamber so unsanitary.

Of course, it was also her professional judgment that he would be dead before infection could set in.

Moynihan's breath stuttered, abruptly and harshly. A sound so painful Margaret instinctively put a comforting hand against his cheek.

But he needed no comfort. Mentally, he had already flown away, and soon his spirit would fly, too, no longer bound by the frail tether of his body.

Margaret's eyes were suddenly awash with tears. She surreptitiously wiped the side of her hand against her eyes, the quarreling voices behind her assuring her that Eamon and David weren't paying attention.

She drew in a clearing breath, looked away from the commander's face, wishing for a good place for a good cry.

Something against the wall sparkled, arresting her glance, and she twitched her wristlight toward it. A transparent flask that looked stronger than glass and purer than diamonds glittered against the metal wall. The liquid within looked like water, with bits of bright-green leaves floating in it.

Margaret pictured the alien giving it to her, then pointing out the gash on her palm. He hadn't let Eamon drink it. Could he have meant them to wash with it?

She leaned over, snagged the flask, and, cupping her right hand, tilted the flask to pour . . .

And didn't. Caution reared up, reminding her that she had no idea what the liquid was or did. She could not begin to calculate what it would do to Moynihan—or herself. The gash in her palm, though shallow, had not fully closed. Margaret did not feel brave—nor, in truth, did she feel afraid. She felt, if anything, fed up.

With abrupt determination, Margaret poured out the liquid into her palm. It tingled with a strange sharpness—strange, because it did not hurt. She tipped her hand, spilling the liquid onto Moynihan's forehead. With that, and two other handfuls, she cleansed his wound again. Then she washed all the blood and dirt from his face.

Stinging pierced her right hand, so sudden and fierce she gasped, but as soon as she felt it, it was gone. Margaret turned her hand over, looking at her palm, and saw that the gash had been healed without a trace of scarring. Her skin was smooth and unbroken, all the harm washed away by the alien's water.

No thought passed through her mind. No emotion heated in her heart. But a rush swept through her veins, electrifying every nerve in her body, and she looked down at Moynihan.

The alien's water dripped down his face, and one large drop slid onto his lips. He opened his mouth, just a little, and swallowed.

Margaret knew it was only an unconscious reflex, but she remained frozen, waiting to see what would happen next. Two, three minutes went by without a sign, yet not wearying her vigilance at all.

Then Moynihan breathed in—not the shallow, rasping breaths he'd usually been taking, nor the stuttering, hurting breaths when his body tried to draw in more air. He breathed in deeply, freely, without trouble and without pain.

"David," Margaret said quietly, her voice a little shaky.

"What?"

Margaret didn't answer; David would have to see.

After a moment, David and Eamon both came treading over the debris-strewn floor.

Moynihan stirred. His eyelids fluttered, he half rolled to his side, and—both hands finding the floor—he pushed himself up.

David and Eamon's clattering footsteps instantly ceased. And though joy took flight in Margaret's heart, it was a silent joy, and she only watched as Moynihan raised a hand vaguely to his head and looked up into their wristlight beams, blinking against the light.

His gaze shifted from David, to Eamon, to her. Then he pulled his hand away from his forehead, and the water on it glistened in the light. Moynihan observed the liquid dripping from his palm a moment, then stretched out his arm. His sleeve, neatly sliced to a point above his elbow, dangled.

The commander looked at all of them again. "What'd I miss?" he asked.

"The apocalypse," said David, his voice strange.

"The aliens," said Margaret. Her voice almost singing.

"We're all going to die." Eamon was Eamon.

Moynihan focused on him, possibly because his statement was the most explicable, and perhaps not even the most alarming. "From what?"

"Starvation."

"Still?"

Eamon turned, aiming his wristlight at the slab of rock that covered the passageway's opening. "We're trapped."

"I see." Moynihan looked very thoughtful and just a little bit lost.

Margaret reached for him. "Let me look at your head. Shine the light, David." She pushed away a wet clump of hair from his forehead and examined where his injury had been. A jagged white scar slashed over his skin, and something in her trembled to remember the deep wound it had been minutes earlier. "Tell me if this hurts," Margaret said, and probed along the scar with her fingers.

He didn't murmur, and when Margaret pulled back, their eyes met. Looking into his gray eyes, as lucid and steady as she had ever seen them, Margaret was sure. "You're healed," she said. "Entirely."

"But how?" Eamon demanded. "He was ringing death's doorbell five minutes ago. I heard his breath beginning to rattle."

Margaret lifted the flask, and it shined more precious than a jewel in the white beam of the wristlight. "The water the alien gave us? It was healing water."

David stooped down, scrutinizing Moynihan's forehead. Then he turned and whacked Eamon. "See what that water can do? No wonder he wouldn't let you drink it. You would be glowing."

"In this miserable hole, and every other miserable hole on this miserable planet, it would be welcome. We could finally see an entire room all at one time."

"You'd see the room. We'd see you. That's the difference in perspective."

"Well, if you can't stand the luck—"

"Eamon, shut up already."

Moynihan laughed low and felt along his scar. "I'm glad I woke up."

Eamon and David went quiet, and Margaret said, "So am I."

Moynihan looked at her, and in the shadows and white light, she saw a flicker in his eyes like a warm, orange flame.

Eamon sat down, making his light jump crazily until he focused it above their heads. "I thought you would be used to our squabbling, maybe even kind of fond of it. We're the dysfunctional family you never had."

Moynihan gave him an analyzing look, much like Margaret had seen him give innumerable mineral specimens from all over Mars.

David settled down by Eamon. "Here, Commander." He held out Moynihan's recorder, and as the commander took it, he continued, "It was in your hand when we found you. There was a transmission on the screen, waiting to be sent. So I sent it."

"Thank you." Moynihan activated the recorder, and its screen brightened with a moon-like glow.

Margaret waited for David to inquire after the transmission, but he only sat there silently. Eamon watched Moynihan, as if expecting him to do something.

The commander slid the recorder into his pocket and said in his scientific tone, "So then, to business." He looked at Eamon. "You say we are going to die?"

Eamon perked up. "Yes. Of starvation. Or dehydration. Or possibly even suffocation."

Margaret looked at the metal-plated walls. That was a new idea to her.

"Well," Moynihan said briefly, and not helpfully.

"Commander," said David, "tell us what to do. I'm discovering I have claustrophobia."

Margaret had never, in all her life, known him to show any weakness about small spaces, but she heard a ring of truth in his voice. She studied her brother closely.

"Colonel," Moynihan said, "fighter pilots rarely suffer claustrophobia. But just to be sure, NASA tested you for latent claustrophobia before putting you on the team. They locked you in a closet, a concrete cell, a worm tube . . ."

"They never locked me in a tomb."

"This is no tomb." But Moynihan brushed his fingers against his new scar, reminding all of them that it very nearly was his. "And," he added, "we will endeavor, to the best of our ability and the end of our strength, to ensure it never is."

It was the loneliest kind of promise, one that could be absolutely believed and yet gave no comfort. Margaret glanced at David, wondering what he thought of it.

"But first . . ."

She looked again at Moynihan, and he passed gray eyes, unusually wistful, over his team. "But first," he said, "tell me about the apocalypse."

XXXV

The cloakroom had been, in its day, a kind of exalted locker room. Now leveled by the mob, it was another wreck, notable among the general wreckage for two features: its gaping lockers, violently forced open, and the long, once-fine bench that still stood, though shakily.

The doors were permanently half-open, unable to slide back or forward. Reuben, nearly flat on the floor, watched through those doors for any movement in the dark corridor. The cloakroom fronted the ruined entranceways that had been sealed with force-shields against interlopers, and they had guessed Karl would enter there.

So Reuben lay still in the darkness and waited. He'd examined Cruz's whole cockeyed plan, rehearsed what he should have said to the congressman about it, and finally reflected that it should have been him, and not Cruz, waiting with Willow.

The air crackled, ever so faintly, and a beam of light penetrated the darkness. Footsteps rapped the hard floor, and then a black figure, armed with the light, disturbed the shadows of the corridor.

Reuben, his cheek nearly touching the cold, dirty floor, watched the black figure pass down the corridor. He did not doubt for a moment that it was Karl.

The footsteps grew fainter, then louder when they creaked on the metal stairwell, and then faded out of Reuben's hearing. He sat up, his foot bumping trash, and went back to waiting.

Wait, Cruz had said, *until it feels right*.

Typical, Reuben thought, huffing in his mind. A moment later, he mouthed the word to himself: *Typical*.

He got up from the floor and slowly counted up to 360. Then he faced the long, rickety bench, planted his foot against its seat, and overturned it with one vigorous kick.

It crashed with a tremendous echo, and Reuben went down a line of lockers, clattering and foraging roughly in them for the sole sake of creating noise.

If that didn't get him the attention he wanted, nothing would. Reuben dodged out the mangled door and quickly made his way to the stairwell. It was blocked from sight by a swinging door, but sounds were not so easily impeded.

Reuben stopped after the next turn in the corridor, just out of view of the stairwell. Moments later, he heard the groan of the stairwell. As the hinges of the swinging door grated, Reuben got going. He made his way in the dark, heedful of the wreck of the ravaged building that cluttered his way, but even more heedful of Karl.

Heavier footsteps mixed among his own, both gratifying and menacing. Reuben led Karl deeper and deeper into the building, striving always to be heard, never to be seen.

Karl's footsteps seemed to grow louder, and Reuben quickened his pace. But Karl stalked closer and closer behind him. As Reuben hooked a quick turn in the corridor, Karl's light beam grazed his shoulder, striking the wall ahead of him.

Sucking in a breath, Reuben lunged for the nearest door. He wrestled it open in a quick, agitated movement and ducked inside.

Reuben snapped on the light and saw, in an unprocessed flash, the remains of an array of desks, and shut off the light again. He had searched this room earlier, remembering it for two things: the demolished fleet of desks and the twin doors, facing each other across the large room. Now he hurried for the second door, intent on escaping into a different hallway.

A metallic scraping warned him, and Reuben lunged for a smashed desk and dropped down behind it. He pulled his arms and legs close, making himself as small as possible.

The door raked open, and then light flooded the room. Reuben stilled himself to shallow breaths.

He felt Karl lurking in the doorway, his eyes heavy on the room. The floor twinged as the doctor shifted, then a leathery rustle rasped the air.

It sounded, to Reuben's limited experience, like a weapon being unholstered, and his breathing nearly stopped. Might Karl have—more urgently, would he use . . .

Probably.

Footsteps creaked as Karl ventured farther into the room. The moment drew out, tightening and plucking Reuben's nerves.

Then the light blinked off, Karl walked out, and the door closed.

Reuben let out a large breath, carefully getting up and moving again in the dark. He found the door he had been aiming for and went out into a corridor parallel to the one Karl now walked.

He paused to choose a new course. Right or left, get behind Karl or get in front?

As he fished for the right answer, he caught a faint but sharp scent lingering in the corridor. Reuben inhaled deeply, and then he knew.

Smoke.

He hesitated. He needed to get moving, to lead Karl off on the wild-goose chase. If Karl lost him entirely, he might go back too soon and interrupt Willow and Cruz. If they failed now, how would they ever be able to save the Mars team? Four lives hung in the balance.

Six, Reuben thought, remembering the sound like a gun being drawn and adding Cruz and Willow's lives to the reckoning.

Then he added his own: *Seven*.

Reuben turned on his heel to dash down the corridor and get between Karl and the stairwell. Then he smelled the smoke again.

It was half instinct that made Reuben spin around again and race after the smoke. He followed it farther and farther from Karl, to the east side of the building and straight toward the back. The rubbish in the dark corridors stymied him a little, but he would not slow down.

The smoke grew stronger, and he tasted it in his mouth, felt it in his throat. It drove out his fear of Karl with a new and mushrooming alarm. Reuben flipped on his flashlight, not worrying now who would see it.

The smoke led him to the long, cold corridor they had first entered, and he arrived at the basement door. Smoke streamed from beneath it, out of all its cracks and gaps.

Reuben kicked the door, and it splintered. He kicked it again, and it flew inward with a *crack* and *bang*.

Smoke billowed out, enveloping Reuben before he could react. He coughed, and through the stinging smoke and the tears that blurred his eyes, he saw living red flames. The *hiss* and *crackle* of their greedy devouring cut clearly through the thick gray haze.

He turned and fled down the long corridors, stumbling over junk in his reckless speed.

At last he burst through the swinging door and stood at the bottom of the stairwell. "Fire!" he yelled. "Willow! Cruz! The building's on fire!"

His shout filled the stairwell, surely reaching the floor above. They had to hear him.

But the echoes of his warning died, and silence crushed him. Images of the fire spreading spun wildly in his mind, and he had a frantic notion that the flames could almost be under his feet, conquering the basement even as the multitude of burning fingers reached upward.

"Cruz!" he bellowed. "Willow! Run! Fire!"

As he stood listening, his breaths coming too rapidly for comfort, he heard only the echoes of his own voice, the rushing of his own blood. And the animal urge to live, a consuming impulse from the mind's primal foundations, refused to endure the danger of the fire, refused to go even deeper into it. But the man knew something greater than survival. Reuben ran up the stairwell.

XXXVI

"And that's it, Commander," the colonel finished. "As soon as the alien sent us through, we began searching and found you not ten minutes later."

Moynihan nodded, but his mind was still soaring through vistas of the yellow twilight and the lowering alien ship and the vast assembly of aliens keeping silent vigil. "That's incredible." It burned in his spirit, driving him to his feet. He began to pace in front of his team, who all sat on the ground. "Do you realize what a tremendous, what a shattering thing this is? It's like discovering for the first time that Earth is an island in an ocean full of planets and suns. It opens up a universe. You are the first human beings ever to meet another intelligent species. You are the first people to travel through time. You saw the aliens leave this planet— heaven only knows how long ago."

A thought shot from his own words, like lightning from a storm cloud, and Moynihan stopped dead, gazing into darkness. "But why would they flee an entire planet because of one volcano? Was Mars even then hostile to life, and this their only city? Was there a series of planet-wide catastrophes?"

"Commander, does it matter?"

The question startled Moynihan, who had forgotten about his team in the heat of his thoughts, and he turned around. Eamon, who had spoken, was staring at him incredulously, and even Margaret and David looked like they were waiting for him to come back to reality.

Moynihan's spirits returned to ground, and he went back and sat down with them. "You're right," he said. "Business." He paused, trying to find where they had been before his detour. "Colonel, that's not quite it."

"What do you mean?"

He gestured toward the obstructed passageway. "What happened there?"

"Another earthquake. I was up there when it began. It seemed like the whole roof was coming down on top of us. There's no telling how much rubble is burying us in here."

"It might have buried the doorway, too," Eamon added. "Or even destroyed it."

That truth washed cold over Moynihan. "So then, after all the discoveries, the aliens, the doorway, my own healing, we are worse off than ever." He shook his head. "I don't know why you came back. You were free and clear."

Eamon threw up his hands. "We came back for you!"

"I would rather you left with the aliens."

"And left you to die?"

"Yes." Moynihan looked at them, at their faces streaked with dirt, marked with bruises and cuts. In the pale, piercing light, their eyes looked too bright, their faces wan. They reminded him of children left alone and wild to their own devices, and he felt an improbable gentleness toward them. "You were not responsible for me, but I was responsible for you. I'd have willingly lost my life so that you three could keep yours."

Eamon looked down at his now-clasped hands. "I said so, Moynihan. I told them."

"Commander," Margaret said, "we didn't come back because of some decision about who should live and who should die. We came back because there are things you have to do, no matter how it ends."

Moynihan glanced around the gloomy chamber. "And this is one of them?"

Eamon looked up. "We're a team."

Before Moynihan could process his surprise, David nodded. "He's right."

Moynihan looked between them, rubbing his scar and wondering what more he had missed. He decided simply to accept the rearrangement of their attitudes. "I suppose we're all in it together, then. And all for it, too." He could not manage the flippancy with which others hid themselves; he never could, and the old bitterness bled into his voice and stained his words. He looked at his team and gave voice to the words that had haunted his heart so long. "I'm sorry."

Eamon shrugged. "We're all sorry for the earthquake."

"But I, Lieutenant Commander, am sorry for . . ." Long habit checked

Moynihan's words, but this truth he had to release from silence. "I am sorry I didn't fight when I should have. I knew Karl meant this team to die on Mars, but I didn't fight him. At least not to the bitter end. I gave up when I could still lose without public humiliation. I could never have won, but . . ." He glanced at Margaret. "But that was one of the things I ought to have done, no matter how it ended."

Margaret met his eyes. "And yet, you're here."

"That I am. And that, I don't regret."

Eamon huffed. "Well, I regret that I'm here, and I still don't know why you're here."

Moynihan's eyes fastened on him. "You want to know? I'm here because I'd rather carry three deaths on my conscience than four. I'm here because, knowing what was coming, I thought I could do some good at the end, and because I knew I could have a few years of great scientific work before that end. I am here because I was ashamed of not fighting Karl. And do you want to know something even more, Mr. Eamon?" Moynihan leaned forward and said, "I am ashamed still."

Eamon's expression was unfamiliar and unintelligible. "You think," the engineer eventually said, "I don't understand? I understand." His voice grew taut. "I applied for this mission the day my divorce was finalized. Marriage didn't work out for me, so I thought maybe fame and glory would. I wanted to stick it to the institution of marriage by proving I was better without it. I wanted my ex-wife and my friends and everyone who had seen my life fall apart to see me famous and all kinds of important. In other words, I joined this mission on the rebound. I have had four long years to think about it, four long years to realize that this"—he spread his arms far apart—"came from my choices as much as anybody else's. And when I remember why I made the choices I did"—his voice fell—"I'm ashamed, too."

Moynihan could not answer, a mix of feelings rousing in him. The colonel's eyes were on Eamon, one eyebrow raised.

But Margaret spoke up softly. "Our parents died on the same day, in the Riyadh ambush. They were both active-duty combat soldiers. Their lives were all about the military. And ours have been about the military, too. It's not strange that, like our parents, we chose to risk everything on a mission so liable to end badly."

David was watching his sister with gentle eyes, and he now shifted his attention to Moynihan. "We all made choices that brought us here,

Commander. We all made mistakes. We've all failed. That's why we all forgive you."

"That's the thing about showing grace," Margaret said. "It's not just that other people need it. We need it too."

Moynihan looked at them, amazed that they would comfort him, amazed that he was comforted. Yet even as his old regret was assuaged, a new grief flowered in him. The world's ancient song of pain echoed all around him.

"There's no sense in being Irish," he repeated softly, "unless you know that sooner or later, the world is going to break your heart."

The words reigned in silence. Moynihan sat quietly, sifting these things, until he felt—deeper than the sorrow, deeper than his consolation—a faint stirring. Like a seed coming to life beneath the hard clods of winter.

Another thought came to him. "But neither," he said with determination, "is there any sense in being Irish unless you are, sooner or later, going to fight." He stood and walked to the stairs, flashing his wristlight on the rock that sealed them into this lower chamber. He swept the light beam slowly over the stone's pitted face, and then down the walls. They were strange walls, covered with a metal tarnished beyond its original color, and right above the stairs, it was warped and bulging.

Moynihan stayed the light on the rumpled metal, his mind turning. Then he gestured at the wall with his wristlight. "If we could trigger a collapse, that stone might come crashing down into this chamber. And up we climb."

"And if we had a transporter, we could beam out of here," Eamon said.

David stood. "Ye of little faith. We will trigger a collapse. We just need to rig an explosion."

Margaret also rose, but Eamon just sat there. "I'd be interested in seeing you try, Killiam," Eamon said.

"*I* am not going to try anything. *You* are going to do it. The blaster charges are explosive. You know they are."

Eamon shook his head. "Fertilizer is explosive too. But you need more than fertilizer to make a bomb, and I need more than blaster charges."

"Look," David said to him. "During the war, when I was stationed overseas, I sat on the court-martial panel of a soldier who had set off an explosion in his barracks and nearly killed three men. People were screaming that he was a traitor, a lone-wolf terrorist. But he said it was an accident. His whole defense came down to insisting that he was an idiot, not a traitor."

Eamon cocked a brow. "Did you believe him?"

"Yeah. Forensics determined that the explosion was caused by a cigarette lighter, a disassembled blaster, and a bottle of beer. It looked more like stupidity than anything else. But that's not the point. The point is that if some fool can accidentally turn a blaster into an explosive, a top-notch engineer like you can surely do it on purpose."

Eamon pulled the blaster from his belt and let it dangle from his fingers. "I've got the blaster. I've got extra charges. I can get the electrical components from one of the wristlights. But where do I get the beer?"

Margaret sat down beside him and drew her med kit to her side. "There is alcohol in the sterilizing pads. And I have other flammable materials too."

"Then we can try this together." Eamon showed a glint of enthusiasm. "Lay down what you've got." He himself yanked a handful of spare charges and dumped them onto the floor. As Margaret rummaged out items from her kit, he took apart his blaster with swift skill.

Moynihan focused on the stairs. He mounted a few until he could touch the twisting metal, and he stroked its ridges and dents, trying to measure the extent of the damage.

"Careful, Commander. It's no good to unblock the passage if you just get crushed in the avalanche."

Moynihan looked back only long enough to see how close the colonel stood. It was near enough that he answered, "If you were truly worried, you would stand farther back yourself."

David laughed. "Probably true."

Moynihan returned to assessing the metal, listening to the sound of Eamon at work and sensing the colonel right behind him. The colonel stood there so long the urge to turn around began to itch at him.

Finally, David said, "I want to ask you something, Commander. That transmission, the one you recorded and I sent, where did it go?"

"To Earth."

"Why?"

Moynihan paused, reaching back to those cloudy memories between the time he'd awakened at the foot of the stairs and departed again into the pain-extinguishing blackness. He hadn't dreamed them, had he?

No. He had made the transmission; that was real. "Earth sent me a transmission first; the habitat computer beamed it to my recorder, and I answered."

"They're not coming, are they?"

Moynihan caught the hope smuggled in the question, and it twisted his heart. "They said nothing about that. They only wanted to know—" Moynihan stopped, suddenly recognizing how ridiculous their inquiry was. When he'd been alone in the darkness, pain hammering in his skull, it hadn't seemed abnormal. "They wanted to know why I joined the mission, and what happened between me and Karl." He cast a look back at David.

The colonel's mouth twisted, and he focused a glare on Moynihan. "They ignore our SOS and send us that? We're dying, and they want—what? An oral history?"

Moynihan shrugged, and behind the nonchalant gesture, a vast puzzlement set in. "I don't know. I don't know why they should care, or ask even if they did."

"Did you give it to them?"

"I think so." Those last minutes before he fell into unconsciousness were shadowy and confused, and he didn't know with any certainty what he'd done. "I gave them something, anyway. I hope it wasn't gibberish."

David leaned back against the wall. The anger died out of his face, and he looked only tired.

"Here!"

At the exclamation, Moynihan looked to see Eamon and Margaret approaching. The engineer cradled their makeshift bomb in greasy hands. The blaster, broken apart and with its insides hanging out, was bound to the extra charges by a web of stripped-out wiring. The whole was slick with clear and white substances that gave it an oily gleam in the light.

"What a mess," David commented.

"A little mess to make a big mess." Eamon jerked his chin. "Get under cover. This will go seconds after I pull the trigger."

Margaret pointed to the opposite side of the room. "There. In the basin where the water used to be."

It seemed as good as they were going to get. Moynihan nodded his consent and cleared off the stairs. As Eamon brushed past him, he asked, "Do you need help?"

"Nope." Eamon raised the bomb awkwardly and, stooping, turned on his wristlight with his teeth. "Just go."

They crossed the chamber quickly. Moynihan paused to make an abbreviated scan of the dry basin, and just as he estimated that it was four feet to the bottom, David jumped lightly down. Then Margaret jumped, too, and Moynihan finally did the same. They hunkered against the rough, greenish wall of the basin and waited for the explosion.

A moment passed by, and Moynihan heard nothing but his companions' breathing. Then a pounding of footsteps erupted above them, and Eamon came leaping into the basin. He landed roughly and dropped down, flattening himself full-length on the floor.

The explosion blasted through the chamber. Moynihan's heart jumped, and as the echoes of the blast resounded, there came a rumbling and the grinding of ponderous stones—wordless threats that made him hold his breath.

A crash like thunder shaking the sky deafened him. The chamber reeled, knocking Moynihan against the basin's rugged wall.

A new sound came, a gallop of falling rocks that began pouring into the basin—a waterfall of pebbles and shale and broken stones.

Moynihan, pressed against the wall, was mostly spared. But the stones pelted Eamon ruthlessly, and the engineer reared up and scrambled to the wall. A flying bit of rock opened the skin below his right eye before he made it.

As Eamon clambered beside him, Moynihan raised his arm to shield his own face. His eyes flitted over his team, and a pang went through him.

A boulder shot over their heads and landed feet away, splintering the floor of the basin with a web of fine cracks. And the waterfall flowed on. Moynihan watched it rain down into the basin, listened to the thunder of its falling above. The rubble began to heap up, covering his feet and forming drifts against his body. Fierce stings peppered Moynihan's leg, foot, upraised arm. His hand was struck with such force that it went numb.

Finally the stream thinned, faltered, failed. As the last pebbles hurtled ineffectually down, Moynihan grasped the edge of the basin and pulled himself to standing. He planted his feet carefully amid the rubble and looked out on the chaos of their creation.

A strange, phantom glow clung to the chamber, revealing everything in pallid half colors. Debris choked the room, burying the floor and the stairs in its great heaps. Slabs of rock half hid in the mounds—one so tremendous it could only be the stone that had trapped them. But when Moynihan looked, he found the passageway was still blocked, filled with dirty, shattered stones of a thousand different sizes.

Eamon joined him against the wall. "It's always hard."

Moynihan glanced at him and then at Margaret and David, also gaining tentative footing and making grim assessment of the scene before them. Before anyone could comment further, Moynihan climbed out.

He tried to stand, slipped at once, and fell into the rubble. It slid, nearly carrying him back into the basin.

He froze, listening to the flurry of stones he had sent over the edge make their landfall. His hands were sunk down in the loose debris to the wrists, his feet and knees were almost buried. Not looking at his team, he ordered, "Stay where you are. This is too unstable for multiple people."

"Looks too unstable for single people," put in Eamon.

Moynihan silently agreed and began to crawl over the mounds of flotsam. They shifted under him, and with every movement he made he heard rocks clatter into the basin. But he slowly progressed to the monstrous rock slab. He climbed onto it, an immovable anchor in the shifting wreckage, and walked it like a bridge.

The far end tilted upward, resting on the unseen stairs. Moynihan balanced on that precarious edge and scrutinized the passageway. It was engulfed in debris, blocked up beyond one sliver of an opening.

His heart began to pulse. An analysis, all too plain, beckoned his mind's exploration, but wild daydreams kindled his spirit. Against all reason, against all the facts, he hoped that his team would survive, that the suicidal charter of their mission would be rewritten, and the end, so long prescribed, be changed. He wanted to live, to write his book and tell their story. And incredibly, but still possibly, learn with Margaret what sort of love could be found, even by them.

He leaped off the slab, plunging into the rubble that filled the passageway. He forded the cold, heavy drifts, struggling upward and sinking deeper into the wreckage with every stride. Down to his calves, his knees, his waist, his ribs.

The roof was close to his head now, and the opening to the upper chamber was before him, choked with debris. He dove in.

A voice called after him, but he paid no attention. He was buried in dirt and rocks, digging through it with chilled and bleeding hands, almost swimming as he treaded it with his feet. The deluging stones leached warmth from his body and filled his sight with a darkness stained by a ghostly luminescence.

And he burrowed on—reaching upward in the cold and the darkness, reaching for the incredible, blazing hope that his team would not die, reaching for life and a future and a love to be learned.

Reaching, reaching, though his breaths turned to gasps and filled his mouth with dirt.

Reaching out of the drowning sea of rock and dirt, reaching out of his own despair.

Fingertips brushing the stars.

XXXVII

The door gaped open, lopsided on its crooked hinges, and exposed the office to the gloomy corridor. Manasseh Cruz sat behind that door, securing for himself a good vantage point through the slit of space framed by the hinges. He peered out into the corridor, vigilant for the man who used to be his ally and always conscious of Willow's quiet breathing beside him.

He wondered how he would explain all this to his wife. Or to anyone else who ever found out about it. It would take a book to justify his actions tonight as the fruit of a mature and intelligent mind. And any explanation that needed a book was, politically speaking, a loser.

Cruz had just returned to plotting how to keep this escapade a secret when a creak interrupted him. He watched, still as he could be, until a beam of light appeared and traced Karl's way to the computer and the transmission. The door opened, then closed on the scientist's shadowy form.

Next up, Jackson. Cruz pondered, with some disquiet, his reliance on him.

Seconds dragged by like minutes, minutes like hours. Cruz leaned his head back against the wall and tried to distract himself with more plotting.

A crash from below caused his heart to jump into his throat. Muffled clanging followed, and Cruz's nerves prickled, but he enjoyed it. He heard the tuneless banging like a call to war, and every fiber of his being was ready to go.

Through the crack between the wall and the door, Cruz watched Karl emerge to stand in the bright doorway of his own room. After a handful of seconds, the scientist stepped out and quietly shut the door, cutting off the light. His footsteps gradually vanished into silence.

The wait was over.

Cruz rose and slipped out from the protection of the door. Willow glided along behind him, and they made the short but momentous trip to Karl's room.

In the brightness of the fully lit room, Cruz reluctantly let Willow move ahead of him and take the chair. He peered at the screen over her shoulder and saw bolded words crowning a column of text: TRANSMISSION TO EARTH FROM MARS COMMANDER MOYNIHAN, 27.03.43.

The text was a string of technical details, and Cruz reached eagerly to skim past it.

"Don't!" Willow snapped.

His hand froze, fingertips nearly brushing the screen, and he looked at Willow.

She pointed at a tiny symbol, crammed tightly into one corner of the screen. "The computer is locked. If anyone tries to use it without entering the key, it will send out an alarm and shut down."

Cruz drew back his hand slowly. "What, then?"

Willow studied the screen a moment, then nodded and stretched her fingers over the keys. "I'll crash the system."

"But—"

He got no further before Willow pressed down on the keys, and the screen winked into blue, and then black. "How is this better?" he demanded.

Willow flexed her fingers. "Congressman Cruz, all these years while you were negotiating with senators and congressmen and the president, I was doing grunt work on government computers. Which of us is more competent to handle this?"

"What are you going to do?"

"The system will reboot in safe mode. We won't be able to tap in to the transmission, but I will be able to slip our ace into the communications system. Dr. Karl will never know what he did."

"Fine," Cruz said.

She was already working.

The screen slipped into one image after another, and Cruz tried to follow Willow's deft manipulation of the system. Familiar names blinked before him—Dr. Karl, Jephthah Baines, even his own—and then segued into technical jumbles.

Suddenly the whole screen changed to blue and then black. "Was that supposed to happen?" Cruz asked, looking down at Willow.

She nodded, concentrating on the screen. "I needed to reset the system."

Cruz, realizing he had been tracking even less than he thought, searched for the best way to ask his next question.

"No luck, then?"

Cruz spun to the voice and found Karl, standing in the open door. He stepped into the room, analyzing them with hard eyes gleaming.

Cruz's first fleeing thought was a half-formed desire to get his hands on Jackson. Then he stepped forward and looked down at the man. "Did you find the thing that went bump, Karl?"

Karl slid one hand beneath his jacket. "Don't question me. I caught *you*."

Cruz shrugged. "So call the cops."

Karl, overlooking that remark entirely, surveyed the scene and asked, "What is this?"

Willow got up from her chair and stood at Cruz's side. "A disgraced congressman trying to get his hands on Moynihan's message."

Karl looked at her. "You're fired."

"I figured."

Cruz took measure of the situation and said, "Run along, Karl. Or stay and watch. We won't make you leave." He turned back to the computer, which was now lighting up again.

"You don't appreciate, Congressman, that I have the upper hand."

The assertion did not impress Cruz in the least, but the granite placidity of Karl's tone turned him back again. "Why?" he asked. "Because you caught me in a place you can't admit you've been?"

"No. Nothing subtle this time. I have the upper hand due to . . ." Karl pulled out his hand from under his jacket, and a gun gleamed, cold and black, in the light.

Willow started, and ice speared Cruz's heart. "You don't mean . . ." A confusion of questions weltered in Cruz's mind—he didn't mean he knew how to use a gun, didn't mean he actually would use it, didn't mean that Cruz might end his life murdered in this forsaken building. But one look at Karl's eyes convinced Cruz he meant all these things and more.

Cruz spread his hands in a placating gesture. "What kind of a solution is this, Karl? You and I have always known how to talk or think or manipulate our way into winning. We knew what all the world's stupid savages never understood—that there's no need to take things from people when you can manipulate them into giving them to you. I'm not saying we were good men, but we were thinking men."

Karl regarded him with chilling quiet. "Don't you think I've wanted to do this before? Don't you think I've wanted, just once, to get rid of people in my way without having to get cute?"

"Think of why you didn't," Cruz said, past the fear sticking in his throat.

"Because I didn't know how to do it without getting caught. Why else?"

"Right." Cruz took up this appeal to Karl's self-interest, trying not to feel the too-quick cadence of his heart, pushing away thoughts of his wife and children. He needed to think, not feel. "Karl, I cannot disappear. A man like me goes missing, it will be the crime of the century. Reporters, the police, the FBI—everyone will go hunting for me. For you."

Willow shied back, until she hit the chair and had to catch herself on the desk.

Karl looked at her, and Cruz moved forward, trying to get Karl's attention back on him. "And they will find me, Karl. Then they'll find you."

"And why would anyone look for you here, Congressman?"

Cruz opened his mouth, but no words came to him. All he could think of was how carefully and how cleverly he had covered his tracks to this forgotten no-place.

Karl turned off his gun's safety with a *click* like a death knell. "And knowing all that you do, your walking out of here could not possibly be good for me. I respect you enough to be sure of that."

Respect. The word struck Cruz with dreadful import; he had a terrible conviction that any opponent Karl could respect he would never endure. Cruz glanced back at Willow, but there was nothing he could say on her behalf. He sent a stray hope Jackson's way and turned to Karl, lifting his chin in defiance of his instinct to duck.

Karl raised the gun.

Cruz looked directly at him, but in his mind's eye he saw his wife and children, and his heart dwelt on them.

A distant shout came shattering into the room. It took Cruz a few seconds to recognize Jackson's voice.

"Of course," said Karl. "Him, too."

Cruz heard Jackson's death in those softly spoken words. Jackson shouted again, and this time Cruz made out his name and, "Fire!"

He repressed a sigh. Idiot diversion tactic.

"Maybe you shouldn't have been so aggressive with the fuse box," Willow said.

Cruz took a quick look at her face, trying to determine if she was playing along with Jackson's diversion or actually believed it.

Karl, eyes and gun still on them, walked forward a few paces until he had both them and the door in view. The next moment, the pounding of feet on metal came from the stairwell.

Cruz did not hold back his sigh this time.

The pounding grew louder, more definite, and Cruz listened with a sense of horrified inevitability, as if watching a car crash he couldn't stop.

Jackson burst into the room, but Cruz was distracted for just a moment as he saw, in the corner of his eye, Willow slide her hand across the keyboard.

"Fire!" Reuben shouted and motioned wildly to the door and stepped back toward it, obviously wanting to lead the way out.

Everyone else stood frozen, staring at him.

Reuben stopped, his hand on the door, and looked at them. Cruz read the truth in his half-wild eyes, and a strange pity surprised him. "I'm sorry to say," he told him, "that we have bigger problems. And now so do you."

"Thank you for joining us," Karl added, and his eyes were even colder than his gun.

Finally, Reuben focused on him and the weapon, and he raised both hands. "We came here for the transmission," he said to Karl. "We couldn't unlock the computer, so we brought you here to do it. But the fire will wipe it all out. The fight's over; the fire takes everything."

"You two stayed in Washington to continue the fight." Karl gestured the gun at Cruz. "You could be home with your wife and children." He shifted the gun back to Jackson. "You could be on your way to a new job in a new city. You chose this, not me."

"Dr. Karl," Willow said, "I know how you hate to lose. But winning like this isn't worth it."

Jackson lowered his hands. "Nothing's happened yet, Karl. We didn't get the transmission; you haven't shot anyone. So let's leave, and it will be as if this night never happened. In the name of God, Karl, let's just leave."

A sense that Cruz had often known in his life, and that had done him all kinds of good, began to burn him. He knew there was no use to any more talk, knew that this window was slamming shut. Tension knitted his muscles, and when Karl turned toward him, instinct took hold. Cruz dove to the floor, grabbing Willow and pulling her down with him.

Gunshots exploded. Somewhere glass shattered, and Cruz, sprawled on the floor, felt nothing. But he'd heard that dying men sometimes felt nothing at first.

Cruz scooted away from Willow and sat up, rubbing his chest in search of blood. His hand stung, but before he could look at it, Karl growled, "Stand back!"

Cruz's head snapped up. Karl pointed the gun at Reuben, who stood frozen in a poise to spring at him. Jackson's face was pale, but his eyes were riveted.

Cruz stood. If Jackson was stupid enough to rush Karl, he needed to be ready to help.

Karl watched them with narrowed eyes. "I am leaving. If I see any of you again, I will shoot you." He jerked the gun at Reuben. "Get away from the door."

Jackson obeyed, coming over to Cruz. Then Karl, never turning his back on them, left the room.

"That might have ended worse," Willow remarked, rising.

"There's still the fire," Jackson said. He looked at both of them. "Are you all right?"

Willow gestured. "He hit the computer."

Cruz turned and saw that the whole computer screen had been blown out, and past its ruins, the mangled inner machinery smoked. He noticed then the filmy shards of glass on the floor.

And on his own clothes. Cruz glanced at his hand, at the tiny nicks in his flesh. It didn't matter.

Reuben looked at the wrecked computer, his mouth and eyes both flattening. But then he urged, "We need to get out."

Cruz pointed his thumb and forefinger into the air, mimicking a gun. "I believe him."

"So do I. But I don't want to die in a fire."

"Neither does Dr. Karl," Willow said. "He won't stay long."

Cruz nodded. "Let him clear out, Jackson. I don't want to be shot."

Jackson stamped impatiently. "You've only seen Karl. I've seen the fire. Let's go." He strode to the door.

Cruz hurried after him and caught his shoulder. "Wait!"

Jackson yanked forcefully out of his grip, and Cruz knew he wouldn't listen to any argument. "Look," he told Jackson, "we leave now, but I'll tell you how we go."

He had no particular idea how they should go, but it kept Jackson from rushing out. "We move out now, slow and quiet, and if Karl is out there waiting for us, we charge him."

Jackson looked over at Willow. "And . . ."

Cruz intervened before he said anything foolish. "And Willow will try to snatch the gun after we knock him down."

Reuben bit down on his lip, but he didn't object. He marched out the door.

Cruz and Willow followed. They crept down the corridor, always close to the wall, but Cruz expected no trouble, and they got no trouble. He knew that Karl, if he had not fled the fire, lurked downstairs.

They reached the stairwell, and Cruz cut around Jackson, taking the lead. When he had taken three carefully placed steps, he realized the stairs would creak no matter how they walked. When he had taken one more step, he smelled smoke clinging in the air. He surrendered to what he couldn't help and descended the stairwell, listening to its groaning and tasting smoke.

At the swinging door at the bottom, Cruz stopped. He tried to pray, but his mind was jumbled with fractured images of fear, and he couldn't distill them to lucid words. So he offered up the fears and a hope and went through the door.

The corridor was dark, and that was a comfort. Cruz angled a path toward the ruined doorways that opened out to the razed lobby. Willow and Jackson trailed after him, their footsteps all too loud.

An awareness that Karl could be skulking anywhere crawled over Cruz's skin. Every second dragged past, until finally they reached their exit–ragged, gaping doorways with night and ruin beyond.

Cruz stopped again. They had not been ambushed this far, and his mind moved to the next logical, but terrible possibility.

"What?" Jackson hissed.

"Doesn't it occur to you that he might be out there, at the end of the escape route, to be sure we don't make it? I'm confident the only reason he left is so that the autopsies will show we died of a fire instead of bullets."

A beam of light shot to life behind him, and Cruz pivoted around. But it was Willow, who stood with the blazing flashlight. "Congressman," she said, "the force-shield is still on."

Cruz turned back and thought he detected a slight distortion of the light where it shot through the doorway. But he had no patience or time for subtlety now. He scanned the floor and, marking a filthy piece of plaster, he kicked it.

It flew at the doorway and then boomeranged back, skittering on the hard floor. "Jackson," Cruz said, "go check the other one."

Reuben snapped on his light and dashed off.

Cruz drew in a breath tainted with smoke, and as it burned in his lungs, clarity burned in his mind. "Karl's gone," he said, but not really to Willow. The crawling itch lifted from him, replaced by a strong need to be gone.

Jackson came running back. "It's up in the second doorway, too," he panted.

Cruz began running before Reuben finished speaking.

Reuben caught up to him. "We're going toward the fire."

"That's where the door is."

"Maybe a window—"

"The windows," Willow interrupted, "are rigged with shock wires. Remember?"

Reuben huffed, "That's illegal in thirty-four states and the District of Columbia."

For reasons he couldn't justify, that struck Cruz as funny. He laughed shortly, until the smoke changed his laugh into a cough.

They ran through corridors that grew dusky with a smoky haze their flashlights could not pierce. The air became heavy, warm, acrid as they raced toward the flames.

The stinging air drew water to Cruz's eyes. He blinked hard, trying to clear it, and suddenly his tears blurred orange. Flames raged ahead.

The walls were on fire. So was the ceiling.

Cruz slowed. Then Jackson swatted his shoulder urgently, and he kicked up his pace.

They ran into a blossoming inferno. Flames crawled across the ceiling, licked up the walls. The floor was warm through Cruz's boots, but its adamantine surface still resisted the fire.

A burning chunk of plaster dropped from the ceiling and broke on the floor. Cruz jumped over it, pressing onward.

His eyes stung fiercely with smoke and sweat, but he strained them ahead. Somewhere was the door out to the alley and the cool night. Willow and Reuben's footsteps beat in his ears, as the eager feeding of the flames surrounded him.

Suddenly, the wall on his right was nothing but fire, and flames crisscrossed the corridor, mounting up from a collapsed section of ceiling.

For a second, Cruz faltered. But he saw clear, free corridor beyond, and he launched himself into the flames.

Heat seared him, and he felt patches of his clothing ignite. Then he was through the fire. Down the corridor, gray light marked the door they had broken, promising them safety, promising them life. Cruz beat at the flame crawling up his shoulder, but he didn't slow.

He barreled through the half-open door into cool air that shocked his body. Collapsing to his knees, he slapped the fire from his shoulder.

Jackson rammed into him from behind, nearly knocking him down onto his face. Cruz heard him fall, and in a hurried glance, he saw Jackson frantically swatting flames on his back, then rolling on the ground as Willow dropped down beside him.

Agony broke off his attention, and Cruz quickly beat out the flames smoldering down his calf. He then stopped, long enough to be sure his clothes were fully extinguished, and turned to Reuben.

He was, with Willow's help, just putting out the sparks remaining on his clothing. When the job was done, they looked at him—dirty head to foot with soot and ash, their clothes singed and charred.

Cruz could only assume he looked just as bad. He tried to straighten and discovered that he was trembling—surely from adrenaline. He would consider nothing else.

"I hurt," Jackson breathed. "But I live."

"I sent it," said Willow.

Jackson twisted a little to see her face. "It worked?"

"I have no idea. But we did manage to try it."

Cruz wanted to feel a little excitement or even a little interest. But he felt only relief mingled with exhaustion.

A crash like the collapsing of walls thundered from the building behind them, followed by the fire's renewed roar. Reuben shuddered a little and stood up, stretching out his hands to Willow. "Time to go."

"And never come back," Cruz muttered, his throat and mouth so dry the words almost hurt. He got up, but as Willow and Jackson started off, he lingered to gaze at the broken door. Smoke drifted out, and orange light danced on the threshold.

The inferno raged on, stronger every moment, and it would soon have everything. Cruz consigned the building to the fire's appetite and faced the alley.

The young dawn did it no favors. Grime hid the ground and coated the bleak walls of the deserted buildings on each side. Trash piled up in reeking heaps, crowning the alley's ugliness. It was as filthy, forgotten a cranny of civilization as Cruz had ever seen, either in his hard-knock youth or the years since the Great Collapse.

And it was, of all the sights of his life, one of those most full of grace. He walked down the ugly alleyway, and it led him out to freedom, to home and family, to life.

XXXVIII

The stones slid and shifted around David, and he still couldn't see what he was aiming for. He reached blindly upward, groping for some kind of handhold. His fingers curled around a loose rock, and he flung it away and quested for something else.

A strong hand gripped his own, and David, scrabbling against the rocks, used it to leverage himself up and out. With a sharp clattering, he scrambled onto a cold, cluttered floor.

Eamon stepped back. "You good?"

"Sure." David stood up, flashing his wristlight over the chamber. Dirt covered everything and seemed to hang in the air, and all the chamber was a wreckage of broken rock. But the light doorway still shone white and pure.

Margaret and Moynihan already stood on its steps, welcome shadows against the welcome light. David joined them, weaving his way down a lopsided aisle formed by two mammoth stones.

Eamon came, too. "Now that we're all unburied . . ." He motioned to the doorway. "I think it leads back to the apocalypse."

"I know it does," answered Moynihan.

"How?" David asked, considering it the better part of valor not to point out that he was the only one who had missed the aliens and their apocalypse entirely.

"It's the only logic that binds all the facts together. Think about what happened to us after we got here. Buildings collapsing and flooding, that army of spheres. The city drove us to this place, to this door. And this door brought you to the aliens' evacuation. It is so simple. They left the door open. Any of their people who missed the evacuation could walk through the time door to a point in time before the ship left. And so none of the aliens missed the ship, even those who did."

David rubbed his temple. "Simple, you say."

"Let me see if I got this," Eamon said, cocking his head. "The aliens loaded up on their spaceship and jetted out of the solar system. But not all of them made it. Someone—Joe Alien—was taking some journey on their spooky phosphorescent highway. He comes back to find the city deserted and gets past the lava to this place. Joe Alien goes through the light door, which takes him back in time to the dead middle of the evacuation. So he jumps to a place on the spaceship and leaves on the exact same ride he missed."

"Precisely." Moynihan swept his hand toward them. "And the same happened with you three. You may have walked through the time door hours ago, but you walked into it thousands of years ago. The alien you described, the guardian of the door—he opened it again. He opened the time door for you to walk through the first time after you walked through it the second time. And no matter who goes through the door, at whatever point in time, he will always arrive before the aliens' evacuation is over. The guardian will always be there. And he will always open the time door again." Moynihan half turned, pointed to the white light. "The door will take us into the apocalypse."

David let his thoughts spin after Moynihan's and caught the edge of a vision of how they had tread time's great cataract backward, and he felt awe.

Awe and just a touch of vertigo.

"So," Eamon mused, and the light was bright in his eyes. "What do you suppose would happen if we altered the patterns so that the time door opens to the future instead of the apocalypse?"

Moynihan looked at him. "Why do you want to go to the future?"

"Because, after what we've discovered, Mars will be settled. It will be explored. All this alien technology alone is enough to start a new space race. If we go into the future, we will find a Mars inhabited by humans. We could live on Mars then. Maybe even find a way back to Earth."

"Maybe. But . . ." David struggled to put his objection kindly. "But we have no idea how many years into the future we would go. Too little time, and we could land before a human colony is established—or at least before it is viable enough to support us. Too much time, and we might just find the ruins of the colony. The alien city will bring humanity here, but that doesn't mean it can make them stay. They might just strip-mine this discovery and leave."

"We may not even reach the future," added Margaret. "We may

guess, but we cannot know what will happen if we alter the patterns. We don't know what we don't know about the time door. Nothing is really simple; things need to be just so to work. But who understands that better than an engineer?"

"So, let me ask again," Moynihan said. "Why do you want to go to the future, Lieutenant Commander?"

Eamon shifted away from David and toward Margaret and Moynihan. "Because wherever we go, you two are going together, aren't you?"

David eyed his sister and then his commander, but their faces were veiled by the brightness of the time door.

Then the commander spoke. "I can hope."

"But I can't. Commander, I've had adventure, and it's been grand, but it's not enough to live on. I've had fame, only to discover it's not really what I want. I want a family of my own. I want a wife. I want kids. And I don't have a chance unless I can get home."

David regarded Eamon, and he felt that he finally understood the engineer. He weighed that understanding against a plunge into the perilous unknown of the time door. Survival, sure survival, lay in a straight path to the aliens' apocalypse and then away with them in their flight.

But Eamon knew that. He just cared about something more than survival. David understood, in his self's deepest core, why a man would hang his life in the balance, rejecting what was certain for hope of what was better. He had held his own life loosely, stacking chances of death in flights over war-riven Mongolia, in testing experimental jets when the peace came, in this whole adventure to Mars.

Because he knew—he had always known, even when danger filled him with the desire to live—that merely keeping one's life was never the most important thing.

Margaret and Moynihan shifted toward each other, as Eamon stood, waiting for a response.

David's spirit surged with sympathy. "You know—" His voice sounded loud, and David met their startled eyes. "Those aliens were spooky. Eyes that glowed like a cat's, skin as cold as metal, those things that came out of their hands. When they came into my mind, I felt like they forced me out. Even my memories of it are broken. I'm not sure I want to jump into their world with no way out. Besides, if we went, I'd never fly again. Not like I want to."

"We'd survive if we went to the aliens," Margaret said, "but then we would be completely in their hands. They would do whatever they wanted with us. I don't think they would ever want to hurt us, but they might decide we were no different than children. Or pets. They might even hurt us without meaning to, like their city did."

Three now in favor, but Moynihan had the deciding vote. David looked at the commander.

Moynihan said, "Lieutenant Commander Eamon."

His tone echoed far-off days and places, when their world was ordered and military and conventional, and Eamon straightened. "Sir?"

"Get us home."

"Yes, sir." Eamon snapped off a salute—the first David had seen from him since they'd left Earth—and he walked to the blazing left-hand column. He drew something from his pocket, no more than a smudge of darkness to David's eyes, and began to twist it against the stone.

"I would have liked to have met the aliens," Moynihan said somewhat wistfully. "It would have made a wonderful chapter in my book."

"Your book ought to be read by people on Earth," Margaret told him. "And this way it will be."

An alarming thought struck David. "Commander, when will Earth learn about the aliens? It could be decades before they send another convoy, and then years after that before they build the colony we're hoping to find."

Moynihan pulled from his pocket what had to be his recorder. "Don't worry about what Earth knows, Colonel."

The light of the doorway rippled, playing on Meg and Moynihan with inscrutable power and purpose. Eamon's voice burst discordantly into it: "That's it!" He swung around the stone column to join them, waving his hands so energetically his tool nearly went flying. "That is what happened when the alien changed the patterns to send us back."

He halted abruptly, and the serene wash of snowy light hushed them. They turned to face the doorway, and David peered into its cool white fires. He longed to see through to the other side, but the light was more impenetrable than any darkness.

"We need to go linked. Physically, I mean," Margaret said. "We need to make sure that wherever we end up, we are all together."

Moynihan stretched out his hand to her, and their hands joined in the brilliance of the light doorway. Two shadows becoming one. Then Margaret reached toward David.

He grasped her hand, not needing in that moment to see what lay ahead. David turned to Eamon and held out his hand.

Eamon stepped over and firmly clasped David's wrist, and they all stood joined at the threshold of the time door.

"One thing I know," Moynihan said, and his voice, strong with a gentle strength, seemed to flow with the bright radiance. "God did not bring us this far, and save us from so much, for nothing. There is more for us. Let's go discover it."

The commander stepped over the threshold, into the blaze of the time door, and they followed him—Margaret, David, and finally Eamon. The light embraced them, free and soaring and immutably itself, and they swam, without effort, its fierce, pure currents.

XXXIX

The newscast played on the north side of the skyscraper, fronting the park. It broadcast to the public the news of the day, which happened to be that the conflagration in the squatter district had finally been brought under control.

Reuben sat on one of the park's benches in plain sight, watching images of towering flames and fire-gutted buildings. He did not feel guilty, not really.

He did, however, feel very involved.

Beside him, Willow shifted. "They could have saved some of those buildings."

"It's what they did in the riots. Created a perimeter, let everything inside burn. At least the perimeter was a lot smaller this time." Reuben rubbed his fingers against the bandage covering his right palm, thinking of fire.

The images playing against the skyscraper flickered, and Reuben looked to see footage of Manasseh Cruz deboarding his jet. Then it cut to his excruciating press conference the day before.

Reuben closed his eyes, but he couldn't shut the images from his heart. He sighed. "I'd hoped to hear yelling from the White House by now, but no. They're dying on Mars, Cruz is picking up the pieces of his life, and Karl hasn't got a scratch. I fought as hard as I could. Wasn't it enough?"

"Reuben . . ."

Surprised by her tone and her use of his first name, Reuben looked at Willow.

And then his gaze turned away from her, as he noticed movement in their direction. Jephthah Baines crossed the grass with swift purpose, and in a moment, he stood over them. "Jackson," he said. His keen eyes moved to Willow. "Ms. Dryson."

"Miss," she corrected him.

"Miss Dryson," he amended. "I need to ask your pardon. I need to take away your companion for a while."

Reuben met the chief of staff's eyes and stood. As Baines turned and walked away, Willow whispered, "'Yelling'?"

He took a glance at Baines's back. "At someone else, I hope." He hurried to catch up.

Baines led him to the street, to a black sedan idling at the curb. He opened its door and climbed in; Reuben slid in next and firmly shut the door.

"Pull out," Baines ordered the driver. "Swing around and come back here." As they peeled into the sparse traffic, the chief of staff relaxed, stretching out his legs and propping one arm comfortably on the back of the seat.

It made Reuben a little nervous, but he knew better than to open his mouth.

"There was a curious item in my inbox this morning," said Baines. "It was addressed to Karl, and yet it came to me. How do you think something like that happens?"

Reuben shrugged, carefully looking out the window to conceal the excitement that suddenly sparked in him. "Obviously some mislabeling in the computer."

"Obviously. This item was, purportedly, a message from Commander Moynihan. It was so wild, though, that I decided it should be deleted as a scam."

Reuben nearly stopped breathing.

"But first," Baines went on, "I made an inquiry to Cape Canaveral. A Colonel Nelson told me that the DSN did receive a transmission from Mars, which they had relayed to Washington. I sent them my mislabeled message to see if they could authenticate it as their own Mars transmission. And it checked out, Jackson."

Reuben looked at Baines. "What did Moynihan say?"

Baines slid a notebook out of his pocket and flicked his finger against the screen.

A voice Reuben did not recognize issued from it, clear but off in a way he couldn't define: *The thing about Karl was, he would do something, and you wouldn't know why until weeks later, after he had* done two or three things more. He spread my old paper all over, made me an embarrassment to everyone—"

Baines tapped the screen. "You know of Moynihan's Sodom and Gomorrah paper, of course."

"Of course." Reuben looked sideways at him. "But how do you know I—"

Baines tapped again, and the voice resumed: "—and I thought I understood. But then . . ."

The voice trailed into silence, one that lasted so long Reuben murmured, "Did he confuse himself?" But unease needled him: Shouldn't Moynihan, by all accounts an estimable scientist, at least sound educated?

Finally Moynihan went on: "Dr. Francis came to me alone and said that the trouble between me and Karl had poisoned the First Names; we were stuck, not even doing our work. He asked me to write a memo, enumerating all the problems and possible solutions.

"And so I wrote. I wrote everything." Melancholia crept into the commander's voice. "I wrote my suspicion that Karl was building the Mars team to be expendable, so he could do what he wanted to them when his time came. I wrote that the best thing would be to oust Karl and put Francis himself in charge. Or even myself. I was a fool, but I trusted Francis. I had no idea that . . ."

A sigh hissed from the transmission. "I don't know why he did it. But one evening Karl invited me to his office and showed me my own memo. He had circulated it to powerful members of government, he said. They all thought I needed to go, he said. And then I saw what he had done. He turned the government against me and made me a liability to them with the paper. It was already a fact that I had jammed the gears of the First Names. Now the memo made it look as if I were scheming to take over the First Names as well, and my suspicions were just part of that. I was beaten. Who can say otherwise?"

Reuben frowned at the rawness of Moynihan's voice. There was a wild edge to it, as though the commander had been wholly disarmed before his emotions.

"I couldn't leave the Mars mission. I was in too deep to ever put it behind me. And the team—three people I had given up on saving, and they were looking for a fourth . . ." He seemed to struggle a moment. "I told them I would be the fourth. But I gave it as a condition that I had to be *in charge. It was supposed to be David Killiam and the team scientist in the lab. Did it look right for a scientist with no rank to be telling military officers, combat veterans, what to do? But if I would be Karl's stupid sacrificial lamb . . ."*

Faint sounds scritched from the notebook, a lull that stretched so long Reuben grew restless. But he heeded Baines's upraised hand and waited silently.

At last Moynihan spoke again, and his voice was steadier. *"I am sending my log. This will stand for my last entry. I am separated from my team, and I know I can't find them; just trying to stand up makes me dizzy. Maybe they will find me, but I can still feel the earthquake, and there is no light or noise here. I seem to be alone. But whatever happens—however this ends . . . Here is my log. Here is our story."*

Moynihan's voice, and all noise with it, cut off. "Dizzy," Reuben said, "and he sounded it. He's hurt. But shouldn't the others . . ." Suddenly something struck him, and he shot a look at Baines. "Earthquake?"

"You would not believe what's in the log. But we will get to that in time. My business at the moment is Dr. Karl. It does not do to hastily credit such serious accusations, especially when the accuser is barely coherent at moments of it, so I went to see Dr. Francis."

Reuben thought of him, the wary scientist with his buried shame. "And what did he say?"

"He confirmed every word Moynihan spoke. So the president fired Karl."

Reuben's mouth dropped slightly open. "Can he do that?"

"Who is going to stop him?"

Reuben considered that a few seconds. "Well, at least we finally know what branch the First Names belong to."

"Better late than never. Very soon we are going to formally request Congress to abolish the First Names, and Karl's shenanigans will make it an easy sell. The hard sell will be getting them to fund a return trip to Mars with a fully staffed team."

Reuben studied Baines, knowing from the seriousness in his eyes not to be happy yet. "Now? Don't tell me you were so moved by Moynihan's last entry—"

Baines shook his head. "No. We won't go back to Mars for them. We'll go back for what they found." He swiped his finger over the notebook again and then held it up, displaying the screen.

Images moved across it, an unsteady sweep of massive buildings looming out of a grim, ashy twilight—enormous, flat-roofed halls, graceful towers, and minareted, many-leveled edifices. The very light was unearthly, rising up in pale mists from the city instead of falling from above, and the buildings were surpassingly strange.

Strange. Unearthly.

Alien.

A powerful sensation, at once hot and cold, struck him. He was suddenly breathless. "That is on Mars?"

"And it's ours." Baines drew back the notebook. "But we need to secure it. We need to put another team on Mars to claim this treasure and put it into our hands. To help achieve that, I am offering you your old position back. Do you accept it?"

"Sure. I mean, yes." Reuben tried to orient himself to this altering reality, Karl gone and a new mission to Mars and an alien city and his old job back . . .

"Your first assignment, then, is to travel south and meet with Congressman Cruz. I want to get his support first of all."

"You want me to follow him home?"

"Yes."

"Today?"

"Yes."

The *thrum* of the car filled a moment between them, then Reuben said, "You know he's salvaging his life down there."

"I know." And Baines's voice, though mild, had no yield in it.

Reuben took a breath. "I suppose I can interrupt him." He felt a bit of guilt for his acquiescence, and even more for his secret gladness. The new Mars team might save the first, and the sooner they left, the more likely they would.

Baines tucked the notebook away in his pocket. "I'll see to it that this transmission is sent to Cruz and that you get a copy. The congressman will want what you're selling, but you should go with the best pitch you've got."

Reuben had doubts about what Cruz wanted, but he kept them to himself. "If I can persuade Cruz to support the new mission, what are the chances it will be sent?"

"Jackson, once Cruz is fighting for the mission, it's one well-presented report and one roll call vote away from victory. He's damaged goods, but he's not out of this game yet."

"Good to know," Reuben said, then laughed.

Baines eyed him. "What?"

Reuben shook his head, looking out at the passing city. "It's just that I never thought those words would come out of my mouth."

"Neither did I. I would like to hear the story, Jackson, but it should probably wait until I'm out of government."

Manasseh Cruz had important things to do. Messages from Washington accumulated in his inbox, spinning around the troubles of these hard years like planets around the sun. His family was in the house, and it would mean something just to be there. And he had all kinds of calls to make, the first deft contacts that would begin the work of securing his power base again.

But he did nothing. He sat against a tree—an old live oak, its twisting, sprawling arms brushing sky and earth—and gazed at the sunset. Above the trees that shielded their property, orange and pink streaked the sky, and the sun stabbed molten rays through the thick tapestry of branches.

Someone tread the grass behind him, crunching a fallen branch, and he knew at once it was not his wife or any of his children. Cruz listened to the newcomer skirt the oak, and then he raised his hand and commanded, "Wait."

The footsteps ceased, and Cruz slowly lowered his hand. "Jackson," he said.

"Had a feeling, Congressman?" Reuben Jackson joined him, settling on the root-ridged earth and looking about. He indicated the sunset. "Another day gone. At least the world's a slightly better place today than it was yesterday. You see, in the exact reverse of yesterday, today Karl is not employed, and I am."

Cruz looked at Reuben. "What happened to Karl?"

"The president fired him."

"I had hoped he'd be arrested. Ah, well, I'll take what I can get. Who hired you?"

"Jephthah Baines—back to my old job as White House liaison. That's why I'm here, in fact. He sent me down. I would have left you alone, Congressman, but—well, you know how it is."

He did. "What does Baines want?"

"First, he wants Congress to abolish the First Names."

Cruz shrugged. "Soon done."

"And second . . ." Jackson stopped. "You've seen Moynihan's transmission?"

"I looked at it long enough to get the gist. Later I'll get the nuance."

"The gist is that they've proved the existence of aliens. When word gets out, the world will explode."

"Then here's hoping it won't get out. I could use some peace." Cruz, surveying the trees and the sunset blazing behind them, felt a vast indifference to the dead gray city of Moynihan's recordings. His heart was Earth-bound, his ambitions in a living city to the north and his dreams in his family's eyes.

"The White House is trying to keep the news in—until we've acted on it. Congressman, the administration is going to ask Congress to fund a new mission to Mars."

Cruz lifted a brow. "Where's the money coming from?"

"I'm not sure. Taken out of the military budget, perhaps."

"If our military is reduced anymore, it won't be able to repel a platoon of determined Girl Scouts."

"Well, there are other options. We could cut other budgets, raise taxes, maybe borrow money from Brazil. But the mission has to be sent, and it has to be sent soon. We know that China has been trying to intercept transmissions over our DSN. We are one hack and one decryption away from losing the secret. Even if it's not stolen, it's only a matter of time before it's leaked. There is viable alien technology on Mars. As a matter of national security, we can't allow any other nation to seize it. We have to get there first. Whatever the cost, it's just going to have to be endured. Better Americans have suffered worse for our security. Besides"—his voice became lighter—"this is America. We can't not make money off discovering alien life."

"That is a good argument, Jackson. Briefly but forcefully presented and tailored to appeal to my own biases and predilections. I was thinking along just those lines earlier. So give my assurances to Jep Baines that when the vote is called, I'll vote in favor. If I'm there." Ready to be done with Mars, Cruz fixed his eyes again on the sky. Dusky blue overtook the orange and deepened the pink to gray.

But he felt Jackson's eyes on him. "You don't understand, Congressman. Baines doesn't want just your vote. He wants you to lead the fight for the bill."

Cruz jerked his head to look at Reuben. "I'm covered in scandal."

"He knows, Congressman."

Baines did. He had learned Cruz's shameful secret one step ahead of everyone else when he'd come to persuade Cruz to keep a different secret. What had Baines said that night? That faith was needed exactly when it was undeserved. And wasn't this faith, to make him leader of their cause in Congress while everybody dissected his failures and sins?

"What should I tell the chief of staff?" Reuben asked.

"Tell him that I'll get his funding approved so fast it will make his head spin." Cruz didn't know if this was kindness on Baines's part or calculation, but he would not miss such an opportunity. He would lead and he would win.

He would justify Baines's belief that he could win, that he was still a man worth betting on.

"Now that I've spoken Jep Baines's piece, I'd like to speak my own. I'm here to make my last stand for the Mars team."

Cruz almost asked him to promise, but the grace he had just received silenced his sarcasm. "What is it you want?"

"I want a supply capsule launched immediately. Just to give them a chance. These years are shameful enough without it being written that we abandoned four people to die."

A chance. Cruz watched as the sun gathered the last of its golden rays beyond the horizon. He wanted to yield, wanted to withdraw his hand from the iron sentence he and Karl had written together. Maybe he had been wrong from the beginning, but it seemed so rational.

"Very well," he relented. "Before the week is over, a supply capsule will be flying through space to Mars. But Jackson, you need to be ready to let them go."

Jackson studied his bandaged hand. "You think it's too late for them?"

"I prefer not to prophesy until after the event. Let's just say that between running out of food and having volcanoes explode around them, their prospects have grown dim. They're in so deep, the door out is probably fathoms above their heads. Donegan Moynihan could easily be dead already. But we won't know until the new Mars team follows them down into the alien city. In the meantime, you need to let them go. You've done everything you could."

Reuben sighed. "I wanted to save them. Looks like I might have to settle for them saving us."

"They gave us the arrow that brought down the dragon. Still, we did our part." Cruz shifted to the younger man. "Here's something for you to think about, Jackson. The only reason they ever ventured into Jeanne was that we ignored their SOS. If they hadn't despaired of coming back to Earth, they never would have gone so deep into Mars. They never would have found the alien city. But they did. They discovered the city, and they proved the existence of aliens. And whatever happens to them now, that glory will be theirs forever."

Reuben glanced up at him. "You know, I don't know much about glory. I never had any."

"I have." And only because Jackson already knew of his drinking, Cruz gave voice to his next words. "I know about glory and about shame." The breeze lifted, whispering cool breaths of spring around them, and Cruz turned his face to it. "You were right about these shameful years, Jackson. That will be indelible in history, too. The riots. The Hungry March. The squatter districts. Paying off our debts with worthless money, millions losing their jobs and millions having their support cut off. When, in the future, people look back on our time, they'll see how low we fell. But they'll also see it as the beginning of a long climb. Our foundation of sand got swept away, and our house collapsed. Now we're raising the house again, and this rebuilding is painful. But the work we do is leading us upward, because we are building on a better foundation." And he could almost see the hard-but-sure ascent against the dusky sky, an arduous rise . . .

"Why don't you ever talk like that in public, Cruz? You might make people feel better."

Cruz stood up. "It's not my job to make people feel better." He hesitated, watching until the last of the sky's blue faded into black, and his vision of their ascent made it a homely thing. It moved him to tell Jackson, "My job is to keep us on the right course, even though it's a hard course. What we have is worth saving. I'll slog through America at its worst for America at its best. My great-grandparents grew up in a dirty village where they couldn't read or write. Today I'm one of the most powerful men in America. That doesn't happen in every country."

Jackson came to stand next to him. "So you took on three hundred sixty million people as your personal case, and I took on four. Which one of us is happier?"

"You're not exactly bubbling with ebullience, Jackson."

"At least I'm not burning with fanatical zeal."

Cruz was amused at the retort. "I know why I chose my case. Why did you choose yours?"

"Because there was no one else to take it up. That's all."

They stood together in a quiet stirred only by the breeze and a bird's distant night song. Then Jackson cleared his throat. "What do you think of Willow?"

Cruz thought only a few seconds. "Well, she's a nice girl, certainly pretty enough and obviously competent, and if I ever get caught doing anything, I hope it's not by her."

A beat of silence, then: "Okay. But do you think she'll be all right?"

"If you mean, will she be fine after losing her job? I'm going to say yes. An intelligent, competent young assistant with her experience should be able to get a job within a few months. If you mean, will she be fine after sending classified documents around town, I'm still going to say yes. She has three points working in her favor. One, she can claim status as a whistleblower. Two, she sent the papers only to people authorized to read them. Three, no one wants their role in this episode examined too closely. Better just to move on." Cruz altered his tone and straightened. "Now, man up and make a move."

Jackson startled at first, then made a noise halfway between a huff and a laugh. "Now that we've opened the topic of our personal lives—"

"We opened the topic of *your* personal life—"

"Which makes yours fair game."

There was an indisputable logic to that, and Cruz let Reuben go on. "So. Is everything all right?"

Cruz glanced back toward his house, and as the oak branches dipped with the wind, he caught a glimpse of warm yellow windows. "It will be." He turned back to Jackson. Shielded by darkness, Cruz said, "I could almost be grateful to Karl. My drinking has been stalking behind me like a shadow for fifteen years. Even after I quit, the terrible secret of what I had done trailed after me, ready to spring. Then Karl dragged my darkness into the broad daylight of the entire world, and . . . he killed the shadow."

Somewhere in the night, a bird called out again, and another bird answered. Cruz listened, and the darkness held no fears, no doubts. He was free in it, now and forever.

A little girl's voice rang out, bright as the sun: "Daddy! Daddy! It's time for dinner!"

Cruz turned his head toward her. "I'm coming right in, Angelica."

"I have to get back to my hotel," Jackson said. "I've got an early flight, and I could use the sleep."

He began to walk away, and Cruz said, "Jackson. Wait." When Reuben turned around, Cruz said, "Come have dinner with us."

Jackson's face was invisible to him, but Cruz heard surprise in the other man's silence. Then Reuben said, "I could use a meal, too. Thanks."

Cruz led him around the live oak, around the wide embrace of its outspread branches. As they emerged on the other side, the house greeted them—sure and solid in the night, its lit windows full of promises.

Jackson paused, and Cruz looked over to see his head was tilting upward. Cruz looked up, too.

The young night filled the sky with gentle blackness, sweetly pierced by a few silver stars flung wide. Hosts and hosts of stars shone unseen, an immeasurable multitude, and somewhere in their intricate, ever-turning dance, Mars bowed and whirled after the age-old pattern.

Cruz lowered his gaze to Reuben and waited until Jackson's attention came back to Earth. With silent accord, they walked together to the house, which pulsed like a beating heart with light and warmth.

EPILOGUE

The light receded, its tendrils uncurling from Margaret's skin to flow away into the unsearchable heights and depths of the universe. She found herself in a shining gray-and-silver room.

The walls were rough, like rock coated with silvery paint. The floor possessed the color, but not quite the gleam of metal, and no spot or streak marred its smooth span. An unmarked steel box—three times as long as it was high—rested to their right, reflecting the room.

"Holy . . ."

Margaret looked at David, saw that he was staring at the ceiling, and looked up.

Platinum beams crisscrossed overhead, arching in diagonal lines. The massive beams gave off light to the chamber below, obscuring the dark vault above. It was Earth-work, fortifying the ancient Mars city against the restiveness of Arsia Mons, and Margaret could not imagine what resources had brought it across millions of miles of empty space.

"You're here."

The new voice made Margaret turn, and she felt the others shift, startled, with her.

On the left side of the stone steps, a computer console shimmered in the light of the time door. A man stood beside it, the chair behind him askew as if he had just started up. He looked about their age, but surely—like the Earth trappings that turned the aliens' rocky chamber silver—he was far younger.

Margaret slid her eyes over the dark, elusive red of his uniform, over the glinting, foreign emblems on his arm and collar. Military—but not hers.

The man of the future walked over and squared himself in front of them. His blondish hair was almost white in the radiance, his blue eyes almost ethereal.

"Do you know us?" Moynihan asked, but the way he looked at them, the question seemed unnecessary.

The man nodded, his eyes inspecting each of them, until they stopped on Eamon. Even in the white blaze of the time door, intensity darkened his eyes.

Eamon met those eyes, and a seriousness creased his features. "Who are you?"

The man of the future only shook his head, then said in a wondering voice, "You look almost as young as I am."

"Why shouldn't I?"

A grin broke onto the man's face, and suddenly he reminded Margaret of someone. Before she could place it, he said, "Not today." Then he stepped back and clapped his hands. "Dr. Moynihan. Colonel Killiam. Dr. Killiam." He stumbled over the last, looking at her as if to make sure he had gotten it right.

Margaret looked at him more closely. With a dumbfounded realization of whom she saw in his face, she shot a look at Eamon.

The man spoke on. "That is what you are—which is now what you *were*. We have known for many years you would be coming someday. And we know your plan would be—is—to stay. But you can't. You must go back. I will send you."

Dismay chilled Margaret, and David demanded, "How far back?"

The man of the future shifted his gaze to him. "Very far from all this."

David drew a deep, almost dangerous breath, and Margaret said, "We've journeyed through hopeless places so long, and now, as soon as we find a place of safety and rest, you tell us to leave."

The man's eyes flicked to her, then Moynihan. "You understand these things, Dr. Moynihan."

Moynihan stood silent a moment, his gray eyes taking measurements. Then he said, "You knew we were coming because we told you. We have—we will—pass down news of this meeting, preparing you to send us back."

"Exactly."

"We won't regret it, then?" David said doubtfully.

A smile flickered across the man's face. "You don't." He stepped away, but then he stopped, his gaze fixing on Eamon again. Margaret thought she saw tears filming his eyes.

Then he surged up the stairs and wrapped Eamon in a fierce

embrace. Eamon looked ready to push the unknown man away, but then he folded his arms over him. A quiet expression, earnest as life and death, appeared on the engineer's face. He looked as if he were listening hard to a distant song, trying to pluck out words of great meaning.

David stared at the two men, Moynihan studied them, and Margaret guessed the identity of the man who would not tell his name.

The man broke away, beginning to retreat back down the steps, but Eamon gripped his shoulders and stayed him. He looked into the other man's eyes, blue like his own, and asked, "Do we really have to go?"

There was no mistaking the tears in the man's eyes now, iridescent with the light of the time door, but his voice was sure. "Yes. You have things to do." He looked at the rest of them. "You all do."

Eamon released him. "Then send us back."

The man walked back to his computer and sped his fingers over its keys. The light rippled, brightened, and he took one step toward them and no more. "Go on through," he said. "Don't be afraid. Just go straight up. You will be all right; I promise you."

Moynihan turned, catching his team in his gaze. "Let's go."

Margaret tossed one more look around the chamber, memorizing this glimpse of the future, then turned to face the light. When Moynihan walked into the blaze, she followed.

Another rush of light, another swirling journey. Once again Margaret stood on the steps up to the time door, but when she blinked the haze from her eyes, darkness surrounded her.

The full meaning of that clapped onto her, and Margaret whirled around, groping. Her hands hit one of the stone columns, and it was cool to the touch. She ran her fingers against the whorled engravings, feeling polished grooves she could not see, and apprehension frosted her blood. "The time door is shut."

Her voice rang in the darkness, in the chamber that she knew was stone again. A beam of light sliced the blackness, throwing a faint wash of light back on David's face. He swept the beam in an expansive half circle, baring dirt-encrusted wreckage on every side.

"I liked it better the other way," David muttered.

Moynihan snapped on his wristlight and made a more thorough survey. At the end of it, he lowered the beam and said, "It looks exactly as it did before we left."

Margaret breathed in deeply, opening her mouth a little to taste the air as well as smell it, and she said, "But it smells different."

David inhaled. "Right. It's mustier, staler. The dirt's settled since the earthquake made this mess. He put us into the future, but not very far."

Moynihan began a new canvass of the chamber. "How can you be sure? In a sealed chamber like this, a whole century could go by without leaving a sign."

David turned, aiming his light at the closed time door. "It's been left alone. There is no colony, Commander. There may be nobody at all. If anyone had come, the city would have brought them here, and they would not have left a discovery like this alone."

Margaret tipped her head toward Moynihan, wondering if he would be able to refute that.

"Whatever the situation is," Moynihan said, "we will deal with it. We must. This time, we can't leave."

Eamon's wristlight shot on, and in its narrow beam he began leaping over the debris with loose agility. "I don't know why you're all worried. And I don't know what there is to talk about. We know what to do: Go straight up."

They watched him go, until Moynihan pointed after him. "To the platform."

They crossed the chamber, toiling through the wreckage and stirring up dust, until they reached the oval of floor that was, beneath all the mess, tinted green and yellow and blue.

Eamon waited for them, restlessly skipping his wristlight beam over the chamber. Margaret shoved aside chunks of rock for space to stand, and David and Moynihan cleared their own way.

Green, blue, and yellow rays shot up from the floor, engulfing the grimy rocks and making them beautiful for just a moment. Then the white light burst forth and carried them away.

It ebbed as swiftly as it surged and left them in the heart of the city once more. Margaret turned, looking at the four stairways sloping upward. Ash caked the steps, brittle and old, and though the city's crooked horizon was dim, time had cleansed it of the crimson stain.

Eamon cut rapidly across the pavement to the nearest stairway. "Straight up, straight up!"

"Commander?" David murmured.

"Straight up, Colonel," Moynihan answered.

Margaret followed Eamon, but more slowly. David kept pace at her right, and Moynihan on her left, and the ash crunched to powder beneath their boots.

After a dozen steps, her muscles began to protest. A little more than halfway up, her breath began to feel short. By the time she reached Eamon where he waited at the head of the stairs, her side was cramping, and her breaths were coming fast.

David panted. "I've been going too long on short rations and no sleep."

"And still no rest for the weary." Moynihan gestured toward the arch and the avenue beyond, drenched in silver light that seemed to rise from the ground itself. On either side of the mighty thoroughfare, great buildings blurred together in shadows. "Let's continue, as long as the city lets us. I want to know, before we rest, whether or not we've escaped the frying pan."

"Right." David pulled the gun from his belt and clicked off the safety.

Eamon frowned, but Moynihan said, "Take point, Colonel."

David took the forward position and moved out. They all followed, falling into a ragged formation.

They passed beneath the arch and had almost reached the black tower when David halted, raising his hand high. Everyone stopped, and Margaret heard a hard scratching, like metal against rock. It was persistent, and fluid, and she knew something was moving against the stone.

Margaret breathed shallowly, concentrating on the sound and letting her sight drift after her hearing. Her gaze listed to the black tower, and then she saw something scurrying over its sheer, glossy wall—a black, bulbous, many-legged thing.

With an awful shock, it registered in her mind as an impossibly large spider. Then the crack of a gunshot splintered the silence of the dead city, and the spider-thing vanished to the other side of the tower.

Margaret looked over at David. Her brother faced the black tower, the gun aloft in his hand and a razor-sharp glint in his eyes.

The silence returned, but it seemed to be awake now, vibrating with the gunshot. Margaret suddenly felt eyes in the ancient, tomb-gray buildings that towered gloomily over the avenue. "Now they know where we are."

"Just so," Moynihan agreed. "Stand your ground, and hold your fire."

David, still watching the tower, said, "Yes, sir." But he didn't lower the gun.

Eamon shifted—impatient, eager—until he was almost rocking on his feet. Then Moynihan lifted up his hand, extending two slightly crooked fingers, and Eamon obeyed the signal and went still.

Margaret heard soft footsteps on stone, a sound more foreign to the deserted city than the scritching of the spider-thing.

"They're coming," Moynihan said.

Margaret stared at the black tower and at the gray buildings beyond, sifting shadows.

"Commander," said David, "there's one coming from the side and others from dead ahead."

"Thank you, Colonel." But that was all Moynihan said.

One shadow detached itself from a rounded dome of a building and shot out into the avenue. David twitched but he didn't fire.

It took a few seconds for Margaret's mind to resolve what she was seeing. The spider-thing was as tall as her waist, its black, metallic surface reflecting back the light. Lights blinked in a steady rhythm at the center of its round body.

A robot.

Movement stirred beyond it, drawing her eyes up just as three figures emerged from around the shadow-cloaked domed building. They, too, stepped into the avenue, into the silver wash of its light.

Two men and a woman, all clad in jumpsuits that were variants of Margaret's own. She scrutinized their faces, their eyes, and though the light painted them with an otherworldly sheen, they were completely human.

David's arm, pointing the gun, dropped.

Moynihan regarded the newcomers, and the low silver light etched every line of his posture with easy confidence. "Who are you?" he asked.

The woman stepped forward. "I am Major Elyse Walls, Commander of the Eve Mars Team. We were sent to plant the American flag over our first colony on this planet, and to claim the technology of this ghost city."

Moynihan nodded his assent to these claims. "Well, then, Major, call over your last man."

She lifted her hand high and beckoned. A moment later, he materialized from the shadows across the avenue and came to them, slinging a long-barreled weapon over his shoulder.

David shoved his gun beneath his belt, propping his hand on it.

The sharpshooter joined the rest of the Eve crew, and the two Mars teams faced each other—three men and one woman on each side, their jumpsuits displaying the blue and green and gray of the U.S. military. Margaret saw the freshness and vigor of their opposites flowing out of their alert eyes, the sure and ready stance of their bodies, and even their clean skin and well-kept uniforms.

And she and her teammates stood ragged and worn-out. Fatigue haunted their eyes, and they were battered and torn, smeared head to foot with blood and ash and dirt. The new Mars team faced them like a strange mirror, opening windows on the past that was and might have been.

Eamon turned toward their team. "They're our replacements."

"But we're still here." David lifted his chin in a defiant tilt.

"Nobody knew you were, Colonel," Elyse Walls said. "Earth tried many times to raise you. So did we, after making planet-side. For a year and a half—"

Margaret looked at her sharply, and Moynihan said, "A year and a half? How interesting. It has been that long since my last transmission?"

"Indeed." Walls gave the confirmation crisply. "Why did you never answer?"

Margaret and David looked at each other, and the amusement in his eyes was warm and familiar—a ray of simpler, happier days. Eamon cocked his head at the major, and his lips twitched.

But it was Moynihan's to answer, and so Margaret now looked at him. With his face set in that blend of calmness and serious intelligence that was at once aloof and compelling, he studied the major.

Then a grin curved Moynihan's mouth. "You'll have to forgive us, Major. We missed your calls. You see, we just got back."

She raised an eyebrow at him. "Where have you been?"

"That is a story I will be glad to tell. But first . . ." Moynihan half turned, and his eyes, shining in the silver light of the alien city, passed over his team. "First," he said, "let there be rest for the weary."

David's hand slid stiffly off his gun. "Amen."

Reuben, cradling a cold punch glass in each hand, made a quick, but careful circuit through the crowd. He passed a congressman, made way for a grand-looking lady, and sidestepped one of the catering waiters. Then he reached the gold settee at the far end of the room, and the woman sitting on it.

Willow, elegant in a sea-green dress, gave him a smile. Reuben placed a glass in her hand and sat down beside her.

For a minute they sat together quietly, watching the people and listening to the conversations and laughter that swirled through the room without touching them. "I have an idea," Reuben said. "Let's play Name the Important People."

Willow pointed to an iron-haired man, barely visible among a cluster of people. "Denn Leponi, Speaker of the House."

Reuben pointed to an impeccably coiffed woman. "Hassy Vance, minority whip." Then he scanned the room in earnest. "Where's Cruz?"

"Elsewhere. I haven't seen him around in at least fifteen minutes."

"That's odd. This is his party. You'd think that if he was going to hold a big bash to celebrate his reelection and invite half of Washington, he'd want to be here to throw it in their faces."

"He must have been called away." Willow raised her cup, but tipped her head toward him without drinking. "The Eve team was supposed to enter the city today."

"I know." Reuben forced lightness into his voice. "The footage will be incredible."

She went on looking at him, unquestionably knowing how distant that was from his real thoughts, but he had wearied of being the voice of complaint. His hope was long gone, buried by the long silence from Mars and by the discoveries of the Eve team: the untouched supply capsule, grounded on the barren, icy slopes of Arsia Mons; the cold, empty habitat, its darkness swelling with sweet music; the rover, abandoned with all its precious food rations. By the time Eve had worked their gradual, deliberate way to the alien city, Reuben had given up on the original Mars team. He expected to hear news of their remains, found in the gray reaches of the monolithic stone city. Then he would mourn, but he was done complaining.

Reuben looked away from Willow's well-seeing eyes. "You know what I wanted," he told her. "But *que será, será*. What will be, will be."

Willow lifted her glass in a kind of toast. "Then here is to the future, Reuben, and to the fight for it."

Reuben saluted her with his own glass. "The well-fought fight."

"The well-fought fight."

They both drank. As Reuben swallowed the cold, sweet-tart liquid, a voice rang over his head: "I hope this private toast is for me. After all, I paid for the caviar."

Reuben looked up at Manasseh Cruz dressed to the full in the doubtful resplendence of black evening clothes. Somehow, he wore it well, like he wore his power and his wealth. "I don't like caviar," he answered the congressman.

"Neither do I. But the formalities must be observed." Cruz stretched out both hands. "Come. I have something to show you."

Reuben stood, Willow rising beside him. "What is it?"

Cruz smiled and walked away.

Reuben slipped his hand over Willow's and followed Cruz into the crowd. The congressman moved confidently through it, receiving and giving out salutations, a train of words in his wake. Though Reuben spoke to no one, and no one spoke to him, he was hard-pressed to keep up. To aid his cause, he deposited his glass on a passing waiter's tray. Then he reached back to relieve Willow of hers.

She held out her other hand, already empty, and smiled at him.

The smile distracted him, so that he nearly walked directly into a woman holding a wineglass, very full of red liquid, and wearing a very white evening gown. He swerved from what would have been an unfortunate incident, just in time to notice Cruz vanishing into a hallway.

He and Willow slipped into the hallway after Cruz. The light was dimmer, and the close halls sheltered them from the noise and the crowd.

Cruz waited for them at the end of the hall, then he swung open a door and bid them enter with a gesture.

They passed inside, and Reuben found himself looking around at Manasseh Cruz's study. He released Willow's hand, self-conscious now that they stood alone with the congressman in his private quarters.

The door clicked smartly shut, then Cruz was walking past them. "Eve reported in," he said, bending over his desk. "They made it deep into the city, all the way to the center."

The news did not excite Reuben, but as he watched Cruz work the computer with eager hurry, heat rose in his blood.

"And so?"

Cruz struck his hand across the keys, then hustled to where Willow and Reuben stood. Just as he reached them, an enormous holograph shot up over the desk. Its solid images moved in deep colors before their eyes, shadows Reuben felt he could fall into, and austere expanses of stony floor.

The images glided past, streaming away beyond the margins of the holograph. A still, misty light grew larger until it commanded the living pictures with a numinous illumination.

The holograph stilled, allowing Reuben to order the strange images into clarity. The misty light shone from two turbulent sculptures, like flames frozen as they leapt heavenward. Before those wild forms and that ethereal light, four human figures clustered.

Once again the holograph shifted, focused, narrowing onto the four humans and reducing the luminous sculptures to a backdrop. Reuben saw their faces, and a shock jolted every nerve he possessed.

The man on the far right—Donegan Moynihan, as Reuben knew and was persuading himself to believe—cocked his head, seeming to look at something behind Reuben. "Is it a go?" he asked.

Reuben checked his impulse to look over his shoulder and watched Moynihan. A voice, carrying from somewhere beyond the image, said, "It's a go."

Moynihan nodded crisply and refocused his gaze, appearing now to look at Reuben and those with him. A thick, white scar slashed his forehead, intimating a story to be told. "I am Commander Donegan Moynihan, of the first Mars team, reporting to Earth after a silence of more than a year. My team is alive and whole, and we have unburied the secrets of Mars."

A beat passed, and Margaret Killiam, standing at Moynihan's right, pushed her dark hair from her face and looked straight forward. "I am Dr. Margaret Killiam, U.S. Army major. You will not believe the story we have to tell."

At her side, Gulliver Eamon waved his hand, snatching their attention. A large scrape reddened his forehead, and one cheekbone was bruised purple. "Lieutenant Commander Gul Eamon—Navy, Never Again Volunteer Yourself. I fully expect some sort of medal."

David Killiam, last of all. "Colonel David Killiam, pilot of the United States Air Force . . ." He stopped, the words dangling, then slowly raised his hand above his head. And against the white light of the wild sculptures, his fingers pointed the victory sign.

Victory over Mars and over Earth, victory over life and death, and victory over long odds.

"He's right, you know," Cruz said. "They won. Somehow, they . . . lived."

Reuben glanced at him, then at Willow, tears streaming down her face. "We won, too." His own eyes were stinging, and he cleared his throat as he looked again at the Mars team, emerging alive from the shadows of the great, dead city, and he felt a mysterious unity with them, across all the unfathomable miles. "We killed the dragon, and they found the door."

THE END

ABOUT THE AUTHOR

Shannon McDermott is an author of science fiction and has been occupied for years with constructing scenarios of the colonization of Mars. Raised by homeschooling parents, she was encouraged in reading and writing from a young age. Always a fan of the genre, she reviews speculative fiction as a staff writer with Lorehaven. Her interests include history, classic literature, and lattes. She lives in the great Midwest, where she does her best to avoid icy weather, sweltering heat, and tornadoes, according to the season.